Empowering time travelers to communicate across decades, an eager and gifted temporal engineer develops a secret mail drop, hidden in plain sight on a university campus. Codename: the Timeslot.

A charismatic physicist and a focused, revenge-driven hacker go to daring lengths to escape the man who murdered their best friend and fiancé—his boss.

A grieving musician in search of closure uncovers her late father's notebook, written before she was born but, impossibly, dated twenty-five years in the future.

Generations later, another engineer, brilliant but disorganized, struggles to repair the abandoned Timeslot equipment after years of disuse. Her unexpected discovery draws this disparate group of men and women into a cascade of events which echo across a century of recent-past and near-future history.

Journals from five intertwining lives, Black, White, Asian, queer, straight, disabled, and not, blend time travel with mystery, revenge, found family, vintage music, sci-fi references, and even a little romance.

THE TIMESLOT

PARADOX

JEFF WOMACK

A NineStar Press Publication
www.ninestarpress.com

The Timeslot Paradox

First Edition, May 2025

ISBN: 978-1-64890-867-5

Also available in eBook, ISBN: 978-1-64890-866-8

CONTENT WARNING:
This book contains fade-to-black sexual content, which may only be suitable for mature readers. Depictions of alcohol use, grief/loss, profanity, and murder/death.

For friends, loved ones, and my own found family. You know who you are.

A Note on Names

To preserve the secrecy of time travel, Temporal Engineers generally use an alias while away from their home timeline. Most keep their same initials for simplicity.

Theresa uses the alias Tia.

Chris uses the alias Charles.

Kiernen uses the alias Kasey.

Amber uses the alias Autumn.

Crystal uses the alias Summer.

1

CRYSTAL
August 1993

I spent weeks cleaning out the house before I discovered the secret compartment.

Unexpectedly, the lowest dresser drawer was crammed full of socks, far more colorful than I would ever wear. I slid the whole thing out to tilt them into the donation box. Shaking the drawer to free the last pair, I felt something shift, just before a false bottom hinged open, and a book fell out among the clothes.

The unmarked tan cover had no title, no call number, nothing.

Three months before, Mom had...faded to silence like the final song on an album. After the funeral, when the flow of her friends bringing food over eventually slowed and stopped, I slipped into a deep funk. No desire to move on, I'd just spun in place, the crackle of static at the center of a record repeating over and over.

My counselor suggested that the grief process could be helped by changing how I thought about the house. Even though I lived there alone, it still felt like Mom's. So, I cleaned and sorted absolutely everything. Like learning to play an instrument, the only way to improve was practice. So, I practiced. I practiced being a self-sufficient adult, one shelf, one box, one drawer at a time.

Sorting and cleaning became the therapy that finally lifted my needle out of that endless groove.

Slowly, I'd worked my way through the entire basement, most of the garage, the kitchen, nearly everything except Mom's bedroom. I knew I needed to build up to it, so I left her room to last. That morning, I'd stood in her doorway, debating between the dresser and the closet. It didn't matter much. Since I was several inches taller, most of her clothes would be donated anyway.

Gently lifting the book out of the box, I opened it to the first page, where handwritten text began. "James was my best friend, and now he's dead." The date didn't make any sense though: July 2018.

An unpublished novel set in the future? As a librarian, Mom lived her entire life around books. So maybe? Except this wasn't her familiar handwriting. It was far too messy. Why go to such trouble to hide it?

Sitting on the floor, the socks forgotten, a story unfolded, page by page: time travelers, friendship, loss, escape, revenge, and even a little romance.

I read until my legs fell asleep. Standing unsteadily, a folded bundle of paper covered with undecipherable math calculations slipped out from between the pages onto the floor. Tucked inside, I found two white rectangles. I used the smaller, a worn piece of unlabeled plastic to mark my place in the book. The larger showed writing in one corner that I recognized *was* Mom's. "Charles and me, 1968." I flipped it over to see an old black-and-white photo of a smiling couple posing on a stair landing. An Asian man in shirt and tie had his arm around the waist of a White woman in a floral dress. She had straight dark hair parted in the middle.

Mom only had a few photos of my dad. Her favorite hung in the hall, the rest stayed in an album. I'd seen them all many times, but never this one. Dad looked the same as in all his other photos, but Mom was so young, her hair longer than I remembered and years before any gray crept in.

On the wall behind them, the bottom corner of an antique picture frame showed. I leaned close and noticed a dog in the painting. Gasping, I sat up straight. I knew that painting! I knew *exactly* where they stood.

I headed out the door so fast I barely remembered to lock up. Parking always sucked near the student union, so I paid for the parking garage. Through hallways, past meeting rooms, the main lobby, and then halfway up the atrium stairs brought me to a landing with a painting of the first dean of the university...and his dog.

I stepped back and held out the photo. It lined up perfectly: the corner of the painting with the brass plaque underneath, the curving handrail to the stairs, all of it. The only things missing were my parents.

The only things missing were my parents.

That hit me hard. My counselor said grief was a road that winds back on itself. On a stair landing, empty except for me and a century-old dog, I didn't even realize I was crying until an older woman passed by and asked if I was okay. I wiped my cheeks, told her I was fine, and walked away, back toward my car, my house, and the book my dad had left behind.

*

CHRIS
July 2018

James was my best friend, and now he's dead. We grew up in an older neighborhood where every year more and more of the original houses were torn down and replaced by larger ones. James's family lived in one of the older houses, and mine lived in a newer one. We were friends since the bus to grade school; the Black kid and the Asian kid from down the block were always together riding bikes or playing video games or whatever.

In the official story, a mugger shot James and his fiancée after leaving a movie theater. I thought I knew what truly happened, but I couldn't prove it. Yet.

James discovered stuff about our employer he wasn't supposed to know—a string of missing engineers going back decades. I didn't want to believe it at first, but he finally convinced me. Either he dug a little too deep, or he didn't cover his tracks well enough.

After the terrible phone call, I rushed to the hospital but paused, still behind the wheel. I needed to function despite the horrific news, to stand up, walk in there and find Theresa's mom. She'd need someone to sit with her and talk to her. I wasn't sure how or where to start.

In that moment, I couldn't do anything for James. He loved Theresa though. It was so easy to imagine him taking my shoulder and leaning in, his usual smile replaced by intense seriousness. "You've got to be there for her because I can't. T's a badass, and she won't want help, but I need to know you have her back."

Keeping someone *off* her back was the best I had right then.

I had to compartmentalize, do what I could in that moment, and worry about later, later.

Taking a deep breath and letting it out slowly, I opened my tablet. The police blotter on the local paper's web page didn't have a byline but two editors were listed for local news. The photo of the second looked younger, probably an intern.

A general search for her name showed volunteer work with a dog rescue charity and included her personal email. From there it was short work to a phone number. I star-six-sevened. After several rings, I expected voicemail, but a tired voice answered, "H'lo?"

Sounding as calm as possible, I addressed her by name and said, "You don't know me, but I need your help."

Her voice cleared, sounding irritated. "What? Who the hell is this? It's twelve thirty at night!"

"I didn't give my name, and I assure you I have no desire to contact you again after tonight. I need help, and I'm willing to pay you for your effort." I knew this had to sound strange, but I had no way around it.

When she spoke next, her voice sounded more wary than annoyed. "Whoever this is, I'm not interested."

Concerned she was about to end the call, I spoke quickly. "Please don't hang up. My friend was killed, and I'm trying to protect his fiancée from the people who did it."

This gave her pause. "What did you say?"

I started again. "A mugger shot my friend and his fiancée earlier tonight as they walked to their car."

"I'm sorry to hear that, but I still don't understand why you're calling me. How did you get this number anyway?"

"In a few hours, you're going to see a police report about the shooting. It's going to say that an African American man, age twenty-four, and an African American woman, age twenty-three, were mugged and shot near the theater on Parks Street. I need her to be omitted—or if it's simpler, to remove the event from the police blotter altogether."

"You know I can't do that."

I'd expected this. "Please check your Paypal."

"Huh?"

I repeated myself more slowly. "Check your Paypal." I gambled that her email address was also her account. Moments before dialing, I'd tapped the Send icon, and it worked. The amount I transferred wasn't huge but could easily be a car payment, maybe two.

"Hang on," she said, putting me on mute. A moment later she was back, her voice wide awake. "Okay. You have my attention."

"Good," I continued, trying to sound as smooth and cool as I could under the circumstances. "If by next weekend, there's no mention in the paper or on the website, I'll transfer that amount again."

"Why are you doing this? No one's ever called me in the middle of the night and offered to bribe me to remove shit from the paper."

"As I said, I'm trying to protect my friend from the people who killed her fiancée. Is that enough?"

"Yeah, I guess it has to be."

"Good. Thank you. Goodnight." I ended the call and let out a tense breath. I'd pulled it off.

Walking into the waiting room, I found Theresa's mom. She rose and wrapped me into a hug. Shorter than Theresa, her braids rubbed under my chin, and her tears soaked into my shirt.

*

THERESA
July 2018

We had left the movie theater, walking hand-in-hand toward James's truck, comparing that film to others by the same director. When a man with a pistol stepped out of the shadows, James shoved me behind him, but I stumbled, pulling us both down. Two *pops* sounded, and then a third before I passed out.

The sound of a door interrupted my thoughts. Chris found me on a shaded patio behind the funeral home. Of the pair of friends, Chris was the smooth one and James was the funny one.

That's what hooked me actually, James's sense of humor. Sometimes it was deadpan sarcasm, sometimes goofy, sometimes innuendo, but his timing was always perfect. He could bust up a whole room with one joke, and I'd seen him do it plenty of times. The day he proposed, I knew he was up to something because he was less funny than usual. What a weird thing to remember.

Chris brushed off a bench and sat eye level with me, running a hand through his dark hair and shaking his head like he didn't even know where to begin. I saved him the trouble. "Was it because of what he found?" He knew that *I* knew about James's research, so I didn't need to elaborate.

"Damn. I've been thinking the same thing. Yeah, probably, but where's the proof?"

"Oh, hell! We both know this isn't the first time! Proof doesn't do much at this point! What jurisdiction would we take it to? And when? No—what matters is stopping him."

I'd snapped at him when I didn't mean to. With everything, of course my emotions were frayed. I was about to apologize when he leaned back against a planter, squinting one eye and tugging at his lip the way he did when his brain was running hard.

"Or…" He trailed off.

"Or what? You got that look. Where's your head goin'?"

"It's an idea, but it's bonkers. It'd require going all in; and I mean *all.*"

"What?"

"No, no. Give me a few days. I need to check some things out first."

"You better hurry."

"Remember, I still work for Temporal Engineering. We have all the time we need."

"Bullshit. You know as well as I do that's not true."

He rose and offered to push me back inside.

*

CHRIS
July 2018

How many time travel stories have a character who gets stranded in the past? This inspired an idea, and I toyed with it for months before pitching it to the boss.

I leaned into his office trying to sound casual, "Hey, I've got a concept for a project, if you have a few minutes."

I had no idea of Vanhanen's real age, of course: old enough to be mostly bald with a little gray around the sides and probably nearing retirement, but who knew for sure? In a time when jeans in the office were commonplace, he always wore a suit: usually gray, in an almost vintage cut, with just enough hand stitching to let others know it was custom.

He responded like I was taking up his time with nonsense. "Mr. Young, you're fully aware all our research outlines come to us along with our funding. I don't make this up as we go."

"I know. I know. This isn't temporal research, or not exactly. It's more of a fail-safe."

I couldn't tell if he looked intrigued or annoyed, but after a moment he closed his laptop and gestured across his large desk toward the other chair. "I'll admit I'm warily curious."

I described a system where a field engineer could drop an envelope in an unmarked mailbox that would jump it back to their home time.

He shook his head with a small frown. "I don't think so. Why would Temporal Engineering ever need such a thing?"

"In case someone wasn't able to return to their own timeline."

"You've been reading too much science fiction," he said in a slightly condescending tone that set me on edge. "That would never happen. We have protocols and safeguards in place to prevent anyone from ending up in the wrong timeline."

I'd been about to speak, but he continued, so I waited until he was done dismissing my idea out of hand.

"And furthermore, there's the Free Jump. A field engineer in any timeline can provide a passphrase at TE along with coordinates, and we send them on their way without question. Didn't we talk about this during your initial training? I'm fairly certain we did."

I took a deep breath before responding and tried not to let my annoyance show. "Yes, we did."

"See? So, what's the concern? Your rogue project doesn't fix anything that's actually broken."

"If you'll give me a second, I'll explain."

He looked at his watch and said, "I have to leave for a meeting in a few minutes. I'm listening, but you'll need to be quick."

"Okay. You said it yourself. The Free Jump."

"What of it?"

"How often does that policy get used?"

"Not frequently. A few times a year, maybe."

"And when an employee shows up with coordinates in hand—does anyone take the time to check the numbers before they jump?"

He squinted, and his tone changed, speaking more slowly, like he was still processing. "Now that you mention it, no. It's always been 'no questions asked.'"

"What if that person we opened the portal for didn't run the formula correctly? What if they didn't carry enough digits? Wouldn't a way to call for help be a good idea?"

"I'm intrigued, but how would you prevent someone using it to gain foreknowledge."

"I guess that'd need to be a policy thing. This would be for emergencies only." Maybe I'd finally gotten through to him, but I had one more point I wanted to make. "You emphasized in our training about the inherent dangers of time travel, and even more about protecting the timeline. This would be a way to add another layer of safety for field engineers."

Looking thoughtful, and even rubbing his chin, he grudgingly agreed. "Very well. I'll approve some preliminary research. Come up with a plan and some designs. If…and I mean *if*, you can get to a proof of concept, we'll talk more."

We set up a departmental account to pay for materials, but the funding was laughably small—not even half of what I'd need. Sometimes I wondered if Vanhanen knew what things cost in the real world. Rather than debate it, I added enough from my own pocket to make up the difference.

I had pages of notes and sketches, but only the start of a prototype when James and Theresa were shot. The morning after the funeral, I sat in the lab, heart pounding, James's research on an endless loop in my memory. If V was responsible, what would prevent him from doing the same to me?

My spark of a brainstorm the day before with Theresa had been this: maybe the best way to get a safe distance from V wasn't to run to some far-off part of the world. What if I fled to a different time? Would that work? *How* would that work?

I turned the prototype over and over in my hands amid a swirl of possibilities in my mind. The mailbox project could be the catalyst! Building it would be a reason to be gone from TE. Using it would allow Theresa and I to stay in contact.

For my idea to work, I'd need a place to, well, work. My staff ID and a believable story about research got me into the facilities archive, where the university stored floor plans for all the buildings. It was dusty and cramped, but thankfully empty of people.

I referenced an overall campus map, overlaid steam tunnels and underground power lines. Buildings without a basement, too far from the power mains, or newer than fifty years old were eliminated right away.

On a crumbling blueprint of the student union, in a round space between foundations at one end, someone had crossed out the word "UNEXCAVATED" and penciled in "CON OFF," along with a door to the corridor. *Construction Office, maybe?*

Walking through the basement of a hundred-year-old building alone at night felt ominous. The curving hallway looked exactly like the floor plan, except darker and creepier. Between a janitor's closet and an electrical panel was a nondescript wood door, damaged at some point, hastily repaired, and painted to match the wall. As quietly as possible, I pried off a crooked board, but parts of the old latch clattered loudly to the hard floor. So much for silence. The door swung in on hinges creaking like a horror movie.

Inside was better than I'd hoped for: a dry concrete floor, a high ceiling with exposed structure, and even lights and outlets. The carpenters who built the union made themselves an office to get out of the weather. It didn't look like anyone had been there since the last bricks were laid.

2

CRYSTAL
August 1993

I read my dad's manuscript all the way through that first night: a fictionalized autobiography—sort of. The chapter where he met my mom was cute and funny. I'd heard her tell the story enough times to recognize it, but it was cool to see it from the other side.

Was there an earlier volume missing that better explained the stuff about the time portal? Near the end, he wrote more about Mom than time traveling. I was really into it (my favorite character was Kasey, the nerdy guy with the big words) when it just...quit.

I turned a page to find the next sheet blank and made a whiny "Ugh!" I flipped to the previous entry and then back to the still-blank next page as if it might make a difference. It didn't.

Sitting alone on my sofa, the house having grown dark around me, I smiled despite the blank pages. It was a smile that was as much sad as happy, but it was a smile. I'd wept countless tears for the loss of my mother and for the hole it had left in my life. This was different. This smile was for a discovery. The manuscript I held in my hands contained a piece of my father, a man I'd never known. In that moment, I felt closer to him than ever before.

I put the book and the photo on the mantel, unsure what else to do with them. Hiding them again in the bottom drawer didn't feel right, not after I'd found them. That moment became a turning point for me. Seeing this glimpse into Mom's past and who she'd been before the life I remember, before her health became our focus, let me see things as part of a bigger picture.

I walked past the mantel every day. Eventually, their presence there became as familiar as the old photos on the wall.

*

CHRIS
July 2018

"We are *so far* beyond hiding and playing it safe," Theresa snapped.

Ostensibly helping pack up her old apartment, I'd just finished laying out my idea for researching out of time. It didn't go over like I'd hoped. "This isn't only about staying safe. I mean, well…it is, but I'm trying to be smart about it. We only get one shot before he knows we're coming for him. We can't go in there with guns blazing."

She shook her head and breathed out through her nose, sharply and dismissively.

"Right now, all we have is James's research and the fact that you two were attacked soon after." She started to interrupt, so I said the next few words louder, "Assuming James was right..." Then I continued in a normal tone, "If we keep on digging into what he was already researching, there's too strong a chance Vanhanen would figure we're onto him too."

"You think you can find what James was after in another timeline?"

"From an earlier point, when V didn't know he needed to be so diligent about security...yeah, I do. It's not a sure thing, of course, but it's our best chance."

"I know you've thought this through and all, but I'm sorry, I'm not interested in spending time in the civil rights era. It was bad enough for Blacks who could walk."

I didn't expect her to draw that conclusion, because it wasn't what I meant. "Actually, I never intended for you to go with me. Remember, Vanhanen hasn't met you. He didn't even go to James's funeral. You should be safe enough here—" I gestured toward her laptop. "—unless you go poking into things best left *unpoked*."

"I can't just sit around on my ass! My grad classes don't start back up until January. What am I supposed to do until then? Watch Netflix?"

"Well, your physical therapy..."

"Hell, no!" She cut across me. "Hell, no! If you're jumping out of this piece of shit timeline, then so am I."

"What?"

"Thirty years oughta do it, don't you think? I imagine by the 2040s they should be able to make me walk again."

"No. Jumping forward is dangerous."

"Look who's talkin'! Aren't you worried about the hate on Asians in the sixties too?"

"On a college campus, disguised as a visiting professor..." I shrugged and trailed off. "I'll need to be careful about where I go and what I do, but it should be safe enough. I mean, technically this is the Upper Midwest, emphasis on *upper*, y'know?"

"Except you don't know, and you're trying to bullshit your way into convincing me, and possibly yourself, that it'll be okay."

"Maybe so, but I need to be as close to the beginning of TE as I can to find any physical records on file, and better the middle of the civil rights movement than before." Theresa rolled her eyes like she still didn't buy it. "Jumping into the future's a whole different kind of danger. You'd create an end of the line within your own foreseeable lifespan."

She answered flatly, "Do you really think I give a shit?"

"Not right now, no; but one day you might."

"That's not your call to make. It's mine."

I saw determination in her dark eyes that I knew I wouldn't beat. She'd won, and the best I had left was a little bargaining over the specifics. "Can I at least talk you into something less than thirty years?"

"What, like twenty-five?"

"Maybe ten or fifteen?" I asked, unsure.

"Twenty-three, and I'm afraid that's my last offer."

"Fine, damn it. Fine."

*

THERESA
August 2018

Chris sure loved his research. Partway through talking I knew I wouldn't convince him it was frivolous, so I shifted the conversation toward future technology to help me walk. A believable reason to jump, and while true, it wasn't the whole story.

The situation needed action, not more hours spent digging through dusty archives.

Chris's invention would allow us to remain in contact, but only if I had access to the equipment *inside* TE. I could have hacked my way in every so often to "check the mail," but eventually I would have gotten caught. A job there solved the problem in a much simpler way.

Frankly, the thought of working alongside the man responsible for James's death terrified me. I knew it was dangerous, and I knew I'd need to be constantly vigilant about sticking to my cover story. One minor slip and he'd be onto me.

But the thing was...enduring all that stress, not to mention the temporal headaches, put me in the position I wanted: within literal striking distance of revenge.

Chris had said "guns blazing" as a metaphor, but it held more nuance from my side. I'd never liked firearms, even before being permanently disabled by one, but I couldn't deny a temptation to roll into TE, shoot Vanhanen, and escape through the portal. It would have been a sort of revenge, sure. But honestly, I wanted more. I wanted it worse. I wanted him to endure years of consequences stemming from the bullet that caused James's death, like I would face. I wanted him *brought low.*

Shit. That sounded dark.

The trouble was I didn't know how to pull it off...yet.

I envisioned myself lying in wait while Vanhanen jumped, then epically destroying the equipment, sparks flying across the lab and everything. Realistically, I'd get the same result with less effort and drama by simply unplugging it. But no, neither of those would do anything more than keep V from returning through the portal to that one moment in time. He could still go to other years, so it wouldn't keep Chris or anyone else safe. Not to mention it would trap me in my future timeline without a way to get back.

I needed to come up with something better.

*

CHRIS
August 2018

Theresa was right. We didn't have all the time we needed.

In the TE lab, I alternated my attention between my time-letter device and completing James's last experiment, when the door opened. Vanhanen turned a lab chair and sat, looking tired. He pointed at the other one asking, "Do you have a minute?"

"Sure."

Maybe he looked *old* more than tired, or looked older than usual, I guess. He rubbed his forehead and sighed as if unsure sure how to begin. "I've been debating this for a while now, years really. With Miss Garcia leaving last year and now James…" He paused, and I realized he'd said James, not Mr. Sinclair, which was unusual. "The department is down to only the two of us now. I'm thinking maybe it's finally time to retire."

I tried not to let the shock show on my face. No, no, no, no, no! Without access to TE, how would Theresa and I finish our plan? How would we escape? He was looking at me like he expected me to say something, but the best I could stammer out was "Um. Wow. That's…uh…sudden."

"It probably appears that way, but I assure you it's been in the back of my mind since before you and Mr. Sinclair started."

I gestured toward a piece of James's equipment. "What about?"

"Go ahead and finish up that last experiment. Can you wrap it up by a week from Friday?"

I thought fast. I needed to buy time. "Maybe. If I put in some extra hours, or I could finish it up the following week."

"Well, get it far as you can." Damn, didn't work. How would he explain a half-finished experiment?

He stood, interrupting my thought, and added, "I'll write you a letter, of course." I must have looked puzzled. One hand on the lab door, he offered, "Of recommendation. No specifics of course, but I can talk about project management and such. That should help for wherever you go next."

Surprised and confused, I thanked him. He nodded and left quietly. I leaned back and looked at the ceiling, thinking about the door for the round room. A replacement was on order through the prototype account but not delivered or installed yet. I still needed to paint it, and Theresa had to set up the electronic lock.

Not to mention everything else we needed to finish before jumping.

How the *hell* were we going to pull this off in only two weeks?

*

THERESA
August 2018

Time travel isn't what people think. There's no blue box, no silver car, and no phone booth.

The universe abhors a paradox. A person can't meet themselves in the past or prevent something they wish they hadn't done, and they can't change anything altering the timeline leading up to travelling to the past. If they try, debilitating head pain will knock them on their ass.

Chris squeezed everything he'd learned his whole first year at Temporal Engineering into a few weeks: time travel theory, temporal coordinates, and operation of the portal itself. Good thing I was a fast study.

Additionally, I learned about change perpetuation. One can't simply jump back in time, make a change, and expect it to be permanent. That's not how it works. A change will walk its way toward the future at the ordinary rate of time. When I didn't follow his explanation, he elaborated, "Imagine you go back in time to January first and paint a big X on the wall. If you go home for a week, then return on January second, the wall will be blank. The change you made, your X, will have moved forward to the eighth during the seven days you were in your own timeline. See?" Barely beginning to, I referred to those lessons as "CP-101."

Being out of time also meant a constant low-grade headache. On returning, it stopped. The time traveler had to remember that their home time, their *timeslot*, marched forward, just like the X on the wall, at the ordinary rate of time.

Where CP got trickier was in electronic records, or worse, people's memories. When I asked why, he shrugged and said, "That's the main thrust of what TE studies: understanding how time works and what'll affect how changes ripple along the timeline. Decades of study...and it still isn't all figured out. Remember, TE isn't part of the history department. The E is for engineering."

Chris sold as much as he could: his stuff, my stuff, James's stuff. We needed transportable, untraceable wealth.

For jumping to the past, he bought all the vintage cash he could find, regardless of quality. It sold for more than face value, of course, but in the 60s, a one-hundred-dollar bill bought seven or eight times as much as in 2018, so he'd still be ahead.

My future finances relied on a stash of actual gold, since its price consistently increased faster than inflation, as well as thousands worth of savings bonds in my new name.

Meanwhile, I worked on our fake identities.

Chris explained how TE field agents always used an alias when out of time. On the off chance they appeared in any contemporary record, there would be no risk of revealing the existence of time travel. Our jumps weren't *remotely* sanctioned by TE, but it still felt like a good idea, even to the tradition of keeping our same initials for simplicity.

3

AMBER
January 2045

I stepped off the bus into a cold wind and tried to avoid putting my crutches on a patch of ice. Despite sitting near the front, everyone else maneuvered past me on the short sidewalk to the door of the student union.

It was the same knee I injured years before—the one ending my undergrad soccer scholarship. This time, the ski patrol found me in a three-foot drift of snow. There was a ride on a sled thing behind a snowmobile, an ambulance, and finally a surgeon telling me I needed a knee replacement.

Dad flew out and got me settled. When I left for the trip, my apartment was in post-breakup *and* pre-vacation chaos, so even worse than usual. The pain killers did their job but made me sleepy most of the first few days. I'd wake up and smell cleaning products or hear him moving stuff around, and I'd yell something like, "Whatever it is, leave it!"

He'd reply from the other room, "But what about all these tools and things? How are you going to clean all this after I leave?"

I called back, "You're assuming I actually clean. That might be your first mistake."

"Okay, but seriously…"

"Whatever. Just don't throw anything away that looks important," and I'd drift back to sleep on the couch. The pain came later, and it hung around for a long, long time.

Moving slowly, I followed the crowd into the round atrium, staying along the edge of the room by the wall. Campus legend held that walking over the brass inlaid zodiac in the center of the floor meant you'd fail your next test. I'd finished grad school three years before, but I still couldn't bring myself to do anything different.

Uncle Kurtis came by with groceries and a cane for once I'm off the crutches. We watched a lot of movies, all three of us squeezed onto my sofa, me in the middle, my leg on the coffee table. After about a week, and once there wasn't anything left to clean, I sent Dad home, insisting I could get around well enough inside the apartment.

Unexpectedly, it was the down time and the boredom that bothered me most of all. I was used to a certain level of physical activity: running, yoga, whatever. I rode my bicycle nearly everywhere most of the year. Not exercising, not even really moving around made me twitchy. The muscles above and below the joint ached from disuse, and the other leg was sore from having to literally carry all the weight.

I skipped the ornate curving stair and followed Tia's directions instead; she always knew where the elevators were. I rode down to a basement I wasn't aware even existed. Past loading and storage, a dim curving hallway led to a dead end and an unmarked steel door, unassuming, painted to match the wall, and easy to miss if you weren't looking, probably intentional.

I'd texted my boss while still in the hospital. He sent back a characteristically brief email response saying he hoped I would have a fast recovery. Yes, he still uses email. A few days after Dad left, I replied, asking if I could work remotely. Since the pandemic in the early 20s, working from home was common, but given the classified nature of temporal research, our boss was a stickler about security and didn't allow it. I copied Tia, and my friend came through for me offering up an alternative project I could do part-time while my knee worked its frustratingly slow way back to 100 percent.

Vanhanen approved, commenting that the room in the basement of the student union was closer to parking than the regular TE office in the nuclear engineering building. I rolled my eyes at that. He never remembered I didn't own a car at all. At least the bus stopped right out front. V probably hadn't ridden a bus since he was a kid—if then.

Tia explained that the Timeslot room was built decades ago, but it hadn't worked in years, if ever. Therefore…fixing it. I swiped my card and the heavy door clicked. Shouldering it open, I felt around for a light switch. The room was maybe twenty-five feet across and *round*, matching the atrium above. It smelled dusty and old, but dry. Along one wall were metal storage cabinets and a small sink. The other side had furniture, covered like in an old movie, but I barely registered the details.

What waited straight ahead brought me to a halt, and the door creaked shut behind me. It was the biggest computer mess I'd ever seen. A long worktable, overflowing, with piles on the floor as well:

laptops and monitors, more keyboards, cards, mouses and random components than I could count, not to mention miles of cabling, a tube monitor from back when computers were beige, and at least two desktop towers. I hadn't seen one of those since I was kid taking apart an old one in Dad's basement.

Pulling off my hat and scarf, I whispered into the silent room, "Holy...shit."

I found a folding chair behind the table and sat, taking the weight off my knee. For a couple of solid hours, I rummaged through computer hardware older than me. Needing a break, I explored the rest of the room before diving back into the tech. The sheet covered a sofa in a vintage shade of muddy brown, and a rolled-up rug. The storage cabinets held a trove of random stuff: even more computer parts (in case I didn't have enough already), light bulbs, a transistor radio, a pair of leather gloves, loose papers, and an electric tea kettle, its age given away by the cloth-wrapped cord and giant plug. Would it still work? All the way at the bottom sat a rusting toolbox with wood-handled vintage tools.

I'd expected something like an IT closet, but what I found was more along the lines of a workroom, or even an office. Someone spent considerable time there as evidenced by the tea kettle and the secondhand sofa. I plopped, as much as my knee would allow, onto the sofa with the papers from the cabinet. This kicked up enough dust to make me sneeze. Mental note: no more plopping.

Right off, I recognized the formula for calculating time travel coordinates. Why would someone do this longhand? They make you memorize it in your initial TE training, but I've never used it since. I waved away dust, flipping pages. The last few appeared to be schematic diagrams. Did they all fit together, or were they preliminary sketches of the same thing? Hard to tell around the mess. I tilted my head, squinting, turning pages over and around.

At best, I understood maybe half—too many unfamiliar symbols and abbreviations. Instead of running off the reactor in Nuke-E like the portal at Temporal Engineering, this tapped into the underground campus power. A drop slot somewhere upstairs led to a mini time portal near the ceiling. Equipment scanned an envelope and routed to the requested point in time.

It was a great idea—simple and brilliant, but the specifics of the system were ridiculously complicated.

I stood, careful of my knee, and crutched over to where I could hold up the schematics in front of the equipment and study both at once. There were cross outs and notes in a second handwriting. Messier and harder to decipher in faded pencil. Below that, was the first hand again. All the way in the bottom right corner of the page, crumbled and almost falling off was a dash and three capital letters, like initials: KRB.

Wait a minute. Was that...?

*

THERESA
September 2018 / January 2042

We weren't ready in two weeks, but thanks to James, it didn't matter.

The hospital staff had given me a sealed bag with everything from his pockets. The mugger had stolen the cash and phone but left the rest behind. When Vanhanen asked Chris for his key card on their last day, he handed over the one from James's wallet instead.

V closed down Temporal Engineering exactly like he planned, but at least a month went by before Chris and I had everything prepped.

My bravado aside, what we were about to do and where I was about to go left me anxious, uncomfortable, almost twitchy. In the nighttime silence of Nuclear Engineering, I looked over my shoulder the whole way to TE until the lock clicked shut behind us. Despite his supposed retirement, Vanhanen hadn't gotten rid of anything yet. Empty desks and covered equipment reminded me more of a storage room than a department that had been truly closed, like it was all just...*waiting*. I shook off a shiver and Chris waved me into the lab.

Alone in the center of the room stood an antique door frame wired to computers, equipment and power. From the control workstation, he set up the jump and input the coordinates, then nodding to me over his shoulder when it was almost ready. Emitters, set into the heavy wood all the way around, glowed purple, brightening to white. Electricity sparked from one to the next until it outlined the whole frame, throwing a flickering glare into the otherwise dark room. The arched opening turned silvery opaque before fading to a cloudy haze as the temporal field formed.

As I crossed the threshold, a buzzing sensation passed through me, uncomfortably bright and loud for an instant. Lights came on in the dark lab on the far side. I called out, "Is someone there?" before realizing it was only a motion sensor. Jumpy much?

The furniture looked exactly like before, but the computers were all updated: smaller and sleeker, with everything wireless. Everything wireless meant no USB connection ports! I sat up sharply, looking back toward the portal, but it had already gone dark.

Methodically, I searched each computer, one by one, focusing on the task to calm my anxiety. On an older machine running a backup system, I found a single empty slot. Muttering, "Shit," after getting the USB stick backwards on the first try, I reversed it and wiggled the mouse to wake the computer. No need to even touch the keyboard, I was a better hacker than that.

In a moment, the software quietly copied itself. Eventually, it would replicate to all the computers on their network. When they reviewed resumes of recent grads, mine would be at the top of the list.

In the outer office, I paused at the hallway door. Chris had made sure the new lock for the round room in the union was the same brand and model as at TE because it included a proprietary connection cable. From the secure side, granting myself access took only a few minutes. It was unlikely someone would show up at midnight, but I still wanted to finish and get the hell out of there.

As the door clicked shut behind me, I felt the first sensation of a temporal headache. Despite all the planning and the papers for a new identity in my bag, heading down the hall away from TE, it finally hit me.

I'd left Theresa Jones behind.

*

TIA
May 2043

I set a bottle of wine on the counter. Calling it a kitchen would have been generous. A year and a half before, I rented the smallest and cheapest wheelchair accessible apartment I could find: a kitchenette on one wall of the living room, and an alcove on the other side barely wide enough for a twin bed and a lamp.

Inflation had been worse in the years I'd jumped over than expected. I had enough to get by, but it'd been tight. Advertised prices still shocked me sometimes; even bottom-shelf wine cost more than several bottles in my old timeline.

Planning on celebrating, I didn't want to dwell on money or the life I left behind. Things hadn't gone perfectly but were good enough. I spent the first few months living like a hermit and studying. Learning every day about the history, and more important, the technology, that had come and gone in the years I jumped over. Old tech information got boring eventually, so I alternated with streaming documentaries about music, culture, unsolved mysteries, anything I could find.

By the 2040s, everything was streaming. Physical media was essentially gone. One bought broadband internet like water and power, cellular wireless that didn't come in through a cable.

Handheld phones were rare. Most people wore a device on their wrist which unfolded or stretched to run apps and such. Some even came with earbuds stored in the corners. The watch, tablet, computer, stereo, game console and home control system were all interconnected and couldn't function separately.

University records showed me transferring from a school in South Africa without accessible buildings. A believable enough story, the remoteness of which made it harder to check. No one did.

In truth, I'd immigrated as a baby with my mother, and didn't remember Africa at all. What I *did* remember was Mom's accent. It embarrassed me that she didn't talk like the other kids' moms, even the other Black kids. After the jump, I let her accent color my speech every day. Not as thick, but enough to sound different and support my cover story. Seeming foreign also helped explain any anachronisms I said by accident.

In order for my sleeper virus to flag my resume, I needed to ace my last year of grad school in the 2040s. I busted my ass and was eventually contacted by a certain shadowy department doing classified research. Vanhanen held our first interview in a tiny, nondescript conference room in the engineering department. He didn't appear to know about my disability beforehand because we had to adjust the chairs to make room. Polite but guarded, he had me sign nondisclosure documents on actual paper with an actual pen before he delved into anything even close to the work he was hiring for.

Vanhanen began with talking about electromagnetics and some of the other peripheral components of what his department researched. He worked his way around to the more theoretical elements of it, but never once mentioned the name of the department or said anything about time travel. A week later, I got called in for a second interview.

I poured the wine and took a sip. Alcohol had been an unnecessary luxury, but I splurged in celebration of landing the job and finally moving to the next step. Hopefully, after a few paychecks, I could afford an apartment not quite so microscopic—maybe one with actual rooms and actual doors. That'd be nice.

After my second glass, thoughts wandered fuzzily toward topics I'd consciously walled off since my jump. I'd needed to focus on catching up, classes, and grades, so I compartmentalized and never dealt with things in a healthy way. The wine let the dam break or at least start to leak. What began as a celebration ended with me crying on my shitty thrift-store sofa, thinking about James, about Chris, and about my mother.

The story I told Mom was that I was in witness protection because I needed to testify against the mugger's gang. It was a thin story, and I knew it, but it was the best I could come up with and it fit my pending disappearance.

I hadn't cried like that since the earliest days in my tiny apartment. When I'd looked for her online, I read about a global pandemic in 2020 and discovered Mom had been in the first wave of casualties, months before the vaccine became available. I felt devastated. I knew I couldn't have contacted her. Explaining my age was impossible, and I'm not sure what change perpetuation would have done with her memories of my disappearance. Knowing she was out there somewhere and doing okay would have been nice—comforting, I guess.

Working at TE meant finally having access to a time machine, but even with it, I couldn't go back and change things. The feeling of being alone was the most crushing. James was gone. Chris was as good as. The job was my first goal, and I'd reached it, but at what cost? For *so* long it was only me on this...whatever it was—quest?—for vengeance. Would it always be?

Even if I worked out a way to stop Vanhanen, to hack the equipment or trap him in the distant past, keeping Chris and all the other engineers safe, I'd still be out of time and alone. Was there any way back to my original timeline, if not my original life?

But no—fixated as I was on V, my secondary reason for jumping remained valid. I'd need to stay in the future if I wanted to walk again; and I *did*. Absolutely, I did.

I downed the last of the glass but decided not to finish the bottle.

4

KIERNEN
May 2067

The director called me into the office. That's where this all started.

But was it? Does one ever know where a story begins? Was it my youthful drive to understand the inner workings of things? Was it my academic overachieving as a means of gaining approval and attention from parents who loved me, but didn't excel at showing it?

Even in retrospect I remained unsure.

I poked my head through the empty doorway and saw her lift a stack of old paper books off a chair by her perpetually cluttered desk. She turned and appeared intent on stashing them in a bookcase which was also overflowing. She momentarily considered the top shelf and four detailed miniatures carefully positioned there:

a phone booth, a silver car, a police call box, and a Victorian era contraption with levers and knobs. Rather than disturb the models, she shrugged and set the books on the floor before gesturing to the seat she'd cleared. Without context, this might seem akin to being called to the principal's office or if I was about to be reprimanded for job performance. That was not the case.

She pointed toward the lab. "We got a message this morning from a field engineer in the nineteen sixties," she began. "He needs assistance."

"Sounds interesting."

"Specifically, the message asked if I could send my best engineer."

I was taken aback. Even though I'd worked at Temporal Engineering for a while, I still felt like I needed to compensate for my youth. I'd graduated high school and college early because that's what "smart kids" did, but it created an unexpected side effect. I was always acutely aware I was younger than the people around me and felt the need to prove my worth, to show I deserved to be there. I was recruited to TE right out of grad school, so it was my first career job. Even though the team there was supportive, I still struggled with my own version of imposter syndrome. After my initial surprise at the director's compliment, I managed to stammer out, "I...uh...I'm glad you think I fit that description."

"Well, you do." She set her reading glasses on the desktop and brushed back a lock of graying hair which refused to stay in her short ponytail. "This isn't going to be an easy assignment. You'll likely be helping invent the Timeslot system with century old tools and equipment, clunky electronics, no computers, and tech like they used for the moon launch. Some people might see it as a challenge, but the limitations could frustrate them enough to throw up their hands and quit."

Was this the opportunity I was waiting for? A chance to shine?

I must have looked like I was about to reply because she shook her head. "Wait. Let me finish. There's more to it than that. Before you go and get enamored with a design challenge, remember what the world was like a hundred years ago. The culture was a lot more primitive. It was a tough time for Blacks. The safety of our engineers is always top priority when sending someone into the field. On a college campus, the chance of life-threatening danger is low, but it was a *very* different world then.

"You can do this assignment, and I think you can do it well, but I want you to understand what you're walking into. Before you answer, you should decide not only how you would do this work, but if you're sure you want to."

*

TIA
October 2043

I'd finally gotten rid of all the cardboard boxes, but my new apartment still felt too sparse—like I hadn't lived there long enough to accumulate much stuff. An accessible unit on the first floor, open from kitchen to living room to dining nook, but all discernably separate spaces, and an actual primary bedroom, with a huge closet too. Cool, hip, armless furniture with metal frames and soft gray cushions replaced the nasty couch I left behind at my old place.

Amber was the first visitor, other than my landlord. Unsurprisingly, she texted she'd be late. Something I'd realized not long after the wheelchair, that able-bodied people don't fully grasp, is that the disabled don't often need extra help as much as we need extra time. It takes us longer to do a thing, or to get from here to there. When Amber had told me about her ADHD and how it made her late, I shrugged and rolled with it.

The slow cooker full of chili didn't care if we ate it sooner or later. I set the door security app to Unlocked, and told her to let herself in. She gently set an assorted six-pack of beer on the counter. "Better wait before we open those. Probably got shook up on the ride over." She removed her bike helmet and ran fingers through her short red hair. "Nice place. This is bigger than mine. Newer too."

"Thanks." It occurred to me to ask, "Don't you and Meg? Y'know?" while gesturing vaguely around.

"Ugh. We keep talking about moving in, but it keeps not happening. Leases and stuff."

I suspected there was more, but let it drop. "Uh-huh."

Behind me, Shadow emerged from the bedroom and jumped into my lap, curling his tail around him. The bend in his tail, and a scar on one ear were reminders of hard-learned lessons from his former life. In short, he was kind of a badass, and I think he knew it. Amber smiled, "So that's the notorious cat, huh?"

"Mm-hmm. Amber, Shadow. Shadow, Amber." She reached in to scratch his ears, and he decided to allow it.

"Why the name though?"

I pointed toward my patio. "The streetlight casts a shadow from that landscaping wall. It was only my second night here, and with his gray and black fur, all I saw were green eyes, *hovering* in the dark. It scared the shit out of me to be honest."

She kept scratching. "A runaway maybe?"

"He was skinny, but the vet said he didn't look like he'd been on his own for long. He already knew the layout of the apartment, so either he ran away from someone, or got left behind by a previous tenant. I think he was looking for new human staff and waiting for me to realize I'd been appointed to the position."

"Yeah, funny." She paused scratching to point toward the kitchen. "That chili smells amazing, by the way."

Over bowls of it she asked, "Okay, spill. What're we watching tonight?"

"That first time we went out for lunch, you said you'd never seen *Star Wars*, right?"

"Yeah…" She sounded unsure. "I've seen little bits of it here and there: spaceships and light sabers and all. My dad was super into *Lord of the Rings* and fantasy stuff in general, not spaceships. There's what—like twenty movies, plus all the series and stuff. Where do you even start?"

"You start at the beginning, obviously."

"But wasn't it all released out of order?"

I put my spoon down, enjoying sharing this with a friend who was interested. I explained in brief about the trilogies, the pre-quels and the sale to Disney.

She looked a little confused and asked, "Wait. So, *which* one are we watching?"

"In the twenty teens, some fans digitized an archived print from 1977, making the only high-rez copy of the original theatrical version. They called it the Silver Screen Edition."

"And that's what we're watching?"

"Yep. It's my favorite, and it's the best way to introduce some-one to the series—wonky special effects and all."

As the twin suns set over Tatooine, my mind drifted. They say it's harder to make friends in adulthood. I'd had several casual ac-quaintances in grad school in my second timeline, but not anyone I would consider a close friend. I was so focused on grades and the eventual job I didn't notice until later.

Somehow, Shadow's appearance coincided with things improving. After working at TE for a while, Amber and I started having lunch together a few times a week. It was so much nicer than eating on the back patio by myself. I heard all about her girlfriend drama, and I shared what I could of my own backstory.

Her revelation about *Star Wars* was part of a conversation about D&D, which came right after a story about soccer. "Y'know," I'd begun, gently teasing, "Most people are either a jock or a nerd..."

She held up both hands. "I know. I know. My dad makes the same joke all the time."

I jumped at the opportunity to invite her over for the movie. I missed having real friends, but if I'm honest, there was more to it. I know I can't ask anyone to help with V at the far end. That's on me. Having someone along the way though... Was Amber that friend? Would we eventually become that close one day? Or was I latching onto the first close human connection I've had since James died? Is it possible for her to be both?

Right after the Death Star exploded and the medal ceremony, Amber asked eagerly, "Do you have the next one too? Can we..." She looked at her watch. "Shit. I told Meg I'd meet up with her. How about next weekend?"

"Of course!"

And just like that, "movie night" began.

*

CHARLES
July 1967

A week previous, I threw a message forward a hundred years in hopes it would land somewhere past V's influence. I answered a knock at the door in the round room to find a skinny

Black guy with chunky glasses frames and short trimmed hair. He was dressed in khaki carpenter pants, a denim shirt, heavy work boots, and carrying a toolbox. We exchanged quotes from *The Time Machine*, and I held the door open. "I'm Charles, by the way."

"Yes, I read your message. I'm…"

I interrupted, "Remember, not your real name."

"Of course. We have protocols for field engineers in my time too. I was about to introduce myself as Kasey, which I assure you is not my given name."

I smiled and nodded as he looked over the components and equipment spread out on the worktable. "You don't look like what I expected, but I guess I'm not sure what I expected."

"Someone older?"

"Partly, but I think the workman getup threw me off."

"I discussed this at length with my director. She thought the safest thing would be for me to look as incognito as possible."

Internally, I let out a sigh of relief. He said "she." Maybe my request went past V's time after all. Good!

"No one ever notices the repair guy. Especially a Black one at this point in history. I might as well be invisible."

"That's smart, very smart."

He smirked. "Well, you did ask for the best."

I chuckled, then looked at my watch. "Y'know, I was going to walk you through my design first thing when you got here, but honestly, I'm starving. Let's have lunch before we get started. I know a great barbeque place."

He seemed like a highly capable engineer, and a genuinely good guy. I wasn't sure how or if I should reveal more.

5

TIA
January 2045

Harsh light flickered through the lab windows, and I heard the deep hum of the time portal as soon as I entered the outer office.

There were no jumps scheduled for that morning. Who activated the portal, and why?

I opened the lab door to see Vanhanen stepping out through the arch. His usual gray suit looked windblown, his tie crooked. Was he even a little out of breath? He straightened, sounding surprised, "Miss James! I didn't expect anyone here this early."

I tugged at a curly brown lock, badly in need of a trim. "Hair appointment this afternoon? I told you about it last week."

"That's right, you did. I didn't see it on the calendar." He turned toward the workstation, typing quickly. The hum diminished as the equipment powered back down. He gestured toward the portal speaking rapidly in a way that was *almost* overly dismissive. "Uh...something needed checking first thing this morning. If I'd known you planned to get in early, I would have asked you to help with it. Well, it's done now."

Did he intentionally stand so I couldn't read the screen? Clearly, I wasn't supposed to witness his early-morning jump, so I never mentioned it again, and slipped straight back into my role as his reliable IT person. What was he up to? I didn't know, but it was the first time since starting at Temporal Engineering that I saw him slip up.

In the weeks following that morning, I wrote an app to create a secondary log of time jumps. I quietly installed it on the TE server, right under his nose. Even if someone altered the main jump log, the backup would be sent to my personal tablet. I'd see every time he jumped, and to when. Eventually, I hoped, a pattern would emerge.

Now, the hardest part—patience.

*

KASEY
August 1967

Considering the ancient technology, we made admirable pro-gress, even in only ten days. Charles and I spent the first few sequestered in the round room in the basement, ideating and sketching.

As a physicist, Charles filled the role of temporal theory expert on our little team, but he was far less adept at fabrication, hence his request for an engineer. At a quick glance, our clothes would lead someone to guess he was the brain, and I was the labor. In practice, it was much the opposite. Charles had the overall design in mind but needed me to execute the specifics and handed over directorship for the build. He willingly accepted any support tasks, no matter how mundane.

Charles had jumped to that timeline ahead of me, in part, to set up accommodations and finances. We shared a small apartment and had enough resources for food and such, but not for purchasing NASA-level equipment.

In that era, ordinary citizens didn't carry a minicomputer in their pocket, which made sourcing the necessary equipment tricky. The required technology was large, rare, and if one could even procure it at all, expensive. We had to get creative.

We stood among a cluster of people outside a nondescript storage building along the far north edge of campus. A man in front of us, with long sideburns, dug around in his pocket and produced a pipe, which he lit with a wooden match. We turned toward each other with matching grimaces and edged to the back of the crowd without a word.

"I can't believe that used to be *legal*," I mumbled, then clamped my mouth shut before saying anything else out of time.

"Hmm?" he asked.

"Nothin', nothin'." I waved it away along with the smoke and changed the subject. "What are you expecting to find here?"

"I'm not sure exactly. I read about it in the campus paper. People call it the University Garage Sale. The article said it's been going on for a long time, but it's not well advertised. Sometimes you can get lucky on random equipment cheap."

As the garage door opened, the crowd surged forward eagerly. I squinted into the dim interior. "It looks like mostly broken furniture."

Charles shrugged. "Let's poke around before we write it off."

Following the crowd into the building, my eyes adjusted to reveal tables and shelves extending farther back than I could see around the crowd. "Where's all this junk come from?"

"Departments replace stuff all the time, but I guess some of it comes from old lost-and-found boxes across campus."

An hour later, we left, carrying an ammeter with a loose handle, an oscilloscope with a scratched screen and a missing knob, the ends of several spools of wire in assorted colors, a bag of conduit fittings, and more, all jammed into a ragged cardboard box. I hoisted it onto my shoulder and followed Charles toward the sidewalk.

"That room's going to start looking like Frankenstein's lab," I muttered.

Once we were away from the crowd, Charles spoke quietly, "We still need a codename for this contraption."

We'd already dismissed CTPS (cross timeline postal service) as too complicated, and TPE (temporal pony express) as too silly.

"I still like Timeslot," I said.

"Yeah, I know. I'm concerned it'd be confusing since it's already a term used at TE."

"Time will tell…"

"I guess maybe it will."

After acquiring the secondhand equipment and repairing it, neither Charles nor I had time to restock our dwindling refrigerator. We walked to a local steak house for dinner instead of the grocery store.

The restaurant was crowded, so we opted to sit at the bar. I was about halfway through a mug of mediocre beer and two or three bites into a thoroughly amazing steak when we were interrupted.

Two locals, dressed in jeans, work boots, and stained T-shirts, stood over us and spoke to each other in a tone we were clearly meant to overhear. They talked loudly about how full the restaurant was and how these were their regular places at the bar. The taller of the pair leaned in. "It'd sure be a shame if anyone was to get hurt 'cause we had to wait for own goddamn seats."

I held up my hands and slipped into a mode of speech he might expect, "Look mister, we don't want no trouble."

Charles took a long time chewing, wiped his mouth, and set the napkin down. "We'll be happy to leave as soon as we're done."

People around us began to stare.

The shorter and heavier of the two spoke more quietly and more harshly than his friend, managing to include racial slurs against each of us and a graphically homophobic suggestion all in one sentence.

It left me scared speechless. In my home time, that combination of bigotry and aggression was known only as ancient history, as distant as muskets or a compact disc. My hands shook as I grabbed the edge of the bar to push my chair back.

Charles's reaction, unexpectedly, did not match mine. Instead of moving to get up, he lifted his beer toward his mouth with the annoyed expression of a man whose patience was being pushed near its limit. Without warning, one of them kicked his chair hard enough to tip it. He landed on his back and the mug shattered beside him. In the confusion, I stood up, but I'm not sure what I thought I was going to do. The restaurant went quiet.

In seconds, the bartender and a middle-aged man (probably the owner) grabbed the four of us and pushed us out a side door into the alley, yelling, "Take it outside!"

The door swung closed and one of them gave me a shove. I stumbled over some broken crates and fell onto the dusty ground by a row of garbage cans. I rolled over in time to see the second one pull a knife and flick it open.

He lunged forward, and I flinched, trying to turn away. A blur of motion to my right, and a long piece of wood lay across my stomach with the switchblade stuck in it.

Charles pulled the board back, spun it, and struck the thug in the head with the other end, dropping him to the pavement instantly. He removed the knife and handed me the piece of wood before rounding on the one who shoved me—the shorter one. He shifted into a fighting stance, holding the stolen knife like he knew how to use it.

My own adrenaline kicked in and I stepped up beside him hefting the board like a baseball bat.

The second thug looked from his friend groaning in the dirt to the two of us, armed as we were, and decided not to stick around. Charles chased him as far as the end of the alley but gave up and returned.

He found me bent over, hands on knees taking deep breaths. "You okay?"

"Yeah. Yeah." I pulled up my shirt and saw my unharmed abdomen. Dropping it, I added, "You saved my life."

"There've been enough dead field engineers. We don't need another." He slapped me gently on the shoulder.

I nodded. "Let's get the hell out of here."

Instead, he edged toward the door, gripping the knob. "No. Enough of this bullshit. I have a better idea."

A waiter had just picked up our plates as we opened the door. The bartender looked up. "What are you two doing back in here?"

Charles smiled and said politely, "We'd like to finish our steaks."

"And pay you for them, of course." I added.

We sat and did exactly that.

Walking home from the restaurant, I asked what he meant by "enough dead engineers."

"That, my friend, is a long story. But after tonight, it's one I need to trust you with."

6

TIA
January 2045

I texted ahead for a table rather than a booth. They had to shuffle around at the last minute, but got it sorted before Amber arrived. That a woman who clearly struggled with tardiness, studied *time* for a living... Well, the audacity of it always made me smile. She insisted if she was ever early it might kill me from the shock. She unwound her scarf and brushed snow out of her hair before setting her ski jacket on an empty seat.

"I'm surprised you ever want to wear that again."

"Eh. It was on top. You know how my place gets." Pointing at the crutches next to the coat she said, "I cannot *wait* to get off those things though. Kurtis already loaned me a cane for later."

I had no trouble imagining it—dark wood with African carving. Amber explained to me once how the palest White person I knew ended up with a cool Black uncle. He'd married her dad's older sister, and with no family of his own was welcomed into theirs. He and Amber had gotten close living in the same little college town.

She leaned over for a quick hug saying, "Missed you."

"You too! It's been so quiet with you not there. V's been gone a lot too."

"More than usual?" she asked.

"Mm-hmm."

"Weird."

After I ordered a veggie omelet and Amber a breakfast burrito, I asked about the Timeslot room. "So how *is* the temporary gig going?"

She looked up from adding cream to her coffee. "Did you know that place even existed? 'Cause I didn't."

"Sort of... There's a blank spot in the power use monitoring software labeled 'auxiliary.' I asked V about it a long time ago. His answer was vague enough to get my curiosity going. Nobody's touched it in years. Is it bad?"

"That place is a huge mess! I'll send you a pic. A whole week and I'm only beginning to make sense of it. At first, I thought it was just a heap of old computer junk. I found some hand-drawn schematics, so there might be more to it...if I can figure out the drawings"

"I notice you're bitching, but you're also smiling. Could you actually be enjoying it?"

She looked sheepish and held up her hands. "You know how I am about vintage tech."

Underneath the constant clutter, Amber's apartment held evidence of both her engineering desire to understand machines, as well as her tendency to get focused on a project. An antique espresso machine, a vintage stereo and turntable, even an upright video game, were each acquired nonfunctioning and repaired after weeks spent disassembled all over the floor, table, counter, whatever. I knew this challenge was comfortably in her wheelhouse. Smirking, I added, "This sounds like a mountain of vintage tech."

"Oh yeah."

When I couldn't wait any longer, and she obviously wasn't going to bring it up, I addressed the elephant in the room. Or is it gorilla? I can never remember. "So...have you heard from Meg?"

She set her fork down and took a long drink of coffee before answering, "No, but I didn't expect to. She's on to bigger and better, right?"

I gave a puzzled look. "Just because she's with someone taller than you, doesn't mean anything. Certainly not *better*."

She squinted like I wasn't getting it and held both hands out in front of her chest. "Bigger."

I glared a little but let it go. Changing the direction of the conversation, I asked, "Did you even tell her about the accident? If you'd given her the tickets, and she went with New Girl..." I trailed off.

"Yeah. I know. Don't you think I've thought about that a million times?"

Of course she had. She said as much at the hospital after her knee surgery.

"The thing is, and I've had a lot of time to think about this..." She took a deep breath. "It's okay. Getting dumped isn't easy to hear. If I'm being honest though, we were over for a while already. We were coasting, and she finally called it quits."

I nodded, listening.

"She used to gripe that the life I wanted was boring. I worked too much, my interests were weird and nerdy, and...I dunno. Maybe it's living here, but she sometimes acted like we were still students, going to bars and concerts and all the stuff in this town catering to undergrads. I mean, pardon me for wanting to be an adult, y'know?"

"Why stick around then? Or did it always feel like things were about to get better?"

"It was momentum as much as anything. We were together for close to two years. You develop a lot of habits in that much time." She fidgeted with her fork. "I guess, not being really happy becomes a habit too. Leaving just felt so daunting. In the end, she accused me of being emotionally absent, but I could say the same about her."

"Mm-hmm."

"The thing is, I'm great at *being* a girlfriend, but I'm terrible at *finding* one. It must be a different skill set. Meg was introduced by a friend-of-a-friend. The thought of trying to meet someone, having to be all smooth and impressive—ugh, I just hate that."

"So, what *do* you want?"

"I want to move on; past the breakup, past my knee and this tediously slow recovery. Sorry, but I even want past the giant heap of computer parts waiting in the basement of the student union." She smirked. "Well intentioned and interesting as they are."

She was finally venting, and I was letting her get it out. She needed it. Between the breakup, the skiing accident, and the knee surgery, she'd had a pretty shitty start to 2045.

*

AMBER
January 2045

Kurtis tried to talk me into going out for dinner, but I refused; it was my turn. Making stew in the slow cooker, I wouldn't be on my feet too long. The conversation I wanted, no—*needed* to have—wasn't for a public place like a restaurant.

He brought great wine. He always did. During dessert and coffee, I brought up a photo on my tablet—a closeup of the initials with a fragment of the diagram visible next to the letters. He looked at it on the table between us for a long moment. "Where did you get this?"

"Is it you? Are you KRB?"

"But how...where could you have found this?"

I shook my head. "Uh-uh. You first. Did you write your initials on the corner of a schematic diagram in the basement of the student union?"

Unsurprisingly, he looked unsure how to answer that, so I spared him the trouble.

"The Morlocks," I began.

"And the Eloy," he correctly replied, looking a little shocked but beginning the next passphrase anyway. "The matches...from the museum..."

"Were strike-on-box only," I responded, both of us smiling.

He scratched his goatee and squinted at me for a second. "I wondered all along, you know. You were maybe a little *too* evasive about the details of your job. I told myself the chances were infinitesimal. Thousands of students every year, and only a handful of positions at Temporal Engineering. Perhaps if you'd been a thespian instead of playing soccer, your acting skills might have been up to fooling me."

"You could have asked."

"How awkward if I was wrong though—standing in your kitchen quoting H.G. Wells for no reason?"

"Okay, fair point." I tapped the photo. "So this was you?"

"Yes, an expanse of time ago. I was younger than you are now."

"But the diagram was from the nineteen sixties." He smirked and waited for me to catch up, "Oh my god, time travel—of course! You were a field engineer?"

"There you go."

TE didn't frequently send people into the past anymore—at least, not that I knew of.

"So you've been to the Timeslot room," he asked.

"I'm supposed to be repairing it while recuperating." I tapped my knee and shrugged.

"Repairing? How bad is it?"

The photo I sent Tia was still on my tablet. His reaction was as shocked as mine but mixed with the disappointment and frustration of seeing something you built broken.

"Do you ever have your work cut out for you!"

"I know! If I brought home the schematics, would you take a look at them? Or better yet, would you come over to the student union with me?"

He flinched minutely at my suggestion. "Bring the drawings over tomorrow night. I'll help you decipher them, but unfortunately, that's the extent of what I can do." I must have looked disappointed because he continued. "You of all people know why I'm concerned about getting too involved, and why I'm reticent to discuss it."

I nodded. "You're worried about screwing up the timeline or creating a paradox."

"Exactly. In fact, it would be best for now if you don't even mention my part in this at all."

"I have so many questions: When did you work for TE? Why did you leave?" I stopped myself with sigh. "But I suppose you won't answer those either, will you?"

"You suppose correctly. However, I have one question if you'll indulge me."

"Sure."

"Who is your employer at Temporal Engineering?"

"He's an older guy, Horatio Vanhanen, but Tia and I just refer to him as V."

Concern flashed across his face, but when he spoke again, he asked, "Your friend Tia works with you?"

"Shit—didn't mean to let that slip."

He gave a small, kind smile. "It's not a problem. You're not in much danger of entangling my timeline by what you say, removed as I am from TE." He turned serious, "But do be careful around your Mr. V."

"Did you know him? Is that why you won't talk about him?" He held up a hand to quiet me.

"No specifics. Just be wary of anything feeling suspicious. Vanhanen is far more concerned with his own wealth than any-thing else—even TE and the people there."

I reached across the table and took his hand. "What do you mean? You're freaking me out a little."

He smiled reassuringly and squeezed my fingers. "I'm glad you have Tia there with you. She sees more than people realize. You two would be wise to watch each other's backs."

Kurtis and I spent Saturday afternoon and evening going through the schematics, component by component, connection by connection.

An hour or so in, it occurred to me that the build he described and the heap in the basement of the union didn't exactly match. Someone had done additional work in the years since.

After he mentioned a particular component, a specific connec-tion port, I jumped in and asked, "Okay, but why not use a VQX coupler instead?"

He sounded annoyed in the way only older people can be with the young and their technology. "Well, I didn't have one at the time."

"Meaning...you didn't have one available in your stash, or you built this before it was invented?"

He smiled, but didn't answer.

"I thought those dated back into the nineties."

Shrugging, he replied vaguely, "Maybe. Maybe even earlier."

"Wait. How much earlier are we talking about?"

He answered with a smirk, "Nice try," then returned his attention to the schematic.

In my head, I began running through how to modernize it but thought it best to keep it to myself. After we finished, he produced an old bottle of scotch. "This deserves a drink of something stronger than our usual grape."

After one sip, I blurted out, "Oh my god, that's good!"

"I'm glad you like it."

It was easily the smoothest whiskey I'd ever had. What could I say? The man knew his booze.

The rideshare dropped me at the student union. I planned to leave the schematics and check on a couple of components we talked about, but I opened a box and idly dug through parts and connections, thinking I'd lay them out for the next day. I knew myself and my own ADHD brain well enough to predict what would happen if I'd stopped to think about it, but I didn't. I got focused, and before I realized it, it was morning.

*

CHARLES
August 1967

Instead of walking from the restaurant to the apartment, we headed to the student union. In the round room, I plugged in the tea kettle and gestured toward the lone chair in the room.

"Have a seat." I flipped over a crate and sat also.

"We should get a sofa in here. Students are always selling them on the cheap," Kasey suggested.

"Good idea." I paused, not even sure where to begin. "The reason I reached so far forward for help, was to avoid the attention of the TE director from my time. I wasn't sure I'd reached far enough until you referred to your director as 'she'."

"I didn't know that'd make such a significant difference, but okay."

"I should back up and give you more context." I rubbed my forehead and continued. "My best friend, since I was a kid, was James, who lived down the street from me. Eventually we both studied here at the university—him in engineering, and me in physics..."

It felt weird to talk about it with someone other than Theresa, as if speaking aloud made it real. Or maybe *present* was a better word. Since jumping to the 60s, my attention had been on other things and telling it to Kasey brought it all back. With it came the frustration and anger, even a bit of the fear. But talking about James also made me smile. We'd had a hell of a laugh when we both showed up for work the first day at TE, neither of us knowing the other had been approached for a secret interview.

Months into the job, James came over and we sat on my balcony drinking beer. He complained about the number of time jumps the director made, and how we still weren't allowed. In that way conversation rolls only when drinking, we made a couple leaps of intuition we might not have made otherwise. James became convinced that there must be another reason beyond inexperience that our director wouldn't let us jump.

That was how it started. James's obsession with the director and his belief in a mystery to solve was the direct result of our alcohol-fogged, late-night conversation.

After we sobered up, he still wouldn't let it go and quietly searched through all the records he could access. He learned the department had been around since the 1940s, but it hadn't been in continuous operation; there were periodic closures and drop-outs in staff. I suggested a connection to the funding cycle of our government contract, but he wouldn't buy it. Eventually, he let his fiancé in on the secret. She was a software whiz and helped him get past the security lockouts.

The teapot whistled. Kasey put bags and water in mugs and handed me one. "If he'd been caught, that would have been grounds for dismissal in my time."

"In ours too."

Weeks passed without James mentioning it, so I thought he'd dropped it. The two of them invited me over for dinner, but it was really to show me what they'd found: partial records, but with enough of a pattern to convince me there was something more going on.

A forty-year-old news clipping showed a story about a woman who disappeared at the university—at work one day and the next just...gone. They never found her. No suspects or even a scrap of evidence. James discovered she'd worked for TE. There was a jump the night before she'd been reported missing. The record of that jump was incomplete.

"Someone altered the log?" Kasey interrupted.

I nodded.

I knew James would say "yes" before I even asked, but I had to know if there were others. He'd found evidence of at least two. One was killed during a break-in at his house, and the other had been in a car crash. Both times the department closed down within months but reopened a few years later with all new staff. James believed the disappearances were TE people who had either been caught digging or discovered something and confronted the boss.

"But *he* was digging, wasn't he?"

I responded flatly, "Yeah. He was digging." It still gutted me to say it out loud. "A week later, while James and Theresa walked to their car after a movie, a mugger stepped out of an alley and shot them both."

Kasey gasped, "Oh my god!"

"He'd been looking so hard for proof of what happened to the missing engineers, and then...and then he became the proof."

"What'd you do?"

"What could I do?"

If we'd run, it would have tipped our hand that we knew what he was up to. I gritted my teeth and walked back through the door of TE, day after day. I kept on working, acting like nothing was wrong, right alongside the asshole who probably had them killed. Thankfully, I guess, it didn't go on for long. Vanhanen played it out much like before—this time announcing plans to "retire" and shutter the department soon after.

Kasey sat quietly, looking shocked, as if unsure what to say, his tea untouched beside him.

"So now you know, and hopefully you understand. This is probably my final jump, my last opportunity to follow the trail James uncovered. The Timeslot is something I'd brainstormed months earlier. It's a solid idea, and I believe it'll make jumps safer for field engineers. It exists now, though, largely to keep attention away from my research in this timeline."

When Kasey finally spoke, he asked with an unexpected smirk, "So you're agreeing to my name for the project?"

A short laugh escaped me at the unexpected change in tone, and I rolled my eyes. "Okay, okay, fine. Timeslot it is."

7

AMBER
February 2045

The power switch on the Timeslot computer lit up when I clicked it, and somewhere inside a fan whirred feebly but nothing more.

I texted Tia.

> **Amber**: *Threepio! This thing's got a bad motivator!*

A minute later, the vid call icon on my tablet lit up.

"Yo, you called?" At first, all I could see was a mass of curly dark hair. When she leaned back, she was smiling over the rim of her coffee cup.

"Do you know old Windows? I mean like *really* old?"

Her smile became a smirk, and her usual accent was replaced by one sounding like a polite British butler. "It's like a second language to me."

I rolled my eyes and dropped my head forward onto the table. When she was done laughing, she asked, "How could I resist such a perfect setup?

I groaned into the tabletop.

She tapped the screen. "Um, seriously, what do you need?"

I sat up and turned the tablet. "Here look for yourself."

"Okay, whoa, that *is* old! Get a little closer."

We worked on it together with the tablet propped on some junk while I typed. After half an hour, I asked, "Don't you have other stuff you need to do?"

"Nah. V's not even here."

"Okay. Are you bored out of your skull?"

"You know it. I'm considering taking up knitting. Hold on... this is weird. Your computer there isn't connected to the computer here."

"Well, this one's been off for a long, long time."

She directed me through a few more operations. "Hmm. It was always set up like this. Someone started a clunky workaround but never finished it."

"But other than that, can we fix it?"

That tugged her out of her puzzlement. "Oh sure. Bring up the list of attached devices. Did you update anything?

"Um." I looked around at the mess of computer parts on the table and the floor. "Yeah?" I responded feebly.

"How much?"

"Kind of a lot."

She made an exasperated sound and rolled her eyes. "Okay, I can walk you through this but it's going to take a while. By the way, you're bringing dinner and wine to movie night—and *I'm* picking the film!"

We worked for another two hours before Tia finally said, "Okay, that should do it. Restart the controller computer, then hit the power switch for the rest if it."

I did, and one by one the components powered on and did their thing. I turned the tablet around. "Thank you *so* much. I owe you one."

"Nah. Just dinner and wine."

"See ya Saturday."

"Later."

About three seconds after I disconnected, the distinctive low hum of a time portal powering up, sounded above me. I kicked the chair away from the desk and rolled backward looking up. Overhead, a familiar purple glow sputtered to life. Before I even had a chance to say, "Whoa," an envelope dropped through the portal and landed on the floor in front of me.

*

CRYSTAL
October 1993

To whoever finds this:

Our house always held just my mother and me. Dad was gone before I was born. She had a few photos of him, but that was it. He was a physics professor at the university, and she was a librarian. That's how they met.

I grew up going to that library almost every weekday. Mom and I had an agreement: I could walk to the library and hang out there until she was off work so long as I did my homework and didn't get into trouble. If I had, there would have been an afterschool babysitter, but it never happened. The quiet kid got access to more books than she could imagine. There was no way I would screw that up.

The only time even close to my being in trouble was when another librarian caught me practicing my viola in one of the back stairwells. (The echo sounded so cool!) Mom found me a rehearsal room after that.

I was a student at the university myself when her cancer diagnosis came, and the phrase "six to twelve months" was used. It was devastating. In fact, the word "devastating" might not be horrific enough. We prepared as best we could, but how do you ever really prepare for something like that?

We'd never argued all that much. Just stupid teenager shit, y'know? But, *wow,* we argued over whether I should finish my last semester of undergrad or stay home with her. Mom won that one. She was right, of course. She lived almost four hundred days after her diagnosis.

Her university insurance provided me with a grief counselor. I couldn't deny I'd come home after Mom's funeral and spent the next few weeks doing damn near nothing. Eventually, the counselor suggested cleaning out the house as a way to revisit the past, and to prepare for my future.

Hidden in a bottom drawer, I found a photo of my parents and an unfinished manuscript my father had written—a time-travel novel set at the university. The weird thing was if I hadn't lost my mom I never would have found this piece of my dad. It's not a trade I'd have made willingly, but it's the one I got.

In the story, there was a secret mail drop at the student union that the time travelers used. Oddly, it was the same spot my parents were standing in the photo—the landing of the atrium stairs above the zodiac. After reading the manuscript, standing there in front of the painting, I nudged the brass plaque with my finger. Same as in the story, it slid up to reveal an opening in the wall, wide enough for an envelope.

Somehow my dad found that, and it inspired his book. Too bad he never got to finish it. I wanted to know if they got the bad guy, or if there was a cool plot twist near the end.

I told you all this so you might understand why I did what I did next.

I walked around the house, finally admitting to myself I was done cleaning. I could have finished up a week or more before. At that point I was screwing around and maybe procrastinating. I knew I needed to move on, but I hadn't done it yet.

Finding the Timeslot, or at least a hole in the wall that inspired it, helped make something click for me.

I grabbed a pen and paper from my desk along with an overstuffed folder. Then, sitting on the couch in my living room, I wrote this letter. All about what happened and what I found and, ultimately, what it meant to me. It was important, but it was the past. When I discovered that slot and imagined dropping a letter into it, I started to think about letting go—letting go in a much larger sense.

Tomorrow morning I'm going to put this letter into the slot behind the plaque, and then it'll be beyond my control. I won't be able to take back what I've written, even if I want to. I will have literally let it go.

In the folder were all the admissions forms for my deferred acceptance to the university's graduate music program Mom made me fill out last year. I'm going to walk from the student union to the admissions building and restart my life.

Thank you for reading.

Crystal Yung, daughter of Emma and Charles

*

AMBER
February 2045

On the sofa in the Timeslot room, I read and reread the letter that had fallen through the portal while, uncharacteristically, wiping my eyes on my sleeve. The woman who wrote it was strong and amazing. Her story was at once both sad and empowering.

Honestly, it made me feel less awful about a breakup and a bad knee. We all have our own drama, but when we learned about someone else's stuff and could still empathize, maybe we weren't as far gone as we'd thought.

I got so wrapped up in Crystal's story about her mom, I had to think my way back around to the obvious fact about her dad. He'd clearly worked for TE. She used the word, "Timeslot," so that must have been in his writing.

On my tablet, I researched Crystal Yung. Public records had a birth certificate from 1969, schools attended through 1988, and inheritance of property in 1993—a too-brief summary of a life, for sure. I kept digging.

A school newsletter listed her name among others in a string ensemble winning a state competition while in high school. All that viola practice in the back stairs at the library had paid off.

The local paper had a brief article about her winning a music scholarship at the university. It included a photo of a slender girl with shoulder-length dark hair and bangs, posing with her viola on her lap. I enlarged the old low-rez image. She was cute, but still in that young and trying-so-hard-not-to-be-awkward phase that comes off as kind of stiff.

University records showed her in the school of music from 1988 to 1992 and starting grad classes in 1994. This matched the letter. She went back to finish school; good for her! I rooted for her from fifty years in the future.

Her parents' names were in the letter also. Her mother had the usual kind of stuff from a birth date in 1943, to schools, degrees, employment, marriage, purchase of a house, and finally her death in 1993.

Crystal said her dad was "gone" before she was born. Dead or left? University records showed him as a visiting physics professor from a school in California. The marriage license and a car registration were the only other things I could find, until I stumbled onto an obituary from September 15, 1969. His cause of death was listed as a motor vehicle crash.

Had Crystal's father been one of the engineers who built the equipment I was repairing? The timing was about right. If so, he'd likely spent hours in this exact room. I leaned back from the screen and spoke aloud, "Who were you, Charles?"

If the room knew, it didn't answer.

8

CHARLES
September 1967

The reference library had heavy dark wood furniture and a built-in help desk that looked at least as old as the university itself.

Facing away from me, all I could see of the librarian was a long dark ponytail and cat-eye glasses on top of her head. When she turned and asked what she could help me with, I was met with the smile of possibly the most beautiful women I'd ever seen. I mean, she was *gorgeous*.

For a moment, my brain shut down, and I had a few agonizing seconds trying to re-engage before stammering out, "Um...do I get microfilm from you?" Not the most suave opening line, but better than standing there saying nothing. Theresa used to claim James was the funny one, and I was the smooth one. Not at that moment, I wasn't.

"Yep. It's all in the back." She slid a clipboard toward me. "Just fill this out with name and date of publication." She pointed to the appropriate spots on the form, while I noticed how pretty her hands were.

A sign indicated a dim side room with microfilm readers. I vaguely remembered using one as a kid, but still managed to load the spool upside down on the first try. I briefly considered asking the librarian for help but didn't want to look stupid. I willed myself to focus. Predigital record storage was a dark and dusty task for a guy who grew up with the internet. Not to mention excruciatingly slow.

There was a previous lull at TE in the mid-fifties. I worked backward, year by year, through university records of research grants until it got interesting. A bunch of listings near the end of World War Two had military contract numbers. No surprise. Buried between paperwork for radio components and tank turret aiming systems was a listing in 1945 for funding of research on advanced electromagnetic field modulation which had been granted to Misters Brennan and Vahn Hannen.

It wasn't an exact match, but sometimes immigrant families simplified the spelling. I took notes and returned to the librarian's desk.

"Back again?"

"Mm-hmm." On the clipboard, I marked the first rolls returned. "Could I get the roll for the university paper from 1945 please?" I asked, impressed at my own ability to form coherent sentences.

"Sure. What're you looking for, anyway?"

I'd prepped this answer in case I needed it, so it rolled out with less stammering. "It was a research grant from twenty-plus years ago which never got documented well enough. I'm trying to track it down."

"Wait." She looked thoughtful. "Did you say Physics department or Engineering?"

"Um...I'm not sure."

She raised one thin eyebrow. "Well, 'Mr. Um-not-sure,' there are internal publications for each department. I can get you the university paper, but for something like that, the monthly newsletters are probably a better bet."

"Can I try both departments?"

"No problem." She spun the clipboard around, dropped the black-framed glasses onto her nose, and filled in the blanks for me. She returned in a moment with more rolls of microfilm.

Oh my god, this woman was beautiful. It didn't even occur to me till later she might have been flirting with me.

The electrical engineering newsletter had a brief mention of the research contract, but even better, there was a photo of two young men in suits in front of some equipment with a caption listing their names. One looked enough like V, that I thought he might be his father or possibly grandfather. The other had a prominent scar on his cheek and, despite his youth, leaned on a cane.

*

KASEY
September 1967

Charles had a passion for his research, to be sure. He walked to the library nearly every day, usually returning with new intel about his nefarious director's past. Something felt off though. Considering the dark nature of the research, he seemed in an unusually buoyant mood.

I knelt on the floor with my head and one arm through a ventilation grate in the wall when Charles returned to the round room in the basement of the student union. He asked, "Are you getting the power hooked up?"

"What?" I replied, yelling, my head still in the wall.

Charles raised his voice. "I asked if you were getting the power—" I leaned back and he paused midsentence, then continued in a normal tone. "—hooked up."

I pointed to a substantial piece of conduit running across the floor that terminated by the worktable. "I finished that earlier."

"Then why?" he trailed off, pointing to the open grate.

"Did you know there's a little thrift store on Center Street?"

He looked understandably confused. "I guess?"

"The woman there sold me this for next to nothing." I produced a transistor radio from under the worktable.

Charles laughed. "My grandfather had one of these in his basement!"

"It needed some repair, but even so, the reception down here is terrible. Too much concrete, or too close to the equipment. I confess, radio is not exactly my area of expertise."

"So again, I ask…"

"I used a piece of surplus cable to extend the antenna. Turn it on."

Charles adjusted the tuning knob until the static resolved into a bluesy guitar riff over a simple catchy beat which left us both bobbing our heads. When the singer joined back in, though, his lyrics were surprisingly grim—about how no one gets out alive.

Charles turned it down, muttering, "That got dark."

I changed the subject. "How'd it go at the library?"

"Oh, um—good. I think I finally found the original contract for the controls used on the portal field. There was a photo of two guys with the equipment. One of them looked like my director in his twenties."

"Huh. Wow. When was this photo from?"

"Nineteen forty-five."

Something didn't add up, so I asked, "Okay, I don't know when you're from."

"Nor should you."

"How old is he in your time?"

Charles squinted, pondering. "I don't know—old—sixties, seventies maybe, certainly not eighties."

"But that photo would have put him born around 1920."

"Maybe it's his father?" Charles brainstormed.

"You saw the photo. How much did it look like your director? Was it a family resemblance, or was it him?"

He sounded pensive. "Hard to say."

I asked, "I mean, how much do you look like *your* dad?"

"My dad's White," he replied, deadpan.

I rolled my eyes. "My father and I are both Black, but no one will ever confuse us for the same person."

"Where are you going with this?"

I gestured vaguely to the equipment around us. "Think it through."

Charles's expression changed. "Damn! Time travel."

I nodded. "Given the evidence, it's a strong possibility. In fact, it might be the solution that makes the fewest assumptions."

He asked, "You have Occam's razor in your time too?"

"Mm-hmm."

"This suddenly got a whole lot more complicated, didn't it?"

*

TIA
February 2045

I awoke to a text.

> **Amber***: If you see V, don't mention the work we did yesterday. I need to figure some stuff out first. More soon. Thx!*

She'd sent it in the wee hours of morning, but kindly marked it low priority, so it wouldn't wake me. Another all-nighter? I could occasionally get in the zone and ignore the rest of the world, but in Amber's hyperfocus mode, time itself ran differently.

It would have slipped my mind anyway. I had a busy morning. Timeline studies from the previous six weeks were coming back around. Equipment had been sent forward, connected wirelessly, to record and synchronize chronometer readings, and all land on the same day. Vanhanen was unexpectedly absent.

At exactly 9:00 a.m., the portal hum shifted into its warmup sequence. Emitters glowed, arcs jumped, and the field formed. A locked plastic case bumped over the threshold and rolled across the lab floor stopping by my feet. A moment later the portal returned to standby mode.

At 10:00 a.m., the whole process repeated, and then again, every hour on the hour until early afternoon. Intervals as short as a minute were possible but required carrying the calculations out to several more decimal places. I'm good, but that would have been showing off.

Between arrivals, I checked my secret jump log. Hard as it was, I'd intentionally left it alone for over a month. I watched data populate down my spreadsheet with a satisfied grin. It faded quickly though as I read it in more detail. Jumps were listed every few days, but they didn't follow any sort of rhythm. Sometimes single jumps, but more often in pairs—sometimes minutes, or even hours apart. I could let the app run longer and log more data, but my gut said it wouldn't make things any clearer.

I'd hoped for a pattern, a way to know when he was going to jump, and to what timeline. If I could know those, I might find a way to keep him from returning. I imagined reopening the portal to where he'd just gone and rolling some kind of destructive device through. If I could sabotage the equipment in the time he'd jumped to, it would trap him there.

The outer door clicked, and I only barely closed the app before V leaned into the lab. "Was the retrieval on schedule?"

I smiled to cover my surprise. "Yep, five hours, six boxes. I was about to start checking the data. The last one is almost done downloading."

He stepped past me and lifted equipment out of each case, setting them in order on the lab table. "There you go." I'd planned to check them on the floor, since they were awkward for me to lift, but it was easier from the table.

"Thanks."

It was sometimes hard to reconcile his small kindnesses with the missing engineers James had researched and what we suspected V was capable of. When it was only V and I there, were we both performing parallel roles, the boss and the IT woman, each for an audience of one, to cover our own personal scheming.

I was never a theater kid, but maybe I should've been. I might've been great. I gave an Oscar-worthy performance nearly every day.

*

AMBER
February 2045

As soon as I awoke, I sat bolt upright in bed, knocking some unknown stuff onto the floor. Crystal's father didn't just work for TE, he'd been a *field engineer*—a time traveler! It explained the thin records. "Charles" was an alias.

After two late nights in the Timeslot room, I'd meant to sleep in but felt too excited to lay back down. I grabbed my tablet off the floor and reopened my research. There was so little on Charles Yung it was almost laughable how obvious it was. I had to remind myself this was before the internet or computer records when a counterfeit identity was much easier to pull off.

Still, if he was a time traveler...

A few days ago, I would have said it wasn't possible. We're expected to minimize contact with people indigenous to the timeline being visited. We can say, "Thank you," to the cashier selling us a soda, but meaningful or memorable contact is forbidden—too much chance of corrupting the timeline. TE training ingrains the message into us very deeply: above all, don't screw up the timeline.

If Charles had a relationship with a woman while he was out of time, it would bring a *lot* of TE policies into question. Not to mention Crystal herself. Where does she fit into all this? A woman who shouldn't even exist.

I texted Tia.

> **Amber**: *Any way to link the Timeslot computer to TE?*

> **Tia**: *Do I dare ask, or will you promise to explain later?*

> **Amber**: *Do you know me or what? Yes. Promise.*

> **Tia**: *One-way or two-way connection?*

Amber: *If I could read TE's database without vice versa, it'd be nice.*

Tia: *Trickier. Discretion I assume?*

Amber: *Yes, please.*

Later, Tia responded. A little unusual, especially since we had plans the next day.

Tia: *Meet for lunch?*

Amber: *Sure. Where?*

Tia: *That sandwich place on Lincoln. Noonish.*

My research on Crystal's father had hit a dead end. Bad phrasing, but true. I brought the obituary back up and even found the accident report. I knew the street listed, a quiet residential neighborhood. A fatal hit-and-run should have had more coverage than a brief mention in the local paper. I stared at the date on the death certificate and the accident report. News to me, but so many long years ago.

Yet something felt familiar about it, September 15, 1969.

My watch beeped and startled me out of my thoughts. Lunch time. Short hair had its benefits—run wet fingers through it and go. In the mirror, I saw a shaggier reflection than I had in years—since before Meg. Leaning in and squinting, I mussed it a little more, then left. Despite my best efforts, I was still slightly late. The knee and crutches kept me from moving as fast as I wanted.

After we ordered, she produced an older model laptop from the bag on the back of her chair. Turning it over, I recognized it. "Hey, isn't this the one I spilled coffee all over?"

"Yep. I *might* have exaggerated the 'ruined' part to V. It still smells like hazelnut. I don't know how you drink that shit."

"I don't know how you drink it black."

She replied, deadpan, "Because I'm such a badass." A wide grin split her face and we both laughed. "We still on for movie night tomorrow?"

"Absolutely. I'm going to bring the stuff and make pizza at your place."

She gave me that *look*, with the eyebrow thing.

"What? Yes, sometimes I actually cook! Pizza's one of the things I'm good at, or at least the results are consistent and predictable."

She held up her hands. "Okay, okay. Any chance of hearing more about this 'secret' research?"

I patted the laptop. "Depending on how things go this afternoon, yes."

"If you're doing what I think you're doing, best wait till after hours." She was always so careful to follow the protocol of not discussing TE specifics in public. Apparently, the habit extended to activities best described as "unofficial."

"Of course. Thanks. I mean it, really. Thank you."

*

TIA
February 2045

Apparently, Amber fully believed I was some hacker extraordinaire who could easily produce a laptop with backdoor access, like I pulled it out of a hat.

It's never that simple.

During my first month at TE, I inherited the unenviable task of cleaning out the storage closet, a completely forgettable job except for one thing. A shipping label, still attached to a box by one stubborn corner, showed a return address in the Caribbean, unusual enough that I remembered it later.

Around that same time, Amber spilled coffee on her laptop. It needed to be replaced anyway; she'd used it for a year before I worked there, and it belonged to two former employees before her. When Vanhanen asked if I could fix it, I told him "No" out of hand, hoping he'd buy her a new one.

Secretly repaired, it showed *four* sets of login credentials. The first was a previous IT person who wasn't nearly as obsessive as me about security. Once into her account, I discovered deeper access to TE files, and even some of Vanhanen's passwords. One got me into an extensive list of shipping records.

I'd searched as thoroughly as I could, the whole time looking over my shoulder, worried V would open the door. Farther and farther down I scrolled, eyes scanning records that stretched back years. Once I'd filtered out suit and tie purchases, I found equipment, supplies, and furniture. Filtering again and again, all that remained was a handful of random packages. I read the records of each of these individually. The first few showed nothing sinister, or even particularly interesting. Apprehensive, but also needing to know, I kept going. In June of 2018, he received a heavy package from the Cayman Islands. Everyone knew the Caymans were where the unscrupulous kept their dubious riches. The customs form read "antiques," but the insurance value was unusually high.

I sat back from the screen, folding my arms to keep my hands from shaking. The date was less than a month before James and I were attacked. Had someone shipped him paper money from an offshore account? A box of cash would be damn near untraceable.

Is that how he paid the man with the gun?

It wasn't definitive proof, but at the time, it was by far the best I'd found.

Scared V might discover my snooping, I buried the laptop in the storage closet, and it stayed there untouched for over a year until Amber needed it.

9

KASEY
November 1967

I kept Charles back from the library one morning because I needed help moving some things. His professorial false identity included a driver's license, something I'd overlooked for myself. While driving to university central stores in a rusty, old, rented pickup without a muffler, Charles asked incredulously, "So you walked in there, asked for the equipment, and they just gave it to you? Really?"

"No one questions the repair guy, remember?" I shrugged. "Besides, I had the proper requisition form." In fact, it had taken a significant amount of bravery on my part to pull it off, but the improvisation about an electrical breakdown in another part of campus must have paid off.

The clerk was a grumpy old White man with a gray mustache

who called me "boy," but we loaded three heavy boxes and were out of there in minutes.

Backing out of the drive, Charles asked about the best place to park by the student union.

"Uh...we have one additional stop first."

"Which is?"

"The Timeslot room needs more than a teapot and a radio," I replied with a smirk.

"Wait, is this the real reason for needing the truck...and me?"

"I can't lift a sofa by myself now, can I?"

Once we carried everything down the stairs, Charles clicked on the radio. The static resolved into a familiar electric guitar. I didn't know the song title, but I was nearly certain that that riff was by Jimi Hendrix. Opening the first crate, I unpacked and set up the new equipment, while Charles assisted by handing me tools in between bouts of "trying out" our new used sofa. Predominantly, he carried on with a detailed description of the previous day's research findings.

"So, I did finally find record of the name change. Not officially, but two different documents from the same department with both spellings. The original research grant should have been enough to keep the two of them employed for at least three years. After only eighteen months, though, the project closed down, but only sort of."

"How does one 'sort of' close down a government contract?" I gestured across the room from under the worktable. "Could you hand me that spool of wire?"

"Sure. The paperwork was sent back early, marked 'unsuccessful.'"

"I sense a 'but.'"

He grinned and pointed as if to say "exactly." "The lease on their lab space never ended. In fact, a few months later, it was renewed indefinitely. Want to guess where their lab was?"

"If it's room 042 in the basement of Nuclear Engineering, I'll acknowledge you're onto something."

"I'm onto something."

I wondered aloud, "It does seem suspicious. Could returning the research contract have been a way to cover something they didn't want to report? Something bigger?"

"You think they discovered time travel by accident?"

"Maybe? It'd explain the weird lease. It wouldn't be the first time science happened unintentionally."

The radio broadcast switched to an ad for upcoming campus activities. Charles shrugged and continued, "His partner, Brennan, is the unsolved mystery. He came home from the war with a Purple Heart and went back to grad school for electrical engineering. No mention of him after that initial article though."

"A falling out connected to the failure of the research?"

"Possible, but if so, he left the university without finishing his degree. We couldn't find any records after 1946."

I was about to ask who "we" were, when the DJ broke in, "You're on 89.9 KCSR, campus student radio. Back to the tunes in a quick minute. This week in history: way back in 1911 was the armistice that ended the First World War. Closer to home, two years ago marks the discovery of the 'pond pirate,' a John Doe found deceased by the lake with only one leg and one eye. Despite valiant attempts by local law enforcement, his ID is still a mystery. It's going to be chilly out there today, folks, so I probably don't need to remind you to *stay cool!*"

The broadcast rolled into the next song, and Charles and I turned toward each other. I asked, "Didn't you say Brennan was wounded in World War Two?"

Wide eyed, he answered, "Uh-huh."

"Did he happen to lose a leg and an eye?"

Charles looked flabbergasted. He dropped onto the sofa staring straight ahead. "No way. No...goddamn...way!"

After a moment, I spoke it aloud, "They never discovered his identity because he disappeared twenty years earlier."

"I'm so glad you hooked up that radio!"

*

TIA
February 2045

Amber was almost on time. She let herself in yelling, "Hey!"

I called, "Don't let the cat out! The little bastard keeps trying to make a break for it!" I rolled into the kitchen as Amber bent down between two shopping bags to scratch that particular bastard's ears. "Well, that's one way to make sure he doesn't escape. Either he forgets he's domesticated, or else he has a girlfriend somewhere."

She rubbed under his chin and muttered, "One of us should, right buddy?" Leaning on a crutch to stand, she set the bags on the counter. I pulled wine from one and noticed a second bottle. It wouldn't be the first time Amber slept on my couch.

I opened and poured, asking, "Am I finally going to hear about the old laptop?"

"Huh? Oh, uh, yes, but we have to back up a little first to when I called you from the Timeslot room. After you disconnected, I powered the system up and *this* fell through." Amber handed me her tablet with a photo of a handwritten letter she'd found. "Go ahead, read it."

I heard her click the oven on and empty the bags, but I was too engrossed in the letter. It was sweet and moving, and I genuinely didn't know what to say. Pulling myself back to the present, I said, "Hold on—she knew about the Timeslot!"

"I know! That's only the beginning," Amber continued, "I've spent the last two days researching this woman...and her parents." She dropped an onion and a pepper onto a cutting board and slid it across to me, saying, "Here, chop."

She told me all about her discoveries while sprinkling flour on my counter and rolling out dough for the crust. Crystal's life story came out in snippets between cooking motions. Amber clearly needed something to do with her hands while she talked. She'd learned pizza-making working for an Italian restaurant one summer in college but didn't do the whole production very often—with the fresh dough and all.

She continued, "Her digital footprint just *ends* in 1994."

"Is that when her mom got sick?"

"No, that was a little earlier. Her mom died in '93. She was registered for classes in spring semester of '94, but I can't find a damn thing after—not a single public record."

"Weird. Something tells me that's not the end of your story, and we still haven't gotten to the laptop."

"Ha ha." She tossed the dough, spinning it in the air. It landed across the backs of her hands; she stretched and tossed again. After the second catch, she flipped it onto the pan, a maneuver that blew little puffs of flour across the counter.

Fingers shaping the dough, she dove back into the story. "Her parents were named in the letter, so I researched them too. Her mom's records were pretty straightforward. Her dad is a different story."

Amber poured a small jar of sauce over the crust and spread it around with the back of a spoon. After a drink of wine, she continued. "Public records show a driver's license, and the university lists him as a visiting physics professor for the 1968 and 1969 school years, but the poly-tech school he supposedly came from has no record of him whatsoever."

Pepperoni slices went on over the sauce. "It's pretty clear he knew about the Timeslot room, maybe even built it. The dates would be about right, but that's a guess. I think the writing she found was actually a journal."

I did my best performance of confusion becoming realization. "Oh shit—a field engineer?"

The vegetables followed the pepperoni, with her smile and a nod. "Nice! You figured it out faster than me. I had to sleep on it before the pieces fit."

I didn't have to figure it out. I already knew. Out loud I asked a genuine question, "But if her father was out of time—hold on— that shouldn't even be possible, should it?"

"According to V's rules of time travel, no. I'm starting to wonder if maybe there's more going on here than we've been told."

Oh, my friend. You don't even know.

I desperately wanted to lay everything out for her, from James and what he found, all the way down to my sketches of a device to disable the equipment on the far side of the portal. I hesitated, though, telling myself I wanted to hear her story first, or that I shouldn't derail the conversation. But that pause for breath held more in it than that. I needed to be 100 percent sure where her loyalty would fall. Absolutely certain. We were somewhere above 90 percent and climbing, but that wasn't close enough yet. Instead, I asked, "So, what'd you find in TE's dusty archives?"

She sprinkled grated mozzarella over everything. "Charles Yung was the field alias of a TE engineer in the twenty teens named Christopher Young, different spelling. He disappeared from the employee list in about 2018. Normally I'd say he quit, but the department closed for a few years right after."

Leaning on the counter, Amber slid the pizza into the oven and set a timer before continuing. "A marriage license was filed in 1968 in Crystal's parents' names. It looks like he planned to stay and live out of time permanently."

"But the headaches…"

"Yeah. I know. I'm not sure how he lived with that."

It can be done. It's not easy, but it can be done.

Scared to ask, but needing to know the truth, I said gently, "What else?"

"I found an obituary from 1969. He and Emma were in a car crash. Hit and run."

Oh, Chris…

My heart sank, and my stomach tightened.

She talked for a minute about how it could have been faked but said there weren't any more modern records for him after 2019 either. In truth, I wasn't fully listening.

I wanted to mourn my friend but couldn't—not right then. I was fighting a losing battle with my eyes tearing up. Amber paused and asked if I was okay. I pushed the cutting board and knife back across the counter. "There's still enough onion smell to bother my eyes." She washed while I dabbed my eyes with my sleeve.

"Here's the wild part—"

I interrupted, with a small waver in my voice, "Oh? We're not up to the wild part yet?"

"Not quite." She refilled both our glasses, and I took a generous swallow. "The date of the accident was the same date as on Crystal's birth certificate. Charles didn't survive the crash, but it sent his wife into premature labor."

"Oh my god."

"It's only a theory because yeah, she shouldn't exist at all, but I think the only reason Crystal was able to survive with half her DNA being out of time is because she slipped into her father's timeslot after he died. It hadn't closed yet because it was still the same day." Amber held up a finger. "If that's true, the reason her records vanish after the spring semester in '94 is because Charles was born in May of that year, and it would have been her end of the line."

Silently, I processed her theory but couldn't find a flaw in it. It made sense, and it explained the evidence at hand. Damn, Chris. If you're gonna screw up, do it up right.

Then the kitchen timer beeped and scared the hell out of us both.

At the table, after my first bite, I realized Amber looked unsure, glancing around the room and down at her plate, picking at the crust, but not eating. Her mood had changed. I could see it in her posture and hear it in her silence—no fast-talking pizza-making chatter of a few minutes before, and I think I knew why. There was more to say. Whatever her story'd been building up to, it wasn't the realization about the Timeslot or the end of the line. What she was about to say was *it*. I set my slice down, concerned, and asked as gently as I could, "What?"

She looked up. "I don't know if you noticed, but there was a date on her letter in October of 1993. From when I read it the day before yesterday, she has about six months to live."

"Uh-huh." I responded, dragging out the last syllable, unsure of where this was going.

"I...I want to rescue her."

10

KASEY
December 1967

We finished the Timeslot equipment, but in order to test the system, it needed a second end. Charles suggested five years, but I asked for an extra month. Past the holidays and into the end of winter break would mean fewer people on campus.

We discussed it in the miniscule kitchen of our miniscule apartment.

"I wish you were coming along," I said.

Charles shrugged. "I'm still researching. I need to figure out how Brennan became the pond pirate. I don't need help on that, and you, frankly, don't need my help on the Timeslot equipment, unless you count listening to the radio and handing you tools as helping."

I sighed. "Yeah, I know. I thought it was going to be the two of us running out the rest of the project—Han and Chewie."

"You realize that's not for another nine and a half years, right? Wait, which one am I?"

"You're Han. I'm Chewbacca. You saved my life, so you get my undying loyalty, remember?"

"I'm just glad you don't talk in grunts and growls."

I imitated a Wookie howl, and he replied with sarcasm, "Hilarious."

Refilling our coffee cups, I said, "I need a couple of hours to finish packing my tools in the Timeslot room." It wouldn't actually require anywhere near that long; what I needed was an excuse.

"Okay, I'm researching again this morning at the library."

Charles researching at the library was to be expected. He went multiple days every week. I still had a nagging sensation that something didn't add up. I couldn't believe he was up to anything suspicious, but I got the feeling there was something he wasn't telling me. Most of the time, I was able to write it off as the secrecy necessary between field engineers. There's only so much we can know about each other without potentially endangering the timeline.

"What are you going to do next month when classes start? Are you really going to teach physics? How far are you willing to sustain this alias?" He'd even attended several staff functions on random evenings over the previous weeks.

"It's a decent enough cover that'll work for a while. If I have to teach some freshmen about distance equals rate times time, that's a comparatively small price." He changed the subject. "Speaking of covers, is there anything else you need for 1973?"

"I'm going to follow the model of what you did here: a bank account, a month-to-month apartment, *and* a driver's license this time. I'm hopeful for a quicker process due to better tech and having done it once already."

"I was going to suggest the barbeque place tonight for dinner, but you'll need to jump before the TE staff leave for the day. How about lunch?" He looked at his watch. "The library opened a few minutes ago, so I should get going."

He set his cup in the sink before leaving, so I procrastinated by washing dishes. Time travel periodically led my thoughts down odd paths. I stood there at a sink in the 1960s and washed coffee mugs. I'd performed that exact action a full century in the future, and it was essentially the same: the shape of the sink, the pattern on the cups, and the label on the bottle of soap were all affected by their place in history, but this simple act was unchanged. In a few days, would I wash dishes five years in the future?

When I thought Charles had enough of a head start, I put on my coat and left. Instead of walking to the student union, I diverted toward the library. Was I spying? Probably. I wanted to learn what I could, even if it was my last day.

I maneuvered around the massive card catalog cabinets in the library lobby, remembering how my grandfather had tried to explain these to me once. He'd even looked up a vintage photo, but I guess the concept never clicked until I stood there. No wonder the research took Charles so long.

The entrance to the reference section sat right on the other side of the card catalog, but I opted for more subtlety. In my home time, I'd found another route through the stacks and the back stairs. I tried to be as inconspicuous as possible.

My hand on the rear door to the reference department, I paused, needing to go no farther. Through the narrow window, I could see between shelves and across the room. Charles held a pile of books and chatted with an attractive brunette woman behind the librarian's desk. I didn't need to hear their conversation to know it wasn't solely about research. He was obviously flirting with her, and from the way she touched his arm when she laughed, she was flirting right back. She pushed her glasses up onto her head and flipped her long hair over one shoulder.

The reverberation of my footsteps on the stairs followed me down and out of the building in a bit of a daze. Before I knew it, I found myself at the door of the Timeslot room, then packing up tools and spare equipment, but it was a mechanical action. My thoughts were on Charles and the dark-haired librarian.

Minimizing interaction with people in the times they visit was drilled into TE employees. Even after decades of study, it wasn't fully understood where the line of significance was. The reason for my repairman persona was to avoid standing out or being memorable. We didn't remember a person passed on the street, or someone met only once, only briefly. If a time traveler became significant enough to remember, they risked altering the indigenous person's history, or worse, creating a paradox.

Surely Charles knew all this. So why draw attention to himself?

I felt awkward during lunch, trying not to reveal my inner turmoil over what I'd seen. I covered it by directing the conversation onto how to source the necessary equipment after my jump. Being in public, we had to speak in generalities, but he gave me some good suggestions, and it filled the time while I filled my stomach with barbequed pork.

I pressed the intercom button next to the door at 042 Nuclear Engineering, carrying my toolbox and a large duffel bag filled with clothes and equipment. A voice answered with a veiled reference to the Time Machine. I gave the requisite answer, and the door clicked open. A man a few years older and a little shorter than me, with curly dark hair, stood from a desk as I stepped inside and held out a sheet of temporal coordinates. "Free Jump."

He took the page and I followed into the lab to watch coordinates input at a control panel covered with switches and dials, then double-checked. The familiar sub-audible hum sounded, and the emitters glowed. Arcs formed, and the field established. Once stable, he said, "You're good to jump." I thanked him and stepped through.

*

AMBER
February 2045

To her credit, Tia did not tell me I was batshit crazy. It was easily within the range of possible outcomes of my confession over homemade pizza. She took me seriously and we discussed how it might be done. If we did this or that, would it work? If we did something else instead, how would that change the parameters? Slowly, across an evening of conversation, the *ifs* disappeared. We finished the second bottle of wine but never watched a movie.

Tia said straight away that V would never allow it, and I agreed. No matter how we set it up, no matter how safe we were, pulling someone out of time—especially someone who didn't work for TE—broke too many of his rules. The need for secrecy was paramount. We ran through a bunch of brainstorms on how to get in and out of TE undetected, but none sounded workable, too many variables. I flopped back on the sofa and complained, "If only we had another time portal!"

Tia got a wicked smile and held up two fingers about a foot apart. "We do. It's only about *this* big, but we have the equipment in the Timeslot room."

I sat up, staring at her wide-eyed, thinking it through. "That just might work." I downed the last of my wine.

I vid-called Kurtis the next day. For an old guy, he was pretty tech savvy, and he agreed to meet. We had dinner at his house, and I repeated the whole description I ran through for Tia, going light on the wine, considering I drank a whole bottle myself the night before.

At the end, he gave me an odd squinting look. Like he was pondering something or possibly weighing how much to say. "I don't think I need to warn you that what you're suggesting is dangerous."

I nodded. "Mm-hmm."

"You probably expect me to discourage you from this endeavor."

I nodded again.

"I'm not. This young woman is, or rather *was*, the unfortunate victim of other people's irresponsibility with time travel. Charles probably shouldn't have pursued the pretty librarian, but they were in love and likely nothing would have dissuaded him. It's truly unfortunate that he died when he did."

I'd expected him to tell me not to mess with time and leave alone things that were fifty years in the past. When he didn't, my words came out in a rush. "Oh my god, I'm so glad to hear you say that."

"I'll extrapolate that you're here because you need assistance in some way. You wouldn't share all this merely for dinnertime conversation. So now, what can your retired electrical engineer widower uncle do for you?"

"Tia has a theory that the Timeslot equipment could be modified to function like the portal at TE. If it could, it would let us mount a rescue in secret."

"Away from Mr. V's prying eyes? Good. Tia's right though. It could be made to function like that, but the conversion would take a fair bit of effort. Remember, with the available power, you'll need another portal in the other time for it to work."

"Yeah, we're aware. That'll be phase two."

I unfolded the schematics across the table and weighed down the corners with wine glasses and coffee mugs.

"Okay, the stuff marked in green is where I made upgrades."

"Well, that's a lot of green."

"I know, I know. A bunch of what you talked about wasn't in the pile in the Timeslot room, and some of it was where I made replacements with newer components."

He looked it over, genuinely studying it. A couple times he pointed at my notes saying something like, "Oh, okay, yeah. That'll work."

"We know we're going to need more emitters and a larger frame, not to mention a more robust set of controls."

"True, but your bigger problem is electrical. You're going to need to tap into a larger power source. If you can't find that, you're not going anywhere." I started to deflate. "Don't concede defeat yet. I have an idea." He smirked. "It's probably technically illegal, or at least against university regulations."

"Not a problem."

"I thought as much. In truth, our legal system isn't equipped to handle the problems at TE. By comparison, stealing some electricity, or even a lot of electricity, is inconsequential."

*

CHARLES
January 1968

I hoped Kasey was okay in 1973. I didn't expect to hear from him for a while.

My research supported what James feared about the missing engineers. Vanhanen's original partner left the department, ostensibly, to return to family on the East Coast, but I couldn't prove he ever arrived or did anything that left a single public record, not even an obituary.

Our pond pirate theory was far more likely. The mysterious dead body gained a lot of newspaper space in 1965. He was described as a mid-twenties male Caucasian with brown hair, a scar across his cheek and ear, and having only one eye and one leg. Published police reports listed cause of death as head trauma *and* poison. He'd also had an unusually high blood alcohol level. This probably furthered the "pirate" label.

I could accept that he'd time travelled, had too much to drink, took a walk by the lake, fell and hit his head—except for the poison. A chemical common in industrial cleaning products was found in his blood, but not in his stomach. Did V get him drunk enough to have difficulty fighting back, before clubbing and injecting him? Whether they walked to the lake together or V dragged him there didn't make much difference. He had no ID; clothes, prosthetic leg and eye were gone. An unsolvable John Doe.

Did he and Vanhanen quarrel over the use of the time portal? Had one of them wanted to charge ahead into the unknown, and one of them wanted to play it safe? Could the disagreement have escalated until it ended in murder?

As shocking as the revelation about Brennan was, it changed little. James had compiled a list of the dormant periods at TE, but it was incomplete. Even if we filled in every blank with a missing engineer, what would we do? Who would we go to with that proof? Were we to become time travelling vigilantes? I wished I knew.

The lease on the TE office and lab space was paid by a

company which existed on paper only. A Mr. H. Vahn Hannen was listed as the CEO, but the most "real" thing was a PO box. It wasn't exactly a dead end, but my research turned up less and less new information over time.

Initially, I thought a fifty-two-year jump would be enough to feel safe, but it hadn't been. I spent the first several weeks incredibly anxious. After the fight at the steakhouse, I felt sure V had sent those thugs, and I barely slept for days. Eventually, as more and more weeks went by and nothing happened, I slowly began to relax. I consoled myself that if he was after me, it would have happened by then, time travel and all.

After Kasey left and I started teaching, it had been easy to fall into an illusion of normalcy. Almost too easy. Especially since my research slowed around that same time. I kept returning to the library anyway, as an excuse to see Emma, an amazing and beautiful woman, intelligent in a quiet watchful way that missed nothing. We talked while I researched at the library, and it was so easy, so comfortable—we just fit. I asked her to a concert without thinking it through. If I had... I don't know.

Would it be terrible if I found solace in a place, and time, where I least expected it?

The concert was only the beginning. More dates followed, of course. Emma and I spent the holidays together—hot chocolate, Christmas stockings, Johnny Mathis on the record player. It was nice, more than nice, actually. It was magical.

*

KASEY
July 1973

CJY,

Assuming the equipment functioned as we designed and this letter made it back to you, you're reading this around the beginning of the summer. I completed the installation in slightly over five months, which was longer than I'd hoped.

I had little to do in the evenings, so I hooked up a radio in the Timeslot room again and often worked longer days, intending to speed up the process. The unforeseen trouble with this approach is that I got significantly ahead of the delivery of components I'd ordered and sometimes waited weeks until I could make more progress. In those instances, I watched a lot of movies. From personal experience, I'd say the music from this era was considerably more enjoyable than the cinema.

How's the research progressing? Any new leads?

KRB

11

CRYSTAL
December 1993

"You've been listening to 89.9 KCSR campus student radio. I'm Crystal, and this has been the Nite Trax. Thanks for hangin' out with me. I've got one more for tonight, and I'll see you next week." I spun the knob and a squeal of recorded feedback resolved into the opening chords of a Depeche Mode song. The next DJ was already there picking out CDs and records. She wore more black than I did, didn't talk much, and ran the station's industrial show that came on right after mine. She mumbled, "Later," as I put on my coat and left.

The radio station had been my one constant for years. Even with everything that happened, I never missed a show. I shouldn't have been on staff since I wasn't a student. The station director was a friend who realized I needed something in my life more than taking care of Mom and convinced the board to bend the rules based on my deferred student status.

I got invited to Thanksgiving with a bunch of other DJs whose families were too far away to go home. The host was vegetarian, which I thought was going to be weird, but she was super cool about it. Pretty much, it was an excuse to try all these different appetizers and have huge amounts of pie for dessert.

I started practicing my viola again. The house felt ominously quiet, and it needed something other than my stereo to fill it. I set up a music stand in the living room like when I was a kid, practicing while Mom cooked. It sounded pretty rough at first. I hadn't ever gone that long without playing. They say serious authors write every day, so I decided to practice, even if it was only a little, every single day.

My student deferral was only set up to go through January, one more month. I felt oddly excited about going back to class.

I'd finally flipped the record and *couldn't wait* to hear what was on the other side.

*

CHARLES
June 1968

The Timeslot worked! I got Kasey's letter from 1973!

He asked about the research, and I wasn't sure how to answer. I still occasionally spent an evening or Saturday afternoon at the library or sending letters out looking for more information. If I'm being honest, though, it's a half-hearted effort at best.

I fell hard for Emma after Kasey left and I slipped more fully into my physics professor role. I loved her more intensely than I realized was possible. A lifetime of headaches would be a small price to pay.

The first few times we went out gave me terrible insomnia. I'd spend hours gazing up in the dark, my growing feelings for her, at war with my TE training to avoid meaningful contact. I could almost hear Vanhanen's voice, "Above all—don't do anything to endanger the timeline." Eventually, the more time we spent together, the less I stared sleeplessly at my ceiling. It gradually dawned on me that I didn't much care about V's opinion. Thoughts of TE, though never exactly gone, eventually retreated to the back corners of my mind. I hoped they'd stay there.

It was unusually cold this past winter, and it lingered well into March. Once it was finally warm enough to go for a walk in the park near Emma's apartment, I took out a ring, got down on one knee and proposed.

She said, "Yes."

*

AMBER
March 2045

Once in a while, the universe reaffirmed my procrastination and general messiness. I sorted the heap of computer parts I'd never thrown away into two smaller piles: contemporary to 1994, and not. The first pile would go with me to build the other end, and the second pile was fair game in 2045. Neither stack looked like it held enough for what I needed. At the university garage sale, I bought some slightly damaged lighting controls from the theater department, and a metal pushcart.

For nineties-looking clothes, I tried thrift stores but had more success in quirky vintage shops. I asked Tia along, saying I wanted company, but mostly because it was no secret she had better fashion sense than me. What she wore on a daily basis was put together, rather than my thrown together look. She even paid attention to stuff like jewelry and nail polish. We ended up in a tiny shop where the saleswoman's pretentious attitude was seriously annoying, but despite being expensive, her stuff was by far the most authentic. I bought jeans, band T-shirts, and a leather jacket that cost at least twice what it sold for when it was new.

Between all this, I attempted to absorb as much of the contemporary culture as possible. I read vintage fashion magazines, book and movie reviews, and listened to early 90s music nearly nonstop. I needed to go beyond simply looking the part. I needed to blend in if I wanted to pull this off. Articles like "Top Ten Quintessentially Nineties Films," fueled movie night for weeks.

The stack of computer parts for the "now" end got smaller each day as I built. Uncle Kurtis came through with some stuff from his basement, and I found the last few things on eBay. If only I could have had packages shipped to 1994. We packed the "then" pile as tightly as possible onto the pushcart, a bundle of two-by-fours poking off the front like a lance.

Eventually, the part Kurtis warned me about couldn't be put off any longer. We needed to power our bootleg time portal. I sat on the floor, grate to the crawlspace already removed when Tia got there. Beside me was a backpack with my tools and a coil of flex conduit as thick as my wrist. She squeezed my shoulder in support, and I appreciated the gesture. She knew what I was about to do scared the shit out of me. It wasn't claustrophobia. It was fear of screwing up and getting electrocuted.

I squeezed through the grate, leaving my feet hanging out so Tia could tie a thin rope to my ankle. Up behind the wall, my headlamp illuminated the chute that led to the slot above, right where Kurtis said it would be.

One earbud in, I tapped the screen on my watch. "Call Tia." Her tablet beeped in response.

"Should we synchronize our watches like in a spy movie?"

"Ha ha," I responded sarcastically and headed into the crawlspace. It narrowed at first but past the curve of the wall widened again. I remembered an old pair of soccer kneepads in my closet and wished I'd worn them. The grit and rough concrete were painful under my knees, especially the fake one.

Kurtis's antenna wire hung overhead, tied periodically to the steel structure. I followed it to where the floor was crumbled and broken, open to darkness below. The headlamp showed an ink-dark tunnel nearly filled with pipes and conduit, and what looked like a century of dust.

"How you doin' in there?"

"I'm to the hole in the floor. I'm going to pull a bunch of rope through for a minute."

Seated on the edge of the hole, I stretched one leg down until my toe touched the rounded top of a large pipe. Weight on it, I shifted and repeated with the other foot, until I was on the floor of the tunnel, an ache in one leg reminding me my knee wasn't fully healed yet.

It hit me where I was—the steam tunnels. Everyone knew they ran under the whole campus, but hardly anyone had ever seen them. They carried electricity and heat from the power plant to all the university buildings. Supposedly, it meant instant expulsion for a student caught down there. Legends of giant rats and cockroaches probably weren't true, but I still wanted to finish quickly.

"I'm in the tunnel! Start feeding the conduit."

"Roger, ten four"

"Seriously?"

I pulled until the rope became taut, then felt the weight of the flex conduit dragging through the crawlspace. When the end appeared over the broken concrete above, I said, "Got it!" Without using my cane, progress along the tunnel meant I alternated which hand leaned on the wall. The mechanics of which let me concentrate on something other than the electrical panel waiting for me. My hand came down on an uninsulated steam pipe. "Ow!"

"You okay?"

"Yeah, yeah, I'm fine. Just a hot pipe."

If the pipe was live, I hoped I was close. Another bend of the tunnel, and the power panel loomed ahead, completely covered with rust. The front opened with a squeal, and my headlamp showed an interior with more spider webs than wires, but plenty of room to add a circuit.

A stout lever along one side would turn off the panel, but it didn't budge. Dammit. I didn't want to do this work with it hot. Both hands pulling only got a tiny bit of movement. Stepping onto a pipe, I leaned my full weight across the lever. It squealed in protest and sifted flakes of rust onto the floor, but slowly tilted down.

My power meter showed it was off, and I breathed a sigh of relief. The actual work was almost anticlimactic after that. I connected the new wiring and conduit and closed the cover. Lifting the lever up wasn't much easier, but at least I could keep both feet on the ground.

Back at the hole in the tunnel ceiling, I grabbed one pipe overhead and set my foot on another near the floor. Climbing the cold, dirty pipes, I kept pausing to brush my hands on my pants.

Up onto the fourth or fifth pipe, my foot slipped. I wheeled around for something to grab, but only found empty air. I yelled and hung on to a dusty pipe one-handed before slipping and crashing to the floor.

I could have landed on my ass or even my funny bone, but I

came down on my bad knee. Pain shot up my leg all the way to my back and I cut off a scream with clenched teeth. Tia was loud in my ear, "Are you okay? Are you okay?"

Eyes squeezed shut and teeth clenched, I managed to respond, "Gimme a minute." I took a ragged breath and opened my eyes. My headlamp was on the floor next to me but still on. My pants were torn at the knee and I could see my scraped skin underneath was starting to bleed. I ripped the hole wider to feel around inside. I don't know what I thought I was doing. I'm no doctor. All I knew was it hurt like hell.

"Amber?" Tia asked hesitantly.

"I fell off a pipe and landed on my knee."

"Oh shit!"

"I can't tell if I damaged it or not. There's not much blood, but a *lot* of pain."

Tia shifted straight into coach mode. "You're going to be all right. Can you stand?"

"Not sure. Probably."

"Give it a try."

I scooted my butt across the gritty concrete until I could hold onto a pipe. All the moving with one leg after the skiing accident came back, and I shifted my good leg under me until I could keep the weight off the injured one while I pulled myself up.

"Okay, okay, I'm up"

"You gotta get your ass outta there. I'll take you to the doctor, but we can't have paramedics climbing back there or this whole thing gets found out."

She was right.

Shoeprints on the dusty pipes led down and partway back up. My gaze followed them up the ladder of pipes to the ragged hole in the ceiling, impossibly high. Oh, shit.

"Can you hop over to right under the hole and grab that new conduit?"

"Maybe? Wait a sec."

Holding the conduit, muscles tense, and teeth gritted against the pain, I hopped my good leg up pipe after pipe. Tia had enough slack in the flex conduit to tug and help me along when I needed it. Slow, but it worked. When I finally dragged myself across the rough concrete at the top of the hole, I collapsed, breathing hard.

Tia's voice was in my ear. "Almost there! Don't quit now!"

"You're not my mom!"

She snorted a short laugh. "You're so close, girl. I can see your light. C'mon!"

Back in the Timeslot room, I sat awkwardly on the floor at Tia's feet and gulped from a water bottle. I was dirty and my knee was starting to swell. Oddly, Tia smiled. "For what it's worth, it worked." She pointed at our cobbled-together time portal control unit. A light blinked for standby mode, and it hummed gently. "Now let's get that knee looked at."

*

TIA
March 2045

Amber probably wasn't aware of my biggest contribution to the adventure—lying to Vanhanen.

I lied to him about loads of other stuff, but specifically about Amber's knee, exaggerating the slowness of her recovery. I kept up a fiction that she had ongoing trouble with her meds; too much and they made her sleepy, not enough and she couldn't stand for long.

The Monday after she fell in the tunnel, he leaned out of his office and asked, "Have you heard from Miss Wells about how the project at the student union is coming along? Shouldn't she be getting close to finished by now?"

"Didn't she text you? I thought she did. She tripped on the stairs outside her apartment building and hurt her knee. She iced it right away, but it was still swollen and painful by the time we got her to the doctor."

"Did he prescribe more bed rest? Do you know how long?"

"*She*, but yes, and I don't know for how long. It depends on how quickly the swelling and pain go down." I lifted my tablet and flipped through texts. "She sent me a photo of the bruise yesterday. It looked pretty gross."

He held up a hand. "No. No, that's quite all right." Maybe it was me, exaggerating a grumpy undertone that was only barely there, when he muttered, "I was hoping to have her back to help prep the for the next series of crate jumps. The telemetry is considerably more sensitive."

I smiled. "I'm already working on them."

"Oh, you are? Excellent." He turned back into his office and didn't say more about it for at least a week.

12

CHARLES
August 1968/November 2019

I didn't feel good about lying to Emma, even if it was to solidify my life with her. Once I dealt with some loose ends in the twenty-first century, her timeline would become mine, and I could fully disappear into the 60s.

Theresa and I had been so focused on preparing for her jump, her new identity, and teaching her about time travel, that my own prep was somewhat lacking. Vanhanen closing TE squeezed the timetable, and I didn't finish as well as I wanted.

That said, I couldn't have completed everything anyway. I needed the weeks of working with Kasey to understand how to make my original idea work. A trip back to the future was inevitable.

I considered sending him a note asking to meet me in 2019

but decided against it. Partly, I worried about further endangering my friend. Partly I felt like this was my thing to do—building this last piece to give me some closure and leave my old life behind.

As part of my backstory, I'd told Emma I needed to return briefly to California ahead of the fall semester. The night before, leaning against our headboard, each reading different books, she took off her glasses and said, "I wish you didn't have to leave tomorrow."

"I know. Me too."

"How long does it take to sell a house, anyway?"

"I'm not exactly sure, but the bank has a buyer who's interested. That should speed things up. It's just paperwork and cleaning out whatever might have been left by the last renters. I'm hoping it won't be more than a couple of weeks." She leaned onto my shoulder, and I kissed her forehead. "I'll be back before you know it with enough money in my pocket that we can start looking for a house of our own."

"Yeah. That sounds nice," she mumbled into my shoulder, clearly drifting toward sleep.

We'd been married a little over a month, and it would be the first time we were apart overnight.

I felt wary about returning to 2019, worried that the lure of smart phones and the internet and the rest might entice me to stay. In my heart I knew I wouldn't, but I didn't relish dealing with the temptation either. I wanted to get in, build the Timeslot, take care of some unfinished business, and get out. She snuggled up against me, dark hair falling over her face, her narrow hand on my arm, and I knew where I needed to be. I sat like that for a long time, her breathing letting me know she'd fallen asleep. The warmth of her on my shoulder cemented that place in time into my memory.

I set my book aside and turned out the light. Shifting onto her pillow, she spoke again, sleepy and muffled, "What about a brick house? I like brick."

The next morning, I took a cab but changed my destination once we were on the way, from the train station to Nuclear Engineering. I jumped to 2019 and found TE dark and closed—as I expected.

Before my jump in 2018, I lived in the basement apartment of a big old house; upstairs were two more units. On the top floor lived the owner's son. Stuart wasn't a bad kid, but he obviously had no interest in being a landlord. He was an undergrad and didn't have the know-how to fix things himself, so he'd always just call a plumber or locksmith or whatever.

I'd wanted to accumulate enough vintage computer components but wasn't completely sure of what I'd need. With too much of my attention on Theresa, I enlisted some help. Stuart and I had a deal where I paid him a finder's fee on computer parts, and he let me store stuff in an old shed behind the house.

Before I left to jump to the 60s, I'd squeezed James's pickup into the shed with a sofa in the back that hadn't sold. When I returned, I found a sealed plastic bag full of papers tied to the door handle.

Chris,

You been gone a lot longer than you thought. Dad's starting to wonder what's in the shed. I told him I rented it out for storage, but that just bought a little more time. You need to get the junk out of there.

I bought all the computer stuff you were after and then some. Eventually, the credit card quit working. There's a list of everything I bought and how much you still owe me for a finder's fee.

I don't want to have to throw all this junk out, especially after all the trouble of finding it, but Dad thinks its worthless shit left by an old renter. He told me to get rid of it by the end of the month or else he would.

Hope you find this note in time.

Stuart

The end of the month had been a few days ago. I lifted a tarp and saw a box full of computer parts, pulled it back more and found another and another and another. Every inch of the bed of the truck not occupied by the sofa had been filled with computer parts.

Clearly, the kid saw my finder's fee as a way to make some extra cash, but damn, this was far beyond what I needed. Flipping through the papers, I groaned at the total. Locked in the truck's glove box was my wallet and stuff from my old life. After months, even turned off, the phone was dead, so I wrote a check and left it in the mailbox.

The truck resisted but turned over on the third try. A kitchen employee questioned me parking at the loading dock behind the student union, but I flashed my staff ID and assured them I'd be done in a few minutes. After numerous loads of computer parts were dumped in the Timeslot room, I grabbed one armrest of the sofa and walked backward, the other end dropping from the tailgate onto the dock. I dragged it like that, letting the far end bump down the stairs all the way to the basement.

After what I paid Stuart, I couldn't afford a hotel, so I slept on the sofa in the Timeslot room.

The owner of a coin shop had kept an eye out for 1960s paper bills while I was gone. I wrote him a check also and pocketed a large stack of vintage currency, a stand-in for selling my fictitious house out of state. I wasn't sure of a realistic sale price in that time and place but hoped it would be enough.

After three days of building the Timeslot, I realized I might be screwed. The tech level in 2019 was so different than what I watched Kasey design I might as well be starting over. A week of working on it, and I was comfortably certain I wasn't going to figure it out. I had more components and bits than I would ever need, but infuriatingly, couldn't get it to work for more than a few seconds before erroring out and shutting down. After ten days, I pronounced time-of-death, covered everything in the Timeslot room with sheets, locked the door, and walked away.

My old key card let me back into TE, no problem. I set the controls one last time and stepped through the portal. Emma seemed happy I was back a few days early and eager to show me some houses she'd already found.

*

AMBER
March 2045

I limped along the sidewalk, pushing a metal cart overflowing with equipment along campus sidewalks at about 11:45 p.m., thankfully empty because of spring break. Tia wheeled behind me, my bag in her lap. "Are you sure you don't need to take the crutches along?"

"Yeah, I'm sure. I'll be fine with the cane."

"But…"

"I know. I'm not as steady with the cane." I said, looking

over my shoulder. "I like to think I'm not as steady on the cane… *yet*."

"Just don't want you fallin' all over yourself on your rescue mission."

I kept pushing the cart and rolled my eyes. I appreciated Tia's concern, but we didn't have time to go back for the crutches, even if I wanted them.

Tia could erase the jump from the log, but there was still a record of the power usage. Since the system reset at midnight, jumping then would be harder to track. The power spike would look like part of the reboot sequence.

She opened the TE door and waved me in. I rubbed my hands together to warm them while we waited. "How long do we have now?" she asked.

"Just a couple of minutes probably. What's on the computer clock?"

"No, I mean before Crystal's end of the line."

"Oh, right. It's the middle of January for her, so, about three and a half months."

"That sounds like a good amount of time. Don't you think?"

"I guess. I just hope it's enough."

At 11:59 p.m. Tia waited by the control keyboard, and I maneuvered the cart right in front of the portal. "You ready?"

"As I'll ever be, I guess." I turned and gave her a tight hug. "Thank you."

When she pulled back, she asked, "For what?"

"For everything. For helping me. For not talking me out of this."

She grinned an understanding smile, and said, "Go get her."

I turned around and the reboot ended. The hum changed as the power cycled. Tia rapidly typed coordinates and hit Enter. The emitters glowed, sparks jumped, and the field sprang into existence. I looked over my shoulder, and at a thumbs-up from Tia, I pushed the cart through the glowing arch.

*

KASEY
January 1978

I stepped through the portal in 1978 into total darkness.

"What the…?"

I banged my wrist on the corner of a lab table. Unfortunately, that hand held my toolbox, which crashed to the floor, popped open and flung tools in all directions with as much associated noise as one would expect. I flinched and ducked, a veteran of watching too many films where so much noise in the dark gets one eaten by a monster. I held my breath and waited. Unsurprisingly, there was no monster. In fact, TE appeared completely unoccupied.

My wrist still stinging, I looked behind me, but the portal had timed out and gone dark. The emitters were off, and the control unit had only one small green light showing low power mode. I shuffled sideways to the light switch by the door. The lab appeared similar to before, except cleaner and emptier. No papers littered the lab tables, no empty coffee cups, no clipboards, no spare ballpoint pens, and the countertop equipment was all draped with white fabric covers.

The door to the front office stood ajar, but it was dark beyond. The staff desks were similarly empty. Not even a calendar on the wall to mark the passage of time in that abandoned place.

Our original plan had been to install the Timeslot equipment every five years. Change perpetuation would mean that from any point, there would be at most a five year wait before the Timeslot system ran straight through from 1967 forward.

I might have run into a snag.

Back in the lab, I checked the readouts on the portal controls. Yes, I came through exactly when I planned, no miscalculation. I collected my tools and dropped into a chair with a frustrated *humph*. Could I have stumbled into one of TE's dormant periods after an engineer "went missing"? My watch read 8:30 a.m. No engineers showing up for work, along with the haunted house feel of the space, supported that hypothesis. Of course, the staff could just as easily have all gone out for breakfast. Impossible to know for sure.

In my own timeline, TE security was biometric. The door leading out to the hallway (as well as the rest of 1978) required an old-style metal key. If I left TE without it, I'd be stuck out of time until the department reopened. Potentially years. I had no desire to live in the 70s that long.

If I could locate a spare key somewhere, I could borrow it long enough to build the Timeslot and be on my way. I searched the lab and staff desks but found nothing. Unfortunately, the most likely place to store a spare key was in Vanhanen's locked office.

One of the staff desks partially obscured a vent in the office wall. I slid the heavy furniture far enough to squeeze behind and squat down. Sure enough, I could see dim light through to the office on the other side. The vent cover came off easily with a screwdriver, but the screw heads were on the far side of the inner vent. I considered kicking it out, but I needed both the vent and the wall undamaged to successfully cover my tracks later. I wiggled and pried for long minutes before it came loose.

Once off, I lay flat on my stomach and looked through the hole. I've always been what people describe as skinny; I got my build from my mother. Right then I was thankful. If removing the vent was "breaking," this would be the "entering" part. My head and left arm slipped through without mishap. I shifted and squeezed my right arm and shoulder through, nearly knocking over a plastic tree, but catching it at the last second with one hand.

Trying to stretch farther in so I could set the tree aside, I realized with shock that I couldn't move. I wasn't able to slide any farther inward, or backward for that matter. I pushed and flailed frantically to no avail. Terrified thoughts of TE staff finding my corpse years later filled my imagination. Stopping just short of panic, my weight on my palms, face an inch from the pattern of the vintage brown carpet, I willed myself to focus and slowed my breathing.

I lowered my forehead to the floor, and reached back with one hand, then both, to feel around the opening in the wall. My belt had caught on a missed screw from the vent. Nothing more. It took only seconds to free it, and I slipped through, rolling onto my back with a sigh of relief.

I used some tape from my toolbox to put the vents back in place. It wouldn't hold if someone pulled on it with determination, but it should stand up to casual viewing. I positioned the plastic tree in front, hoping it would help obscure the vent also.

The locked door was merely the first difference between this office and the one from my own time. In the 2060s it was perpetually cluttered with books and materials for experiments, not to mention personal items. There were signs of ongoing work, and even a sense of humor, evidenced in the four miniatures on the top shelf. In stark contrast, the 1970s office could have come out of a catalog or a store display. The large, dark wood furniture looked expensive. I'm sure it was supposed to—the generic executive office of a rich old White man who wanted the person across the desk to see what he could afford and to feel intimidated by it. That realization did nothing to improve my already low opinion of him.

My search began with the shelves, but they mostly held reference manuals. The top of the desk was empty except for a green banker's lamp, a typewriter, and a letter opener.

The desk's upper drawer held papers and the sorts of things you'd expect in the pre-computer world. In the middle drawer were pens, notepads, and a bottle of bourbon, half full. In the bottom drawer, behind hanging file folders, I found a pistol! The sight made me jump and look around, forgetting I was alone. Gently, I picked up the gun, still in its holster. I didn't know much about firearms, but I could see it was a revolver with wood grips. A glimpse was enough. I put it back exactly like I found it and closed the drawer. Why would that be there?

Still feeling shaken by finding the gun, I sat and clicked on the lamp. A glance at my watch showed me my trip through the wall had taken less time than I'd thought. I could afford to search a little longer, but not much. Reopening the top drawer to hunt more thoroughly, my fingers brushed against an old ledger, leather bound at the corners and worn from much use. I held it up and shook it, but no key fell out. The writing I glimpsed didn't look like financial records. Out of curiosity, I opened it to a random page. What I found gave me a chill, sending goose bumps crawling up my arms.

It was a record of time jumps, all neatly organized with arrivals and departures.

I paged forward. Many, many times, almost countlessly, he'd jumped ahead a few years and then back. Doing that would create an end of the line, dangerous and stupid. He'd have to keep ridiculously detailed records of when *not* to be where. I riffled through the thick stack of ledger pages with my thumb. That's exactly what it was. Hundreds, maybe thousands of jumps.

I flipped backward to the earliest entries. My finger traced down the page, scanning the dates. Near the bottom was a jump to November 12, 1965, followed by a return on the night Brennan became the pond pirate.

Charles had spent hours upon hours researching, and I'd stumbled accidentally onto the proof he and James were after. It'd been locked in Vanhanen's office all along—confirmation that he'd kill for his cover-up. My initial response was to run. The urge felt almost overpowering. I gripped the edge of the desk to stop my hands from shaking. Despite the terrifying old man with a gun in my imagination, there was no reason to assume he was after me, especially not right that second.

If I didn't run, if I lingered *even longer* in a place where I could be discovered, I had an opportunity that wouldn't come again. It took me almost an hour, but I copied the first several pages of the ledger by hand.

No jumps were recorded for months after Brennan's last. V had held off. The next only went forward a few weeks, and back the same day—a test of the equipment, or of his own resolve? Had his resistance eroded to curiosity, or temptation? Jump frequency increased dramatically soon after.

I returned the ledger to the drawer and despite the time of day seriously considered the bourbon in the desk. I even pulled the cork and smelled it. Remembering the pistol, though, I had no way of knowing if the bottle was for V's use, or if it was another way of dispatching troublesome engineers. I put it back into the drawer untouched.

For all my searching, the key still eluded me. Given what I'd discovered, my gut told me not to stay in that time, anyway. Making sure I'd left no sign, I relocked the office door. Back in the lab, my bag and toolbox at my feet, I stared at the time portal. When? When should I jump to?

I could bail out of this whole business and jump back to 2067, but that didn't feel right. Charles was a friend, and I needed to get him the pages I spent all that time copying. But if I jumped to see Charles in 1968, I could potentially be leading V straight to him. Heading back to my original timeline held the same danger. A circuitous route? Maybe one covering all three: more Timeslot installs, a visit with Charles, and finally home.

I knew one date in the 70s that I wouldn't mind jumping to, and it was as good a place as any to start. I calculated the temporal coordinates for May 25, 1977.

While the portal warmed up, I changed my shirt, ripped and dirty from crawling through the vent, to a Pink Floyd concert T-shirt from my previous jump. When the emitters glowed and the field formed, I stepped through the portal, eight months into the past.

*

AMBER
January 1994

The portal opened into a quiet TE lab, and I pushed the heavy cart all the way to the student union. I knew from experience my knee would ache more than usual the next day.

The temperature felt far lower than I'd expected, and my thin gloves didn't offer much protection. I paused in the basement hallway to blow into my hands and rub them together before attacking the lock with my bolt cutters.

The round room looked eerily like I discovered it in 2045. The storage locker, the sink and sofa all looked exactly the same, except no pile of junk on the table. The equipment mounted to the ceiling was in far better condition than I found fifty years on. *Would* find. Whatever. The Timeslot rig looked almost new.

First things first. I removed the old padlock and hasp and replaced the doorknob with a deadbolt. I couldn't risk the noise of a drill to put a second hole in the door. Besides, all the best time machines used a Yale lock.

I worked for two or three hours before lying down on the sofa. I'd never slept out of time before, and I thought I might have trouble, but I was so tired, I fell asleep almost instantly.

*

KASEY
May 1977 / April 1980

I watched *Star Wars* on opening night and went back to see it again the next day.

I'd planned to jump the following Monday morning, but it didn't work out. I lingered in the basement hallway of Nuclear Engineering, toolbox open, pretending to repair a light fixture. When V walked past me toward TE, I tilted my head so the bill of my baseball cap obscured my face. I packed up my toolbox and left, truly invisible as the repair guy.

I slept in the Timeslot room and tried again the next day. I "repaired" a different light fixture a little before lunchtime. When he walked past in the opposite direction at about 12:30 p.m., I grabbed my duffel bag and pressed the intercom button by the TE door. Another woman's voice, another question from the Time Machine. I replied and the door opened. Standing up from behind a desk was the same blonde engineer as in 1973, who'd sent me to 1978 a few days before. However, for her, four years had elapsed.

If she recognized me, she didn't show it. I handed over a page of coordinates, and she entered them without asking any questions.

Hum, glow, arc, field. A wave from the engineer, and I stepped through into the future.

Rather than jumping randomly through time, while terrifying myself by imagining V hot on my tail, I decided to lay low for a while and do another Timeslot install. It was tempting to do it in '77 while already there, but I wanted to put one more jump behind me first.

In my home time, all this (accounts, expenditures, identification) could be traced digitally by a hacker with even a modicum of skill. I relied on the disconnectedness of paper records making my path harder to follow. Almost as an afterthought, I'd created a staff ID for myself in addition to a driver's license. I was glad; it let me use the library.

The reference section was darker than I remembered. Twenty-first century LED lighting would one day greatly improve that space. Charles talked so much about research. I wanted to see if I could dig up anything else to send along with the copied pages. I started with microfilm of the local and university papers. Scanning backward through page after page began to hypnotize me or simply bore me to sleep. I'd only been at it for a couple of hours. I don't know how Charles did it day after day. Actually, I did. It was the pretty librarian.

Leaning my chin on one fist while cranking with the other, I nodded off and banged my forehead on the microfilm reader. I hoped the *bonk* didn't sound as loud in the library as inside my head. I jumped and tried to play it cool but managed to spin the crank handle wildly. I registered the word "missing" slip past the screen.

Rubbing my head, I backed through the microfilm for several

pages, hoping I wouldn't find it, but there it was. A follow-up article from September of 1977: "No further leads in the case of the missing university researcher, Gretchen Whitley. A police spokesman confirmed today was the end of a three-day search by officers and volunteers near the missing woman's home. Police are asking anyone with information to please call the department or campus security."

I cranked back to the original article and felt like I'd been kicked in the chest. Accompanying it was a photo of the blonde engineer who'd twice helped me jump.

I couldn't breathe. I thought I might vomit. I squeezed my eyes shut and gripped the edge of the table. For a long moment, time felt frozen. Behind my closed lids, I remembered her in the office at TE, deftly inputting my coordinates and opening the portal. Then at some point after that, she was just...gone.

Her roommate had contacted police after she didn't come home the previous evening and was still unaccounted for. At the time, there was a required forty-eight-hour wait before a missing person report could be filed. The roommate checked with her employer and not only had she not shown up for work that morning, she'd been gone the day before also. It was enough for the police to start looking. The roommate was quoted saying Gretchen didn't have a boyfriend, and her family lived too far away for an impromptu visit. A search was being organized of nearby wooded parkland where she occasionally hiked. Her parents were travelling from Boston to join the search.

There was a physical description with the photo: height and weight, blonde hair, green eyes, glasses, etc. It also mentioned she was mute. She could hear but not speak. She communicated with sign language or by written note, which was making the search more difficult.

I leaned away from the screen, taken aback. I hadn't even realized, but both times I met her, she never said a word. The verbal security prompt at the door could have been prerecorded. She took the sheet of coordinates and silently motioned me toward the portal. I'd thought she was respecting the "no questions asked" policy.

I felt growing anger. I'd joined Charles on his quest because he'd become a friend, especially after the thugs in the alley. That moment, in the dim microfilm room, staring at the smiling face of a dead woman, it became real to me in a way it hadn't been before.

"You bastard." I whispered aloud.

Did you kill her because she found out what you were doing? Did you dump her body somewhere out of time? Were you planning for this eventuality when you hired her, knowing she couldn't yell for help?

13

AMBER
January 1994

So, here's a list of shit I handled the previous week and a half:

- Built the wood frame for the auxiliary portal.
- Mounted all the emitters and ran all the wiring.
- Set up an account and credit card for my fake ID.
- Signed up for a class that just so happened to include Crystal Yung.
- Set up the computasaurus to control the time portal. (Yes, it was that old. It may have even exceeded *my* fascination with vintage tech.)
- Loaded Tia's portal control app onto the computasaurus. (I thought it worked, but it was hard to know for sure.)

- Bought a textbook—an actual paper textbook. They were expensive even in 1994.
- Slept on the sofa in the Timeslot room.
- Drank a lot of tea.
- Went shopping for more 90s clothes and paid less for a whole bag than a single pair of vintage jeans in 2045.
- Ran the power cable through the crawlspace to the breaker panel. (At least I remembered my knee pads.)

I saved the crawlspace work till last. I knew it'd be tricky, and I'd need a shower after. My research found an older gym building in a corner of campus used only by the fencing team, women's cross country, and some historical reenactment club, but it had locker rooms that I hoped to slip into and out of unnoticed.

With classes not starting until Monday, along with the frigid weather, the sidewalks were nearly empty. Tia had talked me into buying worn leather boots that looked at home in a mosh pit instead of canvas high-tops; more expensive, but thankfully my feet were warm. The rest of my 90s costume must have been effective enough because nobody gave me a second glance.

I dried my hair as best I could with the air hand-dryer thing. This exaggerated the shagginess, but it worked for a college-age woman in the grunge era. I kept my nose stud in, too, hoping it looked a little punk, one less thing to remember going back and forth.

Another of my shopping finds was a gray hoodie to layer under my leather jacket. Pulling it up over my damp hair, I snuck out into the dark winter evening.

The coffee place was big and warm, and it smelled *amazing*.

After days alone in the Timeslot room, I needed to be around other people, even if only as an observer. Seeing advertisements for Strange Brew in the campus paper every day, I couldn't stop thinking about coffee, after having so much tea. As far as I could tell, it was the only coffeehouse in town. Nineteen ninety-four was a decade away from the era of chain locations everywhere. With the cold weather, a hot mug of coffee sounded wonderful.

The décor was themed around "strange" in the name. Surrealist paintings and Escher prints adorned the walls, but the couches and overstuffed armchairs made it inviting and comfortable despite the peculiar art. I sank into an empty chair under a painting of a train in a fireplace and got comfortable.

Warming my hands on the wide ceramic mug, I quietly watched the students around me wearing slim-fitting jeans and bulky sweaters, university logo sweatshirts and snow boots, and an oddly layered ensemble topped with a pom-pommed knit hat. I'd worried *way* too much about my fashion choices.

I closed my eyes and sipped. The overpowering smell of coffee, the background music from Pearl Jam, snippets of conversations around me about classes, movies, romance, all blended together into the essence of that time in history: no smart watches, no tablets, no text alerts. Students studied from bound textbooks or read magazines and wrote in spiral notebooks. I felt myself relax for the first time since I jumped. I was *really* there—in 1994. With the portal work nearly finished, I'd be going to class with Crystal in two more days. From where I sat in the timeline, we had a little over three months to pull this off.

Tia and I had done everything we could to set this particular stage. I just had to walk onto it and give the improv performance of a lifetime. Except it wasn't my lifetime in question, it was Crystal's.

*

CRYSTAL
January 1994

The daily practice eventually paid off. I'd almost caught back up to where I was before Mom got sick.

Tired of playing in the living room, I rearranged some furniture and turned Mom's bedroom into a rehearsal space. My counselor suggested I renovate it to be *my* bedroom, but I just couldn't do it. It felt too weird. Her room was a little bigger, which worked fine for practicing.

I did my first radio show of the semester, and the station director stopped by to say she wanted me to apply for program director. Wow. Didn't expect that. It sounded cool and all, but I wasn't sure how it would fit in around grad school and practicing and stuff.

The semester started on Monday. Despite walking through the cold and snow to class at 7:30 a.m., moving forward again felt great, like finally dropping that needle into a new groove.

I had my first computer applications class, a requirement the university suddenly dumped on us. Even people whose major is playing an instrument invented centuries before the computer need to know how to use one, I guess. Maybe I would learn some audio editing. At least, that might be useful.

From the next row, someone rested a thick-soled, clunky leather boot on the empty seat beside me. Standing, at the end of class, I turned and saw it belonged to a redhead so cute, I was left gaping. She pulled on an expensive-looking leather motorcycle jacket, black like the boots. She wore a nose ring, too, so maybe rich and a rebel. Who knew? I tried not to run into her with my bag while mumbling, "'Scuse me."

She looked up and smiled. "Oh, you're fine." She had a great smile, but what struck me most were her brown eyes. Unexpected, but *gorgeous* against her pale skin and that hair. I tried to give a friendly smile in return. Hopefully, my checking her out wasn't too obvious. I didn't even notice the cane until later.

*

TIA
March 2045

My app revealed something even more surprising and disturbing than an increase in Vanhanen's jump frequency; he was *overlapping* his jumps. Most time jumps are like a plane trip: you go, you're there for a while and you come back. With time travel, you can squeeze into that gap between your departure and return.

So long as you don't jump into a timeline already occupied by another version of yourself, it's technically possible, but it's playing with fire. At some past date, V's younger self had jumped forward to a given moment, but when he eventually aged up to that point, he'd needed to jump out of the timeline before his younger self arrived.

The record-keeping would've been absolutely insane to avoid running into an end of the line created years before. I couldn't imagine. He was essentially living out of order. Filling in between jumps by showing up at TE in some other time when he had to jump away from his main timeline. He'd done it right in front of me, and I never noticed, hiding in plain sight. In my defense, he wore the same style of suits all the time and always had close-cropped gray hair around the sides and bald on top.

There were days where both the calendar and the jump log

were empty as well. Was he trying to extend the number of years he lived across? Why? Even with time travel, you only got eighty-some years of experiential time, at best, and no way to change that. We were temporal engineers, not Time Lords.

Infuriatingly, the list of his time jumps still showed no pattern. My fantasy of swooping in while he was out of time and trapping him there had run out of plausibility. Even if it could be successful, what would stop him from simply repairing the portal, or even building a whole new one and coming after me?

I'd waited for years. I'd watched my stupid app for months, and it'd gotten me practically nowhere.

I no longer cared much about punishing V. I cared about the safety of the temporal engineers—the ones I knew, and the ones I didn't. I'd borrowed that dream from Chris, but it was down to me.

From the outside, that moment might have even looked peaceful, sitting on my sofa with a mug of tea, tablet on my lap and a gray cat curled beside me, but I'd made a grim decision, the darkest of my life.

I couldn't achieve our end without getting my hands dirty.

Following his path through time needed more data. I added a secondary component to my logging app that charted a map of his jumps and how they interconnected. His crisscrossing path through the last century meant that I'd met and interacted with numerous versions of him. If I could find and track the timeline where he was the oldest, he wouldn't be subject to paradox protection.

14

KASEY
July 1980

During my installation in 1973, I stayed in the same building where Charles and I lived in 1967. Cheap, furnished apartments were challenging to find in a campus town, no matter what era you lived in. Mine had been on the top floor around the back, with access off the alley rather than the sidewalk. This *may* have been due to the color of my skin, but honestly, I appreciated the privacy. By 1980, the whole complex was replaced by taller buildings with pricier units. Luckily, I found an inexpensive attic apartment close by. Living with its lack of air conditioning, however, was another challenge altogether.

The 1980 install overlapped the release of *The Empire Strikes Back*. Seeing it on the big screen was a well-earned reward after so many months of field work, not to mention all the bad movies I had sat through in the 70s. Honestly, it was the high point of my time there. I saw it a couple more times, just to sit in the air conditioning.

On a thrift store excursion, I stumbled onto a vintage leather-bound book without a title. Opening it, I half expected it to be hollow, but instead it was blank. I bought it anyway. Sitting shirtless in front of a small fan in my stifling apartment, I took out a pen and began to write.

*

AMBER
January 1994

In class the second day, I realized I needed to actually learn the material, do homework and take the tests if I wanted to blend in.

I didn't see Crystal and sat anxiously through the rest of the lecture, worried she'd dropped the class. I couldn't exactly stand up and look around; the lecture hall wasn't that big. Inconspicuous, remember? If she had, what would I do? I didn't have a plan B. Turning to grab my coat, I saw her in the next row. I tried not to let the relief show on my face.

"Hey, you're behind me this time." Ugh—what a dumb thing to say!

"Uh, yeah." Did she look a little like she'd been caught, or was it my imagination?

She glanced down toward the cane, and I explained, "Skiing accident."

"Uh, that's awful. Over break?"

"Mm-hmm."

"Dude, that sucks. What a terrible way to spend Christmas

vacation."

"Yeah. I mean it could've been spring break, and I'd have missed half a semester."

"I guess that's the bright side." She picked up her bag, thumbed the strap onto her shoulder, and gave a tiny wave. "Later."

I watched her walk away, in a long gray wool coat, ripped jeans, and black canvas high-tops, stepping over and around other students' backpacks in the auditorium aisle. She pulled her straight dark hair out over the collar, and it hung down her back, blowing in the cold as soon as she stepped outside the building. All the photos I'd seen of her were from several years earlier. She'd grown out her bangs, and her lanky adolescent awkwardness had morphed into a long-limbed casual grace. She'd gone from a cute kid to a stunningly beautiful woman.

Much as I wanted to follow her, I was aware of the subtlety necessary to pull this off, so I steered down a different sidewalk. Strange Brew was a better place to study than the library, not as quiet, but...there was coffee. The whole walk there I replayed the exchange after class in my head—awkward at first but got better. As first contacts went, it wasn't bad.

I lingered as long as possible at the coffee place. After finishing the reading for class, I drifted back to the Timeslot room and found a note from Tia waiting on the floor. Vanhanen had been trying to get in touch, and it sounded like he wanted me back at TE.

Somewhere in there I had to make time for homework too. Yuck!

*

TIA
April 2045

The 90s end of the Timeslot must still be functioning because Amber replied to Vanhanen's email immediately after her midnight jump back to the 2040s. "Sorry I didn't respond right away. I've had a head cold on top of everything, and the congestion completely screwed up my sleep cycle. I'm not quite done with the project at the student union, but I can come back to TE on Mondays and Fridays like you asked. I'll reschedule my physical therapy appointments."

All day, while prepping the next experiment, I could tell she was bursting to fill me in. Finally, I suggested, "Hey, want to change movie night to tonight?"

I could hear her relief. "Oh yeah. That sounds great."

"Cool. Bring beer though. I'm craving spicy Indian, and wine doesn't go with vindaloo."

She mouthed the words "Thank you" behind V's back.

Amber gave a long description of her time in 1994. Considering how she wolfed down the spicy lamb and rice, I assumed she'd not been leaving herself enough time to eat. She'd met Crystal and was super excited to tell me about it.

I wanted so desperately to reveal it all right there. Especially after a couple of beers. I knew for sure I could trust her, but I held off. Still in the middle of Amber's adventure, adding mine felt like too much. I could wait a little longer.

But...not too long. V mumbled something about retirement the other day. If he stepped away from TE, I'd miss my chance to rid the world of a monster.

Patience. I needed to let my app collect more data before I could extrapolate his final timeline.

"Final timeline." I liked that. It sounded like the title of a novel.

15

CHARLES
January 1969

Christmas and New Year's came and went and no further word from Kasey.

There were nights I couldn't sleep, worried he'd run into V. I thought through all the reasons why that was unlikely, but I was still afraid I involved my friend in a mess that had gotten him killed. Then I remembered he was Chewbacca. Wookies were notoriously hard to kill, and they lived for centuries.

When I finally received his letter, I dropped onto the sofa in the Timeslot room and felt a knot inside me loosen. It was hard to express the relief I felt.

He planned to return to his original timeline soon, since funds were running short. If he got home safely, I'd be happy—even if he didn't continue the work on the Timeslot or the chase for V. I'd put him in enough danger. I'd sleep better knowing he was okay.

He wrote about jumping into a locked and empty TE department in 1978. I obviously forgot to check against the dormant periods. The dates were in my notes, but we were so excited to test the Timeslot, it had slipped my mind completely.

He sent handwritten copies of a ledger he found in the director's office. He'd circled an entry to draw my attention to it. I let out a breath, deflated. "Son of a bitch." Kasey had found the proof about Vanhanen. An actual written link existed between his jumps and when his partner was found dead as an unidentified John Doe. I rubbed my eyes and wished I could tell Theresa about it.

What did the proof change though? There wasn't a higher authority to appeal to. Vanhanen was the creator of time travel, and within its influence, that made him nearly a god. How do we challenge that? Or do we run and hide forever?

I shook my head and returned to Kasey's letter. He also wrote about a TE engineer who went missing in the fall of 1977, but the body was never found. Was she dumped somewhere out of time as well, or had V changed his tactics? It seemed unlikely she was the only one. James had found another dormant period in the 90s as well.

We already had enough evidence to know he was a murderer. Kasey just provided us with more detail and another example. Theresa was right. No court existed for what he'd done.

Theresa.

I sighed.

Apologies, my friend. I won't walk away from Emma and our life together. I have no plans to return to my former home time, ever. I need to keep her safe and far away from V and his machinations. My life has taken an oddly twisted path to get where I am, but I'm okay with that.

*

AMBER
February 1994

I fell into a rhythm. Work on Monday and jump to 1994 at midnight. Class with Crystal Tuesdays and Thursdays and jump back to 2045 for work on Friday and movie night with Tia on Saturday.

That left Wednesdays as a weird downtime. I studied for class but was never quite sure what to do with myself. I listened to the radio in the Timeslot room until cabin fever set in. Despite the cold, I managed to work out in the old gym a few times. My leg felt better but was still recovering from the setback of falling in the tunnel. On the rare warmer days, I exercised my knee by walking around the university. Slowly at first, but I gradually increased my range into the part of town south of campus. It held mostly bars and restaurants, but not entirely. There was an art supply store, a used record and CD shop, which smelled a bit like weed, and down the block was a T-shirt, jewelry, and gift shop. I bought a cool leather-bound sketchbook, rustic-looking and thick.

That night on the sofa in the Timeslot room, I turned to the first page and wrote. I began with my broken knee, since it felt like the beginning of this story. Farther back and I'd have needed to describe the breakup, which I preferred not to revisit. Slowly, I filled page by page. I'd never been a journaler. Is that a word? Diarist? The quiet routine of it became almost meditative on Wednesday evenings.

This continued for close to a month until our first real exam. The professor called "Time's up," as she walked up the aisle to collect the scantron multiple-choice tests. In a few years, voting would look almost exactly like this.

A student in front of us with short blonde hair stood up and stretched. "Oh my god—that was brutal! Who wants to get a drink?"

Thank you, snarky popular girl for this opportunity!

Slipping on my coat, I asked Crystal, "Hey. Want to go?"

"Um, sure!"

A few people lingered around Blondie, until she announced going to a popular bar/restaurant/live music place in campustown. Crystal and I looked at each other and both shrugged at the same time. She laughed quietly, adorably. I couldn't help but smile.

We chatted along the way—the test, the weather. I'd exercised earlier, and felt the additional miles in my knee, slowing me down. When the rest pulled ahead of us, I took advantage of an opportunity, even though it required a bit of a white lie. I exaggerated my slowness, then gambled. "Hey, if you want to catch up with them..." and I left the sentence hanging.

"It's okay. We were talking, and I don't really know any of them." She paused for thought. "Actually, how would you feel about going somewhere else? Somewhere closer...and quieter."

"Yeah sure." *Yes!*

"Do you like barbeque? I mean you're not a vegetarian or anything?"

"Barbeque sounds great. They serve beer though, right?"

"Yep."

She tugged on my elbow and pulled me down a side street. The restaurant was small and dim, with reclaimed wood on the walls, and we had to order at the counter, but they played great jazz and served some of the best barbeque I'd ever had.

We took our beers to a booth. Suddenly, things felt awkward. Getting acquainted outside of class was new.

I asked, "So…did you go to undergrad here? I just moved here this semester."

"Oh, from where?"

"Chicago. That's where my dad lives." It was true enough.

"Just dad? Parents divorced?"

"Yeah, but it was a long time ago. My mom left when I was a baby. I don't remember her except for some photos."

"Wow. That got personal quick. Sorry."

"Nah. It's okay. To me it was normal growing up with only my dad. You?" She paused as if unsure. I realized I may have screwed up and gone too fast. I already knew her story—the story she was struggling to even start. I knew the ending, too, even farther out than she did.

She pulled one knee up, wrapping her arms around it. "Ugh. It's just…when I tell people this story, they start to look at me differently. I don't want to be 'that girl,' y'know?"

"It's okay." I thought for a second. "Start with something else. Something simple: your major, favorite band, favorite movie, what you want to do after college, last thing you watched on TV."

She smiled with obvious relief. Maybe I recovered from the misstep. "Music major. Nirvana. *Labyrinth*. Professional musician or music teacher. MTV." She listed while ticking them off on long fingers with chunky silver rings.

"Music, huh? What do you play?"

"Well, piano, but all music majors play piano. My concentration is the viola."

"Not the violin?"

"I played the violin at first, but it didn't last. Being tall for my age, my middle school music teacher tried to make me a cellist, but I didn't want to lug around such a heavy instrument. We compromised on the viola. It's okay though. There are a zillion girls out there who start playing the violin when they're barely in preschool. The viola has far less competition. I'd rather be first violist than seventh violin." She took a drink of her beer. "What about you?"

"I don't play any instruments."

"No, I mean 'major, favorite band, etc.'"

"Oh, right. Computer engineering. U2. *Star Wars*. Cutting-edge computer hardware designer. And um...*Northern Exposure*." It was the first 90s era show I could think of. I watched a couple episodes during my research.

"Did you see U2 on their Zoo TV Tour? They played at the stadium. It was great."

"Yeah. I caught them in Chicago." Okay, I actually watched a recording of it, but close enough. I hope they played a show there. "When you saw them, did Bono pull some woman up on the stage to dance with?"

She sat up. "He did! Can you imagine being her? Like, 'hi, just here watchin' a concert with my friends' and all of a sudden...whoa, shit! I'm dancing with Bono!"

"I know. Wild."

"I always wondered if it was as spur of the moment as it seemed, or if some security dude walked along the front row beforehand with his clipboard till he found a girl with long blonde hair." She lowered her voice. "Excuse me miss, but uh...you qualify as pretty, would you be willing to dance with Bono? Mm-hmm, would you sign this form in case you fall off the stage? Oh, and can you act surprised?"

I couldn't help but laugh. The image of it was too amusing. Crystal was funny and sweet and someone I genuinely wanted to be friends with. Friends at least...

The situation felt oddly like a first date. I hoped I could stay focused on why I was actually here. Crystal was distractingly beautiful.

The food arrived, and for a minute conversation paused.

I pointed with a French fry. "You said your favorite movie was *Labyrinth*?" I couldn't hide a bit of confusion. "I guess I always thought of it as a kids' movie."

"And *Star Wars* isn't?"

I ate my fry and held my hands up. "Fair enough."

"We were barely teenagers when it came out. Here was a main character with long straight dark hair like me, written to be both smart *and* brave. It was the first time I ever saw a movie like that, where a woman thinks her way out of all the problems in the story. I wish there were more movies like that, well-written, with cool female protagonists."

My mind flashed to Buffy Summers, who wouldn't step onto the scene for a few more years, and all the amazing fiction that would follow in her wake. Unsure of what to say, I covered with a joke. "I watched it with my little cousins once, a few years ago. Mostly I remember the Muppets...and David Bowie's ridiculously tight pants."

She rolled her eyes. "Okay, yeah. Those pants are kinda scary."

The conversation rolled on like that, easy and wandering. From movies and music to books and school. I filled in a few details from my cover story, but I tried to listen more than I spoke.

Crystal talked about growing up being an orchestra kid and told some goofy jokes about violas. I guess even viola players tell viola jokes. I talked about reading *The Lord of the Rings* and playing *Dungeons and Dragons*. I hoped for accessibly nerdy, not deeply geeky. So long as I didn't mention edition numbers or much about game mechanics, this was safe.

I emptied my glass. "Hey, do you want another beer?"

"Sure."

"I'll buy, but—" I held up the cane. "—I can only carry one at a time."

Back at the table, she asked, "Your skiing accident, was it one of those spectacular wipeouts like you see on TV? At least you'd get a good story out of it."

"Unfortunately, no. I got into some powder along the edge of a run, lost my balance and came down crooked. I'd injured the same knee playing soccer when I was a sophomore. The doctors told me I had to stop playing or I'd risk hurting it again. They didn't say anything about skiing. A person with a regular knee probably would've come out of it fine."

"Dude, that sucks."

"The dumb part was that I didn't even want to go on the trip. I bought the vacation as an early Christmas present for my ex because she'd always wanted to go, but when we broke up, I got stuck with nonrefundable tickets. So, I went anyway, planning to ski a little and drink a lot." I tapped my knee. "Worst Christmas present ever."

She smirked and shook her head. "Yeah, that probably qualifies." I'd just taken a large bite of pulled chicken sandwich when Crystal said, "She? Your ex. You said 'she.'"

I paused midchew. Damn! I hadn't meant to let that slip so soon. I nodded. "Mm-hmm." I swallowed and took a gulp of beer.

"So you're..."

"Gay. Yeah. I hope that's not a problem."

She smiled the biggest, kindest smile and said, "Absolutely not." She slid her empty plate aside and leaned in. I followed. "The story I didn't tell you earlier was about my mom. She had cancer, and she died last year. I deferred grad school to take care of her."

I put my hand on hers almost without realizing I'd done it.

Maybe subconsciously it was the appropriate gesture for the moment. "Oh my god. I'm so sorry."

She shook her head. "Thank you, but no. It's sad, and I miss her terribly, but it doesn't define me. Please don't think of me as 'the girl whose mom died'."

"Absolutely not," I replied, repeating her words and squeezing her hand.

"That's why I hardly know anyone in most of my classes—because I took three semesters off.

She looked down at my hand still on hers and gasped. I started to pull back, thinking I'd done something wrong, but instead, she gripped my arm and pulled it forward. Twisting her head around to read my watch, she said, "Oh shit! Shit, shit, shit, shit, shit."

"What's—" was all I got out.

"I'm going to be late for my radio show!" She pulled on her coat while speaking in a rush. "Oh my god, I'm so sorry. I have to run. This has been great. Seriously, seriously great, but I have to go!" She slung her backpack over her shoulder on her way to the door, burst onto the sidewalk, and took off at a run.

I leaned back in the booth, unsure what to make of that. Despite the odd ending, I considered it a clear step forward. I'd spent a month chatting with her after class, but that night felt different, like she'd finally opened up. I mean, she lived alone in her dead mom's house, and her friends were mostly graduated and gone. Maybe she craved having someone to talk to. Whatever the cause, I felt the beginnings of a deeper connection. Good. We were down to a little over two months.

An inch of beer remained in the bottom of my glass. I picked it up, tapped the rim against Crystal's, and drained it.

I stopped by Strange Brew on my way back to the student union. When the barista asked if the coffee was for there or to-go, I paused, remembering something. Instead of my usual comfy sofa and people-watching in the 90s, I asked for it to-go and headed back to the Timeslot room. I had a sudden desire to listen to the radio.

*

CRYSTAL
February 1994

Shit, shit, shit, shit, shit!

I took off at a dead run. Campus radio was in the basement of a dorm building, thankfully, not too far from the restaurant. When I looked at Amber's watch, it read 7:58 p.m.

Amber. Ugh! I finally managed to hang out with the cool gorgeous redhead from class, but I bungled it right at the end with my impromptu exit.

I burst through the lobby door at 8:04 p.m., according to the red digital clock above the control panel.

The DJ before me, Steven, did the station's new wave and electronica show. He propped his tall, lanky frame in the doorway to the studio, flipped his asymmetrical hair back, and with his customary level of cool asked, "Girl, where you been?"

I threw my backpack in a corner, and my coat followed as I took in massive gulps of air. "I went out after class for drinks because we'd had a huge test, and I lost track of time, and oh my god, I am so, so, so sorry."

He kinda squinted like it took his brain a moment to process, since I didn't leave much space between any of the words.

"Don't worry about it. I put on that one long grungy track you like. You got about—" He leaned his head back into the studio. "—

three and a half minutes. Plenty of time. Catch you next week."

I stepped into the studio and breathed deeply of the scent of vinyl, the smell so profoundly ingrained, I doubted it could ever fade, even if they changed to all CDs. My heart, still pounding from my sprint, slowed, and I felt my stress level drop immediately. A lot of musicians say the stage is their "happy place," but the radio booth was mine—quiet, and I controlled the music.

Another deep breath, and I made a quick circuit, pulling discs and records off the shelves. One went onto the turntable, and the rest in a stack on the counter. I dropped into the DJ chair and put on the headphones. On a secondary channel, I queued up the album on the turntable and kept an eye on the CD time counter. When the last guitar chord faded out, I clicked for a prerecorded PSA and spun a knob to start the turntable.

A track by Alice in Chains played its way through, then I leaned in and tapped the button marked "MIC." "You're listening to KCSR, 89.9. I'm Crystal, and this is the *Night Trax*: rock, metal, punk, and grunge from now till midnight." I read a campus announcement and the weather forecast: cold. While giving the number for the request line, I rested my left hand on the CD player button. "I was talking with a friend earlier tonight about this concert and how Bono pulled some girl up on stage to dance with. Imagine what that must have been like for her. Anyway, here's some U2."

The opening notes of "Trying to Throw Your Arms Around the World" filled the booth. Maybe Amber was listening. Maybe I liked it for the lyric comparing a woman needing a man to a fish needing a bicycle. Maybe I was trying to send a subtle message. Maybe it wasn't all that subtle.

*

KASEY
June 1986/Jan 1992

Despite the generous finances I'd been fronted before leaving 2067, by 1986 the number on that account was becoming concerningly small, and things were getting more expensive as well. I considered squatting in the Timeslot room, but instead, took the cheapest apartment I could find, notwithstanding it was also the shabbiest.

That install went the most quickly and was the least notable. Nineteen eighty-six was three years into the long dry spell between *The Return of the Jedi* and *The Phantom Menace*. I ran the numbers for the time coordinates to land in early 1992—using an actual pocket calculator! Charles had a different vision for the equipment once the Timeslot coexisted with email, but he never worked it out. From there, some other TE engineer would need to take the baton and finish the project.

I had barely enough funds left for one more install and then home to my own timeslot. Even with the classic sci-fi films, I'd had my fill of temporal headaches and vintage clothes, no wireless internet, and no streaming.

In all the previous installs, I first secured entry to the Timeslot room before finding a place to stay. Carrying my duffel and toolbox from Nuke-E toward the student union, I realized there was a problem as soon as I glimpsed the building from across the pond. The entire west end had been encased in scaffolding and plastic, obviously under renovation. Unfortunately, that's also where the round atrium and the room below were located.

I stashed my duffel underneath a stairway and changed into my most well-worn T-shirt. Toolbox in hand, I took a slow stroll through the construction zone.

Good news: they weren't using the round room as a construction office. The old padlock remained in place. Bad news: the basement hallway was cordoned off for renovation. This precluded sleeping in the Timeslot room. From overhearing the contractors, I learned it would be closed through the end of the semester, at least.

That night, sitting on the bed in a cheap motel, I weighed my options. I could wait it out and start the work in few months—maybe. The necessary living expenses without making progress on the project would absolutely strain my remaining finances. I could run the numbers, go back to TE, and request a jump to a year or two later and do the install then. I could throw in the proverbial towel and go home to the 2060s.

I had a reluctance to follow the last option for reasons which were difficult to explain. Even though Charles's involvement had essentially stopped, I felt driven to complete the project. Construction of the Timeslot was originally just a glorified cover story. Why was I so committed to it? The path had gone so far astray of what it sounded like that day in the director's office. Jump back a century and help build the Timeslot, then go home. I sat there ruminating between two options: create or retreat. More accurately: create, *then* retreat, or go straight to retreating.

I began this endeavor with thoughts of, for lack of a better way to articulate it, proving myself. I'd long ago surpassed what could have reasonably been expected of me. I could go home to 2067 and be done with this.

And yet...and yet.

I ruminated until I couldn't keep my eyes open.

I woke up feeling like I wanted to finish the job before heading home. I didn't relish the idea of waiting around for the renovation to finish up who knew when. On a notepad from the desk drawer,

I ran the numbers for a jump to 1994. One year out might not be enough, but two should fall after the renovation was complete.

The formula for time jump coordinates was complicated, even with a calculator. It involved a lot of decimal places. I double-checked, made a minor adjustment, and then triple-checked.

I set my glasses on top of the papers, rubbed my eyes, and scratched my head. I kept meaning to get a trim but hadn't. My hair was well on its way to an afro—very fashionable if I'd stayed in the 70s any longer. Yeah, no.

Despite the cheapness of the motel, the bathroom was clean, and the shower was hot. I stood there for a long time, too long, in the end. The ruminating resumed.

I couldn't know if V was aware of me or my time jumps. The fact that Charles knew about James's discoveries was something Charles always feared Vanhanen had figured out and would try to silence him. I couldn't blame my friend for finding a reason to stay out of sight. I might not be on V's radar, but then again, I might.

If I jumped again right away, it'd increase my chances of running into the director, and two jumps two days in a row might look odd in the records. I preferred going unnoticed, like with the toolbox.

The toolbox! I blended in well enough for short periods, but could I do it for longer? Could I use the renovation as cover? Beyond that, could I find or, honestly, steal, some components I would need? Hmm.

Checking out, I asked the motel clerk for a newspaper. He grabbed one off the desk in back, obviously already read and re-folded. I removed the classifieds and left the rest on the counter. After a minute, he asked, "Lookin' fer a job?"

"No. A cheap, little apartment."

He scratched the back of his head and then his ample belly.

"How long you need it for?"

"Probably only through the semester."

"My brother-in-law's got a basement place over by campus, he was talkin' about tryin' to rent. Here let me call 'im." He dialed the front desk phone and talked for a minute, before putting his hand over the receiver. "Look, it don't have no AC, and no place to park."

"I don't have a car," I took a quick glance out the window at the January weather, deciding the lack of air-conditioning wouldn't be a concern any time soon. "It has heat though, right?"

"Sorta. He says it needs fixin'."

He mumbled back into the receiver behind his hand before asking me, "You got a dog?"

"No." I shook my head, both in answer, and at the ridiculousness of the question.

"Month to month, cash only. Hunnerd n' fifty a month."

"Without heat or air-conditioning? I assume it has water and electricity though?"

"Yep, got those. One a them little fridges too."

"Tell him I'll look at it, and we'll see what it's worth."

In the end I compromised with my new landlord on one twenty a month for the basement efficiency apartment. Before he left, he grudgingly made adjustments to the furnace, amounting to redirecting some vents from the upstairs unit to blow into the basement.

With no furniture and no carpet, bare concrete floor and walls, it was *by far* the most primitive apartment I'd ever been in, let alone rented, but the cost was a fraction of what I expected to pay. I could wait out the renovation if I needed to. I hoped it wouldn't come to that.

That afternoon, I walked through the snowy side yard lugging a huge armload from a big box store. Since the stairs were boarded up, I used a back patio door when I came and went. I thought I'd feel like I was camping the whole time, but a cot, sleeping bag, folding chair, and space heater were what I could get and wrangle home on the bus, something not particularly feasible with a bed or sofa.

More trips through the cold got me got me groceries, kitchenware, and enough else to get by. I ordered equipment for the Timeslot from a catalog using a payphone, and debated whether I needed one in the apartment, ultimately deciding I didn't. After a week or two, I waited on pause again. Damn. I didn't relish the thought of more downtime. Having a phone, going to the movies, or even buying a TV were probably out of my budget. A street address, though, got me a card at the public library, and I became a regular there over the next few months.

16

TIA
April 2045

The secret log showed V jumping *five times* some weeks, and the empty days where he was gone dropped to almost zero.

My mom had been a nurse, and when I was a kid, she explained to me about the patients she worked with in a rehab center. They'd gotten into something which started out fun, but later they couldn't control it and couldn't get away, even after it quit being fun. Was that it? Was the unhinged jump frequency evidence of Vanhanen just trying to *survive* the maze of jumps and ends of the lines his younger self created?

"Maze" was exactly right. The timeline that the secondary part of my app charted was convoluted and frustratingly incomplete. Whenever he arrived from a point before electronic records, it left a gap. If there was a way to know more about his early jumps, it would mean less extrapolation for the app and make my temporal chart far more accurate.

Alone in the quiet at TE, I looked up from my tablet to V's office door, closed and locked, as always. Never once, to my knowledge, did he leave it open. What was so secret to require such diligence? In contrast to the card reader on the hallway door, this had an old-school deadbolt with a metal key. I squinted and leaned closer to read the brand name.

The hallway door clicked and swung inward. I was halfway across the room, my chair facing away from my desk and toward his office. Thinking fast, I grabbed one hoop earring and tugged. When V stepped into view, he found me bent forward, retrieving it from the carpet muttering, "There you are." Looking up, I said, "Good morning," and rolled back to my desk.

He took out a keyring and unlocked the office. "Good morning, Miss James. Have a good weekend?"

"Yeah. I saw that new 3D sci-fi horror film. You?"

"Got in some golf both days."

"Good weather for it, huh?"

"Yes. Finally." He said and disappeared into his office.

Unclenching my fist, a badly bent earring lay on my palm.

Enjoy yourself while you can. I'm coming for you, asshole.

*

AMBER
February 1994

You'd think with literally nothing else to do on Tuesdays and Thursdays in 1994, I might be able to make it to class early. You'd be wrong. I slipped into the seat next to Crystal right as class started, whispering, "Hey."

She replied the same but looked a little uncomfortable. Was that a blush?

For the next forty-five minutes, I listened to a lecture about early computer software; "apps" wasn't a common term yet. I took a few notes, but my mind kept straying.

At one point I realized Crystal was looking at me, wearing a slightly worried expression and fidgeting with her thumb ring. I mouthed "what," trying to look concerned rather than snarky. She shrugged, shook her head, and made a dismissive never mind gesture.

As soon as class ended, I leaned in to say, "I listened to your show," but we both talked at once.

"Wait, what?"

"I said I listened to your show."

"After I ran out on you like that?"

We flowed with the other students toward the hallway.

"Huh? Don't worry about it. No, you had somewhere to be, and our conversation almost made you late. You didn't get in trouble with the radio people, did you?"

She sounded relieved. "Nah. The DJ before me stayed a few minutes longer; that was all."

I felt like the next move was on me. "If you want to continue our conversation sometime...we could get coffee?"

Smiling, she said, "That sounds great. I have to get to my next class, but I have a break right before this one on Thursday."

"Strange Brew at threeish?"

She nodded, smiling. "Awesome." I watched her head down the corridor, possibly admiring her long legs and the way she tucked her hair behind one ear.

What was I getting into? Was there something there? Ugh. I

didn't know, other than I could be making my situation so much more difficult.

When Crystal disappeared out the door, I turned...and bumped into Blondie. "Oh, sorry. 'Scuse me."

She gestured toward the far door. "Did you two get together?"

"What?"

She repeated slowly, like I was deaf or stupid, "Did you two get together yet?"

"Well, we went out for dinner together after the test last week." I held up my cane. "I couldn't keep up with you guys, so we went somewhere else. Somewhere closer."

"Uh-huh, sure," she replied, deadpan.

"Why do you care?"

"You two've been over there on the other side of the room since almost the beginning of the semester. Becca and I have a bet on whether you're together."

"Um. Uh...." *Holy shit. Was it that obvious?*

"She's clearly into you but probably too shy to make a move." She paused and changed her stance, leaning in a little. "For what it's worth, I hope you two do get together, and not only because it means Becca owes me twenty bucks." She straightened and walked away, her pale hair merging with the flow of other students.

*

CRYSTAL
February 1994

I spent a weirdly long time staring into the dark abyss of my closet deciding what to wear. It was only coffee, but I must have tried on, or at least held up and stared at, half the clothes I own. Okay, admittedly, my wardrobe doesn't have tons of variety, largely consisting of black, gray, and dark colors. I considered going shopping but thought I'd frustrate myself even more. How to look nice without looking like you're trying to look nice, y'know?

For over a year, my life had been about taking care of Mom. Then it was about grief and patching the hole in myself her death had left behind, the house, the letter, and all. I wrote that I was going to restart my life. I thought I meant school, classes, and eventually graduation. I didn't realize until later how much it was also about my internal self. Amber was beautiful and cool, sure, but so much more than that. I enjoyed talking to her. I really enjoyed hanging out with her. Seeing her walking into class twice a week made me happy. Happier than I'd been in a long time. She had nothing to do with my past, but maybe, hopefully, something to do with my future.

I finally decided on a longer black cardigan, faded jeans, and a burgundy shirt with some low leather boots instead of my chucks. If the shirt was a little slimmer than I usually wore, or I spent a little longer on my makeup than a typical Thursday, what of it?

I hadn't been inside Strange Brew in months, usually making my coffee at home. I could have grabbed a sofa in the back, but wanting to see the door, I waited in a wooden chair across from the counter, reading *Rolling Stone*, or trying to read, anyway. I kept looking at my watch and spinning the ring on my thumb, the way I do when I'm anxious. Amber usually appeared just as, or right after, class began. Despite my excitement, I didn't expect her to be early.

She showed up at 3:05 p.m. Those five minutes were more anxiety riddled than I cared to admit. Seeing her walk through the door, felt like releasing a breath I didn't realize I'd been holding. Hanging her sunglasses from her shirt, she looked around, squinting from sun blindness. The glasses pulled an already low V-neck even lower.

"Oh, hey! Did you order yet?" she asked, bringing my attention back up.

"No, I was waiting for you."

"Cool. I was hoping you hadn't. It's super nice outside. How would you feel about getting the coffees to-go and taking a walk."

Not what I'd imagined, but yeah. "Sure. That sounds great. It's been cold so long."

She stepped up toward the counter saying back over her shoulder, "I know, right?" Even though she ordered first, my plain black coffee was ready before her latte. "Yeah, yeah. My friend Tia always gives me a hard time about holding up the line with my foo-foo coffee. She claims there should be an express lane for black coffee orders."

I shrugged. "Not a bad idea at all."

The weather was sunny and warmer than it had been in months. I took my coat off while waiting and never put it back on. It was a beautiful day, but possibly I was strolling around campus talking and drinking coffee with a woman I'd crushed on all semester. Sunshine and roses were maybe to be expected.

We walked for a few blocks, chatting, before it hit me. "Hey, wait a minute—your knee. You're walking a lot faster than you did before."

She made a grimace which turned into a smirk. "That night, I *may* have been exaggerating, a bit, to put some distance between us and the rest of the group."

"A bit?"

"A bit. What? It worked, didn't it?"

I shook my head and smiled from being let in on the secret.

Just like at the restaurant, the conversation flowed without effort. I don't remember what all we talked about. The time both flew by and enclosed us in a moment lasting much longer.

Almost back to the lecture hall building, we stopped at some park benches in the sun. Amber shrugged out of her leather jacket, which exposed part of a tattoo on her upper arm: green and gold lines disappearing under her short sleeve.

I was about to ask about it when she leaned in and said, "So right before you left the restaurant..."

I groaned and covered my eyes with one hand. "I definitely remember my headlong exit. Don't think I'll ever forget."

"Huh? No, just before that. You were talking about your mom."

I dropped my hand, looking back at her. "Yeah?" I replied, wary of where this was going.

"What made you tell me? I mean, earlier you said I'd look at you different and you didn't want to be 'that girl.' What changed? If you don't mind me asking."

I knew the exact moment in the earlier conversation when I'd relaxed. It was the same moment when real hope began. "You said 'she.' You didn't have to mention your ex was a woman, you could've been sly about it, but you weren't. You trusted me enough to be honest."

"I've been out since high school. Sometimes I have a hard time remembering to shut the hell up."

"Well, even still. I appreciated it." I finished my coffee and leaned over, tossing the cup into a trash basket. "Wow. High school?"

A breeze ruffled her hair, and she pushed it back. "I had an enormous crush on my chem lab partner. I know, I know. Cliché, huh?" I shrugged. "I was all set to ask her to the winter dance. I'd been psyching myself up all semester."

I interrupted. "Oh no. Let me guess...football player?"

"Close...basketball. He was very tall. Anyway, I was devastated, and my dad happened to catch me at exactly the right moment with 'What happened?' He didn't let me push him away even when I tried. He made tea, sat down with me, and let me cry, and when I was done, he let me talk."

"He wasn't weird?"

"No, not at all. I mean, I was a sporty girl with short hair. Maybe he suspected."

It was easy to imagine the scene, soccer jersey, book bag and all.

I looked at my watch. We still had a few minutes. Knowing what I was about to do, I took a deep breath to calm my nerves. "When my mom was first diagnosed with cancer, I found her on the couch after class. She told me, and we both started crying. Once we calmed down a little, I realized I didn't know how long we'd have together. I couldn't hold onto it any longer. I blurted out, 'Mom, I'm gay.'"

I studied Amber's reaction as I led up to that last word. She listened intently and looked sympathetic during the part about my mom but gave a tiny one-corner smile at my confession. Almost a look of relief. Oh, thank god! I'm terrible at reading when someone's interested. It had been so long, so *very* long. I hoped I didn't misinterpret this (whatever this was) out of wishful thinking. Her little half-smile told me everything.

"Really that blunt?"

"Pretty much." I held up one hand like a puppet "I have cancer." Then the other hand, "Mom I'm gay."

Suppressing a chuckle, she asked, "What'd she say?"

"It must have been so unexpected, she laughed. I got mad and punched her in the arm. It made us both laugh, until we were flopped all over each other on the sofa, laughing and crying at the same time. Eventually she wiped her eyes and said, 'Oh, sweetie, I know.'

"I was shocked. For a second, I thought maybe she saw me kissing Annika in the basement that one time in high school. I was all 'Wait. How?' and she goes 'It was the *Star Wars* poster in your room, if you must know.' I snapped back, 'There are plenty of girls who like *Star Wars*!'" Amber was full-on grinning at that point. She was so pretty. "Mom shook her head, smoothed down my hair, and said, 'Most girls who like *Star Wars* have posters with Luke or Han, or maybe a spaceship, not Princess Leia in the gold bikini.'"

Amber burst out laughing. She laughed until I joined in.

Around bouts of more laughter, she asked, "Wait, wait, wait! You got outed by Princess Leia?"

"Yep. Pretty much."

She put one hand on my arm and rubbed her eyes with the other, still laughing, then looked at me. "That might be the best coming out story I've ever heard!"

*

TIA
April 2045

The makeshift portal activated, and Amber stepped through. Startled, she stifled a scream, hand over her mouth, then dropped it to her chest, breathing hard. "Oh my god, Tia! You scared the shit out of me!"

"Sorry about that."

Draping her leather jacket over the sofa, she asked, "What are you doing here?" Adding with a smirk, "Isn't it past your bedtime?" She unlaced her boots but kept looking over at me.

"I need you to do me a favor and not ask any questions."

"Sure."

"I'll explain later."

"Or not. Whatever." She shrugged. "I know what our line of work means. Sometimes you have to not know in order to not mess up the timeline. And besides, you *did* hook me up with the coffee computer. What do you need? I hope it's quick because I'm seriously tired, and we both have to work in the morning."

I waved vaguely at the Timeslot. "How far back does this thing go?"

That question seemed unexpected. "Um. It's spotty. There are dead patches. I assume from loss of power or damage on the other end. *Ends*. Whatever. There's pretty good coverage from the mid-nineties back into the early eighties. The seventies are hit and miss, and there's a tiny connection to the late sixties." She finished changing and slipped on her shoes.

"But it'll go that far back?"

"Yeah. The signal's not as wide as the others, but it's constant. What date?"

"Anytime in the first part of 1969 should do."

Was that a raised eyebrow? It was gone so quickly I couldn't be sure in the dim room. I didn't see any suspicion again. She stood, switched to the African cane, and woke one of the computers in the jumble of cabling on the worktable. I asked, "How do you keep track of which one does what?"

"Dunno, just do. How do you keep track of all that code in your software?"

I held up my hands, "Fair enough."

Reading off the screen, she asked, "How does March first sound?"

"Great. And you'll shut down the notification to TE?"

"That part's not online yet, don't worry." A few more clicks, and the portal hummed above us. She asked, "Want me to run it up to the slot?"

"Nah. You're not much faster than me these days." I turned toward the door but looked back. "I can give you a ride home after."

"Yeah, thanks! I'll meet you in the hallway to the parking garage."

I slid the plaque aside and dropped an envelope through time, hoping for a little help.

On our way out I asked, "Wasn't physical therapy supposed to get rid of the cane?"

"I've only been to a couple appointments. Hard to schedule around trips to the nineties."

"I'm sure. How's that going, by the way. Any news?"

She grinned a big sly smile. One I hadn't seen on my friend's face in far too long. "We went out for coffee!"

17

KASEY
August 1992

Ibecame exceptionally skilled at sneaking around. When I told Charles people didn't notice the repair guy, I had no concept how frequently that'd prove right. Carry a toolbox, behave as if you know where you're going, and you can hide in plain sight, for months if necessary.

After-hours, the student union jobsite was uninhabited, and getting past security was as uncomplicated as stepping over yellow tape marked "Caution: Do Not Cross." Beyond the plastic dust protection, I was invisible to the rest of the building.

Even with both a hacksaw and bolt cutters, the padlock took a while to get through. Inside, the empty room overlaid in my memory with the version Charles and had I set up together—the radio, the sofa, all of it.

Leaving, I replaced the old hasp with a new, stouter one and upgraded the padlock as well. I prowled through the whole construction site, looking for materials I could eventually use for the Timeslot. I justified it like this: the university was paying for the renovation to the student union, and they were *also* indirectly paying my salary and expense report. Ridiculous, thinking of it as simply "reallocation of resources," but it was that or imagine myself as a time-traveling Robin Hood, which didn't fit the situation as well. Cautious and careful, I never reallocated so many resources it'd be noticed.

Between walking through the construction site every few nights, hitting thrift stores during the day, and the monthly university garage sale, I acquired much of what I'd need. Slower going that way but I stayed out of sight.

In the evenings, sitting in my folding camp chair amidst stacks of materials for the Timeslot and listening to yet another thrift store radio, I filled the journal with all that had happened since I was called into the director's office.

I'd found one of the necessary components was easier to acquire than in the 60s and 70s. Previously, I'd ordered from an electronics supply catalog what could later be sourced from the internal workings of a common microwave oven. By 1992, these were readily available on the student secondary market. Public bulletin boards were full of copied pages listing stereos, books, guitars, CDs and furniture for sale with tear-off tabs fringing the bottom.

The last microwave oven was so big, at nearly fifty pounds, it should have rightfully been called a "macro-wave." I lugged it back to my basement apartment and disassembled it, same as the previous three.

During that walk around the construction site on my first day in '92, I overheard talk about the end of the semester, and I thought they'd meant the spring semester, not the summer one. If I'd understood better, it would have affected my decision to stay. But...the renovation was *finally* wrapping up. Day by day, the protective plastic, most of the contractors and their equipment relocated to another wing of the building for the next phase of the project.

By that time, I had all the components I needed for the Timeslot and felt anxious to get building, knowing the calendar was counting down. The first several weeks in 1992 had been unusually cold. I bought extra sweaters, blankets, wool socks, and rarely strayed far from the corner of the basement closest to the furnace itself. Getting by on a space heater and some redirected warm air from upstairs was something I had absolutely no desire to endure again. It meant I needed to be gone by the end of September, early October at the latest. That gave me about six weeks to build the thing and get the hell out of there.

*

AMBER
March 1994

At the end of class, Crystal leaned over. "Hey, you busy tonight?"

"Nope."

"I'm on KCSR after 8:00 p.m. if you want to come hang out."

It was the kind of invitation I'd been waiting for. Since I'd asked her to coffee, I hoped she'd take the next turn.

I smiled. "Sure! Sounds cool!"

It'd seemed so easy, or at least straightforward, when we planned this in Tia's living room. In the midst of it all, though, it just *wasn't*. It took a level of subtlety beyond my usual instincts. I wanted her to trust me, but if I let it go on too long, I ran a serious risk of her feeling I led her on.

I wished I could be completely honest, but that held heavy risk too. "Hi, I'm a time traveler from the future come to rescue you" sounds *bonkers.* The point where I needed to bare it all and hope I'd prepped well enough was fast approaching. Her end of the line hovered about seven weeks out. Every day, my window got smaller and smaller.

A large part of me felt confused for a completely different reason. Procrastinating in the role of fellow student, allowed me to drag out my real reason for being there— gaining her trust and building toward the big reveal. It was almost believable...until the coffee date.

I couldn't bullshit myself any longer. It started back with Crystal's letter. Eventual perspective let me see that more clearly. Between the aftermath of the breakup with Meg, and the weird doldrum of my knee recovery, I'd needed something to focus on. The letter became *it.* Once I met her...she was all these things I found myself drawn to, and I was falling for her, hard.

Crystal coming out made things even more complicated. If she was straight, I could have written it off as a crush and let it go. It wouldn't have been the first time. But knowing there was even a possibility of something more, that maybe the feelings were mutual, made it even harder. I felt two ways at once: stretched between a rescue and a relationship as surely as I was spanning across two time periods. The longer I knew her, the blurrier that line became. I lay on the sofa in the Timeslot room with my arm over my eyes and thought it all over and over. When 8:00 p.m. came I'd gotten no closer to an answer.

The radio station had a large hallway window that opened into the studio. I watched her for a moment through the call letters painted across the glass. Her back to me, she stretched between controls in front of her and ones far to the right, long dark hair around big headphones obscuring her face. At my tap, she turned and smiled, waving me toward the door. That smile lifted my mood like nothing else.

The studio had a central countertop where the DJ sat: controls in the middle, CD players in a tall cabinet to the left, and turntables on an extension of the counter to the right. Around it, every wall was covered floor to ceiling with shelves crammed to overflowing with CDs and records.

Still looking around, Crystal waved to get my attention, pointed at the ON AIR sign and mouthed the words "one minute" as the song wound down and ended. She leaned toward the mic. "A little Garbage for ya on 89.9, campus student radio." She read a public service announcement and gave the request line number before starting the next song, "Fall Down." I recognized it from my vintage music immersion but couldn't remember the name of the band. It was something weird, I thought. She slid the headphones down to hang around her neck and said, "Hey, you."

The evening progressed through an incredible selection of music, a playlist that flowed from song to song, from end to beginning and on and on. Crystal was amazing. Punk bands like Green Day blended into grunge stuff like Soundgarden. Rarities I didn't know mixed with mainstream radio like the Cranberries. I'd read about the mixtape phenomenon and the level of attention heaped on the art of song order. If someone had said to me, "Imagine an hours-long mixtape, maybe the best you've ever heard. Now imagine sitting inside it as it was being created live and on the fly." That's what it felt like in the booth with Crystal, and she made it look almost effortless, all while holding up an ongoing conversation with me.

At one point, I recognized a distinctive bass line, even though I hadn't heard it in years. "Seasons" had been one of my dad's favorite songs. I almost spoke up saying so, but stopped myself at the last second, aware it wouldn't make sense from that point in time.

When Crystal played the station identification, I looked at my watch. Three hours had buzzed by in a swirl of amazing music. She must have seen me glance down. After starting the next song, she pulled off the headphones and spun the DJ chair toward me, leaning forward, elbows on knees. "Do you need to get going?"

I didn't want to, but I had to. "Yeah. I'm sorry. I have an appointment first thing tomorrow, and my physical therapist makes a big deal about getting eight hours of sleep the night before." I'd made up a believable story, but in that moment, the disappointment in my voice was honest.

She took my hand, lacing her fingers with mine. "Hey, c'mere…um, before you go." She guided us around the CD players to a far corner of the studio filled with shelves of more records. Some distant part of my mind also noticed it was out of view of the hallway window.

Saying nothing more, she turned to face me with a mischievous little smirk. She put her free hand on my shoulder and gently pulled me into a kiss. My hand on her waist slid around to the small of her back.

*

CRYSTAL
March 1994

I have no memory of what I played for the last hour of my set. I may have actually floated home without touching the ground as well. I kissed Amber! I could barely believe it.

After she left, I danced around the studio from sheer happiness. Juvenile and embarrassing if anyone saw me, but no one did. If Amber's kiss was any indication...well, it only ended because after four minutes I had to start the next song.

I wished I could call her over the weekend to hang out, but she'd explained she was crashing in a friend's basement after her breakup and had no phone.

I knew there was no way I'd be able to sleep, class the next morning or no. To avoid annoying my neighbors, I took sheet music, my viola, and some wine to the basement. Two hours later, I finally felt tired enough to go to bed.

Saturday morning, a dream woke me early, and I couldn't get back to sleep. I wish I could say I dreamt of Amber or the kiss, but no. It was strange and hard to remember. I was running maybe? I'm not sure.

Even in her absence, Mom's influence stuck around—work first, fun later. I planned to rent a movie when I finished studying and practicing—and maybe finish that bottle of wine. Late in the afternoon, while looking for my keys, the doorbell rang. Out the window I saw Amber. My heart leapt, but I played it cool, opening the door.

I couldn't help but smile as I stepped out onto the porch. "Hey, you."

"Hey." She had her hands jammed deep into her coat pockets and looked down, before back up at me. "So...I can't stop thinking about the other night."

"I know. Me too." I pointed over my shoulder. "Do you want to, like, come in?"

"No. Er, I mean, not right now. I actually wanted to know if you'd like to go out."

"You mean like on a date?"

"Yeah. Our other time got cut kinda short."

"That's true." I pointed again. "Can I have, like, five minutes?"

She smiled. "Yeah, of course! Take as long as you need."

I motioned her inside and disappeared into my bedroom.

Oh my god! Amber asked me out!

Pulling off my T-shirt, I looked around for what to wear. My jeans were okay, fashionably ripped. I looked in the mirror and pulled out my hair tie. My hair had that annoying line from being in a ponytail all day. Quickly brushing it out, I followed with a French braid, all the while scanning my closet for a shirt. I tied off the braid, did some quick makeup and pulled on a black button-down I found tucked behind a bunch of other stuff I hadn't worn in a long time.

Amber, lingering near the front door, turned as I stepped out of the bedroom. "You look great. I mean, you looked great before too, but wow."

I smiled at her stumbling, awkward compliment. "Thanks. Where'd you want to go?"

"I didn't really have this planned. I just wanted to hang out."

We stepped outside, and I locked the door. Inside my head, I jumped like a cheerleader but did my best not to show how excited I felt.

She asked, "Do you like Indian food? There's that curry place on Lincoln."

"Yeah. That's supposed to be good."

At a crosswalk for a busy intersection, I stepped forward, but Amber put her hand on my wrist to stop me, seeing a motorcycle turning, which I'd missed.

Across, and a few steps onto the opposite sidewalk, she pointed backward with a surprised expression. "Wait. Did we hold hands crossing the street back there?"

"Pretty sure we did." And it felt completely natural and normal, and basically awesome.

She grinned. "Cool."

The curry restaurant had a sign on the door explaining that they were closed due to a plumbing problem in the kitchen.

Amber turned to me. "Crystal and Amber's Excellent Adventure is off to a rough start."

"I bet we can figure something out." I took her hand again, and we headed down the street.

Dinner started with kabobs from a food truck, eaten sitting in a little public plaza while discussing music, movies, and whatever came to mind until it got fully dark and we were cold. Dessert came from the cookie bakery in campustown. Amber had obviously never been there before and acted a little weirded out that it was an option to buy a scoop of dough in a little container instead of a regular baked cookie.

We wandered into a comic book shop, browsing, then laughing at the ridiculously large breasts on the female characters. Amber knew a little about comics, but mostly the odder, non-superhero ones. When the owner's annoyed stare, likely for us not buying anything, became too much, we moved on.

In the shop next door, we tried on increasingly ugly sunglasses until we both giggled like teenagers. Back on the sidewalk, we noted most places were closing except bars and restaurants. I gestured down the street saying, "C'mon."

One entryway area served both Strange Brew and the bar in the basement, the London Underground. I led the way down the familiar steps. The Underground is a British pub-themed place, but more importantly, its patrons are mostly grad students, a little older and a lot quieter. Customers could actually hold a conversation without yelling. The walls were lined with shelves of books, which people can sit and read as long as they like, and the place served imported dark beer.

The tables each had a sign for a different Tube stop, and I headed for Brixton Station in a far corner. I liked it because of the Clash song. The blonde bartender waved as we passed, and I waved back. At the table, Amber asked, "You know her?"

"Kit? Yeah." I wasn't quite sure how this might sound, but I charged ahead and admitted it anyway. "I'm kind of a regular here."

She looked curious. "Huh."

"I get headaches, a lot. They're not migraines exactly. The doctors did all kinds of tests when I was a kid: scanned my whole head, tested my eyesight and hearing, the works, but they never figured it out. Loud noise and smoke sometimes make them worse. So..." I held my hands palm up in a shrug gesture and turned a little side to side.

"Ahh. The quieter bar."

I pointed up as if to say "exactly" before continuing aloud. "Eventually, I discovered that alcohol works better than just about anything else on my headaches."

She smiled. "Now it all makes sense."

"Don't go anywhere. I'll get the first round." While Kit was pouring the pints, she tilted her head slightly toward Amber. I replied with the tiniest of nods. She gave a smile of approval and a subtle thumbs-up, whispering, "Cute!"

I mouthed my response, "I know!"

Carrying the pints to the table, I noticed Amber's jacket hung on the back of her chair. From the first time I'd seen her in class, I thought she was beautiful. With her messy red hair, amazing brown eyes, and wiry athletic physique, how could I not? I mean, c'mon! At first, the motorcycle jacket, clunky boots, and a certain attitude she carried around made her appear distant, though, or maybe "guarded" was a better word. Talking with her after class, I was glad to discover she was different than I expected, nicer.

The night we went out for barbeque, she opened up more, and things started to click. The girl who'd loved *Star Wars*, played D&D, and read comic books spent years studying how the "cool kids" dressed, and when going off to college tried to emulate it. That tough exterior was her public persona, her armor, protecting the soft nerdy center. She wore her armor like that leather jacket, and maybe the two were one.

I just knew I wanted to reach inside the jacket and... Well, I got a little lost in my own metaphor. Approaching the table, carrying pints of beer after an evening of fun and silliness, the armor was off, both physically and (I hoped) mentally.

She looked up, pushed her hair back, and accepted the glass I held out. Sitting down opposite, I took a generous sip and savored it for a moment. Or maybe savored *the* moment.

"What?" Amber asked after a second.

"You fidget with your hair a lot. Did it used to be longer?" I sat up, putting my hand flat on the table. "Oh no, you didn't do the post-breakup cut, did you?"

She laughed a little. "No. Well, same idea but opposite. I used to wear it even shorter. My ex liked it and always talked about how not everyone can pull it off." She rolled her eyes. "Whatever. Since the breakup, I haven't had the motivation to get a trim. A post-breakup grow, I guess." She ran both hands through it and messed it up. "Not sure what I'm going to do."

Quietly, I admitted, "I like it the way it is."

She smiled and straightened. "Really?"

"Mm-hmm. Kind of a red-haired Winona Ryder look."

She was silent for a moment, thinking. "'Fidget', huh? At least it's not twirling. Did you ever date a twirler?"

I laughed. "No. Never did." In truth, I was a little embarrassed to reveal how few women I'd dated.

"I'll admit the hair twirling thing can be cute at first, but, oh my god, it never stops!"

We had at least two more rounds, but I'm not positive. I lost count. Part of me wanted to take her home, but part of me wanted this moment together to never end.

When closing approached, we were among the last few people left, and Kit waved us up to the bar. Amber weaved a little but covered by leaning on her cane. I felt at least as unsteady as she looked, maybe more so. I hadn't gotten that drunk in a long time, which is kind of funny considering how much alcohol I consume. I usually don't feel more than a slight buzz, barely enough to keep the headaches at bay.

Kit flipped her long braid over one shoulder, produced a bottle from under the bar, and poured three shots. I got a glimpse of the label before it disappeared.

"The good stuff?" I asked.

She smirked conspiratorially and slid a shot glass across to each of us.

Looking at Amber but nodding toward me she said, "Be good to her," and drank. We followed. "Now, go home."

Coats back on, we stumbled up the stairs to the sidewalk, hand in hand. It was probably less cute than it sounds, with both of us weaving drunkenly and bumping into each other. After a minute of silent walking, Amber said, "Can I ask you something?"

"You can always ask. But sure."

She gestured back toward the bar. "You, and the bartender?"

"Um..."

"No shit!"

"Once. Long time ago"

"Wow, she's gorgeous!"

"Guys ask her out multiple times a week, and she always politely declines, saying the owner doesn't want her to date customers. I sit right there with a little smile and sip my beer. If only they knew the truth."

"Yeah. If only."

The trip home took a lot longer than the walk there. We stopped to rest a couple of times. One or the other of us would get distracted or amused by something till the other pulled them along. That last shot had finally caught up with us.

On my porch, Amber gripped the rail, swaying, while I dug out my keys.

I don't remember clearly after that. I may have attempted to flirt, but it was about as cumbersome as expected at that point. I think we both had water and aspirin.

Holding my arm, she helped me to my room, and I collapsed on the bed. The last thing I remember was Amber sitting next to me, the light from the hall behind her. I touched her hair, thinking about how I'd wanted to do that since I first met her. I may have mumbled something about how beautiful it was, or maybe how beautiful *she* was. She untied my shoes, pulled them off, and covered me with a quilt.

18

AMBER
March 1994

I awoke on a sofa in 1994, but not the one in the Timeslot room. That one had plain brown upholstery, and this one had an unattractive floral print, but despite that, it felt shockingly comfortable.

I was in Crystal's living room. Moving my head to look around reminded me how much we'd had to drink the night before. My headache would be worse than usual the rest of the day.

The room was decorated in an eclectic mix, things like the furniture obviously left by Crystal's mom, overlaid with a twenty-four-year old's additions. The dining table at one end was completely buried with books and papers. The centerpiece of the room was a wall-sized poster of Nirvana's *Nevermind* album, the one with the naked baby swimming. A yellow sticky note with the word "NOPE" covered his penis.

I heard a shower running but drifted back to sleep. Next was a coffee grinder and the pot gurgling shortly after. It smelled amazing.

Sitting up, I saw Crystal in the kitchen washing mugs, her wet hair combed and hanging down her back over a thick purple robe, bare legs and feet with black nail polish visible under the hem.

She turned toward me and smiled. "Hey, you."

"Hey." I took the mug she held out to me.

"Cream, right?"

"Yes, thanks." I sipped the coffee and it tasted wonderful. She half sat with one hip on the arm of the couch and drank her own.

I had to tell her. I couldn't let this go on longer, especially if things were going where it seemed like they were going. To wait longer would be...

She interrupted my thoughts with a question. "Why are you here?"

For a terrifying second, I didn't know how to answer that. Why was I in 1994? No, of course, she wasn't asking *that*. "We were so drunk last night."

"Um, yeah?" she replied as if I'd stated the obvious, and maybe I had.

"After we got back here and dumped you in bed, I made the mistake of sitting down." I patted the cushion. "This couch is extremely comfortable."

"Oh, I know. Mom used to joke that it was an energy sucker. Don't sit if you have stuff to do."

"It's true. I could not get up and walk home. I found a blanket in your hall closet and crashed."

"Sure, that's fine. No, what I meant was why are you—" She

tapped the sofa. "—here." I must have looked confused because she elaborated. "As opposed to..." She pointed over her shoulder toward her bedroom.

"Oh!" Finally, it clicked. "You were so drunk. You were probably asleep seconds after you laid down."

"I'd have happily shared."

"I know, but..."

She interrupted, "There's a 'but'? Oh shit! Did I misinterpret? I thought things were going really well!"

"They are. I need to talk with you about some stuff before..." I gestured toward the bedroom.

"What? Oh my god, do you have a boyfriend? Was everything just a show?" She was starting to freak out. This was not going like I'd hoped it would at all.

"No. I don't have a boyfriend, never have. It's not like that. Please...please hear me out."

"Okay." She looked tense, gripping her mug.

I took a deep breath. "I know why you have headaches. I have one too right now."

"Yeah. It's called a hangover."

I held up my hand. "There's more to it than that. The headaches are a side effect of temporal displacement."

"Huh?"

"I know about your dad—maybe more than you do. I know who he worked for and where he came from because I work for them too. He would've had the headaches also. He was a time traveler...and...and so am I."

She looked incredulous but said nothing, so I continued. "When a person is out of time, the temporal displacement causes constant low-grade headaches. It's the universe reminding us that time travel goes against the natural flow of things."

"What the *hell* are you talking about?" She stood at the end of the sofa. "You said you were from Chicago."

"I am. Just, not yet. I was born in 2018."

"Bullshit!"

I pulled my shirt up and off my left arm, leaving just the tank underneath, pointing to my tattoo. "When I was a kid, my dad gave me a printed circuit board from an old computer which was man- ufactured the same day I was born. It's what got me interested in computer engineering. I loved it so much, when I was nineteen, I got part of it as a tattoo. If you look, you can see the numbers along the edge with the date."

She leaned in and squinted but didn't sound convinced. "It's only numbers." She stepped back and glared. "What does any of this have to do with us?"

This was going to be harder than I expected. I had to use my fallback plan. Shirt on, I dug in the inside pocket of my jacket.

"You have the headaches because your dad was out of time when he met your mom and when you were conceived. As far as I'm aware that's never happened before."

"How could you possibly know that?"

As gently as possible, I replied, "I work for the same depart- ment, Temporal Engineering. It's how I found this."

I held out her letter, the one she'd dropped in the Timeslot. Seeing it, she jumped back with a little shriek. "Where did you get that? That's not possible! What the hell?"

"I can explain it all, and I might even be able to fix your head- aches, but I need you to trust me."

"What? No! Everything you just said came from my letter. It was all in my dad's book. There's no time travel department!" She pointed at the envelope still in my hand. "Did you somehow find that and start stalking me? You made up that whole story based on what I wrote… For what? To get in my bed? That is *twisted*! And I thought you actually liked me." She was practically yelling by the end.

"I do like you," I responded quietly.

She set the coffee cup down. "I think you should go."

"What? No, I…" The crushing reality of what she said washed over me.

Standing there under her Nirvana poster, she pointed at the door. "Please."

"Okay, okay, I'll go." I picked up my boots and put them on. While tying my laces, I realized I had one chance to make a last-ditch effort, the final play of the desperate. As kindly as I could, I said, "Before I go, can I ask for one small thing?"

"What?" she snapped.

"An envelope."

"Huh?" She dug around on the table and handed me one. I pulled a pen out of my jacket, flipped her letter over and wrote a quick note. I sealed the envelope while she watched and I wrote across the front, "Do not open before April 9, 1994."

I handed it to her. "It wasn't supposed to be like this. I am so, so sorry."

She glanced at it and dropped it on the table. "Fine. Whatever. Just go."

I picked up my jacket and retreated. Glancing back once from the front steps, I could see through the window she'd collapsed on the couch with her face in her hands.

My heart…broke.

*

KASEY
September 1992 / September 1969

Weeks of sneaking around the student union and dodging contractors, months of living in that tiny basement, and the Timeslot installation was finally finished.

Since the beginning of September, the weather overnight became noticeably cooler. On top of that, the stove quit working and I had to grill in the backyard if I wanted to cook. I was so ready to be done with this project.

Despite everything, I stayed through the weekend instead of leaving as soon as it was complete.

Ever since landing in '92, I'd been bombarded with advertisements for a U2 concert at the university stadium in the fall. Originally, I thought I'd be long gone by that time, but when September found me still there, I decided to stay and see the concert, end the trip on a high note.

Before I left for the show, I sat down with my calculator and ran the numbers. First, I tabulated the number of days since jumping away from Charles. The number I came up with was unexpectedly large. I shook my head and double-checked. It was right. Over a year had passed. How was that even possible? One week, one month, one installation at a time, I guess. After the relative date for Charles, I progressed to the formula for the time jump coordinates.

As the first opening band wound down, I approached a scalper near the entrance with tickets in his hand, and he asked, "What you need, my man?"

"What've you got left?"

"I got one or two floor reserved near the back and a bunch in the regular stadium sections."

"What've you got up high?"

"Huh?" He looked confused.

"What's your worst ticket? The one you're probably not going to sell tonight."

He shuffled to the bottom of the stack and pulled one out. "Top row, upper deck."

Even the bad seats for this concert had sold for over forty dollars, and the good ones were scalped for around two hundred. I pulled a ten-dollar bill out of my pocket, and he groaned, "Aw, dude, you're killin' me."

"Would you rather go home tonight with my ten dollars, or that ticket in your pocket?"

He handed it over with a "Shiiiit. You're right."

Even from the nosebleed section, I thoroughly enjoyed the concert.

First thing Monday morning I left my tiny apartment, the camp furniture, and one hundred twenty dollars in cash under an empty beer bottle on the counter. I walked into TE and requested a jump to 1969. V didn't seem to be the type to show up right at 8:00 a.m., but I still felt anxious the whole time.

A few minutes later and twenty-three years earlier, I strode away from Nuke-E with my duffel and toolbox, confident in the knowledge I'd only need to make one more jump before I could take a long break from field work.

Visiting the Timeslot room at so many different points in history had muddied my memories and expectations. I'd been in that room the day before, but the equipment had been far more compact than what was before me.

The sofa felt as comfortable as I remembered. I slouched down and closed my eyes for a few minutes but knew I wasn't going to fall asleep. Sitting up, something white under the worktable caught my attention. An envelope with Charles's initials in the middle where an address would go and the letters TJ in the upper left corner, still sealed. I changed into the khaki pants and denim shirt outfit I wore in the 60s and put the letter in my pocket to give to Charles later.

The walk across campus and parts of town was always interesting when arriving in a timeline, first noticing what's changed from when I just left. I still had a key to our apartment in my pocket, but I didn't even try the lock. Unless Charles's tastes had changed radically, the pink curtains in the window made it abundantly clear he'd moved.

I knocked on the door and stepped back. It opened a crack with the chain across. I realized this was a single woman's apartment in 1969, and I was a lone Black man knocking on her door in the middle of the morning. I put on as polite a voice as I could. "Sorry to bother you miss, but I'm looking for a friend of mine who used to live at this address, Charles Yung"

She nodded tentatively. "We get his mail sometimes."

"Did he happen to leave a forwarding address?"

"No. No, I'm sorry, he didn't." The door began to close.

I spoke quickly. "Excuse me, miss..." She paused. "If I could get your landlord's phone number, maybe he has it."

"Hold on." She stepped away from the door, but left it open a crack. When she returned, she had an address book in her hand. She read off the number, and I wrote it on a corner of the envelope from the Timeslot room.

I said, "Thank you very kindly, miss," but she'd already closed the door.

The nearest pay phone was at a gas station several blocks away. It rang for a long time, and I was about to give up when he finally answered. I explained again about looking for Charles.

"Oh yeah. I remember him, Oriental fella. Nice enough, I guess. Professor or somethin'. Said he was gettin' married and buyin' a house."

Shocked to silence for a few seconds, I managed to ask, "Did he leave a forwarding address?"

He read it off, and I wrote it on the envelope as well. I hung up still stunned by the news. Why would Charles so blatantly break such a fundamental rule of time travel?

The town map in the back of the phone book showed it being past campus the other direction, probably two and a half miles or more. I needed some lunch first, preferably with a strong drink.

Walking toward campustown, something occurred to me which I'm embarrassed I hadn't thought of earlier. I had a wallet full of cash I couldn't use because it was all dated years in the future. Likewise, I had no idea of the date on the coin I used at the pay phone. I could have introduced an anachronism into the change box, and no way to get it back.

Stopping at a park bench, I emptied my pockets and counted a dollar and thirty-five cents I could actually spend. I had a hot dog and a bottle of cola from a food cart, eaten standing in the shade of a nearby building before walking to Charles's new house.

A shortcut took me past the oldest brick buildings in Engineers Row, comforting in their sameness. In the corner of campus where the College of Design would eventually stand, I cut through a still-vacant lot with nothing but the swish of dry autumn grass to mark my passing.

Construction was barely starting on the street where my tiny basement apartment would one day be. I walked on and the neighborhoods changed around me. Postwar brick houses, only twenty years old and just beginning to show their age, led to newer housing built in the previous year or two. Smallish ranch homes with one-car garages populated the blocks I walked through—little slices of the so-called American Dream. A few even had a white picket fence.

The address led me to a one-story tan brick house with some decorative banding in the masonry right below a wide picture window. The roof had a gable over a small porch with a bench and a dark wood door.

I knocked, but no one answered. A driveway led around to a small but well-kept backyard, with a grill, some patio chairs, bicycles leaning against the back of the house and a little flower garden. I stepped over a quirky garden gnome statue in the landscaping to drink from a hose.

Sitting on the front porch, leaning against the sun-warmed brick with my boots up on the railing, I may have nodded off, but engine noise pulled me back to full wakefulness. A cream-colored sedan approached down the block from my left.

I saw Charles behind the wheel, and I stood to wave. When the car was maybe a hundred feet from the driveway, a second, louder engine roared to life off to my right. A quick glance showed nothing but an old blue pickup that had been there all afternoon. As Charles signaled to turn into the driveway, the truck revved loudly with a squeal of tires. I realized what was happening too late and felt stuck in slow motion trying to warn Charles. Grabbing the porch rail, I screamed, "NOOOOOOO!"

The pickup backed down the street, gaining speed, and slammed into the driver's side of Charles's car as he turned into the driveway. The force of the impact shoved the sedan sideways onto the grass and tore off the mailbox, throwing it across the lawn.

Steering one-handed, the driver sat half-turned to look out the rear window, and I got a clear view. An older white man with gray hair close cropped around the sides and bald on top. Though I'd never met him, he fit Charles's description of Vanhanen exactly. Dropping his hand to the gear shift, he drove the truck forward, then shifted again. From the porch stairs, I could only watch as he backed up again, the bed of the truck slamming into the already crushed car.

He opened the door but must have seen me running across the lawn toward him because he closed it again. We had a terrifying instant of eye contact through the back window, and I thought he would target me. Instead, the truck revved and squealed away down the street, dragging a bent tailgate behind.

A spiderweb of cracks covered the windshield, but the glass on the driver's door at the point of impact was completely gone. I reached through to Charles, even when I knew in my gut it was no use. He lay draped across the steering wheel, his face turned away. Feeling for a pulse, but finding none, my hand came away bloody. I gently leaned him back, and recoiled sharply at seeing the side of his head crushed in. Blood ran down all over his shirt onto the seat of the car. I turned away and gagged, vomiting my lunch into the grass.

Wiping my mouth on my sleeve, I ran around to the passenger's side. The woman in the seat was only semiconscious. Long dark hair obscured her face, but I thought she looked like the librarian. She groaned, her arms wrapped protectively around a pregnant belly. From the size of the bump, I realized she was well along.

I gently brushed her hair back and asked if she was okay. She didn't respond, except for more groaning. I didn't see any injuries beyond a swelling patch on her cheek. Internally, though, was anyone's guess, and with the baby, it only made her situation more dire.

I looked back at the house and made a decision. Grabbing a brick from the landscaping, I tossed it through the back door window. My steps crunched on broken glass as I entered.

I lifted a rotary phone on the kitchen wall, hesitating with my finger partway to the dial, unsure whether nine-one-one existed yet. Instead, I dialed zero. I told the operator it was an emergency, and I needed an ambulance for a car crash. She transferred me, and I repeated it all, reading the address off the envelope. The emergency operator asked me to stay on the line, but I only vaguely heard her. Leaning to the side, I peered through the archway into the living room and saw the crumpled car framed in the large front window.

The precariousness of my situation struck me like a slap to the face; the only witness to a vehicular homicide, and I'd just broken into the victim's house. If I was arrested, or even detained for questioning, I had no valid ID, and no way of accounting for my whereabouts for the last year. Added to which was a pocket full of cash and a driver's license from the 90s. I dropped the phone and backed away, retreating through the rear door, whispering, "I'm so sorry, Charles." The receiver, dangling from its cord, swung back and forth.

I lifted his bicycle over the back fence and vaulted after it. Looking down and seeing blood on my shirt, I tore it off and jammed it into my back pocket. Through yards, down alleys and sidewalks, zigzagging through traffic, I rode like the devil himself was at my heels. I had to beat V back to Temporal Engineering if I wanted to get out of that timeline alive.

Stashing the bike on a rack at the student union, I ran inside, sweaty and shirtless, down the stairs to the to the Timeslot room. Between panting for breath, I gulped water from the tiny sink and splashed more on my face.

The stained shirt crammed into my duffel bag, a clean one re-placed it. In the process I disturbed some papers and almost threw them out of my way. When realization dawned of what they were, I cracked a smile for the first time since the crash.

I folded the papers to put them in my pocket, when my fingers brushed the envelope from earlier. Now crushed, with writing on the back and bloodstained on one corner, it went into the duffel. My breath and heartbeat had slowed finally. After more water, I put the bag over my shoulder and locked the door on my way out.

I rode to Nuke-E one-handed, carrying my toolbox with the other, and stashed the bike behind a loading dock. There was no parking lot nearby, but I doubted V would drive the damaged truck farther than necessary. He'd probably dumped it somewhere and was on his way back to TE. No time to stake out the entry, I marched right in and hoped for the best.

The same petite woman with large glasses who'd helped me that morning answered the door again. "Back already?"

"Um. Yes. A quick assignment, just had to check something"

"Not supposed to ask anyway."

I showed her the papers from my pocket—the temporal coordinates for a jump to 1994 I'd calculated during my first day in '92 on the hotel notepaper. Right that minute, though, they were gold. They saved me the time to run the numbers, which made all the difference in my escape.

When the emitters glowed and the field formed, I practically ran through the portal.

*

TIA
May 2045

The doorbell buzzed to my tablet in the middle of the night. Reaching over and tapping the screen, I saw Amber on my doorstep. She looked terrible. I opened without even asking what was wrong.

In the living room, the lights were on low, having activated when Amber entered. She lay curled in a ball on the sofa. For a long time, all I could get out of her was "I screwed up."

She'd walked all the way from the Timeslot room, and it was nearly 1:00 a.m. when she got to my door. She'd held herself together as long as she could but collapsed once she felt safe at my place with me.

Partly on my sofa, partly in my lap, she cried herself to exhaustion. I'd never seen Amber cry at anything—not a sad movie, not even after she fell on her knee in the tunnel.

When she tapered off to intermittent sobs, little by little, she explained. She told me about going out for coffee and about the radio station. I'd heard parts of it before, but the kiss was news.

Her voice gained strength as she went, telling me about going out Saturday night and all that happened. When she got to Sunday morning, she broke down again. Somewhere in there I heard, "She's going to die because I screwed up. I couldn't make her believe…"

I gave her tissues. "Whoa, whoa, whoa. You don't know that. There's still time. She's got, what? Month and a half?"

She sniffed. "Yeah. A little over."

"A lot can change in that much time."

She rolled onto her back across my sofa, one arm over her eyes. "I don't know. I sure hope so."

In the kitchen I heated the tea kettle. "You can stay here tonight, and we can get your stuff from the Timeslot room on our way to work."

An appreciative "Thank you!" came from the direction of the couch.

After a few minutes of silence, not sure if she'd fallen asleep, I whispered, "Amber?"

"Yeah?"

"Come get some of Great Grandma's special tea."

"Specialty?"

"No, special *tea*. Guaranteed to cure what ails ya." I slid a steaming mug across the counter and lifted one of my own. Without even realizing it, I'd used the R2-D2 and C-3PO mugs Amber had given me for Christmas. Too silly? I hoped not.

She sipped and made a face. "What the hell's in this?"

"Rooibos tea and bourbon. Lots of bourbon."

Amber silently drank her tea, stopping to rub her eyes occasionally. Near the bottom of the cup, she sleepily pointed toward the end of the sofa asking, "Um, why do you have a basketful of doorknobs?"

I made something up fast.

*

KASEY
April 1994

My hands shook and I felt ill. I desperately wanted to sit on the first park bench I saw and calm down, but I needed more distance between myself and TE first. I had to hide somewhere other than the Timeslot room. Technically V had access, even if he never went there. I walked away from Engineer's Row carrying my stuff and wishing I'd kept Charles's bike instead of leaving it in 1969.

I slipped into the back stairwell of the library. There was a low-ceilinged space below the last flight that I knew about from my own time at the university. I once accidentally interrupted a Muslim student praying in that secluded spot. I slid my stuff under and followed into the shadows and out of sight.

Leaning back, I rested my head against the wall. As soon as I closed my eyes, the events of that morning replayed in my head: the crash, Charles's bloody face, and my desperate flight from the 60s. I was probably in shock but didn't know what to do about it. I tucked my head between my knees, but it only made my stomach feel worse. Sitting up, I took deliberate slow deep breaths for a long time before I felt myself calming.

Images of the crash intruded repeatedly, and I had to start over with the meditative breathing. Eventually, I relaxed to a point where my hands weren't shaking, and my stomach unclenched minutely, but it wasn't anywhere near what I would have described as calm the day before. Was that the beginning of never feeling fully at ease?

I had a toolbox, a bag full of clothes, plus whatever cash was in my pocket, and that was all I had to my name. I had no way to safely get back into TE to return to my home time. Since V got a good look at me across Charles's lawn, he'd have alerted his staff to someone fitting my description. For the moment at least, I was stuck in 1994.

Opening my duffel bag for more 90s appropriate clothes, I rediscovered the envelope from the Timeslot room. I'd planned to hand it over to Charles and winced again at the thought. The placement of the initials on the envelope made it look like mail, but it wasn't. Not in the way that would make it illegal for me to open it.

With a utility knife from my toolbox, I cut a slit across the end.

CJY

If you're reading this, it would appear you got the Timeslot equipment up and running. I haven't heard from you, so I'm curious how your research went. I've been doing some of my own as well, most recently, tracking his portal use in search of his final timeline. There's a lot of extrapolations in my jump map, especially in the early parts. Have you found any of his early records from your current time or before? If so, please send. They would be invaluable to the accuracy of my map. I hope you're doing well and despite it all, I hope to see you again one day.

TJ

I sat back in wonder. Charles had a friend in another time he'd never mentioned. It sounded like someone who was aware of his efforts, his situation, and also working in parallel on his plot against Vanhanen.

The pages I copied for Charles were presumably somewhere in his house twenty-five years in the past. Returning for them wasn't an option.

Sitting in the quiet under the stairs felt oddly safe, a temporary sanctuary, but a sanctuary nonetheless. I didn't know when the library closed, but I waited until the shadows lengthened and faded to dusk before slipping back out the door.

19

TIA
May 2045

Amber set her bag on her desk and walked behind me with a quiet "Hey." She knocked on Vanhanen's partially closed office door while pushing it open and leaning in.

His "Good morning, Miss Wells" seemed overly cheerful, somewhat forced.

By comparison, her voice sounded flat and tired. "Uh, yeah. So you know, my doctors have okayed me to come back full time, except for my physical therapy appointments. They're still on Tuesday and Thursday afternoons."

"That's great news. We can possibly accelerate the schedule for the next series of experiments. That should please the team in Washington."

She nodded, saying, "Sure. Good," then pointed over her

shoulder. "I'll coordinate with Tia on what we need, okay?"

"Yes, yes. Of course." He glanced at his watch and stood. "If that's all, I need to get to a meeting."

I don't think he understood how few meetings were held in person and how much it tipped his hand to me. His bullshit stretched thinner and thinner.

Back at her desk, Amber looked hollow. I can only imagine the turmoil in her head. I knew she'd pitch in on whatever I asked, but I felt hesitant to lay more on her shoulders. A problem solver by nature, her engineering gene ran deep. She liked a challenge and an opportunity to figure things out. She also needed something to fill her time with *other than* soul-crushing emptiness while waiting for Crystal to contact her.

I asked a simple but intentionally open-ended question, "Don't these meetings seem odd?"

"What d'you mean? Like why run off when he could easily do a vid call?"

"Mm-hmm."

"Well, I imagined he was meeting with other crusty old guys."

I smirked, "Are they also smoking cigars and drinking sherry in your imagination?"

"Ha ha," she replied with sarcasm. "Maybe he can't figure out the app?"

"Nah. I walked him through it a couple of times. Even so, it's unlikely there's somewhere on campus more secure than here. Why leave?"

She squinted for a second and replied, "Okay. That *is* odd."

"It kinda makes me wonder about a lot of things."

"Uh-oh." Amber replied, deadpan.

I mock scowled but, in truth, I was glad she could still give me a hard time. "Maybe I'm nosy, but don't you ever wonder about the mysterious team in DC? Have you ever even once gotten an email from V where he forwarded one from them down the chain?"

This piqued her interest. "Now that you mention it, no."

"For a guy who doesn't trust or utilize modern tech, isn't it a little *too* perfect?"

"He always said it was security clearance; that everything had to go through him. But I see what you're getting at." Amber was quicker than I expected because she added, "Does this have anything to do with the mysterious Timeslot letter?"

"Indirectly, yes," I admitted.

"But you're bringing it up now because?"

"Because I'm starting to wonder what's really going on." If I learned one thing from Amber's story about her last morning in 1994, it was that too much information too fast could backfire. So, I told her briefly about the day I came in early and caught him returning from a jump. I said it made me wonder what he was hiding.

"Wait—when was that?"

"It was right after your knee surgery."

"And you said his schedule's been way more erratic since?"

"Well, that's when I first noticed it. It might have been slowly changing for a while. The last couple of experiments I did almost single-handed he was here so rarely"

"Ugh. Sorry about that."

I waved it off. "It's fine. It was just odd." I needed to pull the conversation away from V's strange schedule. I was working on that. I wanted Amber's help with the DC contacts. "I'm working on a way to track errant jumps. That's what the mystery letter was about."

"And..." She made a *c'mon* motion.

I hesitated. "The DC thing bugs me, okay? A dark mysterious government agency sounds like a poorly written spy novel from the twentieth century." Amber shrugged, but I continued. "I want to know if there's a way to track the experiment results after it leaves here for Washington, or wherever it is they go."

"Yeah, probably."

"Really?"

"Possible, but not easy." The relief must have shown on my face because she added, "You know I'll help you with whatever, right? After all we did together to get me to '94, and you kept V off my back and all? If he found out any of that, we'd both already be fired. At this point, what's a little more sneaking around?"

"Thank you."

"Let's talk about it over movie night. Honestly, I don't have it in me to watch anything where anyone falls in love, or anyone dies."

"That's fair. You doin' okay?"

"Can't sleep. Not hungry. Don't want to think about her. Can't stop thinking about her." She pinched the bridge of her nose. "This isn't my first breakup." I opened my mouth to rebut, and she waved me off. "I know. I know. It just feels an awful lot like one."

*

AMBER
June 2045

It was on the tip of my tongue to tell Tia about the note I left for Crystal, but I didn't. It broke too critical of a rule about time travel. Only my handwritten instructions kept her from foreknowledge of future events. It was flimsy protection against a paradox, and I knew it. Standing there in her living room, I acted in desperation, but I couldn't go back and change it, even if I wanted to.

April ninth had come and gone for her. Either she hadn't opened the letter, or if she had, she was still too mad to reach out. Every day counted farther down, and I hated feeling helpless to do anything about it. We had only seventeen days.

Tia gave me something to concentrate on other than my own heartbreak and worries. Her timing was intentional, and I loved her for it. She knew me well enough to understand that after the initial shock, I didn't need hugs and ice cream; I needed something to do.

In the lab, Vanhanen worked with Tia and I to tabulate the results from the last experiment. Near the end of the day, I asked Tia. "I left my water bottle in your car. Can I walk out with you and get it?"

"Why don't I give you a ride home?"

"Cool."

Safe in the quiet of Tia's van, she guessed, "You didn't leave anything in here, did you? Where we actually going?"

"Still my place." The building was old, and while technically wheelchair accessible, it was kind of a pain in the ass. The elevator and the handicapped parking spaces were at the far end of the building from my unit. Therefore, movie nights at Tia's apartment. Hers was also, most of the time, cleaner.

I pushed her chair, which she usually hated, but it allowed me to go faster and without the cane. The PT had helped, and I could go short distances on my own. The small successes made me impatient though. I wanted the cane *gone.*

I shoved some random junk out of the way to give Tia room. On my kitchen island sat one of the padded shipping containers we sent the data in to Washington, dark green plastic, about half the size of a shoe box. Tia peered inside, remarking, "What am I looking at? 'Cause I don't see anything but an empty box."

"Good. It passed the first test."

She gave me the puzzled eyebrow look.

"The encrypted data we send out is on a wireless drive, in a seamless plastic enclosure. Tampering with it would be obvious."

Tia picked up the box. "So, we'll track the shipping container instead? Clever!"

I worked the molded foam padding loose, sliding it out and flipping it over. I'd hollowed a space in the back, a little bigger than a playing card, and about a quarter inch deep. Taped inside were a battery and some electronics.

"The easiest way to do this quickly was to start with preexisting tech. This was a prepaid handheld, the smallest and lightest I could find. I cut away everything except battery, GPS, and data connection to go even lighter. We'll only get about two days runtime off a charge, but you should be able to track it, right?"

She brought up a list of GPS signatures on her tablet. "Falcon Homing Device?" She smirked. "Seriously?"

I shrugged. "I had to call it something."

"You realize that makes us the Imperials here. Not so sure about that..."

"Huh. Didn't think of it that way." I waved the silliness away. "Whatever. Can you sneak it into TE Friday morning?"

"There's room in my bag. I'll get there a few minutes early. That should work."

"We're going to have to track it Friday evening and maybe Saturday. I hope it doesn't sit on V's kitchen counter till Monday morning."

I wish I could describe a cool sequence where Tia and I passed it back and forth through the lab with tension and near-misses of being *almost* discovered by V, but we didn't. He barely even glanced at it—simply tucked it under his arm on his way out the door. We looked at each other, like 'What the hell?'

In Tia's van, she handed me her tablet and clicked her chair into the driver's position, then said, "Computer." It beeped in response, Tia having set it to sound like an R2 unit. "Run app Tractor Beam." Another beep sounded, and the app appeared on the screen in front of me. An aerial photo of campus and the surrounding town with two blinking lights: us and the box.

I was confused. "Wasn't this whole thing your idea? Are we not taking it seriously? Or is this an attempt to cheer me up?"

"Can't it be both? All we're doing right now is reconnaissance. The B&E will come later."

"Wait, what?"

"Let's figure out where we're going before we worry about how we're getting in."

I let my concerns go for the moment and watched the blinking icons on the screen. The package light stopped moving, and we gained on it quickly. In a moment, we zipped by an expensive restaurant and the two icons almost touched.

"We just passed him."

"Yep. I know. Let me turn around."

Once around the block, Tia spotted V's car—an enormous, old, white luxury sedan from the early 2000s, a vehicle which was, by then, a form of conspicuous consumption itself. "Look at me. I keep putting a diminishing natural resource in this dated mode of transportation simply because I can afford to, but mostly, I want you to see that I can afford to." I shook my head. *Asshole.*

Tia parked nearby, out of sight in the lot for a tropical fish store. This was still a Midwestern college town and it wasn't all that big. We couldn't exactly keep orbiting the restaurant. Too obvious.

We talked for a few minutes before quietly watching the icons on the screen, which were blinking but not moving. Bored, I finally broke the silence, "Look, I appreciate the adventure to take my mind off…things. I do, but how long d'you want to wait?"

"A little longer, I guess. And hey, this isn't just for you. I really am curious to find out what's going on. I think we're being lied to."

"I know."

"If I was only trying to distract you, my diversion would involve more booze." I couldn't help but laugh a little. She continued, "Do you mind if I ask…"

"No, it's okay. I just…ugh… The night we went out was Saturday, March eighteenth, and Sunday morning…"

Tia supplied, "Would have been the nineteenth."

I nodded. "Thirty-four days ago. Right now, it's the twenty-second of April for her. She has until the first of May. I can't stop thinking about her clock ticking down."

She reached over and squeezed my arm. "I wish I knew what to say."

"All the memories, the moments together, even the way she tucked her hair behind her ear… It could all be gone in a week."

She looked thoughtful. "Imagine what that must have been like for her. Someone you trust tells you time travel is real. What would happen if one day I told you I knew magic? You wouldn't believe it, no matter how much you thought you trusted me. And you and I've been friends longer than you and Crystal. You shocked her and probably scared her. Badly."

I nodded. "Probably, yeah."

"Could you go back? Try and talk with her again now that she's had time to process and cool down a little?"

I shrugged feebly. "I dunno, maybe. I'm not sure if it would do more harm than good." We sat in silence for at least a minute before I spoke again. "I...I was falling in love with her."

She responded gently, "I know."

"Huh?"

"I knew from the night you told me about getting coffee. The way you smiled... Girl, you were practically glowing. I hadn't seen that look on your face, maybe ever. Then later...Nobody cries like that for an acquaintance, or even a good friend. That kind of hurt only comes from love and loss. Trust me."

Wisdom from a friend who's been there. Wow, that gave me some perspective. Tia always seemed to have her shit together so well, sometimes I forgot about her own tragic backstory. I rubbed my eyes, took a deep breath and tried to change the subject. "There's an ice cream shop two blocks down. What do you want?" Even though I'm not the type to drown my sorrows in Rocky Road, I'm also not above having some if it's available. Plus, we'd gone straight from TE to our stakeout. I was hungry.

Standing in line, my watch beeped with a new text.

Tia: *"He's on the move."*

"Still want the ice cream?"

"Hell, yeah."

He was a mile or so away when I got back to the van. "Get in. Get in!" I dropped the ice cream containers into the cup holders, glad I hadn't bought cones with points.

"Which way's he headed?"

"North, which is odd. His house is west from campus, and the post office is south."

We followed for ten minutes or so before the symbol stopped moving. We were finally gaining on it when the icon blinked out.

"What?" I snapped at the screen.

"What d'you mean what?"

"The icon for the package just disappeared! It was there a second ago, and now it's gone."

She leaned toward the screen showing only one icon. "Shit." Tia pulled over. "Computer, display time signature minus one minute." The screen blinked and beeped, and the display looked like it did a moment before—one still, one moving. "Pause." She zoomed the display. The icon hovered over a garage, and an address appeared along the bottom of the screen.

"This doesn't make sense. There's no way he lives in this neighborhood. It's way below his standards."

"He doesn't; he has rental properties." She pulled forward and turned off the main road, approaching the address from side streets. Abruptly, she yelled, "DUCK!"

I folded forward at the waist, brushing my head on the dash, feeling around for the seat belt release.

She put one hand on my back. "Stop, stop. Hold still." I froze, my heart thumping. "I thought I saw his car." She peeked up over the dash, "Okay, it's gone now."

The house looked empty. In fact, it looked abandoned. An old, detached garage sat facing an alley at the back of the property. Tia parked next to it and said, "There's a black case in the glovebox. Can you hand it to me?"

It looked like a toolkit for mini screwdrivers. I had one, too, except mine was red. She tucked it under her leg and rolled backwards. At the push of a button, the rear door opened, and the floor tilted into a ramp to the ground.

"Where are you going? Wait! What are you doing?"

She gestured for quiet, then spoke in barely a whisper, "Remember the basket of doorknobs?"

I gave a confused look.

"I need you on lookout."

A regular door sat next to the garage door directly behind the van. Tia put on a headlamp and leaned in, right in front of the knob.

"What..."

Sounds of tools clicking and muttered curses came from behind me but kept my eyes on the alley in front. Curiosity getting the better of me, I aimed the mirror to see out the back of the van and gasped in surprise. Holy shit! Tia was picking the lock!

She told me later her timer read six minutes. It felt like much longer before the door swung in, her headlamp shining inside. My thumb waited on the seat belt button, but didn't click. I stayed on quiet lookout like she asked.

According to the clock on the dash, Tia was inside for only about two minutes. She retreated to the van after relocking the garage. Tossing her tablet into my lap, she clicked her chair into place behind the wheel with more force than was probably necessary. Her expression clear despite the dark alley—she was shocked, but moreover, she was pissed.

As the van crept toward the street, Tia spoke, almost to herself. "Oh, hell! It is so much worse than I thought!" She pointed toward the tablet. "Look for yourself."

"That photo looks like a hydraulic press, but what's the other thing on the workbench?"

"It's an electromagnet—and it was still warm."

"Wait! What does...?" I flipped forward through the images, dumbstruck: debris under the press, a metal trash can filled with the crushed remains of our last several mailers, and shattered hard drives.

I had no words.

At the next stop light, Tia held up the GPS tracker. "I thought it'd be best to grab this."

*

TIA
June 2045

Amber stood awkwardly in my living room eating ice cream like she wasn't sure what else to do and, understandably, looking shocked. She gestured vaguely toward campus with the plastic spoon and asked, "Why? Why would he? Oh, my god—all that work!"

I pointed to my sofa. "Sit." I was about to turn the tables and I desperately hoped it would work. "For the sake of our friendship, please hear me out."

She looked puzzled. "Huh? Of course!"

"What we found proved that research into the mechanics of time maybe isn't the real purpose of TE."

"How can you possibly know that?"

I held up my hand. "Vanhanen isn't who you think but, technically, neither am I."

Her head tilted, her response a little sharper. "Wait. What happened to your accent?"

"That wasn't my accent; it was my mother's. She was South African, but we immigrated when I was little, and I grew up here. My name is not Tia James. I was born Theresa Jones. My fiancée wasn't killed in a car crash. We were shot as we walked down a sidewalk after a movie."

One hand over her mouth and wearing a stunned expression, but she was still with me. Good. I had to keep going.

"James discovered stuff about his employer he shouldn't have seen: missing former employees and years of coverup. He shared it with his best friend, Chris, who worked for the same department, and with me. His boss found out what James knew, and he paid someone a literal box full of cash to make it look like a mugging gone bad." I tapped the wheel of my chair. "Except they didn't quite finish the job. Afterward, Chris and I needed to get as far away as we could."

Amber slid across the couch and grabbed my hand.

"How come you never told me?"

"I spent the last year trying to figure out when and how. Just when I was finally sure it wouldn't freak you out, you told me about the letter from Crystal."

"Ugh." She looked down and shook her head.

I tousled her hair. "It's okay. It solidified for me how much you were willing to break the rules."

She met my eyes with a smirk and squeezed my hand.

"Crystal's letter also showed how much our stories overlapped. See...when Chris and I went into hiding, it wasn't by fleeing to different countries. It was by fleeing to different times."

She jumped up. "What?"

I waited. This was the moment of go big or go home. She paced back and forth, began to talk, stopped, paced a little longer, and ate more ice cream looking confused and surprised, but not angry.

"Sit down and I'll explain the rest. Or get your PT laps around my coffee table, I don't care...just, please, don't leave."

"Oh, I'm not going anywhere. I need to hear this."

I sighed. "I jumped forward in time, and Chris to the past."

"That means one of you worked for TE. Wait... How would that work? When... Was it Chris? But that would mean his boss was..." She sat back down, stunned. "Oh, shit."

"Yeah, oh, shit is right. I took the name Tia James when I jumped to 2042, and Chris took the name Charles Yung when he jumped to 1967."

She slumped. "Charles was Crystal's dad."

I nodded. "Mm-hmm."

"That's what you meant by overlapping, wasn't it?"

I nodded again.

"But why? Why would V do that?"

"He's been covering something up for years. I'm still not sure exactly what, other than dead former employees. Clearly, he's willing to kill to keep it hidden."

"Is that what happened to Crystal's parents? Charles, er, Chris, knew too much and had 'an accident'?"

"Probably. I only learned about Chris's death when you told me about Crystal."

"Oh, shit. I'm so sorry."

I shrugged. "He was supposed to send word through the Timeslot, but he never did. You told me why."

"So why send the letter? Wait. You were trying to catch him before... Damn, that's risky."

"I needed V's earliest time travel records. He's jumping more and more frequently. The guy who shows up to work on any given day is almost never the one who left the night before."

"Whoa. He's interlacing his timelines?"

"Bad. Ridiculously complicated. I've been running a secret logging app on the TE computers for a while now. It's trying to extrapolate the order of his jumps. The early jump records should help fill in the blanks. I'm trying to find the timeline where he's oldest."

"Why?" she asked, dragging the word out slowly, sounding like she suspected the answer.

This next part was hard to say out loud. "If I can find his final timeline, it wouldn't create a paradox...to..." I trailed off.

"Whoa!" She stood up and shook her head as if to make sure she heard me right. Seeing my stern expression, she continued. "Oh my god! You're..."

I responded with more grim determination than sadness, "He killed the man I loved."

"You're serious?"

"I followed him here from the past, created a whole new identity, and even cut myself off from ever seeing my mom again just for a chance at him."

"And you've been working for the guy all this time? Holy shit!"

I nodded. "I needed access to TE to get close to him."

"Wait. What are you planning to do? When?"

"I don't know yet."

She stepped back. "I can't be part of this, no matter how much it sounds like maybe he deserves it."

"I'm not asking you to. I'd never ask you for something like that. This is on me."

"So why are you telling me all this?"

My voice sounded rough in my ears. "Because I needed to be honest with you...finally. I wanted you to know the whole story. Because when it happens, I need you to understand why. But more than that, I want you safe, and I want you to stay out of the way."

A slow blend of emotions played across my friend's face. A long moment later, she laid her hand on my shoulder and simply nodded.

*

CRYSTAL
April 1994

Not wanting to drink alone, combined with the isolation of living by myself in grad school, eventually pushed me back toward the Underground, despite my reservations. My last time there had been with Amber the night before things went horribly, horribly wrong.

The familiarity of the surroundings felt oddly comforting though. Nothing ever changed in the Underground: same quirky décor, same signs, same bookshelves. I considered a table—Knightsbridge was open—but that was still isolating. I craved conversation.

Since Kit was working, I sat at the bar. She poured a dark pint without me even asking, pushed the glass across, and followed with a veteran bartender's leading question, "You've been scarce."

"I was out of town for spring break. A group of music grad students drove to Minneapolis to see the symphony. We got a tour of the auditorium and backstage and stuff too."

Kit's hands never stopped wiping the bar, putting away glasses, and so on. "Sounds cool. Spring break was weeks ago though. I thought maybe you'd been busy with the cute redhead."

I shook my head and couldn't help looking disappointed.

"Shit, I'm sorry. She seemed cool."

"I thought so too. Things got complicated, and I'm not sure she was quite who I thought."

"Girl, things always get complicated."

I gestured between us. "We weren't complicated."

"*We* weren't really together," she responded quietly.

"Okay, true," I conceded, and turned to hang my sweatshirt on the back of my chair. She gestured toward my Nirvana T-shirt.

"Where were you when you heard?"

"Huh?"

"Where were you when you found out—about Kurt Cobain?"

"Oh. I'd just gotten home from class, dropped my stuff on the couch, and clicked on the TV. I caught the last few seconds of MTV News. There was a black-and-white photo of him with his guitar, and I heard Kurt Loder's voice say, 'He was twenty-seven.'" I shook my head. "I knew what twenty-seven meant. I knew about Jim Morrison and the rest, but I didn't want to believe it at first. I kept whispering 'No, no, no,' and flipping channels until I got to CNN. I kinda sank into my couch and cried."

"I was on my way here and caught a radio news report. I had to pull over for a few minutes before I could drive the last few blocks. We played their albums over and over that night."

"Yeah. I dug out all the old B-sides and demos in my collection along with what the station had and did a tribute show on KCSR."

"Nice. Wish I'd heard it."

I took a long drink of my beer, but before I could say more, she continued. "I had this school assignment when I was a kid. We were supposed to ask our parents where they were when they first learned about the Kennedy assassination. I remember being surprised how vivid my mom's memory of it was after twenty-whatever years. She knew exactly where she was and what she was doing. Do you suppose we'll remember Cobain's death like that?"

"Kurt Loder saying, 'He was twenty-seven'? Maybe."

Kit did a newscaster's voice, "Where were you on April eighth, 1994?" Someone waved from the other end of the bar, and she slipped away to pour their drinks.

I stared into the glass of beer, the color of which reflected my mood. The argument with Amber had been devastating. I cried most of that day and hadn't slept well since.

I could say it was the first time since Mom got sick that I had feelings for someone, but on that level, the truth was more like first time *ever*. There were girls in undergrad, but it was casual and mostly on the sly. One of them was Kit. Amber was the first one I fell for. Why did she have to go and screw it up?

All that sci-fi bullshit about time travel! Shaking my head, I drank again. I was so freaked out that morning, and things went so wrong so fast. One minute I was making coffee, the next we were yelling at each other, and I was throwing her out. Okay, I was doing most of the yelling. But still.

In the weeks since, I kept returning to one thing that didn't add up, something I'd been too upset to question at the time: Why did she sleep on my couch?

Somehow, she found my letter and created this weird fiction based on it, even stalking me and looking into my past. But if it was really as sinister as it sounds, what was she after? If sleeping with me was her goal, it would have been shockingly easy that night. I was drunk but would have willingly, happily gone to bed with her. Why the couch? That's the part that haunted me.

The only thing I could fathom was that she'd tried playing a longer game. By not sleeping with me, she set something up for later. But it didn't feel like an explanation that fit, too Hollywood. Why would anyone target me like that?

It didn't make sense, and that was probably why I had so much trouble letting it go. If she was just psycho...well, everyone has a crazy ex story. Except she appeared completely normal right up to the end.

I finished my beer and left a tip under the coaster, zipping my sweatshirt and waving to Kit as I left. Back home, I clicked on lights and slumped into one of my dining room chairs. I treated that space like a giant desk, and it overflowed with books and papers.

I knew right where the envelope was. The same corner where I set it that morning more than a month ago. I picked it up, like I had so many times before; for a while, it had been every night. I sat in the same chair, holding the envelope, unable to open it, unable to destroy it, just staring. It was the only thing I had with her handwriting on it. Printed in block capital letters, it read, "DO NOT OPEN UNTIL APRIL 9, 1994." By now, that was weeks past.

I shook my head, set it back down, and turned off the light.

Pajamas on and hair in a ponytail, I was brushing my teeth when the lightbulb finally came on. I stood up straight, eyes wide reflecting back in the mirror, foamy toothbrush still in my mouth. The date! I started toward the door, but spun back, dropped the toothbrush into the sink, wiped my mouth, and ran barefoot to the dining room.

I scooped up the envelope with one hand and fumbled for the light switch with the other. Looking at the familiar writing, Kit's voice echoed in my head, "Where were you on April eighth, 1994?"

I tore it open, and my letter slid out. On the back was more of Amber's blocky handwriting.

Crystal,

On April 8, 1994, Kurt Cobain's body will be found above his garage, dead from a self-inflicted gunshot wound. A famous photo will show his legs and shoes on the floor through the window. I am very, very sorry. Please get in touch.

Amber

Holy! Shit!

I dropped onto the couch, rereading her brief note. My brain ran through numerous possibilities of how she could have broken in and planted the letter, each more convoluted and improbable than the last. Every train of thought brought me back to the question of *why*. Why would she go to such extremes?

Occam's razor though. Was I at a point where the simplest solution was that Amber was telling the truth? What if...?

I flipped the paper over and saw my own handwriting. A letter I wrote and cast away as part of my grieving process. I reread it and noticed something. I reread it again to be sure.

I took Dad's manuscript down from the mantle, and soon I was wrapped in his story just as much as I was wrapped in the blanket on my sofa. Amber had slept under that same one. I searched for something specific in the story, a term Dad used in his manuscript that I didn't mention in my letter. The name of the time travel department: Temporal Engineering. Amber said it during our argument that morning, but I didn't remember until I held her note, my letter, and Dad's manuscript together.

Sure enough. A few chapters in, he mentioned it while he and Kasey were in the Timeslot room. That meant Dad's writing wasn't a manuscript. It was a journal!

Oh, Amber.

Oh my god, I'm so sorry I didn't believe you.

20

TIA
July 2045

After my big reveal, Amber seemed quieter than usual. Not exactly distant, but noticeably different. We skipped movie night for a few weeks, and I wondered if our conversation was still echoing in her head every time Amber, V and I were in TE together.

The next experiment took more setup than was typical. We needed a container to jump into the past at a moment when TE was empty, connect wirelessly, and run through a series of digital operations. It sent emails, transferred money, downloaded and uploaded data, before rolling back through the portal, only to repeat the process at several different points in the timeline.

This took a fair bit of coordination between hardware and software. Amber and I were both knee-deep into this build before we discovered the garage. Over the weeks since, she slowly worked back to interacting with me like before, so it surprised me when she picked up a component, turned it over in her hands and let it clatter back onto the lab table, saying, "Why should I even give a shit?"

I'd been in this role for two years, and I needed her to understand the nuances of it or we were both in real danger. "Because right now we both need to keep our jobs." I said, irritation in my voice. "If we get kicked out, neither of us get where we want to go."

She held up her hands, "Fine, fine, okay. You're right. If there's any chance, I need to make sure I can take it. How do you do it... every day, knowing what he's capable of? What he did?"

"You just do."

The hallway door opened, so conversation shifted back to the design of the motorized wheels. Vanhanen stepped into the lab a moment later in shirt and tie, having left his coat in his office.

The three of us worked on the project all morning, each component vying for limited space in the container. It needed to work like a remote-controlled car, but without a remote. Amber was supposed to be adapting motors for the wheels, but she seemed unmotivated and directionless. I had to pull her back on track a couple of times.

We could have easily done the job without V's presence or assistance, but he usually (at least acted like he) wanted to be part of the work to better understand it. It was more of a token contribution than ever before. With Amber being off-center, I carried most of the weight.

The top half of the containers held a modified computer and battery. She'd done this fussier part of the design a month before. I worked on the sequencing all afternoon while they built the other two cases. Amber was short with him and didn't cover her irritation well.

Alone together at lunch, I tried to appeal to the need for subtlety.

"I know, but it's so hard," she responded.

"Take a deep breath. Center yourself. Reach out with your feelings, or whatever the hell it is you need to do to get your shit together, but do it. I'm not interested in all my work and waiting getting screwed up because you're being pissy!"

Me snapping at her like that must have been out-of-character enough to get her attention. She looked guilty, held up both hands saying, "Okay. You're right. I apologize. I'm stressed about Crystal and can't stop thinking about her."

So that was it. It wasn't me or our conversation, after all. Or at least it wasn't the most present thing in her mind. Gently, I asked, "There's not much time left now, is there?"

"Two days."

"Wow. Are you going to jump again?"

"I don't know. I...I just don't know."

That afternoon went better. While we prepped the experiment, V mentioned Amber walking without her cane. They chatted for a few minutes, and she talked about her PT appointments and how glad she was to be almost done. Around three o'clock, V had retreated to his office, I was troubleshooting the control app, and Amber was rummaging for a specific tool in the storage bin when an alert popped up on my screen—one that hadn't appeared before. I whispered, "Amber!"

Head in the bin, she yelled, "What?"

"Shh! C'mere. Look at this."

I held up the tablet showing a message from my Timeslot monitoring app. A letter had come through.

The origin date was April 29, 1994.

*

AMBER
July 2045

If Tia hadn't laid her hand on my arm and aggressively whispered that I needed to chill the hell out, I might have run all the way from TE to the student union, bad knee or not, but she did, so I didn't.

After I'd gotten over my initial shock from her giant confession, my respect for her resilience, patience, and mental strength increased exponentially. I couldn't even imagine what she'd gone through. I'd acted like a whiny little bitch that morning and desperately needed a reminder from my best friend.

I walked into Vanhanen's office, covering my excitement by exaggerating how tired I felt. When he looked up from his tablet screen, I said, "I'm going to take off early, okay? I've had a headache all day, and I think I'm coming down with something."

"Oh, okay." He acted a little surprised, understandably. It wasn't exactly cold season.

"I don't want to get you two sick, so I'm probably going to stay home tomorrow too."

"That sounds like a good plan. Get some rest. Maybe have some chicken soup." He chuckled at his own little joke.

"Yeah, maybe."

He added, "Just coordinate with Miss James before you go, about the experiment progress," while turning his attention back to his tablet.

"Of course. I already did."

He nodded but didn't look back up.

At the student union, I took the stairs rather than the elevator—a little hard on my knee, but I couldn't wait. A small white envelope with my initials waited in the middle of the floor. I leaned on the arm of the sofa to bend and pick it up. With shaking fingers, I tore it open. The note was brief and weirdly cryptic.

BRX

430

430

What the hell? Confused, I dropped onto the couch, forgetting again about the dust and coughing at the cloud it raised. Of course, I'd hoped for a letter where she described a change of heart and professed her love, or even one where she wanted to see me again, but this made no sense.

At first it reminded me of a library call number. A quick search online showed the format wasn't quite right for either Dewey Decimal or Library of Congress.

Given that the letter was sent on April 29, the numbers could mean the thirtieth. Not sure why it was written twice though, unless the second one meant time. So, 4:30 p.m. on the thirtieth? Okay, possible.

Could the letters refer to a TV or radio station? Crystal *was* a radio person, after all. A search didn't come up with anything that was local to the university in the 90s.

Three capital letters made it look like an airport code, but that didn't check out either. A few more searches brought back frustratingly large numbers of possibilities, thousands.

Why would Crystal do this? It felt like a movie scene where the protagonist had to contact someone secretly and knew the bad guys might intercept it.

I texted Tia.

Amber*: Call me when you have a minute. This is puzzling.*

I'd already examined the envelope and started on the back of the notepaper when my watch beeped for a vid-call. "Yeah, so check this out." I held up the weird note to the screen. Tia was at a table in the lab. She gave the note a look as confused as I felt.

A typed message scrolled across my screen. "Don't want V to hear." She pulled her hair back and pointed to a wireless earbud but kept typing. "Why send a note like that?"

"I know! Not what I hoped for at all!"

"Sure it's her?"

"I don't know who else it could be. But why the spy game? Is she making me jump through hoops for some reason? To see if I'm serious?" I slumped back on the sofa. "She's making it so damn hard to save her life."

Tia tapped away on the other end. "What have you tried?" she typed without looking at me.

"Uh. Library catalog numbers, TV and radio call letters, and airport codes."

"Good guesses. No hits so far?"

"None...or thousands, depending on how you look at it."

She gave a little laugh. "Let's think it through before we worry about the big number."

"Why would she—?"

Tia cut me off with a head shake and typed again. "Ask her yourself later. We can maybe solve what, when, or where. Probably not why."

"The four-three-zeroes might mean four thirty on April thirtieth. That'd be the day after she sent the note."

She nodded, her curly, dark hair bobbing along. "Makes sense. Okay, that's the when." She scowled at the screen, scratched her chin, and looked back at me. "You're right. Hell of a lot of hits."

"Is there a way to pare them down by category? I mean…"

"Sure. Start with something you both know. What'd you talk about?"

"Tons." She glared at me in the call window. "Okay…" and I listed off all the categories of what I knew about Crystal, the things we talked about after class, at the barbeque restaurant, when we went out for coffee, and the time we tried to get curry, but ended up wandering around campustown.

Tia latched onto that last one. "Where'd you go? What'd you do?" The sounds of her typing never paused on the other end. I walked her through the whole evening, finished up describing pints at the Underground and walking home drunk. I paused there rather than delve into the heartbreaking next morning.

"Hold on. The bar design was based on the London Tube?"

"Yeah?"

"Does Brixton Station mean anything?"

I squealed, "YES!" and she winced. "That's the table where we sat that night! All the tables have a Tube stop sign over them. We sat at Brixton Station. Oh my god, thank you, thank you, thank you!"

She was smiling on the screen. "What ya gonna do?"

"Jump at midnight, and maybe this heroine will get the girl!"

"Are your nineties clothes still there?"

"Yeah. Hadn't thought of that." I pawed through the duffel bag left on the sofa weeks ago.

"Call me if you need anything, okay?"

I looked back up at the screen. "Of course. Seriously, thank you so much."

She nodded and typed one last message before signing off. "Go, get her. Good luck!"

*

TIA
July 2045

I tried to focus on the sequencing for the remote and the preprogrammed data connections for use during jumps but couldn't stop imagining Amber, excitedly getting ready for one last jump to 1994.

V called, "Miss James, can you help me with something in here?"

I rolled my eyes at the interruption and how stereotypical it is when the older boss couldn't do the simplest things on computers. But no, that trope was decades in the past. In the 2040s, even someone in their seventies or older would have lived with computers their entire adult life. Except he hadn't...

In the office, he turned his tablet stand so we could both see it and tapped the screen. It was a web page I didn't recognize—a security company logo and an archive of dated subfolders.

"Click on the subdirectory for last month and see if you can open the file that's highlighted."

I did, and it appeared to work without issue. A video image filled the screen. The washed-out colorlessness of a night-view camera showed an alley and a garage. I gasped involuntarily when I recognized the scene. The back corner of my van crept into view along the right side of the frame. I glanced up from the screen to V's stoic face.

"Oh no—keep watching." His tone sounded almost snarky. Back on the screen, I rolled down the ramp and started picking the lock. He moved the slider to the right. "We can skip forward. This part is boring."

I was speechless. He'd had a surveillance camera in the alley, and I'd missed it. My initial anger quickly gave way to fear. I'd been caught crossing a man who wasn't above killing those who got in his way. Not outwardly angry, he sat still as stone. Did he look like this when he sent the thugs after James?

I rolled back from the desk.

"I don't know how you found that address, nor do I particularly care. What you saw in there or what you *think* you saw—isn't even the half of it. You're poking your nose into things so far above your pay grade, you couldn't even comprehend. Not to mention the betrayal of trust I've put in you working here the last two years."

With memories of the hydraulic press and a bin full of crushed shipping containers, I only managed to stammer "I...uh..."

"I'm sure you're aware this is breaking and entering, and I could easily have you charged. However, as nothing was stolen and with no prior record, the local court would most likely let you off with a slap on the wrist."

His hands had been in his lap since he last touched the screen. His right arm and shoulder lifted, and in a flash, I *knew* he had a pistol. Was that how I'd die? All movement in slow motion, my brain had shifted into overdrive. I reached for my wheels but couldn't make my hands go fast enough. Would he shoot me right there in his office—my blood splattering on the back wall? That didn't seem like his way. He was too fastidious. Would he hold me at gunpoint and force me toward the portal—jumping me to who knew where? Maybe even into my own past?

His hand cleared the edge of the desk and opened.

It was empty.

"Give me your key card and get the hell out. Leave your tablet on the desk and go. I don't ever want to see you again."

The finality of it felt like a punch in the stomach. I watched my hand shakily set the key card in his, not turning to face away from him until I was almost to the hallway door. My chances of revenge had evaporated, but all I could feel was relief at escaping with my life.

Later, away from TE and after I had a chance to calm down from those terrifying moments replaying in my head, I found they'd planted a seed of thought.

21

CRYSTAL
April 1994

Four thirty came and went. I didn't expect Amber...yet.

After finding the reference to Temporal Engineering in Dad's book, I kept reading. I'd read it twice before, but that time felt different. Knowing it wasn't fiction, and beyond that, knowing it involved someone I cared about, meant I paid far more attention to details I'd glossed over before. The villain of the piece in particular, scared the shit out of me. If he was still the director in Amber's time and he found out about her jumps to 1994... Well, she'd put herself in a lot of danger just to meet me, and she was putting herself in even more danger coming back.

I'd made my note as cryptic as possible in case anyone but Amber found it. The Underground had a wall-sized poster of the whole Tube system, each line and each station labeled along with an abbreviation used by London Regional Transport.

I didn't wait at the Brixton table though. Too dangerous. I'd asked Kit to do me a favor from behind the bar. When Amber got there, she'd pass her a note. If an old, bald guy in a suit showed up, she'd call my answering machine at home.

The note told Amber to meet me at the park benches on campus. With her habitual lateness on top of using the cane, I didn't expect her before 5:00 p.m. at the earliest. I was there at 4:15 because I couldn't contain my excitement, alternating between spinning my thumb ring and looking at my watch. No closet-diving apparel decisions, just an ordinary everyday black hooded sweatshirt and tee with jeans.

When a familiar figure stepped into view around a nearby building, it took everything I had to not sprint down the sidewalk and sweep her into a hug.

She smiled broadly when she saw me. Same leather jacket, same shaggy hair, with coffee, but no cane, only a tiny hint of a limp. She sat, facing me. I took off my sunglasses to look her in the eyes. I wanted to begin with how sorry I was, but I needed to start with my most important question. Depending on the answer we'd see where things went from there. Without preamble, I asked, "What does TE stand for?"

"Huh? It's for Temporal Engineering."

Relief swept over me. I slumped back in the seat and blew out a long breath. I grabbed her hand and she eagerly squeezed back. "It was in my dad's writing, but I didn't mention it in my letter. I was pretty sure you said it that morning...before I threw you out." I swallowed. "I'm really, really sorry, by the way." She laid her other hand on top and held mine in both of hers. "After I opened your letter, I put it all together, but that was only a couple days ago. It clicked when I realized the thing about TE." Amber sat quietly holding my hand, so I continued. "I thought it all through. Like, analyzed it. Weeks had gone by since that awful morning, and I could process more clearly. You were never anything but nice to me, and I feel guilty it took me so long to see it. You didn't give me any indication of being creepy or weird. And if you were really stalking me, like...like I accused you of, you wouldn't have slept on my couch."

She cracked a smile. "It's an extremely comfortable couch."

It took me by surprise, and I laughed out loud. I asked, "It's all true then? The time travel and everything?"

She nodded. "Yes. Absolutely. The only things I ever lied to you about were some dates, so it looked like we were about the same age, and the story about staying in a friend's basement."

I let that last part go and dove into my biggest question. "Okay, but why? Why did you travel here? Was it some kind of mission or experiment? Certainly, it wasn't just to meet me."

"Actually, it was," she responded quietly still looking down at our hands before meeting my eyes, seeing my surprise. "I have a theory. If I'm right, and I'm nearly positive I am, you're in danger and the longer you stay in this timeline, the worse it is."

I wanted to jump up and yell, "What?" but I didn't. Freaking out was what happened the last time.

Huh. *Time*. Yeah. "Please...just tell me what's going on."

"I'll tell you everything. We have no time for bullshit." She took a deep breath and let it out. "Each of us has a home time that we're born into and are supposed to return to after a time jump. That home time moves with us over the years, and at TE, we call it a timeslot."

"I thought the letter drop thing at the student union was the Timeslot?"

"It is. They're both called that. I tried to tell you some of this before…" She let go with one hand and pushed her hair back, unsuccessful at tucking it behind her ear. "Your dad was a time traveler. He jumped back about fifty years and met your mom. We're supposed to minimize contact with people in the times we visit, but for some reason, he didn't. As far as I can tell, you're the first child of a TE engineer out of time. When your dad died, you slipped into his empty timeslot, because the universe didn't quite know what to do with you."

I started to speak, but she held up her hand, so I waited. "No, I promised I'd tell you everything. There are only a few rules of time travel. You can't create a paradox, and you can't meet yourself. If you jump into a time where you already were, you'll die. You'll just cease to exist. If you're in a timeline your younger self will jump into later, you have to get out before your younger self arrives. We call that point your 'end of the line.'"

"Yeah, some of this was in my dad's book."

"Right. The trouble is…by occupying your dad's timeslot, you're also subject to his end of the line."

"Okay." I said dragging it out, still thinking. "So, I'm an inherited time traveler?"

"That's not a bad way to put it." She paused and rubbed her eyes.

"What?"

"You're twenty-four, right?"

"Yeah," I replied.

"Your dad was twenty-four in 2018 when he jumped to 1967. That, plus the time he lived in the sixties before you were born, plus your age, means his original timeslot lines up with mine in 2045. That's why I got your letter."

"Okay. That makes sense, I guess. Twenty forty-five though. Wow!" I grinned at the thought of it. She looked tense, so I asked, my smile fading, "Is there something else I'm missing?"

She repeated herself more slowly, sounding determined. "Your dad turned twenty-four in 2018."

"That means he was born in 1994…" My voice trailed off as what she was getting at slammed into me like a wave. I felt a massive chill down my back but managed to whisper, "Oh shit! His birth is my end of the line, isn't it?"

Amber nodded and squeezed my hand. "I was on a temporary assignment repairing the Timeslot while my knee healed. As soon as I got it running, your letter fell through. I researched you. When I figured out about your father…and his timeslot…"

"You tried to rescue me? Why? You didn't even know me. It was years in the past for you."

She gave a small, one-shoulder shrug. "Something about your letter, your honesty in talking about your mom. Holding it in my hands and reading what you wrote, made it personal, like I knew you a little bit, and I didn't want you to die. You seemed nice and normal and cool, and you didn't do anything to deserve to just be gone one day."

As the depth of that barely started to sink in, I asked, "Okay, but I don't understand why you went to class with me and stuff. Why not just tell me? Or is this one of the things TE has rules about?"

"Oh no. I broke a hell of a lot of rules to get here. My rescue attempt was…uh…unofficial. If my boss knew what we did, I'd be fired."

I couldn't help but sound shocked. "Dude! Your boss doesn't know! So why not tell me when you first got here? Why keep going to class?"

"I thought it'd be more believable coming from someone you knew."

"But why drag it out so long? You could have told me weeks before."

She steeled herself, like this part was harder to say. "I...I didn't expect to fall for you. It made things so much more complicated. I kept putting it off because I enjoyed hanging out with you. I felt terrified that as soon as I told you, it'd change things. Lying on your couch that night, I thought I'd let it go on too long. Then I tried to tell you, and...shit, I screwed it up." She kind of slumped on the last sentence. I half expected her to apologize again.

Before she could, I spoke up. "So, yeah...can we go back to the 'falling for' part?"

Shyly, she said, "Um, sure?"

I lifted her chin and looked straight into her big, beautiful eyes. "Yeah. That."

I thought she might kiss me then, but she didn't. Instead, she looked puzzled and asked, "So why the *Mission Impossible* shit? Why not write me a regular note? It took me an hour to figure it out."

"Hmm. Sorry about that. The thing is, I think I know more than I think you think I know." I paused a second while that sank in, but she still looked confused. I took Dad's notebook out of my backpack. Stuffed inside was my letter with Amber's note on the back, and the photo of my parents. I showed her the photo.

"These are your parents? Wait, they're right by the..."

I nodded. "Mm-hmm. Dad's journal has way more in it than I wrote about. His best friend was killed, and he and the friend's fiancée escaped into different times."

Amber responded, wide-eyed, "I just learned that part myself recently. My friend Tia who works at TE with me—that's her. She was Theresa, James's fiancée. I never would have made it here without her help."

I asked, "Is your boss a guy named Vanhanen?" She nodded. "Then you're in serious danger. That's why my note was so vague. I wanted you to be able to figure it out, but not be obvious if he found it. He's killed TE employees before. That's part of what Dad and the other engineer were working on—research in the past. I'm nearly positive he caused the crash that killed my dad." My voice shook by the end, but I had to get it out, had to tell her what I knew.

She gave a small nod and squeezed my hands. "I think you're right. I also think we need to get out of here." I zipped the notebook and photo back into my bag. She pulled me to my feet and held tight to one hand like she was afraid she'd lose me if she let go.

We headed down the sidewalk together, and I said, "I noticed—no cane."

"Yeah. A month of PT when I needed something to concentrate on that wasn't you."

"Sorry. Er...you know what I mean." A few steps farther along, I asked one last question, dreading that I already knew the answer, "When is it? When's the end of the line?"

"Tomorrow."

"We really *don't* have time for bullshit."

The student union loomed ahead of us. We passed the fountain and entered the atrium with the zodiac. I followed her through back corridors and down stairways. In a shadowy curved hallway, she unlocked an old door painted to match the wall.

Amber held the door open; beyond, I saw a table, equipment, and an old sofa. Entering the room, my headache abruptly disappeared, and I went weak in the knees. I can't even describe how amazing it felt—like suddenly gaining superpowers, or...being relieved of a weight you've carried so long you forgot what it was like before.

I lost my balance and Amber caught me, her arm around my

back and my hand on her shoulder. Right at that moment, I'd have been okay with sitting on the concrete floor, but she pulled us over to the sofa before I collapsed.

I was literally crying on her shoulder, Amber asking repeatedly what was wrong and trying to brush my hair away from my face. My sobs diminished, and I leaned back, but still had tears streaming down my cheeks.

I tried to reassure her there was nothing wrong. Well, nothing new anyway. I wiped my eyes saying, "It's okay. I'm okay. I've just never *not* had a headache before...except when I was drunk. It was... It's a little overwhelming."

Her arm, still around my back gave a slow, gentle hug, released, and rubbed between my shoulders. She shifted and turned more toward me, her leg pressed against mine, our faces nearly touching, and she paused. Her eyes looked bottomless in the dim light. "Are you *sure* you're okay?"

Not breaking eye contact, I nodded minutely. "Yeah. I will be."

Except for those four minutes behind the record shelves, we'd never sat this close. I wanted to pull her even closer. What was she waiting for?

"I..." she began, whispering.

"Shh. I know."

When she didn't lean in any closer, I did. We kissed, and for a long time nothing else mattered.

*

KASEY
April 1994

The loading entrance at the student union was as poorly monitored as ever. I walked past storage rooms behind the kitchen, and down the stairs to the lower hallway. The one kitchen employee I encountered took a quick glance at the toolbox and never even noticed the duffel over my shoulder.

I had a moment of shock and fear seeing the padlock and hasp gone, and the doorknob replaced by a deadbolt. Someone had changed it! I felt my situation worsen. Every other time I'd been to the door of the round room in the basement, I'd cut off the old lock and let myself in. Moreover, it was never left unlocked either, so I don't know what brought my hand to rest on the rim of the deadbolt, but it did, and the door swung open. Stepping in, I locked it behind me. My attention momentarily drawn to the work light left on near the table, I saw movement in my peripheral vision and jumped in surprise at seeing two women on the sofa!

It startled me so much, I grabbed a screwdriver out of my pocket and pointed it like a weapon, yelling a highly uncharacteristic, "Who the FUCK are you?"

The redhead stood up carefully, disentangling herself from the blanket and held up empty hands. "This isn't what it looks like."

The brunette, still on the couch, giggled quietly. "Actually, it's pretty much exactly what it looks like."

The redhead glared at her, before turning back to me. "Morlocks and Eloi. The pedestal of the Sphynx…"

I responded by rote, but still puzzled, "Was the entrance to the underground."

"I'm Autumn. I work for TE. This is…uh, Summer." The brunette looked confused for an instant but stepped in beside her friend. They were both in jeans and rumpled T-shirts, barefoot, and with noticeable bedhead. Maybe it really was just what it looked like.

The brunette, Summer, standing a few inches taller, said quietly over her friend's shoulder, "Um…that's just a screwdriver."

I looked down and realized I was still holding the tool threateningly. I mumbled, "Right. Sorry." I slid it back into my pocket.

Past the two women, I noticed an expanse of additional equipment. A makeshift time portal had been built in the center of the room, with a frame of simple 2x4s and a messy bundle of cables connecting it to the worktable. Through the arch of the inactive portal, I saw far more gear on the table than when I left it. "What the hell did you do with my equipment?"

"Your equipment?"

"I built it. I finished it a few days, er...I mean, two years ago."

"A few days for you, but two years on the calendar?"

"Right."

Autumn appeared to be the leader of the pair, or at least the more talkative. "I jumped here and made modifications almost four months ago. Four months cumulative time."

I walked past them toward the equipment, stepping around the portal. Examining it all over, I saw the new portal added onto the Timeslot system, but despite the chaotic look, it was ingeniously constructed. It didn't appear to compromise the Timeslot at all, merely added on to it. It even had its own power supply. Squatting down to see the AC connection, I asked, "This took you four months?"

"No, this took me about two weeks."

"Two weeks!" I said, impressed. The Timeslot builds had taken me months, but that included sourcing materials.

She pointed vaguely with her thumb, "I built the end in the time I jumped from, and I brought everything with me for this one. I only had to assemble it."

"Why not use the portal in TE?" I scratched my head. "Hold on, hold on. TE doesn't know about this, do they? No, of course not, otherwise why build it. You're jumping in secret, aren't you?"

Autumn talked over her shoulder toward Summer.

"Remember the part where I said this was unofficial?" She waved in my direction as if to say "See?" "I'll explain, but I need you to listen before you go running back to V."

I'd walked around to the far side of the worktable to examine the controls when she said this last part. I straightened up so fast it probably looked like I'd been shocked. "I'm not going anywhere. I've never met this Mr. V, and from what I hear, I don't want to." A memory of him and Charles's crashed car flashed through my mind. I clenched my jaw, trying to focus on the moment.

"That must mean you're from farther out than me," she said.

"You know I can't say." Oh, but I was curious. Were these ladies wrapped up in this too? Possibly here to finish what Charles and I started? Was the enemy of my enemy, my friend?

Autumn stepped over beside the portal, touching the frame gently, almost protectively. Closer to the work light, she looked naggingly familiar, but I couldn't quite place her. She asked, "I'm sorry, I didn't catch your name."

"That's because I didn't say it. I'm Kasey."

Summer gasped from behind Autumn. "*The* Kasey?"

"Not exactly. Kasey is no more my given name than you two are really Autumn and Summer, but it's the alias I've lived with for a while if that's what you mean."

Summer walked around her friend, her hand brushing Autumn's on the way past, until she stood across the worktable from me, into the light of the lamp. "You worked with Charles. You were his friend."

"Yes, I did. I was," I answered, sounding unsure.

"He wrote about you. Said you were a brilliant engineer."

"Wrote? What do you mean wrote?" I felt increasingly wary of where this might go.

"He was my…"

I cut her off with a waved hand and turned my head away. "Do *not* bootstrap the timeline! I can't know when you're from or who you were to Charles! Didn't you learn about paradox avoidance in your TE training?" I glanced from Summer, who looked frustrated and a little confused, to Autumn, who looked anxious and concerned, and then back to Summer.

That's when I finally caught it. It was in her eyes—her exotic, slightly Asian eyes. Oh no, Charles. Oh no. His wife had been pregnant at the time of the crash. Summer wasn't going to complete "He was my..." with the word, "friend." She was going to say *dad*.

I watched him die hours before, his child unborn, and now she stood before me in the Timeslot room. Things just got even more complicated.

Autumn slid in next to Summer, a hand on her back. "No, she didn't. I work for TE, not her, but she's wrapped up in this as much as we are."

I said numbly, "She shouldn't be here."

"In sight of classified TE equipment, or within earshot of discussions about time travel, or like...here at all? Because the answer to all of them is no, she shouldn't, but she is. That's why I'm in this timeline." Autumn glanced up toward the Timeslot. "She called for help, and I'm trying to fix things."

Her hand slid down into Summer's. I understood then or at least began to.

*

CRYSTAL
April 1994

Saying I called for help was maybe a bit of an exaggeration, but it appeared to be working, so I went along with it.

Dad described Kasey as a slender Black man in his early twenties with glasses and short-cropped hair. His shaggy afro clearly hadn't seen a barber in a while. How much time had gone by for him? Kasey rubbed the back of his neck and said to Amber, "Are you hiding from Vanhanen? Is he after you? That's why you didn't want me to tell him I'd seen you, right? Then why not go already? Jump and get away! Why...kill time?" He gestured vaguely toward the sofa. This made me smile a little to myself.

"Because the system resets at midnight, and a jump then is less noticeable and harder to trace."

He pointed a finger as if to respond but thought better of it and closed his mouth. A moment later, he said, "That's clever. You're probably right."

"Um, yeah! I've been jumping twice a week all semester!"

Kasey and I responded in unison, facing her from two different directions, "What?"

She shrugged. "I still had to work two days a week in my own time."

Wow. She did all that...for me. It still felt so odd, like, what drove her? She'd said falling for me was unexpected, but this much effort started before she even met me. And I was *so* shitty to her... But right that moment I stood in the super-secret Timeslot room, the one I thought was fiction until a few days before, and I held Amber's hand while she talked with a guy I'd believed was also fictional.

Kasey spoke, "Believe it or not, you aren't the only ones on the run from your director. It's highly possible he chased me here from another time. I suspect we're in more danger standing around than we would be leaving a traceable jump. At least we'll be gone if we jump now." I noticed he switched to saying we. Had an alliance been formed, even if only temporary?

"I need to send a quick response through the Timeslot," he continued, "Then maybe we can all get the hell out of Dodge."

He took a battered envelope from his pocket and slid out a folded letter. Sitting at the worktable, he flipped it over and began to write. Amber tugged my arm toward the sofa. She sat and pulled her boots on. I did the same. Our heads together while lacing, she whispered, "Do you trust this guy? How do you know who he is?"

"He helped my dad build the Timeslot."

Eyes wide, her head popped up, swiveled to Kasey and back to me. Still whispering, she asked, "Built?"

"Yeah. They did the original installation in the sixties. It was all in Dad's journal."

Amber got an "oh shit" look on her face, but before she could explain, Kasey walked over to us. Gesturing toward my backpack, he asked, "Have you got a blank envelope or some notebook paper in there?"

"Paper, sure. Probably not an envelope though." I dug out a single sheet. He thanked me and folded it into an origami rectangle that tucked in on itself, staying closed around the letter.

Back at the worktable, he studied the crumpled envelope. The back was covered with writing, but I wasn't close enough to read it. He and Amber exchanged some questions and answers about "relativistic time" while Kasey scribbled more notes. He ran a few numbers on a large calculator and double-checked before nodding at the screen.

Unexpectedly, he shoved the table sideways several feet, being careful not to bump the portal. At one of the computers, he typed a string of commands, followed by numbers from the back of the envelope. He set the chair on top of the table, legs straddling the equipment. Satisfied it was sturdy, he hit Enter, climbed onto the table, and up to the chair, the folded letter in his teeth.

A low-pitched humming sound began, and I noticed a purple glow up near the structure at the uneven ceiling. He stretched up and grabbed the edge of a beam to steady himself. Right above him hung a wood rectangle with cables running to it. The middle glowed intensely bright. I squinted but kept looking.

Kasey took the envelope in his free hand, reached around and above the wood frame, dropping it. There was a flash and a brief change in the hum, but it never fell through. Was that what happened to my letter? *Duh.* Of course, it was. How else would Amber have found it?

Watching him on the table, Amber shook her head with a quiet chuckle. "Huh. I never thought of that. I had a friend take it upstairs and put it in the slot."

In the silence following her comment, the door rattled. All three of us turned and stared. Someone was at the door and found it locked. Amber said what I was thinking, "Oh shit!"

Kasey jumped off the table, the chair clattering loudly to the concrete floor. While sliding the worktable roughly back into place, he asked Amber over his shoulder "Do you have coordinates ready for your jump?"

"They're saved in the computer! It's set to advance the coordinates each day so I always hit my timeslot, and I don't have to recalculate each time." She ran over to the keyboard, typed quickly, and clicked the mouse. A different humming sounded, louder and deeper. She looked up, and seeing me next to the portal, yelled, "Get back! Grab our stuff!"

The rattling of the door turned to a pounding.

"Is there a way to delete the jump log?"

"Not from here until after the jump! Wait—but I can shut down the far end once we're through!"

Points around the edges of the wooden frame glowed purple

as the hum swelled. The glowing brightened and sparks flew between the points until it chained all the way around. Swirling light filled the opening and obscured my view of the others.

A startling BOOM shook the door, loud and terrifying over the hum of the portal. My backpack on one shoulder, I grabbed Amber's jacket and edged away from the door. Kasey still stood by the computer, but Amber stepped into view around the far side of the portal frame. She caught the thrown jacket one-handed and grabbed my arm with the other. Yelling, "C'mon!" she pulled me toward the glowing portal right as the door crashed inward, splinters of broken wood frame skittering along the floor between our feet. I had no time to turn and look. A loud pop sounded behind us as we dove through the portal. I felt dizzy, and we crumpled to the concrete floor. Amber jumped up again in an instant, pulling me off to one side.

We were in the same room, but different. It was dark and quiet, ominously quiet after the cacophony seconds before. Amber activated one of the computers, light from the screen illuminating a worried look on her face. She clicked and typed frantically, swearing under her breath. Seconds later, muttering, "Screw it!" she reached behind the computer and grabbed a bundle of cabling.

Before she could do more, the portal crackled loudly, blinking and throwing off sparks from the upper edge. She held up a hand to shield her eyes, and I did the same. The field wavered and fluctuated, before closing in on itself from top to bottom, like a popped soap bubble.

"He didn't make it!" With a frantic edge to my voice, I asked, "Can't you reopen it?"

She let out a long breath. "No. There's no signal from the other end. It was unplugged or damaged."

"Is there anything we can do?"

"No, but it's okay; trust me," Amber replied, her voice sounding calmer than mine.

"What?"

She didn't respond but clicked on a lamp and dug through a bag on the floor. Standing with an oversized watch in her hand, she tapped it against her arm, and the strap curled itself around her wrist. The screen lit up like a tiny computer. She pulled one corner to make it wider, plucking something from another corner and sticking it in her ear.

"Call Kurtis."

Oh! It was a phone!

"Hey!" She sounded relieved, but also trying not to make it obvious to whoever was on the other end. "Yeah, yeah, everything's fine. Remember the design you helped me with last winter?"

22

TIA
July 2045

The app that monitored the Timeslot didn't understand I no longer worked for TE; late in the evening, it beeped to my tablet for the second time in two days. The origin date read April thirtieth, 1994—Crystal's timeline. Damn.

I texted Amber before I noticed a scan attached to the notification. In the middle were my initials. A flash of hope that it might be from Chris ended by seeing KRB in the upper left. Not sure who that was, but the letter was definitely for me: Tia James/Theresa Jones, no middle initial.

A text response came back right away.

Amber: *Things got chaotic. Back sooner than planned. Brought a friend!*

Tia: Awesome! Need anything?

Amber: No. Heading to K's.

Tia: Why?

Amber: Close by. My place might not be safe.

Tia: What?!

Amber: Remember the chaos I mentioned?

Tia: Girl...

Amber: Too much to type. Tell ya when I see ya.

Tia: Breakfast?

Amber: Yeah. Bagel place at eight.

Tia: Be safe.

Amber: Have you met me?

And that's where Amber ended it for the night. I couldn't stop imagining the letter on the floor of the Timeslot room.

The cable let me bypass the card reader, and the door clicked open. Amber's word "chaos" left me wondering if I'd find the room in shambles, but I didn't. It looked exactly like I remembered. One corner of an intricately folded note poked out from under the sofa.

TJ,

It is with deep regret I must tell you of the death of our mutual friend, CJY. He was the victim of an intentional hit and run by the very man he was investigating. We can only surmise he knew of C's findings and decided to silence him. As to the research you requested, I unfortunately no longer have it in my possession. A copy was in C's house, but I do not recommend trying to retrieve it. I only barely escaped that timeline myself. However, the original is in the desk drawer of the inner office on or after 01/15/1978. As to our mutual friend, perhaps we will meet one day somewhere in time, and raise a glass to his memory.

KRB

I gripped the letter and my eyes welled up. It hadn't told me anything I didn't already know, but I ached for the loss of my friend. As the last of our trio who knew the truth, and despite bringing Amber in on it, that moment felt profoundly lonely. I wiped my eyes and turned to leave.

My wheel made a gritty *crunch* sound, concrete chips on the floor and more near the back wall. A hole the size of a quarter with a ragged edge was paler than the rest of the concrete, definitely new but too high to reach. Backing toward the door, I noticed a chunk of wood ripped away at the top of Amber's portal, exposing the wiring. The way it lined up with the hole in the opposite wall looked like a gunshot from near the door had hit both.

This must be the chaos Amber texted about. No blood, no signs of struggle, but shit had gone down in this room, and Vanhanen was at the heart of it, for sure.

The letter from KRB held a time and place. They'd put a tool in my hand, and I needed to use it. It was too good an opportunity to pass up, even if I couldn't do much with the information right then. I desperately hoped V hadn't changed the security lockouts yet. Only one day had passed. By Monday morning? For sure. The window was rapidly closing to learn about his past jumps. I needed to haul ass!

The empty corridors in Nuke-E that late at night made me jumpy. My hand hovered above the elevator button, about to press it, when I heard it move in the shaft. Looking up at the readout, the down arrow appeared, and then the B lit up for basement.

It could have been anyone. It could have been a late-night grad student, or someone on the cleaning crew pushing a mop bucket, but I got the hell out of there anyway. The hallway to the right led to exit stairs, and the one to the left turned a corner not far down. I headed left as fast as I could.

Grabbing the edge of the wall with one hand and my wheel with the other, I skidded around the corner and stopped just out of sight. Behind me the elevator door opened with a *bing*, then followed by ominous silence. Quietly, I lifted my tablet and tapped the screen to activate it, thankful I hadn't zipped it into my bag. The elevator door rattled closed, followed by footsteps on the hard floor, loud in the quiet hallway. Tapping the camera icon, I edged the lens around the corner. On the screen, V paused in front of the elevator, before turning and walking my way! He looked furious, with fisted hands and one shoulder of his suit torn. Tablet back on my lap, I spent a terrifying moment with my hands poised over my wheels, waiting, listening desperately. The footsteps sounded again with a shuffle but quickly receded. I braved slipping the lens around the corner just in time to catch him exiting through the far door.

When the adrenaline hangover hit, my hands shook, and I felt a wave of nausea. Eyes shut and stomach in knots, I willed myself to take several deep breaths, and then several more before my heartbeat slowed to something like normal.

Once my own trip down the elevator and the door to TE were behind me, I felt marginally better, but still jumpy. I'd hacked my way back into the department I was fired from with intent to use their equipment and steal sensitive information. I wasn't exactly calm.

The lights were off in Vanhanen's office, but I could see well enough through the window to recoil at the normally pristine space which held a ransacked mess of papers, books, and things thrown around wildly.

I ran coordinates for the date KRB listed, including the extra decimal places to arrive a minute after midnight. Just in case, I calculated the return trip coordinates as well and saved them to my tablet.

The startup sequence initiated, the emitters glowed, and the field formed for 1978. Normally, I'd never take anachronistic tech with me, but I wasn't going farther than the office, and I needed the camera on my tablet.

Empty lab tables and desks and covered equipment made it obvious I'd jumped into a TE dormant period. The space had the same haunted house feel as when Chris and I first jumped away from 2018. I shivered at the thought. As expected, I found the office closed and locked. Head lamp on, and tools out, I set the timer. Four and a half minutes, getting better.

Inside was starkly clean compared to 2045. I opened drawers until I found the ledger and took less time to photograph it than to pick the lock. Sliding the book back into the drawer, I disturbed a second ledger. Hoping for more time jumps, I eagerly opened it across the desktop.

Instead of time travel dates, it contained a record of investments. Each expense coincided with a return jump in the first ledger. I stared in stunned silence. I'd finally discovered the proof James was after. Infuriatingly, I'd found it one day too late.

For all Vanhanen's preaching during TE training about avoiding information which could change the timeline, that's *exactly* what he was doing. He'd used the time portal for future knowledge and financial gain and had been doing it for decades.

That was it? The whole time it was all just about money. Son of a bitch!

I exhaled sharply and shook my head—so stereotypically in character of a rich old white man for money to be the heart of it. The research front kept the university from looking too carefully at why he needed so much electricity, and temporal engineers were only pawns, disposable as soon as they got too close to the truth.

Or was he driven to do what he'd done to remain the only person with this power of unlimited wealth? Was this obsession another remnant from his younger days in a long-passed era? Was the control of the wealth the real issue worth killing for?

His reign over TE was absolute, but it extended not much further than that tiny department in a nondescript university basement. Talk about a little tin god.

Either way, the cover-up was infinitely worse than what he was hiding.

I felt a strong impulse to steal both ledgers, and leave Vanhanen to jump blind, probability ensuring he'd eventually cross his own former timeline, but I couldn't. It'd create a paradox. Taking them farther than the office door probably wasn't possible.

Returning to the first page, I photographed the whole thing.

*

CRYSTAL
July 2045

"I can't go back, can I?" I asked, hearing fear in my own voice, after ten minutes of walking. I kept seeing things I recognized, or that looked completely different. I shut up about it once we left the student union, because everything was at least a little different. I felt overwhelmed. Holding Amber's hand as we walked, I must have squeezed tighter and tighter, because she stopped and asked if I was okay.

I thought I would be, with the time travel and everything, so long as we were together. After everything that happened in the Timeslot room... It was just so much more than I expected. Amber seemed tense, but not as terrified as I was. I pulled her into a tight hug. I needed reassurance, comfort, or validation. I didn't know, but it came out as the question about going back.

She spoke softly by my ear, stroking my hair. "You know you can't. If you'd stayed, you'd be dead."

I squeezed tighter. "I know. I know. Just...promise me it's going to be okay."

She pulled back to look me in the eyes but kept her arm on my shoulder. "I promise you I'll do everything I can to keep us safe. I travelled fifty years to keep you from getting erased. I'm not going to let anything happen to you now."

I sniffed, not realizing how close to tears I was. "I just really needed to hear that."

"I was so focused on getting us out of there, I didn't make sure you were okay. People usually go through months of training before making their first jump, and I grabbed you and dragged you along. Sorry, that was probably jarring." She squeezed my arm, and I nodded before she started walking again. "We're going to my uncle's house tonight. We'll be safe there, and we can figure out what's next."

"How far?"

"About two miles. Sorry, I don't have a car. We could take a rideshare, but I'd rather not have a traceable record if I can avoid it."

"I understand. Is your knee okay? For that much distance, I mean."

"It's a little long, but I'll be fine."

Despite her reassurance, the limp got slowly more noticeable the longer we walked.

At a smallish gray brick home in an older neighborhood, a grandfatherly Black man with a gray goatee opened the door. Amber stepped forward and gave him a one-armed hug before half turning to me. "Crystal, meet my Uncle Kurtis. Kurtis, Crystal, my girlfriend." She gave girlfriend the slightest hint of a question. I nodded enthusiastically.

Girlfriend, huh? I found I liked that a lot.

He waved us inside, and Amber sat at the table. Kurtis smirked and stage-whispered to me behind the back of his hand, "You weren't expecting a Black fellow, were you?"

The unexpected silliness of it broke my tension. I mimicked his gesture and smile and whispered back, "Actually, I was expecting you to have red hair." He ran one hand across his smooth scalp, then laughed and pulled out a chair for me.

Turning toward Amber he said, "I like her." To both of us he asked, "Tea? Or something stronger?"

"Stronger," we replied in unison.

While he grabbed glasses and a bottle, Amber said, "Kurtis used to work for TE. In fact, he helped me design the portal we used."

"So that's why..." He smiled a knowing smile and nodded. Drinks poured, he handed us glasses. I didn't know much about whiskey, but, wow, it tasted good, smooth and a little bit smoky.

Amber set her glass down and began the tale, starting with my letter and ending with us jumping through the portal. I noticed she left out the part about Kasey. Sure she had a reason, I didn't interrupt. "Tomorrow morning, I need to talk with Tia about her tracking app and which version of V came after us. If it was from an earlier timeline, I could be in trouble."

Later, in the dark of the extra bedroom, snuggling together, I asked quietly what I'd been thinking since we got there, "Somehow, Kurtis is Kasey, isn't he?"

"Mm-hmm."

"Why doesn't he remember us?"

"He might remember, and isn't saying anything, but also, he might not. Time travel's funny that way. A change doesn't automatically zip down the whole timeline. It walks along at the ordinary rate of time." She explained change perpetuation as best she could, briefly, before adding, "Except when it doesn't."

"Huh?"

"That's part of what TE studies. Sometimes changes reach farther or happen faster than we expect."

I'd begun to nod off, and Amber must have realized. She kissed me gently and put an arm over me. I inched closer. Her head on my shoulder and my hand on her arm, we fell quickly to sleep.

23

KASEY
April 1994

The frame splintered and the door flew open, slamming loudly against the wall. Vanhanen stood in the opening. He had more strength than I would have imagined for a man of his age to have kicked a door open like that. Reaching inside his jacket, he pulled out the revolver from the desk at TE.

Autumn grabbed Summer's arm and they dove through the portal. At the same instant, V raised the pistol and fired. Since he stood behind them, they wouldn't have seen. Far enough through, and they may not have even heard.

I slipped under the worktable, which unfortunately, put the portal and V between me and the door, but it was the nearest cover. I could only barely hear his steps over the ringing of my ears in the oppressive silence following the gunshot.

Peeking over the table, the portal field blocked my view of him except for one hand almost touching the frame. I hoped that between the brightness of the field right in front of him, my dark skin and a black T-shirt, I'd blend into the shadows.

The field illuminated the shadowy innards of the control computer on the table. Its side panel was missing, and the back of the hard drive was visible. Taking it would keep V from following them or tracking their jump. I pulled, but it didn't budge. Damn! We were still decades away from click-in drives. The footsteps shuffled around on the other side of the portal, and I could see one shoulder and arm around the edge.

With the screwdriver from my pocket, as quietly as I could, I removed the screw holding the hard drive in place. Once loosened, the screw fell into the bottom of the case with a metallic *clack*. The tiny sound clear and distinct in the quiet room.

V 's face appeared around the left side of the portal. I ripped the drive out, dashed to my right and dove behind the sofa, shoving my duffel ahead of me. In my peripheral vision, I registered the portal field as still active, but fluctuating near the top. Had he shot into it? The hum sounded increasingly irregular and choppy. It should have collapsed when the computer errored-out without a hard drive. What drive had I stolen?

Another shot, unbelievably loud and echoing, and a spray of concrete dust erupted from the wall above me, leaving grit on my back and in my hair. Crawling to the other end of the sofa, I found a piece of wood from the kicked-in door frame and threw it across the dim room. The hollow *bang* hitting the storage lockers created the distraction I'd hoped for. I sprinted for the door.

*

CRYSTAL
July 2045

I woke with Amber still squished against me. It was great...for a while.

After thirty minutes of lying there listening to her breathe, I needed to get up and stretch. I carefully extracted myself, pulled my jeans on, and wandered to the kitchen.

Kurtis was already up, dressed, and having coffee. I guess it's true about older people getting up early. "Oh, that coffee smells good!" I slipped onto a barstool at the counter. Without asking, he filled a cup and set it in front of me.

"Cream?"

"No thanks, black is good."

He smiled a little. "Me too. Amber puts in almost as much cream as coffee."

"Yeah, I know."

When I came in, he'd been reading something on a flat computer that looked like a datapad from *Star Trek*. Simple things like sleeping in the guestroom or having coffee were unchanged from my time yesterday, fifty years before. Even the older guy reading the paper with his coffee wasn't too different, except the paper wasn't paper anymore. I was going to need a crash course to fit into this new time. I'd talk to Amber about that after the current crisis passed.

That reminded me. "Hey, in case I didn't say so last night... thanks. Thanks for letting us crash."

"Oh, you're welcome." He took a drink of coffee and gestured with his cup. "How much did she tell you about...about why she didn't want to go straight home last night?"

"She told me everything. All about V and stuff."

He nodded approvingly. "Good, good."

"After pretending to be just another student for so long, she seemed relieved to get it out." I skipped the part about her first attempt and me throwing her out. I also skipped the part about Dad's journal. Not sure what that knowledge might do to the time-line. "We sat and talked into the evening before we jumped. She answered all my questions about the future and what was waiting for us there—*here*, I guess. She wanted to make absolutely sure I understood what was going on before we left. She said, 'We have no time for bullshit.'"

Smirking, "That sounds about like how she'd phrase it." He poured himself more coffee. "How are your headaches?"

I couldn't help but smile. "Almost completely gone. What's left might be from stress. I don't know. I felt better the moment we walked into the Timeslot room."

"That can happen. It's the proximity to the equipment and a latent remnant of the portal field."

"Well, whatever it is, I'm happy for it."

"Amber told me last night she thought she should go to work this morning like usual."

I tensed up. Sensing it, Kurtis immediately added, "If he's jumping as much as Tia tracked, the V who'll show up at TE today is almost certainly not the one that chased you through the portal last night."

It wasn't clear to me who he'd been after, Amber or Kasey. Either way, he still showed up. I wondered what Kurtis's memory of that night might be like. Did V arrive with the gun, but Amber and I weren't there? Change perpetuation confused me.

I stood saying, "I'll go wake her."

Amber had pushed the covers back since I got up. Pausing in the doorway, I watched her for a moment before entering—pale muscular legs with scars on the left knee. Her Pearl Jam T-shirt, twisted and pulled up at one side, gave a tiny glimpse of flat stomach. Even with her hair going everywhere, she looked absolutely adorable. I almost hated to wake her.

*

KASEY
April 1994

In retrospect, I should have fled through the middle of the student union, since he was unlikely to shoot at me with people around. Instead, I ran out the way I'd come in—behind the kitchen. Still, a rich old man like V most likely wasn't familiar with the service corridors or where they led.

I leapt off the loading dock and sprinted across campus, avoiding sidewalks and lights, through grass and landscaping until I was sure enough I'd eluded him to stop and catch my breath. I crouched in the shadow of a mammoth fir tree. Behind the English department, I guessed. My mind spun panicked questions, but I tried to compartmentalize and focus on the most immediate concern: I needed a place to hide. The Timeslot room was out of the question. He saw what was built there and could potentially go back to it.

I'd grabbed my duffel in my flight out the door but left the toolbox behind. My ID and cash were all now usable again. On a crumpled envelope in my pocket, I'd written the phone number for a landlord in 1969, and the address of Charles's house.

Charles's address! If the dark-haired girl was who she looked like, and *if* she hadn't moved in the ensuing years, it was at least worth investigating.

All the windows were dark in the house as I approached, but

it was also after midnight. The occupants could simply be asleep. Aware of what this would look like if I got caught, I was extremely cautious. The landscaping was shaggier than I remembered, and the patio larger, but otherwise the house looked almost exactly like it had a day or two before in 1969. Shrubs and flowers covered the spot where the crash occurred, giving no clue to what'd happened there so long ago.

I crept into the backyard and found the rear door locked, the pane repaired, and no key under the mat. A one-car detached garage had a side door left ajar. I slipped inside, into an even deeper darkness. Feeling my way around to the far side of a small hatchback, I pulled a jacket out of my duffel and sat down on the concrete floor. Finding the hard drive in my pocket, I stashed it in my bag.

I spent the night like that, on the floor of Charles's old garage, cold but hidden for the moment. I tried to tally how long I'd been awake and found I couldn't. From '92 to '69 to '94 and TE to Charles's house to the Timeslot room and back meant I'd been awake for a day and a half at least. Still pondering this, sleep overtook me.

24

TIA
July 2045

Kurtis's electric convertible pulled up in front of the coffee place and stopped under a "No Parking" sign. A tallish woman with a long dark ponytail got out, followed by Amber squeezing out of the small back seat. They kissed, gently and slowly. Pulling back and looking into each other's eyes, Amber said something, and the woman, likely Crystal, nodded before getting back in the car. Kurtis leaned across to wave as he pulled away.

Amber watched them drive off before joining me at an outdoor table. Handing her a cup of coffee, I asked, "So that's Crystal, huh?"

"Obviously. I'll introduce you guys next time. After...y'know." Despite being the only ones at the outdoor seating, she leaned in and spoke quietly to catch me up about their last evening in 1994.

When she finished, I pulled put my tablet, unfolded the larger screen, and opened my secret log app. "I had adventures of my own last night."

"Wait. Where'd you go?"

"Nineteen seventy-eight."

"What!"

"I got an answer to my letter in the Timeslot."

"From Charles?" she asked, shocked.

"No. From a friend of his. He told me where to find V's early jump logs. There was a ledger in his desk…"

"In 1978!" She interrupted, sounding shocked. "Holy shit. Wait, did it work? Did it help your app?"

"Oh yeah." I spun the tablet around so she could see. The jumps were color coded by verifiability or extrapolation. The screen showed *far* fewer extrapolations than the day before.

I didn't know how to bring up getting fired or the other ledger, for that matter. So much of my plan hinged on working at TE. I was about to say, "There was more," but Amber spoke first.

She asked, sounding intense, "Does it show where he jumped to from April thirtieth, 1994?"

Scrolling and double-checking, my finger followed a line of data across the screen. "Oh shit. Here."

*

CRYSTAL
July 2045

As far as I could tell, Kurtis's car appeared to be mostly driving itself, which seemed so sci-fi to me. I couldn't understand why Amber wouldn't want to own one. At the next stoplight, I asked, "Can we, um, swing by the student union?"

Kurtis's tone sounded wary, dragging out his response. "Why?"

"After everything last night, with V and the gun, then the jump, I was in kind of a daze when we left the Timeslot room. I didn't even realize until we were at your house that I'd left my backpack behind."

"So, you want to go back for it?"

It felt uncomfortable admitting it, but I replied, "Right now it holds literally everything I own."

Kurtis signaled, and the car turned toward the union. "I'm sure you're aware, the room is almost certainly locked."

"I know. I know. I thought of that too. We left so fast I can't remember if Amber did anything with the door to lock up. It just swung closed behind us. She grabbed my hand and led us out of there in such a hurry, I probably couldn't find that basement hall-way again on my own if I tried."

He smirked. "And you're hoping I know where it is?"

"Yeah? Sorry. Even if it's locked now, show me the way into the basement, and I can walk back later and get my stuff."

"Sure. Understand, though, my knowledge of the building's layout is decades out of date. I could easily lead us to a supply closet full of toilet paper." He laughed a bit at his own joke. We entered the parking garage, the bright morning sunlight dimmed, and he continued, "Why not go tonight? Amber can let you in."

"I woke up early this morning, and thinking about all this, I couldn't get back to sleep. Amber..." I swallowed. "She saved my life, and I'm incredibly glad to be here with her..."

"But..."

"Right. But...I realized I'm entirely dependent on her for eve-rything now: food, money, a place to stay. She and Tia are going to set me up a new identity, but it'll take some time. For now, I'm not sure how to feel about all this yet. I thought if I could do this one small thing myself instead of asking her for more help…"

Kurtis smiled kindly as the car stopped. "I get it. I do. It's okay." He pointed his watch at a jumbled bar code on the wall above the parking space, then followed with several taps. He turned and saw me looking. "It doesn't matter what time you're in, the university still wants you to pay for parking."

Tapping his watch again, the convertible top extended and clicked back into place. From the narrow trunk, he produced a dark wood cane and headed into the building. He hadn't used one at home, but maybe this was more walking than before. Down hallways and past the round atrium, he paused in the food court, speaking quietly, "Now, I usually came at it from the other side, by the loading docks, but that"—he nodded toward a narrow hallway in a corner of the dining area—"should lead us where you want to go."

A college-age guy wearing a uniform shirt and balancing a tall stack of empty trays swept past us and down that same corridor. We followed. No sign marked it as "employees only," but they looked to be the only people who used it. Two tight corners, one right after the other, made it so we couldn't see the kitchen, but I could hear and smell it at the far end. A few steps past the offset, Kurtis led us through an opening to a narrow stairway going down. That must be it.

We passed empty racks and carts at the bottom of the stairs near large storage rooms on each side. Beyond, the corridor dimmed rapidly, clearly less well used. I followed him around two more corners, and after the second, the walls began to curve. I asked, "Does this look familiar?"

"Mm-hmm."

Following the hallway, I continued, "See, we didn't end up in a closet full of…" I shut up when Kurtis abruptly laid a hand on my arm. We'd come far enough around the curve to see the Timeslot room door standing open a crack, and a narrow sliver of light cut across the dark corridor floor. I mumbled quietly, "Oh, shit."

Kurtis approached the door and pushed it open but immediately shoved me behind him with his other hand. A second later, I understood why.

An older man in a gray suit sat behind the worktable, examining the computer.

"Well," Vanhanen began into the silence, speaking in an even tone, like a teacher schooling a misbehaving student. "It would appear someone's been making unauthorized use of TE equipment. But I'm sure you don't know anything about that." His gaze shifted from me to Kurtis before continuing. "The university forced me to start hiring minorities in the nineteen seventies, and the disabled around the turn of the century, but I don't remember hiring a Black man with a cane. You'd think I would; it might have fulfilled both categories. Since I don't, it means you used someone else's key, and either you stole it, or they breached TE security."

I felt Kurtis's hand on my elbow, and a gentle push as he stepped backward, but I couldn't take my eyes off the man in the suit.

"Not so fast." He lifted a pistol from behind the computer and gestured with his other hand for us to step forward. We did, and the door fell shut behind us with a creak of the hinges.

"You bastard, Vanhanen," growled Kurtis.

"Now see, there you have me at a disadvantage. Unless…oh yes. Did I chase you out of here last night? Except no, that was 1994. The years weigh heavy, don't they?"

The barrel of the gun swung toward me, looking *enormous*. I'd never been so scared. Frozen with fear, I clung to Kurtis's arm.

"But you? Who might you be?" Vanhanen asked.

My heart pounding, I managed to reply, "I'm nobody." My voice sounded small and unsure.

"I think not. In this time, Amber Wells was tasked with the repair of this equipment." He gestured around vaguely. "It appears she went a little overboard. Are you her roommate? Friend? Girlfriend?" He said this last with a hint of distain. "Really now. Did she bring you here to show off? To impress you? Seduce you? Did you two make a quick trip through time...somewhere romantic?"

His tone sickened me. I'd encountered it before—the note of a man who is both disgusted and aroused by lesbians and who covers his confusion with cruelty. I responded as flatly as I could manage, "No."

He gave a theatrical shrug, saying, "No matter."

Switching the revolver to his left hand, he typed with his right. A few clicks, and the equipment began to hum. Immediately after, points around the wood portal frame glowed and the field formed. V stepped around the control table and gestured with the gun, motioning us toward the portal. Neither of us responded, so V leaned closer and commanded, "Move. Now."

When Kurtis stepped forward, he spun his cane, so it came up under the older man's wrist with a painful sounding *crack*. The pistol flew across the room, and V chased it. Kurtis ran around the portal to the worktable grabbing at cables plugged into the back of the computer. The hum wavered, but the field remained in place. In the corner of my eye, I noticed V step from behind the sofa to my left, aiming the pistol at Kurtis.

That's what finally broke my fear paralysis. I saw what I needed to do, and I acted. Sprinting forward, I scooped my backpack off the couch by the strap and whipped my arm around, swinging the heavy bag at Vanhanen's head.

It hit more on the shoulder, but the impact threw off his aim enough he never pulled the trigger.

Shaken, but still determined, he stepped sideways shoving me with his elbow. It knocked me off balance, and I stumbled, hitting the base of the portal frame with my foot. With one hand on my shoulder and one arm across my stomach, he shoved me backward. Kurtis looked up, yelling and stretching out the word, "Noooo!" as if in slow motion.

My wrist banged sharply on the side of the frame, my hand going numb. The portal emitter shrieked in one ear, and then everything went black. I fell and hit my head in the dark.

*

TIA
July 2045

Amber stood and I had my hand on the corner of the screen to fold it, when the tablet beeped again.

"Campus security alert. Active shooter situation. Suspect is a Caucasian male in his seventies or eighties. Last seen on the sidewalk between Mechanical Engineering and the library. Do not approach. The suspect is armed and dangerous. University students and staff advised to remain indoors."

"Where'd you park?" Amber asked quickly.

"Down the block, but there's no way we'll get through, even with my pass." I brought up a live view and saw security blocking off streets and rerouting traffic.

"We need to get to TE."

"Yeah, no shit. How's your knee?" I backed away from the table.

"Good enough."

Heading out at a jog, Amber pushed, and I navigated us around traffic, campus security and police.

We were barely into Engineer's Row, when a wave of nausea rolled through me. Amber's pushing slowed at the same time. "You okay back there?"

"No," came a terse reply through gritted teeth. Almost to a park bench, she let go of my chair. I coasted to a stop, turning enough to see her collapse, grabbing her knee. A headache exploded behind my eyes; both of us groaned, doubling over and holding our temples.

It felt akin to the temporal displacement headache I had every day, but ten times worse, maybe a hundred. Amber whimpered, curled up on the bench, and I hung sideways trying hard not to vomit.

I don't know how long we sat like that. When it finally subsided enough to look up, there was no one around—empty sidewalk all the way to Nuclear Engineering.

With both of us pushing, we made it slowly to the TE door. Amber dug in her pockets, unable to find her key card. "Don't you have yours?"

"No. I was going to tell you this earlier, and then we were running here, and then…" I trailed off not sure how to describe what happened on the sidewalk. "V made me give it back."

"Wait. Why?"

"He had a security camera hidden behind the garage that recorded me breaking in."

"Whoa!"

"The camera only got the back corner of the van. He didn't seem to know you were there."

"What'd he say?"

I grabbed my tablet and elbowed her out of the way. Reaching under the housing to plug in the cable, I replied over my shoulder, "He fired me."

Her jaw dropped open. "Holy shit, I'm sorry. When…When?"

"Day before yesterday. After we got off the vid-call." I shook my head. "Right now, we got bigger things."

"Okay. Later, I want the whole story."

"Deal."

I logged into the lock controls I'd set up during my first minutes in the 2040s, and we were in. Amber dropped into her desk chair. "What the hell happened out there on the sidewalk?" I held up a finger for "just a sec" and looked through the lab door. The portal was timing out and shutting itself down. From behind me, I heard Amber. "Again, I ask, what the hell? Did V finally snap, go on a shooting spree, and escape through the time portal?"

"Maybe?" I responded unconvinced. "Hold on." I drilled down to a tier of apps buried deep on my tablet, ones I didn't use often. I signed in twice, the second time against a very short countdown clock.

"Do I even want to ask?"

"Probably not."

Building security footage of the basement hallway appeared on the screen. I adjusted the slider until I saw movement. Vanhanen walked down the hall looking a little dazed and a *lot* pissed. Outside the TE door, he switched a pistol to his other hand and pulled out his card. Quicker than I had thought possible, another man came around the corner and rushed him from behind. The second man grabbed the back of V's neck, pushing his face crookedly into the door. The two struggled, and the second man grabbed the gun away. His back was to the camera, but I could see he had dark skin and a bald head. Oh no…

With the pistol shoved into his back, V stopped struggling and held out the key card between two fingers. The Black man took it and swiped it. Doing so, he turned far enough I could recognize him. They entered TE and passed out of view of the camera.

Amber sighed, "Shit." She slumped back, looking paler than usual, tapped her watch with an unsteady hand, and used voice control to call Kurtis. It rolled straight to voicemail. She slipped out of her jacket, hung it behind the door, and rubbed a hand across her forehead. "I'm...not feeling great."

"You mean you feel sick, or you're worried about Kurtis?"

"Huh? Both, I guess."

I checked the lab computer log for the last jump—blank. "Damn." How had Kurtis done that? Or did V erase the log? I brought up my secret app and there it was, showing a destination date and time. The app couldn't log how many people passed through, only arrivals and departures. Logically, they'd both jumped. TE had no other exit. A glance into the storage closet ruled that out too.

Amber *did* look like she felt ill. I got her some water and asked her about the jump date from the log, December thirtieth, 1977. "No, sorry. I don't know why that would be significant."

Over her shoulder, I noticed I'd left the security video playback running. I saved out the portion we watched, but right as I closed it, I got a feeling that something was off. I opened the saved portion and rewatched it in reverse from the end at high speed.

Amber and I backed away from the door, followed by minutes of empty hallway. On the third time through, I finally saw it. Between the time V and Kurtis entered TE, and when Amber and I did, there was a flicker. After the flicker, the bulletin board across the hall was different. I couldn't read it at this range, but the colors and arrangement of notices changed. Still random, but a different random.

From when we came into the frame, back to the moment of the flicker, put it at the same time as our headaches out on the sidewalk.

Amber made noise about going home and checking on Crystal. She promised to text later. The hall door clicked shut behind me, but I was focused on the implications of what I'd seen on the recording. What would cause a change like that?

A change. Cause a change.

Time travel.

"Oh shit."

Something altered the timeline shortly after Kurtis and V stepped through the portal, and I didn't know if there would be lingering effects, or how they would manifest. Later, I might not even remember. And Amber had already left...

I reopened my tablet and typed. I'd have preferred to leave TE and write somewhere, anywhere other than where I'd been fired from, but not fully understanding the situation, I thought it best to stay close to the portal. I typed for hours, recalling everything about TE back to the day I caught V jumping at 7:00 a.m. I saved the file to my tablet and two different cloud backups. Unsure of what the timeline change would do to digital records, I printed a hardcopy to take with me. It wasn't like I cared whether I used up V's printer paper.

25

CRYSTAL
Date unknown

Iawoke in total darkness, and the back of my head hurt. Despite a bump, I wasn't bleeding, or at least my hair and scalp didn't feel wet. How long did I lie there on the concrete floor? I felt cold, even wearing my sweatshirt. Zipping it made my left arm hurt. The skin on my wrist felt sore and hot to the touch. I found a scorched hole in my sleeve as well.

I tried to stand but felt woozy and thought better of it. Instead, I crawled until I found a wall. Leaning on it, I got slowly to my feet and shuffled sideways until I felt a door, and beyond, a switch.

Light on and squinting, I saw the inside of the Timeslot room. Memory rushed back of the fight with Kurtis and V, which made me immediately tense and look around. No—I was alone. Whatever happened to Kurtis or V, they were gone.

I remembered stumbling, and...and then nothing, I guess. Obviously, I fell and knocked my head on the concrete. Where'd they go after I blacked out? Kurtis wouldn't have left a friend unconscious on the floor, but V had a gun. He could have forced him anywhere. Did they go out the door or through the portal? The portal looked broken, the wiring on one side torn and hanging loose.

I took a few cautious steps and sat on the edge of the sofa. I replayed the scene in my head: Kurtis at the worktable, V coming in from the left with the pistol, and me hitting him with the backpack. The portal would have been right behind me.

V shoved me backward. My left arm hurt. That side of the portal was damaged.

Oh no.

My head dropped into my hands with the realization that *I'd* been the one to go through the portal, not Kurtis or V. My backpack still lay on the floor where I'd fallen, a few feet past the wood frame—my stand-in in a mental reenactment, lying alone on the cold dusty floor.

Or not alone. From a shadow at the base of the frame, I picked up a charred and torn leather bracelet that had been on my left wrist, the large silver bead blackened and deformed. Had it snagged on the wires when I reached out to catch myself? The burn on my wrist supported that theory.

With the machine broken, there was no way to tell where I was, *when* I was. Worse, there was no way to get back. I didn't even know how to use the equipment. I was trapped in an unknown time.

Two days before, I woke up, made coffee, and went to class like a regular college student. I had good grades, and there was a girl I liked. Then... Shit.

I'd convinced Kurtis to show me the way to the Timeslot room because of the backpack. Why had I been so concerned about notebooks and pens? Except it wasn't the contents. I'd needed validation I could be independent, even in the unfamiliar future. The bag could have waited, like he suggested. Vanhanen wouldn't have found us, we wouldn't have fought, and I wouldn't have fallen through the portal. Who knew what happened to Kurtis? Had V shot him? He was sure trying to, just before...

If only I'd come back *later* for the backpack.

I hugged my knees to my chest, too dazed to even cry. I didn't know how long I sat like that, my thoughts constantly returning to Amber. I had to believe she was out there looking for me. I half turned toward the other end of the sofa. We were together, right there, what—yesterday? My hand touching the cushion came away dusty. How much time had elapsed for the rest of the world since then?

At a point when I felt myself nodding off, I stood carefully and explored the room: bare concrete floor and walls, steel structure overhead, brown fake-leather sofa, with a plaid blanket, a small radio, a worktable heaped with various computer parts, and storage lockers containing more random computer bits—light bulbs, a plug-in tea kettle, a box of tea bags, a chipped porcelain mug, and a rusted toolbox with the name Kasey scratched on the lid.

This last gave me pause. Kasey...Kurtis. Amber said they were the same guy. She made up names for us when we met him, and he'd said Kasey was an alias. Was it TE protocol to not use your real name out of time? But then why'd Amber used "Amber" when she met me? The answer was obvious; her trips to meet and rescue me were unofficial.

Beyond the storage lockers, I found a little sink. Turning the faucet, it hissed harshly and ran rusty water for almost a minute before it cleared. I rinsed the mug and drank, not realizing how thirsty I was until I started. Carefully removing my sweatshirt, I got a better look at my wrist. Painful, but not serious. At least I didn't think so. It looked like a bad sunburn, but with a ragged scratch through the middle. I rinsed it in the sink for a long time. The cool water felt nice, and I hoped it was getting clean. I thought of the tube of ointment and bandages in my medicine cabinet, but it sat two time jumps and unknown years away. I found a dark-blue bandanna in my backpack I'd once used as a headband. I tied it loosely around my wrist and pulled my sweatshirt back on.

Uncomfortably dark with the lights out, I copied Amber's strategy of pointing the worktable lamp toward the far wall. I tried to get comfortable on the sofa, glad I brushed the dust off earlier. As tired as I felt, I couldn't sleep; my gaze kept returning to the door. Plain gray metal with substantial hinges and a big steel handle, it wasn't anything special, or particularly scary, but it still felt *ominous*. I wasn't sure if I expected V to come crashing through, waving a gun, or for Amber to show up and find me.

I was temporarily safe. Doing anything toward getting back to Amber was impossible until I left, but leaving meant abandoning that safety. This realization mostly just pissed me off.

I didn't even know what year I was in. According to what Amber told me about not meeting yourself, all I knew is that I *wasn't* anywhere between 1969 and 1994. Dad's journal said his research spanned back to the 1940s, and Amber was from 2045. The computer equipment ruled out the pre-sixties era, so somewhere in a fifty-year gap between Amber and me. Damn.

I finally managed to sleep. I have no idea how long or if it was even night. For a room with a time machine in it, it sure lacked any way to tell the passage of hours...or days.

*

KASEY
May 1994

Light through the side window woke me. Stiff and cold, I slept about as well as one would expect on the floor of a garage. The passenger side window of the hatchback next to me was down. I reached through and opened the glove compartment. Under a stack of homemade cassettes, I found a registration card: Crystal Yung. Charles's daughter, or his widow? Guessing by music selections, Nirvana, the Breeders, etc., the vehicle belonged to a woman in her twenties, not her fifties.

I'd planned to remove a window screen or, as a last resort, to break out the same pane again. I didn't see or hear anyone around in the early morning light. I needed to go that moment or wait in the garage until night. What if the mom was home? If she was, where was her car? On the street? Why give the kid the better parking spot? It didn't add up.

Bag over my shoulder, I crept across the yard, feeling horribly exposed in the early morning sun. At the sound of a car, I flattened myself against the back of the house, but it continued down the street. I tilted a flowerpot by the door hoping for a key underneath, no luck. That's when I noticed the same garden gnome in the landscaping. Gently lifting it, I found a tarnished brass key in the dirt below. I opened the screen door, tried the lock, and I was in.

The layout of the house matched my memories, despite changes to furniture and decorations. I'd only been in the kitchen and front room before, but this time I quickly searched everywhere, even the basement, before I let myself believe no one was home.

Returning to the kitchen, I took a banana from a bowl of fruit on the counter. Eating it and looking out the window, I realized anyone outside would see me as well. I immediately ducked down, and pulled the curtains closed.

A group of framed photos hung in the hallway: Charles and the librarian together, a wedding, a baby photo, a studio photo of mother and teenaged daughter, finally what was probably a senior picture. I flipped the last one over and found a label, "Crystal—Class of '88."

So Crystal was the daughter—Summer from the Timeslot room. Interesting as this was, it didn't solve my predicament of being trapped out of time. Solve it? Perhaps not, but if no one would be returning home any time soon, a place to crash certainly helped my situation.

Closing the remaining curtains, I found only one bedroom had a bed. Instead, the other had a music stand, a jumbled stack of sheet music on the dresser, and a viola—slightly larger than my sister's violin—on a chair.

In the living room, a massive Nirvana poster covered one wall, and the dining table looked like a study nest, littered with papers, books, highlighters, and an abandoned coffee cup.

Most of the basement was one big, nearly empty room, laundry at one end, storage at the other, and far less cluttered than I expected for living there twenty-plus years. Through a doorway was a space that could have been a tiny guest bedroom but, at the moment, held only a mattress and box springs leaning against the wall.

Obviously, Crystal's mom didn't live there. The car, the poster, and the bed all pointed to a lone occupant. Why?

Finding an extra blanket on the sofa, I considered the mattress in the basement but grabbed my duffel and headed to the shower first.

*

TIA
July 2045

When my alarm woke me, I experienced a weird moment of double vision. I fumbled to turn it off and lay there looking at two identical cats regarding me from the foot of the bed. I squinted and tried to focus until they resolved into a single cat, who yawned hugely and went back to sleep. I rubbed my eyes and considered seeing an optometrist. My vision had always been good.

Was it tied to the odd headache the day before? Hold on, had that happened, or had I been at work with Amber like a regular day. If I concentrated, I could remember it two different ways. I rubbed my temples, and squeezed my eyes shut.

I found I could remember two versions of things farther back too. Had Amber and I broken into Vanhanen's garage, or did we sneak into his house after he went missing?

Missing?

What the hell, Tia?

Did Amber fix the Timeslot, or was it still on my to-do list?

Did she jump into the 90s to rescue Crystal, or were we busy writing research grant proposals?

Sitting on the edge of the bed, the double vision faded, but the double memories remained. It didn't take a time travel scientist to see the connection to the day before. The thing is I was a time travel scientist. This sure looked like paradox after-effects, which meant we were in uncharted territory. TE training included detailed information about how to avoid a paradox but shockingly little about what to do if you found yourself in one.

Before leaving, I reread the printout from the day before. I remembered it all, but most of it was accompanied by a nagging in my head, suggesting something different had happened.

I found a key card in my bag, so I decided to get ready and go to work like half of my memories said I should. I wasn't prepared for the changes at TE. The desks in the outer office had been replaced with comfortable living-room furniture. The door to V's office was gone, and Amber and I each had desks inside. Part of me knew we'd renovated a few months ago, right after V disappeared.

Again? Disappeared?

I rubbed my temples, trying to remember. The previous winter, Vanhanen quit showing up, no email, nothing. After a week, I hacked his computer. A week later, we snuck into his house. Then I reported him missing to the police. We spent the next few months getting university approval to transfer control of the department to Amber and me. They found old paper records in storage, and we claimed the Horatio Vanhanen we worked for was the grandson of the one who opened the department. They eventually granted it but raised the cost of our lab space. Not surprising.

But I also remembered catching V returning from an unscheduled jump, creating a secret log app, learning to pick locks, tracking the package and breaking into his garage, Amber's skiing accident, Crystal's letter and the subsequent visits to 1994, not to mention getting fired by V a few days earlier.

I got to TE late but still earlier than Amber. I'd intended to ask how Crystal and Kurtis were doing but didn't. Seeing her hair brought me to a stop. It was super short again, like when she was with Meg. It got shaggy after their breakup, and she kept it that way for a 90s look. In my alternate memories, though, it was always short. Which timeline was I living in? What had happened—or not happened—in this new version? When Amber went home the day before, I'd have thought all her attention would have been on her new girlfriend, not on getting a haircut. I desperately wanted to ask about Crystal, but if there *had* been a paradox, I couldn't be sure what might make it worse. I'd wait and hear what she remembered, unprompted.

I waited all morning and then all afternoon.

As far as I could tell, she had *absolutely no* memory of the original timeline, only the alternate one. I was shocked, angry, and sad. Amber had such love for Crystal. I saw it in the way she talked about her, in how destroyed she'd felt when she thought she'd failed her, and in the tenderness of their goodbye kiss.

All day I kept almost saying the wrong thing. To the point that Amber asked me if I felt okay because I seemed off. I covered by saying I hadn't slept well. I couldn't understand why I remembered things from before the paradox, and Amber only after? Why the difference?

And then I worked it out. Despite living in the 2040s for three and a half years and coming to consider it my home, I was still technically out of time, but Amber was back in her original timeslot. Was that enough? Did returning to your timeslot after a paradox realign your memories with your home timeline? At the moment, I didn't have a better theory.

So, the bigger question was what happened to Kurtis and Crystal?

And where the hell was Vanhanen for that matter?

When Amber left at the end of the day, I stayed behind, lying about some unfinished work. I checked my secret log, and that's where things got weirder. The database it created of departures and arrivals was complete up through the previous week, but many of V's jumps since January were grayed out in the records. I could see them listed but couldn't access the details.

Temporal headaches didn't kick in until you left TE. Since the computer sat in the same proximity radius, maybe the app had records of both histories, but didn't quite know what to do with the conflicting information.

In front of the portal, I glowered through its empty arch as if trying to stare it down or intimidate it into giving up the truth about Vanhanen. Was he lost somewhere in time? I'd originally planned to trap him in the past. Had that happened without my intervention? Had the paradox swallowed him? Had he run up against an end of the line?

All that time and effort, planning and scheming, and he'd slipped through my fingers anyway.

Shit.

26

CRYSTAL
June 2022

I felt better rested but still pissed off.

I'd been thinking about Mom right as I woke up. I do that sometimes. Not a dream exactly, closer to a memory.

There was something she spoke about only a couple of times while I was growing up. She believed that sometimes when you lived through bad shit, it prepared you for what came later, and surviving hardened some inner part of yourself. Later, when you needed it, you could reach deep inside and touch that obsidian core to channel a little of its power to the surface, even if only as a reminder that whatever you were up against wasn't as bad as the bad shit you'd already faced down and conquered.

Ironically, if that's the right word, Mom's cancer and death was the bad shit I lived through. At about twenty-two, I'd been abruptly thrust into being the full adult in the situation: dealing with insurance, bills and everything, all on top of taking care of Mom. It was too much to even begin to describe here in brief.

Suffice to say, being stuck somewhere in time and cut off from the woman I loved absolutely qualified as bad shit, but it wasn't the worst shit I'd gone toe to toe with.

I put my hair in a ponytail, laced up my chucks, grabbed my backpack, and opened the door. The empty hallway had barely enough light to see the bulky electronic lock above the handle. Stepping back, I let go and it closed smoothly. The hinges had creaked and stayed ajar in 2045, but this door seemed almost new. Looking around the room for something to prop it with, I considered the old toolbox. On second thought, walking away and leaving the room open for any random person to either get in, or remove the prop and lock me out, felt...wrong.

Kneeling in the door opening, I found a slit along the side of the lock. Squinting at it, I heard myself use one of Mom's favorite expressions, "Hold the phone!" then I modified it to be my own. "Dude! Hold the freakin' phone!" One sneaker jammed against the heavy door, I dug in my backpack for Dad's journal. Between chapters, right where I left it, was a scuffed white plastic rectangle that *just maybe* wasn't a bookmark, after all. At the hotel in Minneapolis when we saw the symphony, they gave us a key card for our room, but none of us knew how to use it. The woman from the front desk had to explain it.

Running it through the slit, a small panel on the lock lit up. "Yes!" I tried several more times, but it always went dark after a moment. It clearly had electricity, but there was no way to know for sure if it'd let me back in once it locked. I finally had to give it a try. The door slipped closed, and the lock clicked audibly in the quiet hallway. I swiped the card and spent a tense few seconds waiting before the light changed to green, and I pushed the door back open. I let out my held breath and felt a knot of stress loosen.

Down the hallway I paused. Right before messing with the lock, I'd thought of Amber as "the woman I loved." That was new. The realization made me smile despite the situation.

Upstairs, I'd braced for people to be dressed in *Star Trek* futuristic fashions which would make my clothes look as dated as a hoopskirt...but they weren't. In the food court, I saw guys dressed pretty much like they always do: jeans, T-shirts, sneakers, baseball caps. The girls wore black leggings and tank tops; some had jeans so tight I wondered how they got them on or off. Others wore short shorts or loose boxy jeans with frayed ends and crop tops. Everyone had impossibly thin laptops or tablets and flat little mobile phones.

A wide TV screen on one wall played a recorded loop of advertisements and student information. I sat at an empty table to watch. After an ad showing summer hours for the university bookstore and a map with campus vaccination locations was a commercial for an outdoor performance of *Mid-Summer Night's Dream*, listing dates in June of 2022.

The screen continued to play, but I barely noticed, trying not to show my shock. The portal had dropped me twenty-three years behind Amber, and twenty-eight years ahead of where I'd come from. Why not split the difference evenly? Or for that matter, why not some other completely random time?

Needing some fresh air, and to clear my head, I wandered away, up the stairs and through the lobby with the zodiac. Tall, arched windows filled the space with early afternoon sunshine and a view of clear blue sky. Sunglasses on, I walked out the door into the summer of 2022, grabbing a campus newspaper out of habit from the rack in the entry. As I stepped over a curb, I noticed something odd—an old surgical mask in the gutter. Why would that be there? There wasn't a hospital nearby. Weird.

A short walk north brought me to the wide lawn in the middle of the university. From a bench in the shade, I could see the buildings facing central campus. Most had been a century old or more when I knew them in the 90s and they were still there. Still the same. The familiar setting made the time shift even harder to believe.

I opened the paper, and the differences became real and obvious immediately. Saying I felt shocked didn't even begin to cover it. The top story was about Congressional hearings over the previous president and how he'd incited an insurrection on the capitol when he lost the election a year and a half before. From what I read, he was behaving like a gangster in a movie, or maybe even a toddler, not the president. And yet almost half of Congress still supported the guy? I couldn't even fathom. I remembered learning about Watergate in school. This sounded so much worse.

The current president seemed okay, but he'd inherited an extensive mess. He'd signed a bill on gun control, which was good. I read several pages into the paper before coming across an article about the pandemic. The number of sick and dead was—well, I didn't even have a word for it. And people'd somehow *gotten used to it*? Between that article, and a couple of public service ads from the university, I learned about the symptoms and how contagious it was. I looked around and zipped my sweatshirt up over my nose. A vaccine had been produced, available at no cost, but a surprising amount of people were all weird about taking it. The university PSA listed locations and times to get the shot, but required a current student ID. On the back page I found a listing for a homeless shelter offering the single-dose vaccine, no questions asked.

*

KASEY
May 1994

Iknew I couldn't stay at Crystal's house indefinitely. As tempting as it sounded, people would soon wonder if I was an intruder, or worse if they put my presence together with her disappearance.

I found a bicycle hanging in the garage, which I borrowed. I considered looking for a key to the car, but not only was it an old gas engine, it was a stick shift. Successfully driving it would be nearly impossible. I rode toward campus, intending to look at rental listings in the campus paper, when I passed the basement apartment from 1992.

As far as I could tell, it was empty. I walked into the side yard to look through the window. I half expected to see the things I left behind: beer bottle on the counter, camping cot and all. But no—I knew better than that. Change perpetuation. That hadn't occurred in this timeline.

I debated riding past Nuke-E or the student union but thought better of it. Much as I wanted to get away, I thought lying low for a while would be the safest.

Back at Crystal's house I was confronted in the driveway by a neighbor wearing a shirt and shorts in a matching print, those old-lady sandals, and a fanny pack. She was easily old enough to be my grandmother, if not my great grandmother.

"What are you doing in Crystal's house? Where is she?"

I had to think fast. "I'm house sitting for Crystal." I remembered the viola. "She's on a trip for a music class." Whew!

"How do you know her?"

"I'm a friend of her friend Autumn. Red hair?" I gestured toward the top of my head. She nodded and I thought I'd appeased her, but the interrogation continued.

"How long will she be gone, and why are you house sitting this close to the end of the semester?"

"I'm only here for the week." I almost said, "She'll be back next weekend," but I caught myself. I hoped a week was enough time to find somewhere else. "Um…my roommates are huge partiers. Crystal let me stay here while she was gone so I could study for finals where it was quiet."

I thought the concept of a studious Black guy might confuse her a little, but she rolled right onto a new line of questioning. "Does she know you're using her bike?"

"She offered me her car if I needed it, but I can't drive a stick. The bike was a consolation prize."

She harrumphed. I thought I'd successfully navigated the conversation when she added, "Now don't go cuttin' across my yard when you leave."

Had this woman really told me to get off her lawn? "I wasn't planning to."

"Well, see that you don't," and she turned and disappeared back into her house.

It took most of the week to get in touch with my old landlord. Yes, the place was available and, no, it still didn't have air-conditioning. At least he didn't raise the rent. I'd closed out my bank account before leaving 1992 and took the last of it with me in cash. I'd be okay for a little while but had to figure some things out fast.

I had an internal conflict between my guilty moral compass telling me to leave, and my survival instinct insisting I shouldn't pass up an opportunity. Crystal and Autumn had jumped to another timeline. Despite knowing she wouldn't be back, stealing her things still felt wrong. In the end, the survival instinct kept me around. I initially planned to take only items which wouldn't be noticed. On my second day, I realized that if I was careful about what I took, I could help perpetuate the illusion of Crystal being out of town.

I filled a suitcase with sweatshirts, a denim jacket, socks, and any other clothes gender neutral enough that I might be able to wear. I took several pairs of jeans and a coat as well which I later sold to a consignment store, telling the woman behind the counter that my ex-girlfriend left them behind when she dumped me.

Stuffed in the bottom of a drawer, I found more than a hundred dollars in cash. A jar of coins in a closet held almost another fifty. Everything else I thought I could use, or by taking would save me having to buy later, got piled in the hall: a few random hand tools, some cookware, an unopened tube of toothpaste, things like that. During that week, I ate everything in the kitchen. Someone going out of town wouldn't leave food in the refrigerator, right?

In digging through the desk, I finally learned the fate of Crystal's mom; she'd died of cancer the previous year. I read a copy of her obituary and suffered one last pang of guilt about scavenging her house.

It took me multiple trips on the bike with my duffel and the suitcase to transfer everything. I mentally debated at length, while riding, whether to keep the bike or not. I desperately wanted it, but the ease with which I imagined the grumpy old neighbor lady talking to the police after Crystal was discovered missing dissuaded me. The bike hanging back in the garage where I'd found it, would help deflect attention away from me.

I wasn't sure about CSI technology in 1994, but I scrubbed the whole house before I left, hoping to remove any fingerprints or errant hairs I might have left behind. More than that, I personally needed to *not* look like the house-sitter that the neighbor could describe. On my last trip, I grabbed a pair of scissors, shaving cream and razors from the bathroom cabinet. The first night in the basement apartment, I shaved my head.

*

CRYSTAL
June 2022

My old life, despite its problems, was more privileged than I ever realized. I lost my mom to cancer, but I'd become a homeowner at twenty-three and had enough money left from her life insurance that I could concentrate on being a student and not also have to work. I never once had to worry about my next meal. Had things suddenly changed?

Despite the warm weather, I shrugged deeper into my hooded sweatshirt, hands in the pockets, and entered the homeless shelter. I didn't know what to expect, but the building reminded me of a church or a community center more than whatever my Hollywood fueled anxiety created in my imagination. An older woman by the door politely asked me why I was there and pointed to a small table where a broad-shouldered man sat, wearing blue nurse's scrubs.

He asked with a smirk and an accent I couldn't identify, "Here to get shot?" At my puzzled look, he continued, "No one ever laughs. Maybe that joke's not as funny as I thought." He shrugged and ran through a bunch of questions about allergies and if I had a previous Covid shot. I'd prepared a whole story about how my bag got stolen and my driver's license with it but ended up not needing it. He said, "Here's where I would usually talk about insurance, and ask to see an ID, but that won't be necessary. The state program which puts us here doesn't require any of that. I don't even need your name. I only need to report a total count of doses given."

I felt relieved. "Oh, Okay, good." I'd imagined myself filling out the form with "none" under address, and it felt unnerving and depressing. Rolling my sleeve back down, he handed me a vaccination record card and a package of masks. "The shot can take up to two weeks for full effectiveness. We recommend continuing to mask until then."

"Thank you."

"Ask the woman by the door, but I don't think they start serving dinner for a couple more hours. Later on, you might have had to stand in line for the shot, but at least you could have had something to eat while you were here."

Not wanting to wait around that long, I walked to the grocery store. I knew I had limited cash, so I only bought enough for a few days: fruit, ramen, bread and peanut butter. I hoped the tea kettle in the Timeslot room still worked. Putting on one of the masks before going into the store felt weird and awkward. Once inside, I saw a few other people with them as well, so it wasn't so bad.

I rearranged my backpack to make room for the groceries. I had two textbooks, various pens, a calculator, and a wallet with my driver's license (twenty-plus years expired), a debit card, a video rental card, and after buying the groceries, about forty-five bucks in cash. I had a place to stay but food was quickly going to become a problem.

I needed to find a way home, or rather, back to Amber. My original home was closed off to me. The portal in the Timeslot room looked broken, and as far as I could tell the Timeslot was too. I had no idea how to run them even if they *did* work. There was a Temporal Engineering department on campus with a functioning time portal, but it was overseen by a madman who'd tried to shoot Amber and I in the back.

Returning to the student union, I realized it was almost evening. Yes, the tea kettle worked, and after eating some noodles, I searched the room more thoroughly. Behind the sofa I found a crumpled dust cover. Moving it threw off a cloud of dust and exposed a black gym bag.

I unzipped carefully and pulled it open to find a pair of jeans, followed by a tank top and a black T-shirt with the Joshua Tree cover on the front. Amber had the same one. Underneath lay the gray V-neck from the day we got coffee. Hold on, somehow this was Amber's bag! I felt myself tearing up. I couldn't help it. Wiping my eyes, I kept looking: socks, underwear, even a toothbrush, razor, and tampons. I mumbled, "Amber, you may have just saved my life."

Lifting the whole bag onto the couch, I felt something bulky in a side pocket. I found a thick brown leather journal, which looked to be handmade, with a strap to tie it closed.

Inside was a diary in the same blocky handwriting as her note about Kurt Cobain. I read for over two hours, alternately smiling and crying. She went through so much to get to my timeline and then so much more to save me. She didn't even know me when she started. At the part where we fought and she left, I had to stop for a few minutes. I couldn't read from crying so hard. I still felt so shitty about throwing her out. Intellectually, I knew I couldn't have known, but I wondered how things might have gone differently if I'd heard her out.

Lacking tissues, I washed my face in the little sink and calmed down before reading to the end. In her last entry, she wrote about decoding my message with Tia's help before leaving to meet me. The last half of the pages were blank. I closed the book and held it tightly to my chest. It made my connection to Amber physical, not just a memory. She held this and wrote in it, here in this exact room, probably in the exact spot, closest to the desk light.

I turned toward the empty opposite end of the sofa,

remembering how we'd snuggled there well into the evening, and, eventually, I'd asked about our earlier conversation. "So, If I'm sharing my dad's timeslot..."

"Mm-hmm. Come home with me, and you'll sync back up with where your dad's original timeslot would be if he'd survived. But since he didn't, it'll be free and clear for you."

"Are you sure?"

"No. This is...theoretical, but what I know backs it up. If you stay, though, I'm even more sure you'll die. Look, I know we haven't known each other all that long, and we missed a chunk of time in the middle..."

"I'm in."

"That's it? Just like that?"

I'd had a flicker of regret about abandoning the house after all the work to clean it up—but the work wasn't about the house. It was about Mom. It was about me. Mom was gone, and I didn't have any other family. Amber had offered me a place to belong where I wouldn't have headaches, not to mention she'd be there too.

"Yeah. Just like that."

My fingers had slid gently down her leg as it lay across mine. When they brushed against her scars, I stopped. Before I could pull back, she laid her hand on top of mine, explaining how the skiing accident was worse than she'd let on. Her knee replacement surgery in 2045 didn't exist yet in 1994.

Despite the injury, she'd walked through time, to find...me. There are moments when we realize how much someone means to us, and then there are the rarer ones where we see how much we mean to that other person.

This amazing woman swept into my life with a story that should have been unbelievable, except it explained so much, and arrived at exactly the moment when I was ready for her. Under the blanket in the semi-darkness, we held each other quietly after the conversation dwindled, her head on my shoulder, hair tickling my nose. I didn't mind at all.

Alone in the Timeslot room, I pulled on her U2 shirt. It smelled dusty, but I didn't care. With a pen from my backpack, I reopened the journal to the first blank page and began to write.

27

AMBER
August 2045

Ihad the weird dream again—being chased by an older man in a suit. He looked like Vanhanen, but I never got a clear view of his face. No pistol this time, just running hard, but moving in slow motion. The dark-haired woman was with me again, holding my hand. My knee hurt like hell, the surprise of it waking me before we got to the time portal.

Some version of the same dream happened three times. I never used to remember my dreams at all. When I did, it was usually random nonsense and never a repeating one.

The prevailing internet wisdom suggested keeping a journal. Dreams were evanescent and easily forgotten, confused in your memories later. Writing them down helped make the process of understanding them more tangible. I gave it a try.

Stress could be a cause of disturbing dreams, yet they didn't start until months after Tia and I took over TE. We'd had to justify our existence to the university that hadn't looked into the department in decades. We covered our expenses and paid ourselves with what little was left in TE's accounts after Vanhanen disappeared. He'd done something fishy with the books, and which funds were his, versus TE money was unclear. We only told the university about what we absolutely had to, of course. If I'd gone skiing instead of giving Meg the tickets, this would have all started while I was gone. I'm glad it wasn't dropped in Tia's lap alone. It was tricky enough with both of us.

Since then, we tried to legitimize the department, but dealing with century-old security clearances was a lot of trouble. We hoped to eventually publish our findings, but that held its own difficulties. Even mentioning time travel gets one laughed out of most scientific circles.

Having troubling dreams as well wasn't helpful at all.

*

CRYSTAL
June 2022

It felt oddly comforting to know companies still gave junk away from tables outside the library at the beginning of the semester. Fall semester had much more, but still. I got a water bottle with a fitness club logo. The next booth had stickers for a local pizza restaurant, which I used to cover the logo on the water bottle.

I scored a whole box of granola bars for applying for a credit card. I filled out the computer pad thing with my old address and the name Summer Yung. It was denied of course—insufficient credit history—but I still got the granola bars.

At the end of the row was a mobile phone company. Noticing the logo on the back of the display phones, I stepped closer, which also brought me into the orbit of the sales guy. My age or a little younger, with blond hair, and a name tag reading, "Chaz," he looked exactly like the sort of salesperson a boss would think might connect with college students. "Looking at the new iPhone, huh?"

I tapped the logo. "Oh, not really. My mom had a computer by them when I was a kid."

"Was it one of those all-in-one things where the case was transparent blue or whatever?"

It hadn't been, but I couldn't admit I remembered a beige box from before the sales guy was born. "Yeah, I think so."

He pointed at the phone in front of me. "We've got the iPhone eleven free when you sign up for a two-year contract or the twelve for an extra hundred bucks." He spun the stand back around and rolled into his sales pitch about the features of the phone. Most of it went over my head, but near the end he talked about the web browser app and its built-in virus protection, or some such. He tapped the icon on the screen, and it launched software displaying the phone company's web page. Like double-clicking an icon in Windows, I followed it well enough. The professor for the class I took with Amber had a whole unit about the World Wide Web and how it would eventually connect nearly everything. I guess she was right.

"My bag got stolen with my phone in it, but it was technically my mom's old one, and we're still working it out. Thanks though." I hoped my explanation was vague enough to let him know I wasn't going to sign up right away.

He smiled and reached under the table. "That's cool. Not to-day. Here's a brochure. The prices and my card are on the back for whenever you're ready to replace your old one." I edged away, but he leaned in and spoke more quietly, "Hey, you want a T-shirt?"

"Okay?" I said a little unsure.

"See—the trouble is, I'm at the end of the row and without a giveaway like granola bars most people pass me by. My boss wanted me to"—he did air quotes—"flirt with some pretty students and give away a T-shirt if they act interested." He slid a rolled-up bundle of garish magenta across the table. "You're the first person to talk to me in at least an hour. I'll tell him you looked interested."

There was also a surprising amount of stuff available for free to students if you read the daily paper carefully enough. I never paid much attention when I *was* a student, for lack of time. Some department or another was always having a reception with free food. Once you got over the social awkwardness of eating and leaving, it was no big deal. An electric-car dealership gave away hot dogs on Saturdays, churches had free barbeques—as long as you could ignore a little proselytizing—and on and on. I walked into a sandwich shop because of a wide jar on the counter labeled, "Free." I thought they were tea packets, but up close I discovered they were condoms, the uselessness of which made me laugh a little, despite the situation.

You needed a student ID for the university computers, but the public library had a free workstation. My old address and a believable story about losing my ID got me a temporary library card.

Even with all that it was still hard. It sucked, actually. I slept on a sofa in a hidden basement with no bathroom. I had to sneak upstairs and use the one in the hallway behind the kitchen. I was constantly hungry and constantly looking over my shoulder for the man in the gray suit.

Amber's journal led me to the old gym building at the west edge of campus. All those years later, it remained underused and had no security to keep nonstudents out. I looked the right age to slip in, shower, and slip out every few days. If no one else was around, I even washed and rinsed some clothes.

I spent a lot of time trying to make sense of the computer equipment in the Timeslot room. Once I got through the tangle of cords and picked out the random parts which didn't connect to anything, I discovered *two* systems on the worktable. Separate, but similar.

The larger one had a fat power cable coming in through a grate in the wall by the floor that ended at the broken portal. Some of the connections to that computer had clearly overheated, leaving black scorch marks on the case above the plug. Even to my untrained eye, it looked hopeless.

The smaller computer had cables running up to the little portal overhead, but it had no cover panel on one side. Had it blown off? No, I was being dramatic. I found it in the junk pile, intact. Someone had removed it and never replaced it. Looking inside, I wondered why there were so many wires not plugged into anything.

I researched in the library section about computers. The books were all old, but so was the computer needing repair. I studied photos and diagrams, making sketches to take back.

Eventually I plugged it in. After a series of beeps, the fan whirred and the screen blinked. A Windows error message appeared: "Hard drive failure." That explained the unplugged cables; the hard drive had been removed! I searched every pile, the storage cabinets, and even under the couch cushions. It was nowhere to be found.

*

TIA
August 2045

The outer lock clicked, and the door opened. Amber slipped into the office and dropped into her chair looking exhausted.

"You okay?"

"I haven't slept well in at least a week. I feel like I can't catch up."

"I hate when that happens to me. You tried the over-the-counter stuff I assume?"

She nodded. "And booze, but that only made it worse. I'm considering seeing the doctor if it's not better soon."

*So...*about the same time as the paradox, interesting. Keeping that thought to myself, I asked, "Is it getting the proposals out by Friday?"

"Maybe." She looked thoughtful and added, "We should go celebrate once the job is done. Or... We haven't done movie night in months."

She was right. We hadn't—in either timeline, but it wasn't what I was in the mood for. I wanted to hang out and talk with my friend, not sit and watch a movie together. "Going out sounds nice."

"I'm supposed to have dinner with Kurtis this Saturday. Maybe he wouldn't mind postponing."

"Sure, text him and ask."

I'd already tried to contact Kurtis and got no response, but I couldn't exactly say so.

She nodded and fiddled with her watch, before sitting up, back in business mode—a side of Amber I hadn't seen before the paradox. Except for her chronic tardiness, she did it surprisingly well. She'd gotten us an opportunity to submit multiple research proposals and had a line on publishing our findings in an actual science publication. It was for peripheral work of course, not time travel.

I didn't know Kurtis all that well, but he was smart and cool, even for an old guy. Crystal, I'd never actually met, but I didn't want either of them to die. The not knowing, the unsolved mystery of it, wouldn't leave me alone.

Presumably, Crystal disappeared along with V and Kurtis, except she wasn't in the video with them at the door. Somewhere between dropping Amber off at breakfast and entering TE, she'd disappeared.

Could V have forced Crystal through the portal into her own past? My grim realization in the aftermath of being fired suggested V had done that before, maybe even repeatedly. Had he turned the time portal into a device to make problems disappear? It explained why some of the missing engineers were never found.

And Vanhanen himself? No clues. In the original timeline, he'd stepped out of the view of the security camera and into TE a few minutes before the paradox, but in this one, he'd disappeared like *smoke*.

28

CRYSTAL
June 2022

I'd read a book in school, set in the early twentieth century, about a protagonist who had both African and Caucasian ancestors. Even though she was legally considered Black at the time, she was pale enough to pass as White. That word, "pass," was a huge deal to the characters. *Pass* undetected. *Pass* through White society. *Pass* yourself off as something else.

As a biracial kid with hazel eyes, brown hair, and no real connection to Chinese culture, it resonated with me intensely. My report was more about my own observations as someone who spent her life "passing" than about the plot of the book. I got an A.

In retrospect, the similarities between my own experiences and the protagonist were more superficial than I thought at the time. I'd never seen racism against Asians as bad as Black people in America. I didn't try to hide being Chinese, but it was pretty hard to tell from a quick glance at me.

As a kid, it could have led me to feeling like a misunderstood outsider, but it didn't. My young brain enjoyed having a cool secret, and my overactive imagination enjoyed feeling like some kind of spy. It sounded so silly to write it out later, but it made some other things make sense—or at least gave context.

When I was finally honest with myself about why I didn't feel the same way about the boys in my class as most of my friends did, I thought about that book report again. I'd been pretending, "passing" for so long that I didn't even realize at first. I wondered later if that's why it took me such a long time to come out.

I noticed same-sex couples on campus, on that first day in 2022, far more than in the 90s. They weren't just the punk hair and studded-jacket crowd either. Most looked like regular students. Like me. It made me happy, honestly. If twenty-eight years had that much change, what would 2045 be like for Amber and me?

I also thought a lot about that awful day when she tried to explain time travel and I flipped out and told her to leave. Was the concept of someone else, someone I trusted, having their own secret knowledge a shock to me? *Maybe*, but I thought that was a bit of a stretch. More likely, it was just me. Did my nervousness at my own romantic inexperience make it easier to believe an even crazier story than the simple truth that she wanted to be with me? Did all those things together contribute to my over-the-top reaction that morning? Probably. I desperately hoped to talk through it with her eventually.

Living in 2022, though, I still needed to pass. I needed to slip undetected through a university summer semester while living illegally in a forgotten basement. I'd passed for so long by that point, I was good at it. Put your sunglasses on and act like you belong there.

*

KURTIS
September 1994

I tried fixing light fixtures in the basement hallway of Nuke-E periodically for a few days, but no one came or went from TE. Charles said there was a dormant cycle in the 1990s. Had I inadvertently caused it by leading Vanhanen to the Timeslot room, and the fight and chase that ensued?

I was supposed to be heading back to my home time, not trapped in the past and locked out of TE. Lacking a key card, I was stuck. Once I got past the immediacy of finding a place to stay other than Crystal's house, this realization hit home like a kick in the head. Every night, all the varied and random elements of my former life ran through my mind while trying to sleep. Simple things like the bicycle I left on the rack behind Nuclear Engineering, all the way up to the family I might never see again, and everything in between.

My relationship with my parents had been awkward since my accelerated path through school began, but I was always close with my sister. Kayla latched onto the violin at a young age and was great by high school, amazing by college. My own full-ride scholarship let my parents put all the money they'd saved for education toward her tuition at the elite private music school she'd always dreamed of attending. There, she got even better. It gutted me that I might never see her again, might never get to hear her play another note.

These thoughts kept me awake and led me to the questionable

decision of alcohol before bed. This didn't work out as I'd hoped. I found myself intoxicated, standing unsteadily in the basement hallway at the door to TE. I had no way of knowing how long I stood there or how late it was. Eventually, footsteps sounded behind me, but I couldn't tear my eyes away from the hated door and its hated lock. It wasn't until the security guard cleared his throat that I looked toward him. In a voice which was gentler than I expected, he said simply "Excuse me sir…you shouldn't be here."

Replying, "No. No, I shouldn't," I turned and walked away from Temporal Engineering.

Sobering up on the trek back to my tiny basement apartment, I came to a realization. I could either mark time until my cash ran out, or I could do something, so, I did something.

It took numerous calls and interactions with a kind of shady character I never would have dreamt of associating with in the past, but I finally created a new identity for myself. I became Kurtis Blake, a name TE had no record of, past or future. I'd never actually liked the name Kasey all that much, but it had worked well enough. The new identity also took most of my available cash.

I got an intern job at a local electrical engineer's office, while I "finished my degree." I was overqualified, but a false identity including a university degree cost more than I could afford. Borrowing the idea from Charles, I "transferred" from a college in another state. It was far easier to pull off.

In my original timeline, I finished high school and college early, so even after working at TE for a couple years, I still looked the right age. I could endure one more semester of classes, but I had to remember not to do anything so advanced it revealed my future knowledge.

One of the engineers at my office even talked me through how to improve the heat in my apartment. Despite the size, I decided to stay there for a while. It was cheap and it let me save money. Future knowledge should help once I had enough saved to start making some shrewd investments.

*

CRYSTAL
July 2022

Amber hadn't found me yet, and it left me worried. What could have been keeping her away? Had she run into Mr. V and been fired? Or worse? All this thinking about her made me feel my isolation more strongly. I missed Amber constantly, but beyond that, I craved something familiar. Something normal. I considered walking by my house but thought it would probably only depress me. Right at that moment, it was the last thing I needed. Instead, I wandered into the music building. A few steps inside, I faintly heard an orchestral piece I recognized. I followed the music to the auditorium and listened to a rehearsal, sounding the same as it had last semester, twenty-eight years ago. I slid down the wall to sit on the floor in the hallway. Eyes closed, my mind drifted to how it was probably the same a century earlier when it was new and would still play the exactly like that two or three or a hundred centuries down the line. The timelessness of the music transcended my own troubles.

Mom used to complain that I got moody when I hadn't eaten enough. Was that my problem? I'd been rationing my food, but my cash was running lower and lower. I decided to get dinner at the homeless shelter like the vaccination nurse suggested. The food was okay. In fact, it reminded me a lot of my middle school cafeteria. A creepy older dude with a tangled beard at the next table wouldn't stop staring at me though. I ate fast, stuffed some rolls in my pocket, asked a staffer to stop the guy if he tried to follow me, and snuck out the back.

I took a shortcut toward the student union through a neighborhood I didn't know well. In a little strip mall, among a cluster of dark windows, a pawn shop still had its lights on. With only a few bucks to my name, I was going to pass it by. I didn't need to look at things I couldn't afford. My hand, pressed against on the window, still wore the three silver rings I had when I jumped. The one on my thumb was a Christmas present from Mom, so there was no way I'd ever consider selling it. The other two I'd bought from a place at the mall and didn't have the same sentimental attachment. Inside, I found a jewelry case with similar rings for around forty dollars. According to the sign explaining store policies, selling mine to the shop would get me maybe five bucks.

Disappointed, I turned to leave when a display of musical instruments caught my attention, mostly electric guitars with a few others mixed in but no violas. In a far top corner hung a mandolin, a four-string, rather than the usual eight. I'd seen one played a few times. Smaller than a guitar, bigger than a ukulele, this one was finished in an odd shade of green, like appliances in the 70s. The woman behind the counter, presumably the owner, saw me and I gestured toward it. "Can I?" I asked. She nodded.

As I gently plucked a couple of strings, soft notes sounded in the quiet space. It was horribly out of tune, but the instrument was solid and the tone was good. That feeling, my fingers on the strings, felt so...normal amid the weird turn my life had taken, so good. I'd missed it so much!

A minute of plucking confirmed something I half remembered. Mandolin tuning matched the violin, but nothing else is tuned like a viola, so what did I expect? Mom tried to teach me guitar at one point, but it wasn't tuned like that either. I hadn't played a violin since I was a kid, so remembering the tunings took some concentration. I sat on a tall stool and set my backpack on the floor beside me.

Someone had previously tried to tune it like a ukelele and botched the job. On my lap, I went through all the strings and adjusted them one by one. Without an electronic tuner or even a pitch pipe, I had to guess, but it sounded better than before. Out of habit, I ran through some practice exercises from my viola. Even plucking rather than bowing, it still felt great holding an instrument and making music.

I transitioned into a piece I knew well, one which I thought might work plucked. When I finished, I heard clapping. I looked up, surprised to see the owner and some customers standing around watching me. It was embarrassing to get caught doing something for personal enjoyment like that. Part of me wanted to slink out of there, but I thanked them politely and hung it back on the wall. The price tag said, "Kermit the Mandolin, $100." It might as well have said a million.

I sighed and picked up my bag, only to run into the woman from behind the counter, middle-aged, with gray hair in a ponytail. "That thing's been hanging there for years, and you're the first person to even look at it, let alone play it. I dust it every month, but that's all the attention it ever gets." She scratched the back of her head as if unsure how to continue. "You ever play one of those before? You sounded good."

"No. It was my first time."

"No shit? You some kind of prodigy or something?"

"Huh? No. I used to study music at the university, and I played the violin when I was a kid. It's tuned the same."

"Used to?"

"Uh...it's complicated."

"Ain't it always?"

"Yeah. I guess so. Well, thanks." I gestured toward the mandolin. "Y'know."

"Hey, hold up."

"Hm?" I half turned back.

"You probably didn't notice, but I made two sales while you were playing."

I shrugged. "Ok..."

"Come back tomorrow and play some more. We can talk about the price on the mandolin."

So, I did.

I returned to the pawn shop every evening for the next two weeks and played for an hour during their after-work busy period. The owner said she'd sell me the mandolin for half price. I didn't have the heart to tell her there was no way I could afford even that.

But I played anyway. It gave me something to do—playing music, which I loved, and learning a new instrument, which was cool. I read up on technique at the library, and I started to improve.

My mind wandered while I played, and I came to a realization, probably overdue. Amber must not have known what point in time I got thrown to, or she would've come looking for me already. It'd been a little over three weeks and still no sign. I needed to do something toward finding my own way back, but I didn't know what. Walking toward the student union, I had an idea.

The night I spent in 2045, Amber and I walked to Kurtis's house. I remembered the way well enough to get close. From there I'd have to go by my memory of the house, gray brick with stone at the corners. I sighed. Not right then, it was getting too dark.

29

TIA
August 2045

My tablet beeped with a new text.

Amber: I still can't get in touch with Kurtis.

Tia: How long?

Amber: I've been trying for a week, but it was at least a week since I talked to him before that.

Tia: Want a ride?

Amber: How'd you know?

Tia: 'Cause I know you. Give me fifteen.

Amber: *Thanks!*

No convertible in the driveway, so Amber looked through the window of the garage and shook her head. "Empty."

I used the ramp to his back door, left from his wife's illness. Amber reached past me at the top and pressed her thumb on a security pad. Pushing the door open, she called, "Kurtis? Hey! It's Amber and Tia. You home? Kurtis?" Her footsteps headed up the stairs.

I opened the refrigerator. It didn't look like someone leaving for a vacation. I saw fruit, eggs, leftover containers, all the usual things in any fridge; even a tiny carton of cream for Amber's coffee. It was unopened and the expiration date was more than a week away.

His tablet lay on the counter, folded and off. Opening it, I found a local news article from three weeks past, the day before the paradox.

Hidden under the tablet, I discovered a piece of paper, face-down. I'd only read, "Part of me remembers being Kasey…" when Amber's sneakers sounded in the hallway, and I slipped it under my leg. On the other side of the counter, she pulled out a barstool and sat. I spun the tablet around, tapping the date.

She squinted. "I don't think he went on vacation."

"No. Me either."

"Because of the tablet?"

I pointed over my shoulder. "Groceries in the fridge."

"Oh, shit. Thanks. I didn't even think of that. I found a full laundry basket, and an empty suitcase in the closet." After a quiet moment, she added, "I'm getting worried."

"Yeah. Me too."

While I drove, Amber called to report him as a missing person.

*

CRYSTAL
July 2022

The library computer provided me with Kurtis's address, a map, and a view from the street. Definitely the same house, and so much better than wandering around in the dark. I finally *was* learning to appreciate twenty-first century technology.

The walk toward Kurtis's house had taken longer than I remembered. It was a Saturday, so a car in the driveway seemed like a good sign. The man who answered the door was Kurtis, but he was far younger than I'd last seen him and far older than the time before that. This Kurtis was maybe in his fifties. I'd met him three times, but they were all out of order and only a few days apart for me, years for him though. Would he remember? If he did, I'd look exactly the same, even down to my clothes. Amber's summary of change perpetuation said probably not.

"Hi. I'm Summer. This may sound weird, but I'm looking for Kasey Browne. Are you him?" I knew he was, but I wasn't sure how else to start the conversation. Looking startled, he stepped outside and pulled the door shut behind him.

In a low but intense voice, he asked, "How do you know that name?"

Where to even start? "I'm here because of Charles Yung. I..."

He cut me off with a waved hand. "No that's not possible." He rubbed his forehead and leaned back on the handrail. "Except it is, isn't it? Charles died a very long time ago and Kasey disappeared soon after...but maybe not for you."

"Look, I know Kasey was Charles's friend." I paused and he gave a small nod. This next part was a gamble. "I met him once, in...uh, in the basement of the student union." His eyes snapped to mine. "He helped my friend and me escape."

He squinted and asked, "You're with TE?"

"It's complicated."

"Isn't it always…" He lowered his voice. "With time travel?" I nodded, but he continued before I could reply. "You said 'escape,' so that makes me wonder who or what. If you and your friend were out of time, you'd have said 'return' or possibly 'jump,' which leads me toward a question of who you escaped from. At this point, you don't need to say more. I know exactly who."

"Yeah," I said quietly.

"And since your friend isn't standing here on my front steps with you, it makes me wonder if your friend is stuck out of time, or more likely, if you are. And furthermore, given the who, you can't simply march into TE and request a jump."

I was taken aback at the speed and accuracy with which he grasped the situation. Amber said he was smart but may have undersold him. "That's about the size of it, yes."

"Well, unfortunately, I don't have a key to TE right here in my pocket. If I did, I'd have used it long ago. He glanced toward the door. "Much to my own loss that would have been."

Was he going to help me or not? Maybe he couldn't help even if he wanted to. His gaze alternated between me and the door a couple of times, deliberating. After a long exhale, he continued, "It's not like I have all the answers hidden away in a floor safe in my closet."

Footsteps in the entryway caught his attention, and he half turned. A woman opened the door and poked her head out. She had vibrantly red hair, brown eyes and freckles. Twenty years younger and she could have been Amber's sister. Shocked and glad I didn't need to speak, Kurtis explained, "This is Summer, she's here from the engineering department at the university. We're almost done."

"Okay. Don't be too long. Reservations are at 6:00 p.m." She disappeared and closed the door, but not before I caught "Why don't they just come to the office?"

Kurtis smirked, which told me heard it too. "We're going out for dinner for our anniversary tonight. I need to get changed."

I headed back down the stairs. This hadn't helped at all. "Well, thanks anyway."

"Hey, did you ever jump somewhere just for fun? I once had to jump to the seventies, so I picked the date *Star Wars* opened. I got to see it on opening night, even though I couldn't ever tell anyone."

"No." I said softly. "We never got to do anything like that."

As I got to the bottom of the steps, he said, "I hope you find your friend."

I walked away, headed vaguely to the pawn shop, feeling like I wasted my time and replaying the conversation in my head. Why had he mentioned *Star Wars*? How odd. And the comment about a safe?

I stopped dead in my tracks.

Oh, you clever old man!

A block or so down the street, excited yells of, "Push me!" sounded across the wide green lawn of a neighborhood park. A teen girl stood behind two kids on swings, pushing with one hand and holding her phone with the other. I psyched myself up and walked over to the babysitter.

"I, uh... I lost my phone. Can I borrow yours for a second? Promise, I won't steal it."

She shrugged and handed it to me. It felt so thin and small I worried I might drop it. I tapped the same web browser symbol the phone salesman used and typed "*Star Wars* opening date" at the search bar. I got a bunch of stuff about TV shows, sequels and an amusement park. Backing up, I added the word, "original." Bingo! In huge text, the search revealed "May 25, 1977." I carefully handed the phone back and thanked her.

"I thought you needed to make a call. Whatever." She rolled her eyes and returned to pushing the kids. Was I that dismissive as a teenager? Probably.

On the whole short walk from the park back to Kurtis's house, I debated whether I wanted to do this. Except for copyright infringement and underage drinking, I'd never really broken the law. Okay, that wasn't true. I got a speeding ticket one time, and it freaked me out. Mom didn't even blink, telling me not to pay it late or they'd tack on an extra fee.

The house in sight, I slowed my pace until I could see the empty driveway. I didn't even try the front door but headed straight to the back where a side entry to the detached garage was unlocked. The spare key on a nail, even hidden behind a ladder, only took a few minutes to find.

In the house, I stayed back from the windows, concerned about spying neighbors. The upstairs bedroom had two closets, but neither had a floor safe. I even checked the linen closet outside the bathroom, not there either. Frustrated, I headed back down but found a little office near the front I'd missed before.

Moving a box of rolled drawings revealed a keypad with buttons arranged like a phone. I typed 5-2-5-7-7, triumphantly expecting it to pop open...but it didn't. I felt a surge of stress tighten my stomach and tried not to panic. Thinking for a moment, I tried 0-5-2-5-7-7. It clicked and a little light turned green.

The safe held a folder with passports and another marked Will. Setting these aside, I found a book, worn on the corners and no title on the spine. Inside was a handwritten journal dating back to the 1960s. Flipped open, I read about installing the Timeslot in

1980. Oh my god, he really was Kasey! Was that what he meant about finding what I needed?

Beneath the rest, sat a gray metal box. It had plugs along one edge and a sticker on top with the brand name and data capacity. The missing hard drive!

My hand on the back door, I paused, looking over my shoulder into the kitchen where the refrigerator hummed quietly. What would it hurt? Opening it, I saw more food than I'd had in weeks. Tempting as it was, I didn't want to abuse his generosity by filling my backpack. Considering the way he'd lied to his wife about me, I doubted she knew about Temporal Engineering. I didn't want to put him in an awkward spot by stealing their food. In the end, I grabbed three apples out of the fridge, some canned soup, and a few other random things from the backs of cupboards where I hoped they wouldn't be noticed.

I ate an apple while walking to the pawn shop. I couldn't wait to plug in the hard drive and read the journal, but I had to play first.

*

KURTIS
July 2045

Some distant part of me remembers being Kasey, and an even more distant part remembers Kiernen. I've been Kurtis longer than the other two combined.

When I first landed in this timeline, my end of the line seemed impossibly far away. Too far to imagine, let alone worry about. Not so, now.

When Amber laid a photo of my initials on the table between our glasses of wine, I knew things had come back around. When she asked for help with the Timeslot, that solidified it.

Helping Amber meant the possibility of getting off this particular train before it was too late. I'd resigned myself to my fate years ago, determined to live the best life possible, despite knowing when it would end.

But now...perhaps there was another way out.

*

TIA
August 2045

In the quiet of my car, I smoothed Kurtis's letter across my knee. Not only was he former TE, but he was out of time and had been for years. I felt surprised, and a little dumb that I hadn't put that together sooner. The letter implied he'd been unable to return to his home time. It was written the day before the paradox. Had he known what he was heading toward? Maybe he suspected? I wished he'd included more in the note.

That brought me back to the mystery of Crystal. An hour had passed between dropping Amber at breakfast and Kurtis and Vanhanen entering TE. Where had she gone? Did the paradox simply zip her out of existence? I hoped not. If she was out of time when it happened, would she be like me—stuck with two sets of memories? What if she wasn't here when the paradox happened?

On a hunch, I powered the van back up and headed toward the student union. The Timeslot room door clicked shut behind me as I hit the light switch and gasped at the mess. It hadn't looked like that the last time I was there, but no—that was in the other timeline. I made my way around the room as best I could among the clutter. The portal still had a chunk of wood missing along the top from the bullet, but it had additional damage too. A loop of wires hung loose from one side, looking scorched and burned.

The worktable overflowed with computer parts. On the floor below, I found a key card and a dark wood cane. Was it the one Kurtis had loaned Amber? Was it her missing key card? I wished I knew.

It appeared as if the room held evidence of *both* timelines. From one timeline was the portal Amber built to visit 1994 and rescue Crystal, albeit now broken and unusable. From the other timeline, in which she never went skiing or hurt her knee, the mess of computer parts still covered the worktable.

When Amber texted me, she didn't say the portal had been ruined. Was that part of the "too much to type" she'd referenced? She didn't mention the torn wiring at breakfast either.

Or...was the damage to the portal connected to Crystal's disappearance and the missing hour?

I desperately wished I could ask Amber what had happened. For that matter, I wished she could remember all of the previous eight months like I did. Even a time machine didn't help me fix this or get my Amber back. I could try to tell her and hope for the best, but I didn't want to risk further alterations to the timeline. If time travel sci-fi had taught me one thing, it was that even trying to make things better, I could end up making them far worse.

30

CRYSTAL
July 2022

The hard drive plugged in, and the computer booted right up, but it rattled annoyingly. Maybe a screw was missing? Twenty-first century computers usually required a login and password. Surprisingly, this one didn't. I double-clicked the only icon on the desktop, Timeslot Control. A dialog box appeared with choices: isolated mail scan, schedule scans, send to specific date, send to relative coordinates, and diagnostic.

Diagnostic sounded like a good place to start. A message popped up, "Timeslot is currently offline. Do you wish to initialize?" I clicked Yes. A low hum sounded above me, and another message appeared: It has been 28 years, 3 months, 17 days since your last diagnostic. This may take a few minutes. Continue? Again, I clicked Yes. There was no change to the screen except the word "processing" appeared at the bottom edge of the dialog box.

"Huh," I said to the empty room and computer with the rattling drive.

Kurtis's original name had been Kiernen, and he'd jumped to the 1960s from the 2060s. Wow! I had a hard enough time imagining twenty-eight years of change. What would a century be like? It wasn't lost on me that this was the third time I was sitting on a sofa paging through someone else's diary. I read until the computer beeped that the diagnostic completed and reported finding no issues.

I shut it down but felt I should keep reading. Kurtis said what I needed to know was in the journal and on the drive. I made tea, returned to the sofa, and read to the end. Folded inside the back cover I found a piece of paper covered with intricate calculations.

Unable to determine their purpose, I sat back and wondered what Amber would do in that situation? She'd think her way out of that shit, that's what. If something bugged her, she'd poke at it until she figured it out. My immediate problem, though, was that I couldn't keep my eyes open any longer.

Papers back in the book, I curled up on the couch. Ambering my way back to the future could wait until morning.

*

KURTIS
August 1995

By the time I'd lived as Kurtis for most of a year, I finished (or retook, depending on one's perspective) my last semester and got my engineering degree. The company I worked for part-time offered me a full-time job. I took it, of course.

As expected, staying in the basement apartment allowed me

to save up. I bought a used soft-top 4x4 and made plans to move out the next month. Despite the work on the furnace, the winter was still cold. It remained a basement, after all.

The best part of the last year was when I discovered a way to treat the temporal displacement headaches—acupuncture. I'd never tried it before, even though it had been far more accepted in my home time than in the 90s. I found an ad for a local clinic saying they treated migraines. I tried it and was pleasantly surprised at the results. While not gone, the constant headaches were greatly reduced. My acupuncturist said my treatment varied from most migraine sufferers, but I told her from the outset my regular doctor couldn't quite figure it out either. Not exactly true, but close enough.

*

CRYSTAL
July 2022

Immediately upon waking, I knew where I'd seen calculations like Kurtis's before. Frantically digging through my bag, I repeated, "Please tell me I saved that. Please tell me I saved that!" Tucked into Dad's journal behind the photo were the loose pages from the bottom of the dresser. I held them up next to Kurtis's: different numbers, but the same formula. I was finally getting somewhere!

I spent most of the morning trying to decipher those calculations. I had always gotten good grades in math, but this eluded and frustrated me.

The university library felt comforting in its sameness. It had been my babysitter for years. I crossed through an open space in the center of the lobby where the card catalog cabinets used to stand, but otherwise it looked much like I remembered. Not being a student, I couldn't check anything out, but I could browse all I wanted.

I pulled several math books from the shelf, hoping the formula didn't require calculus. I'd hated that class. With those first few books, I struck out, but I kept looking, sitting in the aisle on a black, movable stool. I eventually found part of the formula in a book titled, *Arithmetic for Physics*. I copied the relevant info. I'd been hunting for hours and decided I'd had enough math for the afternoon.

Walking into the pawn shop, I almost tripped over a girl with pink hair in a pixie cut hanging a flyer on a bulletin board right inside the door.

"Oh. 'Scuze me, sorry."

"No problem."

I read over her shoulder. "Open Mic Night. New performer every fifteen minutes. Thursdays from 9:00 p.m. to midnight. No cover." It was at a bar northwest of campus, near the College of Design. It'd had a different name in the 90s, but I'd been there a few times.

"Open mic, huh?"

She turned and smiled. "You should come. Summertime's kinda slow on weeknights, so we're starting it back up through August." She thanked the owner on the way out the door. I got the mandolin, took my customary seat on the tall stool, and started to play.

Once again, I lost myself in the music. I warmed up and played for an hour, not thinking about the hard drive, or anything other than my fingers on the strings. Even thoughts of Amber, while never completely gone, retreated from the forefront to willingly take a back seat to the music. For a little while, I could step away from the drama of my situation and simply enjoy playing.

The owner clicked off the sign. I stood and she waved me back down. "Tonight was supposed to be your last night, wasn't it?" I nodded, and she looked thoughtful for a few seconds, leaning on a display case. "I don't know how to say this other than to just ask it. In all the times you've been here, you've worn maybe three different shirts, that's it. You're homeless, or near enough, aren't you?"

Seeing no chance of successfully lying and no real benefit in doing so, I was as honest as I could be. "Near enough, yeah."

"And you kept coming back here and playing, even though there was no chance you'd ever have the money. Why?"

I shrugged, feeling uncomfortably scrutinized. "I liked playing. It was something to do just for fun, instead of worrying about food or whatever."

Pointing to the sign the pink-haired girl left, she said, "If you play at that you'll make a few bucks in tips, and that'll mean couple days of food, won't it?"

I shrugged again. "Yeah, probably."

She walked over, grabbed the price tag, and pulled it off. "Then take it and go. Maybe come back and play sometime, or pay me the fifty once you make it big."

I stared in open-mouthed shock at her unexpected act of kindness, finally stammering out, "Are...are you serious?"

"Yeah. Sure, kid."

I couldn't stop myself. I jumped off the stool and hugged her, thanking her profusely. This seemed to surprise her, and she hugged me back stiffly and awkwardly. "C'mon. I need to close up."

I zipped the mandolin into its case and, holding it tight to my chest, thanked her one more time before heading back to the Timeslot room.

31

KURTIS
October 1997

So much has happened since I last wrote in this journal. I've been here for over three years and managed to make a life for myself. Moving out of the basement apartment felt like leaving behind the last of an old situation. From there I tried to look forward. I got into bicycling, I discovered home-brewed beer, and I joined a book club. I still think vaguely sometimes about returning to the 2060s, but if I can't, I can be satisfied that I didn't spend my time here just sitting around.

I passed the Principles and Practice of Engineering exam, which subsequently got me a promotion and a raise. That, along with the money I saved living in the basement apartment, channeled into investments in tech companies I knew would do well, since they were still around in my original timeline.

Even after only a year, I had enough for a down payment on a house—gray brick with stone at the corners, a sizeable dormer bedroom upstairs, and a timbered gable on the front. I close next week. It's not large, but I don't need it to be.

In the evenings, if I felt introspective, I had to admit that even if TE was open and running, I wasn't sure how I'd get back. After everything, it was highly unlikely I could walk in there and ask for a jump, especially one so far forward. Beyond that, in the 2060s I remembered, there was no sign of V; the directors were middle-aged women. I didn't want to jump back, only to have him chase me and subsequently endanger the rest of the staff. No, I had to either sneak through or sit tight.

*

CRYSTAL
July 2022

As noon approached, I walked off campus to a patio area between restaurants, the same place Amber and I had eaten kabobs on our date. Perched on the edge of a planter, I took out the mandolin and played. I'd never done this before, but I was pretty sure trying this on campus would get me kicked out. I left the case open on the ground next to me, its message universal.

I ran through my warmup exercises and the classical pieces I'd played at the shop, but they felt out of place in a public courtyard on a sunny day. I switched to a classic rock song I remembered my mom playing. A couple smiled as they walked by, recognizing it. One even came back and threw a handful of change in the case. I thanked him but never stopped playing. He wasn't the last.

I'd earned money! Like, actual cash I didn't bring with me from 1994. Which was good because that'd run out, and my stockpile of ramen was almost gone.

The only reason I managed as long as I had was because of Amber. When I tried on her jeans, they fit well enough in the waist and hips but were laughably short. I cuffed them almost to my knees, thinking they could work as capris. One of the pockets felt bunched; straightening it, I found three twenty-dollar bills. They were from the 90s, but they bought groceries just fine.

Food, math, music, and repeat. That was my life for a while. Eat so I could concentrate on math. Practice music so I could play for the money to eat.

It resulted in hours of playing every day and getting up to speed on the mandolin far more quickly than if I did things like working and going to class.

I missed my radio show though. Kasey's antenna extension lay under the pile of computer junk, which I'd reconnected, but the little radio still only picked up the campus station. The first song to emerge from the static had been a banger, though, with a chorus about someone's weight in gold, and a verse that managed to include the word "rapacity." I wished I could have heard the whole thing or had a way to play it back.

Given the number of Chili Peppers and AC/DC T-shirts walking around on campus, 90s music hadn't gone extinct. Good, because I remembered them well enough to play, unlike the new stuff from the radio.

After going through what felt like a hundred math books, I found the rest of the formula in a calculus text. I groaned. It was a step toward deciphering, but it was going to be harder than I'd hoped for. I still needed to figure out the big numbers in the formula variables.

Kurtis's page of calculations were probably the ones he wrote in 1992 for '94 but didn't use until he was trying to escape V in

1969. The paper had a motel logo in the upper corner. The '92 to '69 jump must have been discarded after it was used.

My dad's was harder to account for. Was it his jump from 2018 to 1967? If so, why run the calcs on paper? Why not have the computer do it?

Unless... Oh, shit, unless... Was he was trying to leave as little trail as possible? He'd deleted Theresa's jump from the computer after she was away but couldn't delete his own. Maybe there was more of a record when the computer did the number crunching instead of entering raw coordinates?

The big number on Charles's page was larger than Kurtis's. Why? Longer jump? I scoured the backs and margins of the pages until I found a quick calculation with 365.25 in it. Were all the numbers a quantity of *days*, not months or years? Did they calculate time jumps based on a benchmark date, measuring forward from that point? That'd be strange, wouldn't it?

On my pocket calculator, I divided by 365.25, and roughly subtracted to get to a date in the 1940s. The other one was surprisingly close. I ran both again, more specifically, taking into consideration how far into '68 and '94 they were aiming for, based on dates of the journal entries. This was much closer, only off by a few days. The benchmark was about one hundred twenty days from the end of 1943. I was finally getting somewhere!

I played some celebratory chords on the mandolin. Time to switch gears. I'd been prepping fifteen minutes of solid material and nearly had it. The order was as important as a mixtape: a vintage rock tune, a familiar classical piece, two 90s songs, or maybe put one of the 90s pieces first. Plus, I wanted to have at least one extra—just in case.

*

KURTIS
April 2003

A year and a half ago I opened my own engineering office. Initially the office was a spare bedroom in my house. Small jobs led to bigger jobs.

Un-mysteriously, my stock market portfolio always did well above average. This meant I wasn't relying on the engineering practice as my only source of income. It made it easier for me than for many who go out on their own. It also meant I could afford to take a couple jobs I knew wouldn't be profitable, because I thought it would lead to projects that were.

Once it picked up enough momentum, I hired an engineer right out of college who'd worked for my old firm two summers before. We tripped over each other in my spare bedroom for six months before we moved everything into a small office nearby.

So why write again after so many years? Yesterday, we finally landed the big fish. A new research facility at the university with a ton of equipment that meant work for us for at least two years, plus needing to hire a couple more staff.

I also realized I'd been so busy with the firm, I hadn't even thought about TE in over a year. My future knowledge for investing, sure, but not the actual department or Vanhanen himself. I'd known for years I couldn't jump back, but *not* looking for him over my shoulder crept up on me so slowly, I hadn't even noticed.

32

CRYSTAL
July 2022

I followed a vague line of people into the Hip Joint, under a sign with a dancing cartoon skeleton, mentally bracing myself for the stink of cigarettes and what it sometimes did to my headaches. I'd been planning on sneaking into the old gym the next morning to shower the smell out of my hair, until I passed a prominent "No Smoking" sign on the door. Skeptical they could possibly enforce that, I inhaled deeply. Holy shit! The place smelled like crowds and old beer, but not tobacco. The future was looking better and better.

Pink-pixie-hair stood behind the bar. I asked where performers signed up and she pointed me to a line at the back. A bearded guy in a black "Staff" T-shirt barely looked up from his clipboard when he asked what my act was.

"I play the mandolin. It's kind of a mix of classic rock and nineties..."

He cut me off, "Name?"

"Uh...Summer. Summer Yung."

He tore a slip of paper from his pad and handed it to me. "Here y'are, 11:30 to 11:45 p.m. Be ready a few minutes early." He gestured to the next person in line to step forward, and I got out of the way. Eleven thirty? What the hell was I supposed to do for three hours?

The place had begun to fill up, so I took the last empty chair at one end of the bar. I asked the bartender for water and took a sip. On the next stool sat a muscular, dark-haired guy with tattooed arms, a Batman T-shirt and a guitar case by his feet. Maybe that wasn't the best choice of place to sit...

He half turned toward me and I thought, *Here comes the cheesy pickup line.*

"Wow, that's a...very small guitar." Okay, not what I was expecting.

"It's a mandolin, actually."

"No shit? Can I see it?" I shrugged and unzipped the case. He looked in but didn't reach for it. "Cool. You pick that color?"

I laughed a little. "Uh, no. I wonder why anyone would pick that color. But, hey, the price was right."

He laughed a little and sipped his beer. "This your first open mic?"

"Yeah, they stuck me almost at the end. Makes you wonder who the last guy pissed off."

He laughed again, fuller, saying with a smile, "Yeah. That'd be me."

"Oh shit! Sorry."

"Nah. 'S okay. I always ask for the last slot. It lets me think of the rest a ya as my opening acts."

He lifted his beer and drained what was left. The tattoos on his arm were mostly Aztec imagery—that round calendar thing. I took a sip of my water. He looked at it and asked, "Here, let me get you a beer or something."

And...there it was.

"That's okay."

"You sure?"

I was saying too much too fast, but I couldn't stop. "Look, I know it's only a beer, but there's this social construct where if I let you buy one, I'm either interested in more than drinks, or else I'm leading you on so you'll pay. I'm not either of those. I...I have a girlfriend."

He stared at me for a second with an odd expression, probably trying to catch up on what I'd said. He laughed and slapped the bar between us. "Well, shit! Joke's on me! Girlfriend, huh? She gonna come watch you play?"

I'd worked out a story in case I needed it. "Unfortunately, no, she's studying in London for the summer."

"She's hot?"

"Uh, yeah, smart, athletic, with red hair..."

He interrupted, "Redhead? Oh, you gonna have your hands full you ever piss her off."

I couldn't help but grin. Something caught his attention over by the door. He called to the pink-haired bartender and gestured toward me, "Hey Jess, can you get her a drink? I'll be right back." He made his way through the crowd to a couple who'd just come in. He swept the woman into an enthusiastic hug and gave the guy a fist bump over her shoulder at the same time. "I haven't seen you guys since forever!" I couldn't hear their responses over the crowd.

Jess made her way over, wiping the bar. "What'll ya have?"

"Oh, I don't know," I said stalling.

She pointed to the empty seat. "Don't worry about Marco. I've known him a couple of years. He's okay. You know why he takes the last slot? So he can walk anybody to their car if they need it. The guy's a high school math teacher. If he's buying, it's just a drink."

"Oh, okay. Do you have a stout on tap?"

"We do—or in a bottle."

"Draft please."

She nodded and stepped away, right as the first performer took the stage. That first sip of the darkest of dark Irish beers...oh, dude. I closed my eyes and relished it. Kit asked me once about my affinity for that particular brand, and I'd needed a moment to think. How to describe something so abstract? The closest explanation I could find had been, "It's aggressively comforting."

That pint was my first alcohol since the night Kit and I talked about Kurt Cobain, and it went to my head fast. I alternated sips with water and turned to watch the performer, a jazz saxophonist, who was quite good. He was followed by a comedian who wasn't, and two girls with ukuleles. Not together. Two separate acts one after the other. Had ukuleles become, like, a thing in the years I jumped over?

The couple Marco knew came on about halfway through the night. The husband sat and played guitar quietly, but rapidly gained momentum. His head of shaggy dark hair nodded over a long cool improv piece. His wife joined him when it morphed into a Led Zeppelin song, and finally into "Somebody to Love" by Jefferson Airplane. To do justice to those vocals took an impressive singer, but she pulled it off.

And after a few more, it was my turn. As I stood, Marco whispered, "Break a leg."

"Thanks."

On the stage and seated, warm under the lights, I said, "Hi. I'm Summer." I launched into "Losing my Religion." I'd debated which song to start with, but ultimately chose REM since the mandolin part was so recognizable.

Going on so late meant the audience had had a lot to drink, and they were easy to please. A group of tipsy friends near the front tried to sing along. By the second song, "House of the Rising Sun," other people began singing, too, like a big campfire moment in a movie. Before I knew it, I'd run through my set. The man at the back gestured to keep going. I glanced at the clock and had a minute or two left. Radio instincts for avoiding dead air kicked in, and I idly strummed some chords that shifted into a plucked version of a short viola piece I knew well. I upped the tempo to make sure it fit.

A petite brunette hovered by one corner of the stage. She held up a camera and shrugged, pointing between me and it. I nodded but continued playing. She knelt and took a few shots, using only the stage lighting, no flash. The piece ended and the audience applauded, like, a lot. The photographer mouthed, "Thank you," and I nodded again, smiling. I thanked the audience and stepped down, high-fiving Marco on his way up.

He opened with a Cure song, "The Blood" with its signature flamenco guitar. He played a mix of classic rock and newer stuff, too, but his thing was speed, and the audience responded enthusiastically. When Jess brought me some more water, I leaned in, gesturing toward the stage. "He's really good!" She simply smiled and nodded in response.

A few minutes before midnight, he held up one hand up to shade his eyes and looked for the man at the back. "We got time for one more? Okay, good." He shifted his gaze over to my end of the bar. "Hey, girlfriend! You still out there?" Not sure where this was going, I waved. He played some chords, which I recognized from "Can't Find My Way Home." It had been one of Mom's favorites. "You know the words to this one? Come on up and sing with me." I felt Jess's gentle hand on my back, giving me a shove toward the stage. At that point, how could I refuse?

I don't sing often. I'm too unsure of my own ability. Walking to the stage, I told myself it would be like karaoke. I'd done that before. He looped through the intro again while I got the mic, just in time to start the first verse. I couldn't hear whether people sang along, but the drunk friends in the front laughed loudly at the line about being wasted. We finished the last chorus to wild applause. Marco bowed with a flourish and got me to do the same.

While I zipped up my case, Jess leaned across the bar, holding out a folded handful of cash. "Here. Your share of the tips." I'd almost forgotten.

"Thanks." I'd count it later, but I knew I saw a five in there. Case on my shoulder, I turned and bumped into Marco.

"Hey, thanks for being a good sport! That was really fun."

"Yeah. Yeah, it was. Thanks for asking."

"I hope you come back next week." Behind him at the bar, Jess's pink head nodded agreement.

"Sure, yeah. Okay."

In the crowd moving out the door, I walked right behind the photographer, holding the hand of a taller girl with dyed hair. Seeing that, I realized, beyond just how much I missed Amber, that I'd had more human interaction that night than in several weeks. Despite being pretty much an introvert by nature, it felt refreshing to be around people again. Heading toward the student union, still humming the tune by Blind Faith, a memory stopped me in my tracks. Marco taught math! Could he help in my ongoing struggle with the time coordinate formula? Maybe?

You betcha I was going back the next week.

*

AMBER
September 2045

My watch beeped from the edge of the sink. I was nearly done showering, simply enjoying the warm water. I got out, then wrapped in a towel, I read the text.

> **TIA**: *"Meet me at the union by the zodiac. I'll bring break-fast; you bring coffee."*

Peculiar, but after exerting so much mental energy to send proposals the previous Friday, we deserved a break.

I found Tia waiting in the atrium when I walked in carrying two big travel mugs. She had a bag on her lap from a local bakery. I mumbled, "Good morning," and tried to hand her one of the coffees, remembering at the last second which one *didn't* have cream.

She shook her head. "Nope, follow me," then headed away from the busier parts of the union to an elevator where she pushed the down arrow.

The door creaked as it moved, and my bike helmet hanging from my bag got in the way of it closing. I jostled around in the small space, still holding both coffees. "Can you at least tell me where we're going?"

"Remember the auxiliary category in the power use spread-sheet?"

I shrugged. "I guess?"

"Well, this is it."

"Okay, but why are we here at eight"—I blinked at my watch—

"fifteen on a Monday morning?"

"Because it needs fixing, and you're the hardware expert," Tia said with a smirk.

"It could have waited…" I suppressed a yawn.

"It's been waiting for a while. We don't have anything pressing, and I thought it might be an interesting change."

I followed her into a basement I didn't even know existed.

Wait…or did I? I wasn't sure. Déjà vu?

In a curving hallway, Tia stopped in front of a heavy steel door painted the same color as the wall. She swiped her access card and it clicked open. Inside and lights on, an old sofa, some storage lockers, and a worktable covered with computer junk greeted us.

She gestured to a folding chair, which I slid over with my foot then sat and traded a coffee for a wrapped bagel breakfast sandwich. After a bite and a drink of coffee, she began. "In the nineteen sixties, a TE engineer built this place. He had an idea for sending a letter, should a field engineer ever be stuck out of time. There's a slot in the upstairs hallway which leads to a mail chute, and a miniature time portal in the ceiling."

I craned my neck to look up into the shadows between the steel beams. "Does it work? Wait, sorry—dumb question. Wouldn't be here if it did. Did it ever work?"

"I found a design in the records outlining a system to send a note to another timeline, much like a regular jump. I think he originally planned for equipment to read the letter's destination and program the portal accordingly, but he never finished it."

I munched on my sandwich. Sipping coffee and swallowing, I pointed over at a wood arch with visibly damaged wiring. "What's that then?"

"That…was an unauthorized experiment."

Noticing the scorch marks, I added, "It looks like it burned out. Hope nobody got hurt."

"The Timeslot and portal are separate. I don't think the portal is salvageable, but…"

"Timeslot? Cool name. How did you even know about this when I didn't?"

"I found a reference to it in some old records but didn't have time to come check it out until recently. I was going to tell you, but we got busy with the proposals, and then… Kurtis went missing."

His disappearance had hung over me for days. I still held out hope he'd gone on an unannounced vacation. "So, you brought it up now to help distract me, er…us, from obsessing over where Kurtis went?"

Tia looked caught, asking awkwardly, "Um…is it working?"

"It's okay. I appreciate the thought, and you're right. We don't have much else going on at TE right now." Tia gestured dramatically toward the worktable. "Why not? Yeah, let's give it a go." I stood to get into it when my knee popped loudly. My joints cracked all the time, but it *hurt* just then, and it felt achy the rest of the day. Weird.

What followed ended up being far more than one morning of work. Under all the junk were some hand-drawn diagrams for the equipment. Some looked older than others, and in multiple handwritings. I pointed it out to Tia who said that Charles, the original engineer, must have had some help.

*

CRYSTAL
July 2022

I'd made enough money from the open mic plus playing in public to treat myself to a load of laundry. Unfortunately, I couldn't wash everything unless I wanted to sit around and wait naked. Pulling the black tank top out of Amber's bag, I held it up. I'd worn all her other shirts many times but skipped over this one. I was never a tank top girl, thinking I didn't have the figure for them.

I stripped off my old T-shirt and pulled it on. A memory surfaced of Amber in my living room. It was the morning we fought, and maybe that's why I hadn't thought about it before—a clear image of her showing me her circuit board tattoo. Some corner of my brain, despite my hangover and confusion about her startling time travel story, noticed the muscular arm under the tattoo and thought she looked great in the tank top.

The Timeslot room had no mirror to show my own lean shoulders in the same place Amber's had been. The black, ribbed fabric fit snugly across my abdomen and breasts, but not uncomfortably tight. Well, not physically anyway.

I had a mental disconnect between the figure on athletic women like Amber with their muscle definition and their toned stomachs, and my own body which I always just thought of as too skinny. I sighed and grudgingly acknowledged that *maybe* the only real difference between her figure and mine was a few inches of height. Standing there wearing her clothes was proof enough.

I wore it all morning while working on the formula and practicing the mandolin. Maybe I wanted to practice the tank top also. Finally psyching myself up, the rest of the clothes in the backpack, I headed out. On the sidewalk, I walked past a girl wearing an outfit almost like mine, and it looked great on her. Maybe that should tell me something.

*

KURTIS
July 2006

The room was big but crowded. Traffic made me late, and I squeezed in at the back with everyone else not early enough to get a seat. Meeting space at a community college must be scarce. Perhaps that explained the expansion project.

I shrugged out of my jacket in the quickly warming space, trying not to nudge anyone more than necessary. Whoever was supposed to announce the firms selected for the project was even later than me.

In only a couple of years, this would all be done by email. It probably could have been done that way then, but old rules carried on by momentum, and there we stood, crammed into a conference room waiting for the announcement in person.

The woman ahead of me shifted, and I inched to the side to see the podium around her long red hair. Maybe I'd met her, or at least been introduced at another of these meetings. I couldn't remember her name, but she worked for one of the larger engineering firms. Far too successful to be in competition with us.

A team of people squeezed to the front and talked for a few minutes, thanking us all for being there. I listened and I sweated. When they finally made their announcements, we weren't on the list. I filed out of the building along with everyone else *not* selected and found myself holding the door for the red-haired woman.

"Thank you. Hey, I'm sorry for not remembering, but have we met?" she asked.

We stood in the shade at the edge of the parking lot and talked for a long time. She'd left the big firm and gone out on her own. We'd been trying to land the same projects for over a year and never knew we were each other's strongest competition.

Before parting, I gave her my business card. To my shock, she called me a week later, wanting to partner on a project which required minority- and women-owned businesses. We went out for lunch to discuss it. It was a long lunch.

As one might expect, it didn't end there. She was brilliant and funny and gorgeous. I'd focused so strongly on my engineering firm, in part, to keep my mind away from TE. Elizabeth, for the first time, pulled my attention away from work. Not all my attention though. Eventually we merged her company and mine under a new name in a new building. Around that same time, she moved in with me—and before long, we were married.

33

CRYSTAL
August 2022

Imade my best guesses. I'd studied the goddamned formula for weeks. I triple-checked my calculations for the number of days after the benchmark and accounted for how long I'd been in 2022. I ran the formula through until I got the same exact answers four times in a row. I recopied the whole thing onto new clean paper torn out of a notebook from 1994.

When I wasn't mathing, I learned a couple new songs, practicing them in the Timeslot room or playing them in the plaza area of campustown. The money was barely enough. I bought the cheapest ramen, the cheapest peanut butter, and the day-old bread. I knew it wasn't sustainable. My jeans felt loose, which told me I'd lost weight, not that I had much to spare. In a couple weeks, summer semester would be over. I couldn't keep this up into the fall.

Thursday evening, I got to the open mic early and grabbed the same seat and the same time slot as before, smirking at the double, or triple, use of time slot. When Marco arrived, I asked for a favor. "Jess said you're a math teacher, right?"

"Yeah?" He sounded wary. Admittedly, it was an odd conversation opener.

"I could use some help on a math thing."

"Okay, very random. Just so you know, technically I'm on summer vacation, but now I'm curious."

I unzipped the pocket on my case for the papers. He laughed. "What the hell? You brought it *with* you?"

"Um. Yeah?" I unfolded the pages on the bar between us, and he leaned over it.

After a glance, his gaze snapped back up to me. "Holy shit. Last week you were this shy girl playing the mandolin, now you're asking me about high-end math? What's next?"

Remembering his T-shirt from the week before, I deadpanned the first thing that popped into my head. "I'm Batgirl."

This elicited a bigger laugh than I expected, but he countered with "Batgirl's a redhead."

"Robin then? There was a female Robin, wasn't there?"

Still chuckling, he said, "Yeah, there were a couple." His attention back on the paper, he asked, "This is a weird-ass equation. Why do you really need this?"

"It's for my girlfriend. She's not actually in London. Her team's lost contact with her. Sorry, but the rest is classified research. I shouldn't even be getting outside help, but..." Unsure of how to continue that sentence, I tried to communicate the importance with an expression, but maybe I just looked like a lost puppy. He nodded and returned to the page. I ordered beers for both of us, even though it took most of the rest of my cash. If he deciphered the equation, it'd be worth it.

"Oh man, you were *so* close to acing it," he said after a few minutes of using his phone as a calculator.

"Ugh. I knew the calculus was gonna get me."

"Nah. Your calc was spot-on." He pointed to the other side of the equation, well up the page. "You got the order of operations wrong way up here and it screwed you all the way down."

"Wow, okay."

"Order of operations will get ya if you're not careful." He scratched with my pen for a second. "Do it like this. Chunk out the numbers from there and you'll be fine."

"Oh my god, thank you!" I gave him a one-armed hug, holding my drink with the other.

"Hey, no problem. Maybe I should get a sign. 'Will do math for beer.'"

Before I could answer, the first act stepped onto the stage— one of the ukulele girls. I considered bailing, but I found I wanted to stay. Some corner of me wished I could stay friends with him and Jess. If this worked, I'd be twenty-odd years in the future, and the only person who'll know me there will be Amber. It felt like starting over, again. But also, if it didn't work, I'd need the money.

I played my set, switching out one song so I'd end early again. I leaned close to the mic after the applause and said, "Thanks. I have hope you guys can get Marco up here a couple minutes early. Can you help me with that?" They applauded loudly and someone tried chanting his name, but it died down when he stood and headed toward the stage with his guitar.

He put the strap over his shoulder as he asked, "You have hope?"

"I have hope."

I strummed the rhythm part of an old Bauhaus song, banking

on him recognizing it. The way he rolled his eyes and shook his head told me he did.

"Hope? Seriously? You're exposing my Goth roots, girlfriend. Not sure how to feel about that."

I shrugged. "I told ya. Can you take this part?" He strummed the chords along with me; then I dropped out letting him run through the phrase twice more before I joined back in with the melody. "Hope" was a weird and simple song with no verses and a chorus that repeated eight times, but it took two musicians to play. Emboldened by the applause the previous week, I took a deep breath and began. The song carried us along for the next three and a half minutes. A few in the audience even joined in by the end.

I found I had hope about a lot of things.

*

TIA
September 2045

Even with both of us working, fixing the Timeslot took until Friday. Every time she looked at the diagrams, I worried she'd recognize some of the writing was hers, but she didn't. Maybe it *is* true that all engineers write alike.

It was on the tip of my tongue, a hundred times over, to confess everything I knew about the paradox and the alternate memories. But I didn't. Something held me back. Still afraid of screwing up the timeline? Or more afraid of Amber not believing me?

All assembled and ready to power up, I backed away from the table. "In a minute you're going to flip the switch, and that thing's going to work." She nodded but looked confused. I continued, despite backing toward the door, "When it does, something's going to fall through. You need to read it, and when you're ready, I want you to call me, no matter how late."

"Tia. What's going on? What are you talking about? Is this why you've been so quiet all week?"

"There's more going on here than you remember, and I believe you deserve to know, but I also believe you need to learn it for yourself."

She stepped around the table. "What the hell, Tia? What aren't you telling me?"

"I'm asking you to please trust me. Can you do that?"

That softened her annoyance. "Of course, but—"

I held one hand up to stop her, while turning toward the door. "As soon as I'm gone, start the machine, read the letter, and call me later." I left, desperately hoping I'd done the right thing.

*

CRYSTAL
August 2022

Money in my pocket and back at the Timeslot room, I didn't feel like I could sleep, despite the late hour. I reran the formula and produced a new set of coordinates. Leaving them on the worktable, I took the journal to the sofa and wrote.

Before leaving for the open mic, I had vague plans to start the Timeslot in the morning. I don't know what I was thinking. Maybe the possibility of Marco solving the equation hadn't fully sunk in. Once I had the coordinates in my hand, I was far too excited to sleep.

I wrote Amber a brief note saying I was okay, and the date where I was marooned. I turned on the computer and ran the control software. The portal above began to hum and glow around the edges. I typed and double-checked the coordinates. I crossed my fingers with one hand and tapped Enter with the other.

A message popped up: "Initializing." Following Kurtis's lead, I set the folding chair on the table and climbed up onto it, note in hand. The portal nodes threw electric arcs between them, and the field opened. Holding the beam overhead, I reached out to drop the note through.

The field fluctuated wildly, the hum irregular. An emitter an inch from my wrist shot sparks in every direction. I jumped back, lost my balance, and tumbled to the floor with the chair on top of me.

Above me, the portal became even more unstable, throwing bigger sparks and stinking like ozone. I quickly put the chair back up only to realize I'd dropped the note when I fell. I spun in place looking frantically on the floor but not finding it. The portal seemed about to collapse. Thinking fast, I grabbed the journal off the sofa, climbed onto the chair, and dropped it through. Not even three seconds later, the emitters flashed brightly, flickered and sizzled to black.

Cradling a bruised elbow and looking up at the scorched portal frame overhead, I said aloud to the empty room, "Well, shit."

34

AMBER
September 2045

"Tia?" I called after her. "Tia!"

What...the...hell?

I slumped onto the couch, the dust making me sneeze. Why did she leave like that? Something weird was going on. If I trusted Tia, and I did, then I needed to just go with it.

Cables and connections double-checked, I powered up the computer. Once the app opened, it showed choices for Destination, Passive, or Active scan.

Selecting the last option, I clicked Initiate and stepped back. The portal above hummed while the system ran through its start-up procedures.

Setting the folding chair so I could see the screen, I leaned back and crossed my ankles on the worktable. How long did Tia mean for me to wait? No sooner than I had that thought, the humming sound changed and a message appeared. "Incoming. Origin: August 5, 2022. Addressee: none. The portal field sparked open, and a brown rectangular bundle dropped through onto the floor. A book, bound in leather and tied shut.

How could Tia have possibly known?

I gently untied the leather strap and opened the cover to find a journal. The first entry was dated the previous winter, January 2045. I ran my thumb along the edge, riffling through the pages. It looked almost full, but the handwriting changed halfway through. The first in chunky printed caps, and the second in cursive. I hadn't read cursive since I was a kid, but it was beautiful. Flipping back to the beginning, it occurred to me how much it looked like my own handwriting. It's a well-known stereotype that all engineers write alike.

I sat gently on the sofa so as not to raise a cloud again. The writer talked about recovering from knee surgery after a skiing accident and got a vid-call from her friend Tia.

Wait, what?

They talked about work which sounded exactly like TE. I flipped back to the first page and looked at the date. It was right around the time V disappeared. Plus... Meg and I had planned a ski trip, but after we broke up, I gave her the tickets.

What the hell was I holding? I flipped randomly through the first half of the book, studying the handwriting. Before long I found one of my distinctive capital *G*s. How could that be possible if I didn't remember writing it? And what about the origin date on the screen? I was only four years old, living in Chicago with my dad in 2022. I rubbed my forehead, staring at this strange object in my lap and fighting my gut instinct to call Tia. She'd specifically said to read first, then call.

I remember my dad saying, "Sometimes the only way forward is through." I got as comfortable as possible on the old couch. Flipping back to the beginning, I started over, distancing myself from thinking of it as me. It was me, but at once, not-me also. Dwelling on that confusion held me back. I needed to learn what was in the journal and, ultimately, who wrote the other half and why.

I read about a life I had no memory of. I'd had adventures in another timeline. I met and fell in love with a woman I don't remember. How could I forget something like that?

I looked up Crystal on the old computer in the Timeslot room, exactly like my counterpart in the journal, hoping for a photo of her. I thought seeing her face might jog some hidden memory.

I found the same teenage photo with the bangs and viola. Cute, but it triggered nothing. I dug in the university archives and came up with an ID photo. I zoomed until it filled the screen, pixelated. I squinted and stared for minutes straight. Deep in my mind, I felt maybe the faintest tickle of recognition, but not quite even a tip-of-the-tongue moment. It felt maddening. Had my subconscious hoped for something that wasn't really there, or did she look even the slightest bit familiar?

I decided to try something that wasn't in the journal. I ran the ID photo through face recognition software, searching the university archives from the late 80s to the mid-nineties. It found an orchestra photo, but a pale speck in a sea of black clothes and instruments didn't help. I let it run longer, and it returned only one more hit—a student project with photos of campus architecture. In front of one building, two women sat on a park bench drinking coffee. One sat sideways on the bench, long straight dark hair held back with sunglasses on top of her head. Her companion had messy shorter hair and faced away from the camera. I zoomed in and gasped. The lines of my circuit board tattoo were blurry but visible on her upper arm, right below the sleeve.

Had the photographer captured us while she told the story about Princess Leia? I zoomed back to her face—the natural expression, not posed like the viola photo, seen almost in profile...

Then recognition did strike—the brunette woman running beside me in my dreams!

Oh. My. God.

How was that even possible?

I stared, unmoving, unblinking at the screen, my eyes burning. It felt like a long time before I called Tia.

*

TIA
September 2045

My tablet beeped a little after midnight. Excitement at finally talking to Amber about all this again kept me from falling asleep anyway. I turned on a lamp and tapped the screen.

Amber's eyes looked red, and she sniffed before speaking. "Please tell me what's going on."

"You got the letter?"

"Letter? I got a whole goddamn book!"

I sat up. "What?" On the screen, she held a brown leather journal. "It was just a letter before."

"Yeah. I know. I read about it, and then I found it folded up in the back." Underneath all her other emotions was an edge of annoyance. I needed her to know I was on her side. She waved it and asked, "What the hell? You knew about this, and you didn't tell me!"

"Shh, shh. Please, just answer one question, and I'll tell you everything I know. What's in the book?"

"It's a journal in *my* handwriting that I don't remember writing, and there's a second half that was written by Crystal."

"Oh, holy shit. I didn't know that existed. I only knew about the letter." She stared at me intensely through the screen for a moment before I spoke, "As far as I can tell, you and I survived a paradox, but I'm not sure what happened to Kurtis or Crystal."

"Wait. That's not supposed to…"

"I know, but it did. Or at least that's the only explanation I can work out."

"How long ago?"

"I first noticed the changes about six weeks ago. I woke up one morning with conflicting sets of memories. Two versions of everything since last winter."

"Six weeks! Wait—last winter! Why don't I remember it, and why didn't you tell me?"

"I wasn't sure what happened at first. Once I figured it out, I… I went back and forth every day between wanting to tell you and worrying about screwing up the timeline even more."

"Is that why we fixed the Timeslot this week? So if there was something to find, I'd find it?" Her tone and expression began to soften.

"Yeah. It wouldn't have come through if it'd create a paradox. If you got the letter, I'd be safe to tell you everything." I sighed. "You have no idea how good it is to be able to talk to you about all this. I've slept like shit for weeks. Actually… Hey, are you okay to ride to TE? There's something I want to show you. It'll explain why I remember and you don't."

"It's midnight on a Friday night. The sidewalks are full of tipsy students walking home right about now. I'll be fine."

The TE door opened and I smelled coffee. "Oh my god, great idea!" Amber waited on the sofa with two steaming cups on the table. Facing her, I held both her hands. "Thank you for not being pissed at me."

"Oh, I was for a little while, but your reasons for staying quiet made sense. I guess at this point it doesn't matter much." I took a mug and sipped.

She leaned in. "Look, I know there's stuff you want to show me, and I want to hear all about the alternate timeline, the paradox, and how we survived, but right now, Crystal's stuck in 2022. She's hungry and she's been living in the Timeslot room for weeks."

"Twenty twenty-two? But she's okay?"

"I mean, yeah, I guess."

"She and Kurtis disappeared at the same time. I was worried she…"

"V shoved her through the portal in the Timeslot room!"

"What?"

"She banged the frame with her arm and tore out the wiring when she fell through. That's why she was trapped there with no way to fix the Timeslot room portal and too scared of Vanhanen to come to TE."

I held up one finger, saying, "Hold on." I pulled a thick printout from my bag and set it on the coffee table. "This is what I wanted to show you; it's *my* journal. The thing is, right now it's the middle of the night in both timelines, so there's not much we can do for the moment. Let's trade journals, drink coffee, and both get caught up."

*

AMBER
September 2045

To my utter shock, Tia's journal revealed the depth of her hatred for Vanhanen, and, ultimately, the reason why. Honestly, I can't say I blame her. Reading certain sections, I found myself peeking at her over the top of the printout, surprised at a side of my friend so well hidden I didn't know it existed.

Not to mention she was out of time and had been for over three years. In the journal, she joked about her Oscar-worthy acting skills. If anything, she may have sold herself short. I'd had absolutely no idea.

To jump twenty-three years with no hope of a return trip, driven by rage and a chance for revenge, was a level of badass I'd never imagined existed outside of books and movies. To have Vanhanen disappear into the folds of a paradox must have been crushing. I couldn't even begin to imagine that kind of loss.

At the end of Tia's journal, I poured more coffee, took a sip, and leaned back into the sofa, not sure how to feel about what I read. She'd intended to *kill* our boss. Maybe his disappearance spared her that. I didn't know, too confusing and too close to philosophy for that late at night.

My eyes drifted almost closed but popped right back open and focused on a black leather motorcycle jacket hanging behind the door. "Tia?"

She looked up from the journal, marking her place among the cursive script with a fingertip. "Hm?"

I pointed. "That jacket. How long's it been hanging there?"

She gave a small smile. "About six weeks."

"Is that?" I set the cup down and crossed the room, my knee aching again as I did.

"Yeah. That's the one you wore in the nineties."

My fingers trailed over the worn leather, from the shoulder down the wrinkled sleeve. "Why didn't it disappear along with my memories?"

"Proximity to the portal equipment bends the rules. It still hung there the day after the paradox, but you walked right past and never saw it."

"Now that I know about the paradox, I noticed it?"

She shrugged. "Maybe?"

I slipped it on and looked at my reflection in the dark lab window. It fit perfectly. Not my usual style, but I liked it—a lot. Something in the pocket felt stiff, like a piece of cardboard. I pulled out a round bar coaster, with a Union Jack logo and "The London Underground" printed on one side. On the back, in cursive, were the words, "Meet me where we drank coffee. —C"

*

TIA
September 2045

Amber's gaze shifted from the coaster to me, looking lost. "How do we help her? I can't go. I was four years old in 2022."

"You can't, but I can."

"Wait. You're only two years younger than me..." She paused, sounding unsure.

"That's what it says on my ID, but no. I jumped from 2018 to 2042. August of twenty-two is free and clear for me."

"You'd do that?"

"Of course! You'd do it for me, wouldn't you?"

"Well, yeah, but..."

"What, 'cause it's all dangerous and shit?" Her expression told me that exactly matched what she was thinking. I continued, "Twenty twenty-two was a dormant period. TE closed for a few years after James died. When Covid hit, V left it closed longer than usual. August is barely past the pandemic lockout in the software, but well before he reopened the department. I still have the lock cable that'll let me back in, so no problem."

"You already thought this through, didn't you?"

"I did, yeah."

She stood and reached for the bottom drawer of her desk. "No," I said firmly, knowing what we found there after V disappeared.

"You won't even consider it?"

I shook my head. "Absolutely not! You know how I feel about guns."

"I know, but..."

"But nothin'."

Amber shrugged and let the matter drop. Good. I didn't have it in me to debate her right then.

It was nearly dawn when we left TE and headed to my place with Amber's bike in the back.

Too short of a time later, I awoke to the sound of the shower. On my way to the kitchen, I noticed the leather jacket tangled with the extra blanket on my sofa. Shadow lay sprawled across both, asleep. Despite being summer, Amber never took it off after she'd tried it on. Had she slept under it? If the jacket gave her a feeling of connection, a tangible link to her other self, then good for her.

In the original timeline, Amber had made pizza in my kitchen and talked about her research on Crystal, then rescuing her. Had we come back around? Yes, but not quite a full circle. Not yet.

Wrapped in a towel, Amber poked her head around the corner

to ask, "Hey, can I borrow a T-shirt?"

"Sure. Closet." I pointed vaguely, even though she knew where. Dressed and hair wet, she grabbed a waffle straight out of the toaster, tossing it back and forth between her hands to cool before taking a huge bite.

Her mouth full, she mumbled, "Thank you. I'm starving." She chewed and swallowed before commenting on the laptop on the table. "What's with the antique?"

"I brought this with me from 2018. It's mostly hacker shit, but it has the door access from that time."

"How much longer to recharge?"

"Probably another hour or so. Why?"

She glanced at her watch and grabbed another waffle, heading for the door. "I'll be back by then."

I ran the dates in my head the night before but did it again on my tablet just to be sure. I'd jumped from October of 2018 to January 2042, and lived there three years, eight months and ten days so far. That put my original timeslot into June of 2022. Close, but not *so* close that jumping to August would risk losing my memory from before the paradox.

The bigger risk would be having less headache. Staying could be tempting. But no—the past held nothing else for me. James, Chris, and Mom were all gone. Different reasons, but all dead all the same.

Despite my general stance against firearms, I'd bought a stun gun right before leaving my original timeline with no idea what the world might be like where I was headed. The political climate in 2018 had become unbelievably shitty under the US President at the time, and I feared it being worse in the future. As it worked out, the former president lost the next election, things eventually turned around, and the stun gun hadn't been touched since. I replaced the batteries and slipped it into a pocket of my old denim jacket.

Not late, for the first time possibly ever, Amber showed back up with a bag of vintage clothes: a T-shirt from a brand of hard seltzer I vaguely remembered, black leggings, and checkerboard slip-on sneakers.

35

CRYSTAL
August 2022

Very well. Plan B.

In Kurtis's journal, TE field engineers used passphrases from *The Time Machine* by H.G. Wells. The library had multiple copies. I curled up in the comfiest chair I could find and read it—twice. You can get through it in about three hours. Most of the characters not having names made it confusing and weird, but once the story got to the actual time travel, it improved.

Trying to sleep that night I debated going back to the library the next day. My best moneymaking day for playing in public was Saturday. Reading instead of playing would be a gamble, doubling down against my own future hunger. I needed to know the book backward and forward if I was going to bluff my way through TE on Monday morning with a page full of coordinates, and a head full of H.G. Wells.

A sharp banging sound jolted me awake Saturday morning. It scared me so much I jumped off the couch, heart pounding and breathing hard. It came again. Someone was knocking on the door! This had *never* happened before. As far as I knew, no one else walked down this hallway. I'd lived every day with the fear of being discovered. Having a place to crash meant all my money could go to food, and I was barely able to squeak by. If I lost the Timeslot room, I'd be screwed.

The pounding sounded again, louder than before. I quickly pulled on a pair of jeans, looking around the room, wondering how to carry everything if I was about to get evicted. While jamming clothes into Amber's bag, the knocking stopped and changed to a quiet scratching noise by the door.

Tip-toeing closer, I noticed a curved line of white under the edge of the door. Maybe three inches long and barely protruding into the room, a bar coaster from The Underground. Flipping it over I saw my own writing on the back and had the door open in a heartbeat. "Amber?"

Except it wasn't. A Black woman in a wheelchair moved away from me, around the curving hallway. She turned a head of curly dark hair to look over her shoulder, "Crystal?"

"Yeah. Where's Amber?"

Turning, she lifted one hand in a reassuring gesture. "She sent me. She gave me that coaster to prove it. I'm Tia."

I sighed, relieved. "Oh yeah, of course." Amber said she never would have made it to 1994 without Tia's help. I pushed the door all the way open. "Uh. Come on in, I guess."

"We got your journal, clever to send it."

"*Desperate* more like. The Timeslot wasn't stable. I only barely got it working and it ran for under a minute before it blew out."

She looked up and winced at the scorched frame. "How'd you reach it anyway?"

"Stood on the chair on the table. Kasey did it that way in '94. He sent a message right before…well, before everything went sideways." I sat on the edge of the sofa facing Tia, my hands clasped between my knees. "Please tell me where Amber is."

"She's still in 2045, but since she was born in 2018, she couldn't come herself."

"Right. The end of the line."

She nodded. "Mm-hmm."

I saw her notice the hurried packing. "When I heard you knocking, I thought I was about to get kicked out by security." I fidgeted with the edge of the bag. "If you're here you must have access to TE, right?"

"Yes, but…"

I interrupted. "Can we just go? I've been waiting so long." I shoved the rest of my clothes into the duffel bag and reached for the zipper.

"Yeah, we can go whenever you want. I can get us into TE. Amber and I are co-directors in our time."

"But what about V?"

"That's where it gets complicated. Before we go, I need you to listen to me for a few minutes. It's important." Tia told me about Kurtis and Vanhanen on the video recording, and how she and Amber got headaches on their way to TE. She explained about finding a log of a jump, and the way the bulletin board changed on the video. "So, as impossible as it sounds, there was a paradox, and the three of us survived, but Kurtis and V are missing. It changed the events of the last few months, going back to Amber's ski trip, or rather, the one she never went on."

"What?"

Tia nodded sympathetically. "You and I remember everything from before the paradox because we were out of time when it happened. I...have memories from both versions." She paused sadly, as if wary about continuing. She took my hands in both of hers. "I'm so sorry. Since Amber was in her home time when the paradox hit, her memories got altered along with everything else, including jumping to 1994. She lost all memory of her time with you."

"What? No! That can't... That's not..." I pulled my knees up, hugging them, stunned. "No...no...no..." I slumped forward, face in the crook of my arm at the shock of it. *Unthinkable!* How could she forget? Going to class and having coffee, the long kiss at the radio station... How could those moments be gone? I'd been so close, so goddamn close! What would have happened if I'd waltzed into TE on Monday like I'd planned? I couldn't even imagine.

I felt Tia's gentle hand on my leg, and I looked up. "If it's any consolation, she stayed up all night reading the journal and cried her eyes out. She found the leather jacket and hasn't taken it off since." I sniffed and nodded, so she continued, "She desperately wants to meet you. She'd have jumped through the portal in the middle of the night if it'd been possible."

"Meet me" though—as if it was the first time. For her, it would be.

"Ugh! I've been dreaming about falling back into her arms ever since I landed in this timeline. Everything I've done was to get back to her. Knowing she was out there kept me going when I lost my old life in '94. We barely escaped V in that timeline, only for me to get dumped here in this shitty basement!"

"Let me tell you a few things about Amber: She's perpetually late, she puts a stupid amount of cream in her coffee, her taste in movies is usually good, but her skill at housekeeping isn't. She has a big heart, and in all the time I've known her, I've never seen her happier than when you two were together. She's not usually a crier, but I've seen her in tears over losing you. Twice."

I reflexively put my hand over my mouth.

"Yeah. So even though the memories are gone, the potential is still there. What you had isn't lost, so much as it needs to be rediscovered." I leaned forward and hugged her. I didn't even know why, but she hugged me back without question.

I sat back, and she said, "Let's go, okay?"

"Just a minute." I'd already packed my few clothes but added the two remaining journals along with my notebook into my backpack, next to the mandolin case. I paused, having a thought that gave me reason to smile. I crossed to the little sink and brushed my teeth, then threw the brush and toothpaste into Amber's bag and zipped it.

I took one last glance around the room that had been my sanctuary and my prison, gave a quick nod, and followed Tia out the door.

*

TIA
August 2022 / September 2045

Crystal looked around inside TE for the first time, having only read about it before. In the lab, I powered up the portal. "You still have those coordinates?"

"Well, yeah, but…"

"But nothing. You worked your ass off for those." I pointed at the screen. "Enter them, and let's go home." As the emitters glowed and sparked to life, I typed in a new sequence I'd devised to delete our jump from the log. I nodded to Crystal. Bag in one hand and mandolin case in the other, she stepped through the portal with me right behind.

Amber stood waiting on the other side, wearing the leather jacket and holding the journal, practically bouncing with anticipation.

Barely through the portal, Crystal exclaimed, "Oh my god, your hair—it's so short!"

Amber touched it self-consciously, "I know. I know. I never quit cutting it in this timeline. I could grow it again?"

Crystal dropped the duffel and set the mandolin on top. Stepping toward Amber with a small shrug, she said, "Or not, whatever. It looks cute either way."

Behind me, the portal wound back down to standby. I ran the shutdown sequence, barely looking at the keyboard, and the equipment silenced completely.

Crystal tentatively stepped close but paused. "Y'know, it's okay if you want to take this slowly. I understand we're kinda off the edge of the map."

"Beyond here, there are dragons?"

Crystal smirked. "I sure hope not."

Amber took her hand. "My counterpart, the *me* in the other timeline... Even if she never had time to say it, she loved you."

"Yeah. It was in the journal." Crystal blinked wet eyes. "I never had time to say it either."

Amber stood on her toes and brought their faces almost even. "Let's start from there and figure this out."

Crystal nodded, bent her head, and they kissed. That explained the random tooth brushing. After a minute, I cleared my throat. They turned toward me with identical sheepish grins. "You two are too cute. Can I give you a ride to Amber's place?"

"Yes, please," said Crystal.

"And Amber?"

"Hm?" she replied without taking her eyes off Crystal.

"Don't take her straight to bed, okay? Give her a chance to take a shower, put on some clean clothes, and eat a decent meal."

On hearing this, Crystal just grinned.

After dropping them off, I returned to TE and checked the log for a jump about six weeks prior, and another one seven months before that. Coordinates for the first were sent to the portal workstation, and I pocketed hard copies of the second, plus a third.

Minutes after the paradox headaches hit us, as the portal had timed out, I'd read the first destination date to Amber, who didn't recognize it. Weeks later, it remained my only clue pointing to V and Kurtis.

There was no way to know other than to jump.

Through to the other side, the lab looked exactly like the night I broke into the office. I positioned myself facing the empty portal and waited. At that moment in time, TE sat in a dormant period, but "dead zone" fit my mood better, especially with what was coming. I was so ready to be done with this shit.

When the portal glowed again, I put a hand in my jacket pocket. Roughly shoved by Kurtis, Vanhanen emerged and seeing me, he yelled, "What?" He attempted to twist out of Kurtis's grasp but stumbled right toward me and the stun gun I jabbed into his chest. An electric crackling noise sparked against his shirt, stinking like ozone and scorched fabric. He convulsed and fell to the floor at my feet, unconscious.

Kurtis looked dumbfounded but clicked the safety on the pistol and set it on the counter. "I thought I had him, but I appreciate the assist."

After all this time, I thought I'd be nervous, but instead I felt cold and still—a dark angel of vengeance. I looked up at Kurtis and asked, "I think you know who I am and why I'm here, right?"

"I do."

I rolled an office chair next to V's limp form.

"You're Amber's friend, Tia, but I eventually deduced you were also Charles's friend, Theresa."

I nodded. "Yes. So you know what he did?"

Kurtis lifted V under the arms, grunting at the exertion, and let the older man flop into the seat, his head lolling first to one side and then forward.

"I know a considerable amount about what he did, possibly more than you. But yes, Charles told me what happened."

"And *you* told me what happened to Charles. See... I'm also T.J."

He looked shocked for a second before shaking his head. "You'd think I might have worked that one out as well."

With a roll of packing tape from a different pocket, I bound V's arms and legs to the chair and put a piece over his mouth. I handed Kurtis one of the coordinate printouts. "Would you enter these please?"

After a moment of clicking, he stopped, frustrated, tried again, and shook his head. "I'm getting an error light for the safety pro-tocol." I described the control sequence to override it without once taking my eyes off V's limp form.

I turned his chair toward me, his back to the portal, and slapped him hard across the face. Damn, that felt good!

Immediately awake, he struggled against the bonds but stilled when he focused on me. His eyes went wide, then immediately narrowed with staring hatred. "Horatio Vanhanen, the things you've done are well outside the channels of any justice system." Behind him, the portal hum strengthened, and the field opened. He tried to sit up. "James Sinclair was my fiancée. He discovered too much, and you hired someone to kill him. They shot me too, maybe only to cover it up, but here I still am."

Kurtis stepped around the portal and stood beside me. "You murdered Chris Young in an intentional car crash. I witnessed that one personally. You poisoned and bludgeoned your partner, Johannes Brennan, and dumped his body in the lake. You killed Gretchen Whitley, a mute woman in your employ, and these are just the crimes we know about."

"Enough. No more dealing out death to hide the source of your riches. This is the end of the line, asshole." He struggled and made muffled sounds, but I left the tape over his mouth. My hands pushed ineffectively on the arms of his chair, immobilized by a crushing pain in my head. I couldn't shove him back him an inch. The harder I tried, the more excruciating my headache became. I collapsed and spoke in a breathless whisper to Kurtis. "Shit! I've met an older version of him, so I can't create a paradox."

V chuckled behind the tape until it became a cackle. Kurtis gently rolled me back and squatted down to look V right in the face. "Fortunately, I'm not encumbered by any such meetings."

The laughter stopped and V's eyes grew wide. With one smooth motion, Kurtis stood and shoved the chair bearing V backward through the portal. A horrible buzzing squeal was followed by a blinding white flash that left us both squinting and blinking. The portal timed out and shut down before we could see again to gaze through the empty arch, now still and quiet.

Somewhere along the line, Vanhanen had figured out he could use the time portal as a weapon. We'd turned it against its creator.

There was a time when I despaired of ever having people around me again, let alone one willing to step in and do the horrible thing I couldn't. "Did we just?" I began but was too flustered to finish.

"Yes. Yes, we did. It'd been coming for a very long time. I wondered if I'd live long enough to see it."

Unsure, I asked, "Are... Are you glad you did?"

"Yes," he said simply, before asking, "Where *did* we send him? I didn't have time to check."

"A few months ago, I came into work early one day and caught him returning from an unscheduled jump, and it made me suspicious. Indirectly, it's what started this whole chain of events. I sent him back to collide with himself at that same moment."

"How's that possible? Wouldn't it create a paradox?"

"Yeah... See, Amber and I are already living in that paradox."

He leaned heavily against the countertop. "Whoa." Silently, we both continued staring at the portal and then around the room as the moment stretched out awkwardly. Finally discovering something else to say, Kurtis asked, "What about Crystal? Is she okay?"

"We got her back this morning. She's fine."

"From when?"

"She spent about six weeks stuck in 2022." The whole story was far too complicated to tell, so I just said, "She finally managed to send word by the Timeslot."

He looked relieved for Crystal but still unnerved by the whole situation and responded flatly, "Charles always imagined it helping someone stuck out of time. It's unlikely he guessed it'd be his own daughter."

Kurtis returned the pistol to the drawer. I pocketed the tape, the stun-gun, and the printed coordinates, but when I said, "Let's go home," Kurtis shook his head.

"I can't. From the timeline you're about to jump back to, I'd only have about two months. I was born in November of 2045."

"Oh, hell! That's right." I said, sitting back. "It was in the journal."

"I was out of time in 1994 when V chased me away from the Timeslot room with that pistol, and I have been ever since. I made my peace with it long ago, knowing the date of my own death, but when Amber asked for help with the Timeslot, I saw a chance." He tapped his watch and accessed a set of temporal coordinates.

"Where are you going? Er...when?"

"My own timeslot is too far forward of the world I remember at this point, and besides, I don't want to risk forgetting anything because of your paradox." He carefully set the dials on the control panel, threw switches, and the deep hum sounded from the portal arch.

"What do I tell Amber?"

His gaze snapped up. "You can't tell her anything. If she knows you saw me, she'll try to launch another rescue mission, and it'll end in disaster." I nodded, understanding. He was probably right. "I want her and Crystal to have a great life together and not worry about me. Besides, you'll see me again before long, I just won't know *you* yet."

In front of the arch, Kurtis took my hand and spoke sincerely, "I can't thank you sufficiently for all you did for Amber and all you did for me, but thank you anyway."

He turned and disappeared through the portal.

I rubbed my eyes, feeling dazed, almost numb. I finally got what I'd wanted ever since waking in the hospital and hearing that James had been killed. Why did it feel so hollow? So unfulfilling. Was it because I sat surrounded by the work of a man whose life we'd abruptly ended? It didn't feel real—the thought of having murdered someone. And this was definitely premeditated. Who would ever know though, or care? There was no body, no evidence, no forensic team combing through the room, like in a movie. There was only the familiar hum fading to silence as the portal shut down.

The coordinates on the last printout were for my own jump home.

I drank more whiskey than I usually ever would in one night, and certainly not alone. It made my sleep restless, and I woke with a headache. A bigger one than usual.

Sleep didn't come easily for weeks after, remembering Vanhanen rolling backward toward the portal, a look of utter shock and rage on his face. He couldn't quite believe someone had finally beaten him after all these years. Only in the absolute last second as the chair wheels bumped over the threshold was there anything like fear in his eyes, and then he was gone.

I did, eventually, quit seeing his face behind my closed lids, but years passed by before I truly believed we were out of the woods.

36

CRYSTAL
October 2045

Planning to stay in 2045 permanently, we all wanted my new identity to be as flawless as possible. It relied heavily on the last few experiments before V's disappearance—the ones with the self-operated remote computer. Unfortunately, that all happened in the other timeline. So Tia talked Amber through it from memory, and they tried to re-create it together. It needed to jump and connect to the internet at various points to create records of my life as if I'd been living it all along. They had to invent a kid born in September of 2020, right in the middle of the pandemic. A complex operation, but they were nearly done.

Everything in the 2040s required an ID, a credit card, a membership fob, etc., etc. I couldn't even get a bus pass without an ID. So until then, I used Amber's old bike. I hoped to talk her into a car eventually, but I wasn't going to rush things.

Until January and grad classes, I had a lot of downtime. Tia hooked me up with a ton of historical documentaries she watched her first few months in the 2040s. Amber took a couple of weeks off work to get me settled, help with my crash course in the last fifty years of history, and let's be honest—hang out and revel in our new weird relationship.

I locked the bike outside Nuke E and looked at my watch: early enough to walk over to the coffee cart near central campus. Summer weather had lingered late into the fall, and I still felt warm from the ride. I changed my usual order to iced coffee, handed over a reusable cup and tapped Amber's credit card.

Carrying my drink toward TE, I remembered Amber and I walking through the same part of campus with our coffees that day back in 1994. I'd passed through there on my way to the old gym and the laundromat in 2022 as well. Dreams about those weeks still woke me in the middle of the night, but it happened less and less. The trauma of that time was finally fading.

Navigating contemporary fashion turned out to be more challenging than I expected, especially if I wanted to stop dressing from Amber's closet. Her style was more athletic at home than what she'd worn in the 90s, so I had to find my own way. Right then, jeans in a current style, sandals, purple-chrome nail polish, and a haircut a few inches shorter and more in line with the times. Supposedly, the halter-tank-crop-top things were very fashionable too—retro 20s, Amber called them. Whatever. My pale stomach wasn't used to being quite that exposed. I'd picked one a little longer than she suggested. At least it was black. Pausing back at the bike, I pulled a loose shirt over it. Amber had stopped me the day before, as I was starting to button it, saying I shouldn't. Ugh, fashion again! Only my sunglasses and my silver thumb ring were from the 90s. There was no way I'd ever part with that. I glimpsed my own reflection in the windows of Nuke E before opening the door and imagined Tia's smiling response. Something like, "Shit, girl, you've gone native!"

I walked into TE in the middle of an intense debate. Amber and Tia hardly ever disagreed, let alone argued.

"It's way too dangerous." Amber said, sounding frustrated.

"It's just equipment, like a tool."

"Some people make the same argument about guns."

"That's different."

"How?"

"Time travel equipment isn't available to the general public. And I absolutely wouldn't want it to be."

"No, of course not. It's just... We only barely got Crystal back safely, and V is who knows where." I stood quietly in the lab doorway, wondering where this was going. Amber picked back up. "All I'm saying is V could still be out there. If some version of him realized we have control of the department, there's nothing stopping him from jumping here, and I'm sorry, but that scares the shit out of me!"

"This isn't *The Flash*. A time fragment is highly unlikely. It's theoretical at best."

Amber gestured toward me. "So was Crystal and her dad's timeslot, but there she is."

Tia sighed loudly. "I still think it's better to add a bunch of safety protocols than to destroy it."

"Destroy?" I interjected, shocked.

"I actually said 'dismantle.'"

"Fine. Whatever."

"So, you're okay with this? At least for now?"

"Not really, but I don't think I'm going to out argue you here."

Amber squatted by the portal where two bundles of cabling attached to the frame, one for power and one to the computer. Tia frowned, folded her arms and stayed still.

In the second before she grabbed the cable, I yelled, "No! Wait!" But I was too late. She pulled and immediately froze up, all her muscles clenching. She groaned painfully and tugged again, eyes squeezed shut and teeth clenched. After a moment, she pried her other hand off the cables and fell backward to the floor, holding her head. An outsider might think she'd been shocked, but I knew better.

Kneeling and touching her arm, I repeated, "Are you okay? Are you okay?" She only groaned in answer. More gently I asked, "Didn't you hear me yell 'wait'? You had to know it wouldn't let you create a paradox! Kiernen will come to work here in like, twenty years, and two you have to send him to the past."

Tia rolled up behind us, speaking to Amber, "Your girlfriend's smart."

Breathless and sounding annoyed, she responded, "I know. I know. I thought I could keep us safe by taking it offline for a while." I squeezed her arm appreciatively before she continued, "Guess not."

"Guess not." Tia repeated.

"After he's gone?"

"That's a long time from now, but yeah. If you still feel this way in twenty-two years, go ahead and take it apart. I won't stop you."

I sat back and finished my coffee, the straw slurping loudly. "So, where'd you want to go for lunch?"

*

TIA
July 2047

Some things never change. Amber was late.

I picked a microbrewery we went to on Fridays after work sometimes, but not often for lunch. Being summer vacation, Crystal joined us too. She slid her sunglasses up onto her head as she slipped into another chair under the patio umbrella. Her tank top revealed a tattoo I'd heard about from Amber but hadn't seen yet: an alto clef. "Always the violist, huh?"

She touched it, smiling and replied, "Yup!" Her other shoulder had a vintage clock face, permanently set to 4:30. It was one of the first things she did after establishing her new twenty-first century identity.

We chatted until Amber joined us, taking off her bike helmet and running her hands through her hair, longer even than in the other timeline. Waiting until we'd ordered and had our drinks, I said, "I met with the spinal surgeon again."

Amber's glass paused halfway to her mouth. "What'd she say? Wait. Was this the scheduled one at the end of the PT?"

Crystal sat forward. "Yeah. What'd she say?"

"Well, the short version is that my physical therapy plateaued because I'm reaching my point of —" I did air quotes. "—maximum potential improvement."

"Oh no!"

"She had my X-rays and some charts and all, but what it comes down to is I'll be listed in her report statistics as 'moderate recovery' rather than 'full recovery.'" Amber reached across the table and gently squeezed my arm. I patted her hand and continued. "With how the PT was going lately...well, I could do the math. The chance of full recovery was always low, and something like this was the most likely outcome."

"I know, but..." Crystal trailed off.

They both looked so sullen, like they weren't sure what to say. I didn't want this to be the downer it was becoming. I smiled and tried to emphasize the bright side. "Look. I knew going in that this was experimental. I beat the odds even getting to be part of the trial. Where I am today is miles, hell, light years beyond where I was. I mean, check this out." I pushed back from the table and turned so they could see me lift one leg and cross it over the other, then wiggle my toes in my sandals. "No, I'll never walk unaided, but I'm trying not to think of it in terms of only one version of success." I pointed at both of them. "And I don't want you to either, okay?"

"Is this a 'less than you hoped for but more than you expected' kind of thing?" asked Crystal.

"Yes. Far more than I expected. I have full sensation in my legs. My mobility is way beyond what it was. I can even stand and walk a little, so long as I have something to hold onto." Using the words 'stand and walk' filled me with more joy than either of them probably understood. Loss of mobility is a pain in the ass. Permanent loss is devastating, and then it's a thing you slowly learn to live with. To have someone come along years later and give even part of it back is...miraculous, unlike anything else that'd ever happened to me.

When Chris and I discussed hiding out in time, he didn't want to stick me in an era with bad conditions for Black people. I wanted to jump forward specifically because I hoped for something like this, where I'd find medical technology advanced enough to help me out. That hope took a back seat for over three years, but with Vanhanen gone, it came back with a persistence, and I started looking into options.

Seeing Vanhanen roll through the portal was a relief, but it was a dark end. It didn't bring James or any of the others back, it just stopped V's horrible selfish process which began a hundred years earlier.

This though...this was the beginning of something amazing.

*

AMBER
September 2052

Crystal and Tia washed dishes in the kitchen, while I went to get the papers from the floor safe. I paused at the mantel in the living room. A framed black-and-white photo hung above it: Crystal playing the mandolin, wearing my T-shirt, her face partly obscured by shadows and long hair. After we set up her new identity, I used the same technology to track down the photographer from the open mic night and convinced her to sell me a digital copy. The mandolin itself sat in its customary place next to the handwritten journals, the brown one Crystal and I had written in, a black one that was Kurtis's, and a tan one of Charles's. Tia's typed entries completed the set—hand bound in green leather by Crystal. My fingertip slid lightly across the spines, and I marveled at the near misses that brought us to where we were.

Not *all* of us. Charles was gone, many years before I knew about this story or found myself swept up in it. His chapters remained valid though, integral to the longer tale. Much as I wished Crystal could have met her father, Kurtis had carried living memory of the car crash that killed his friend, and that locked it in time, unchangeable. Kurtis himself never reappeared. When he'd been gone a few months, Tia suggested Crystal and I move in and consider it extended house-sitting rather than letting the place stand empty. My old apartment was a little small for two anyway.

The previous month marked seven years since I reported him missing. We long ago moved all his clothes and stuff into boxes in the basement, but some of his collection of African art still hung on the walls. The papers in the safe were from his lawyer who notified us after he was declared legally dead, since I was listed as executor of his estate. I closed the safe and stood, whispering, "Kurtis, wherever or whenever you landed, I hope you're okay. I miss you, old man."

I heard voices from the kitchen over the clink of dishes and stopped in the hallway to listen. The banter between my wife and my best friend cheered me up.

"No. C'mon, spill!" asked Crystal.

"What?"

"Don't be coy. I saw Mitchel after school in the teachers' lounge, and he said you guys went out."

"Yeah, so?" Tia sounded a little bit defensive, but seeing her dating someone after so long, made me happy for her.

"So? He seemed super into you when we all had dinner after the fundraiser thing. I'm just an old married lady..." Tia snorted audibly. "Who wants to live vicariously through her single friends."

I smiled a little at the 'old married lady' comment. Crystal had been ecstatic when her history studies got into the Obama years, and she learned we could get married. I waited, also wanting to hear about the date.

Tia sighed. "If you must know, we took a cooking class together. It was nice. We made Chicken Cordon Bleu and laughed about whether the teacher's French accent was real or not."

I set the envelope on the dining room table, still listening. Crystal asked, sounding conspiratorial, "So...was there any...dessert?" A sharp *smack* followed, probably Tia snapping her with a towel. I covered a grin with my hand.

I called, "C'mon guys. Let's do the thing."

They emerged, Crystal carrying a tray with three cups of coffee, in the *Star Wars* mugs. BB-8 had been added to round out the droid trio. In the film, he's described as one of a kind. So was Crystal, and I don't mean just because she's awesome and I love her. As far as we know, Crystal's the only person ever born of parents from two different timelines. And I can say that with some authority. Tia and I are arguably the world's leading experts in time travel, but since the research is all classified, who really knows?

Crystal tapped the large tan envelope with a slender finger. "C'mon, open it up."

I took a deep breath and let it out slowly. "We're here tonight to read the last will and testament of Kurtis Robert Blake." I unwound the string from the little button and slid the papers out onto the table. Lifting the top one I began to read out loud. The top paragraph was a bunch of legal stuff, so I scanned down to Distribution of Assets. "He says here that he bequeaths twenty thousand dollars each to a series of charities on the next page."

Crystal picked it up and scanned the list. "There's got to be at least twenty names here. That's like, half a million dollars!"

Tia gestured toward the papers. "Just keep reading."

"There's stuff here about if he died before he retired, what should happen to his company, but that doesn't apply." He'd sold the engineering firm to a group of junior partners years before.

"Tia? He left you..." I tilted the page and pointed to a number.

"Holy shit, that's generous. I thought I was only here as a witness!" She looked shocked but smiled too.

I continued, "The house, property and remaining assets he leaves to me...and spouse if such a person exists."

Crystal interjected, "Yeah, she does. Does it give a number?"

"The lawyer said there's a statement." Shuffling through the pages until I found it, I blinked and squinted, not believing my eyes. I turned it toward Crystal. "Am I reading that right?"

She leaned in. "Um...that number has eight digits."

Tia slid the paper over and spun it around. "Did you have any idea Kurtis had that kind of money?"

I felt stunned but managed to sputter, "No. None at all. I mean...he always had great wine and whisky at home and usually insisted on paying when we went out. I guess I never thought about it. He seemed so normal. He was just Uncle Kurtis, y'know?"

Crystal took one look at me and knew where my thoughts were heading. She turned so we sat face-to-face and said, "No. You're not going to feel guilty about this. Kurtis wanted you to have that money, or he could have given it to any one of a hundred other charities." I struggled to speak, to protest, to say something starting with "But..." She stopped me with a finger on my lips and a gentle "Shh."

Sometimes I forgot Crystal was no stranger to grief. She'd walked that road long before we ever met. She pulled me into a hug and spoke quietly by my ear. "Think of all the good we could do with that money."

I leaned back but didn't break the embrace. "Your charity idea about instruments for kids who can't afford them!"

"Sure. Or if there's something else you'd like to do, that'd be fine too."

I hugged her tightly and whispered, "Oh my god, I love you."

Tia opened a corner cupboard and produced three small glasses and a bottle of Scotch probably older than me. Poured and passed around, she said, "Kurtis once told me we would drink to Charles's memory, and we never did, so tonight, we drink to them both."

Three glasses clinked together over the table in a gray brick house by three women, to honor two men who had gone before, or as much "before" as was possible when time travel was involved.

*

CRYSTAL
May 2055

I looked in the mirror and fidgeted with my hair again and then with my dress...again. Amber hugged me from behind. "You look awesome. Stop worrying. You're going to be great."

It was Replay Orchestra's first concert ever, and the kids' nervous excitement had spilled over onto me. I'd directed bunches of concerts for the high school orchestra, but somehow this was different. For many of these kids, it would be the first time they ever played in public.

I'd wondered aloud to Amber once about putting instruments to use rather than sitting in storage indefinitely. That little idea stuck with me. With Kurtis's money behind it, the program took off. No kid was ever turned away. If they wanted to play an instrument, we'd find it for them. If they stayed with the program, they took the instrument home.

I stepped back into the rec room where the kids were warming up and thanked a parent volunteer. The program had innumerable volunteers. We herded them out to the grass where folding chairs waited, arranged in an arc. One day I hoped this program would warrant a concert in an actual auditorium rather than the lawn of a retirement home, but we weren't there yet. Beyond that, there was another reason I'd asked this particular facility about hosting the concert, and it wasn't only for the built-in audience. Well, it was, at least a little bit.

After the kids took their places, I walked to the front, baton in one hand and an instrument case in the other. The young musicians all snapped to attention, and I gestured for them to relax. Turning, I noticed Tia and Mitchell in the audience, as well as friends and other teachers from the high school.

"Thank you all for coming. We're all here because of a love of music. These new musicians have worked hard this year on the pieces we're about to play. The thing I want you all to remember is that this isn't for class credit or an easy A. Each of these kids just wanted to play music. It's that simple. To everyone who donated instruments, or money, or your time—you're the ones who made all this possible."

I moved an extra chair to the front and sat with the case on my lap. I had to tell the next part in a way which wasn't exactly true, for the timeline to make sense to everyone else. "My um...my mother used to say that music saved her life. At a time when she had nothing, someone reached out and made it possible for her to play." I opened the case and lifted out the familiar green instrument, checking the tuning although I knew it was perfect. "This is a four-string mandolin, an odd instrument by most measures, in an even odder color. It was given to her by a generous stranger, rather than letting it silently collect dust in the corner of a shop." Somewhere in the back of the quiet crowd, I heard a small gasp. "For her, for me, it made all the difference in the world."

I didn't know what change perpetuation would do to the former pawnshop owner's memory, but I had to try. I researched her before selecting the venue and felt happy in that moment that I had. I finally got to return that kindness.

I bent over the strings and played.

*

TIA
June 2067

Amber leaned into the TE office with an expression of mixed emotions. She took off her glasses and rubbed her eyes. "I just sent Kiernen into the past."

The date on his first journal entry had told us this day was coming. When our system flagged his resume a year and a half before, we knew we couldn't *not* hire him. He was a brilliant engineer and grasped time travel theory faster than most. I'd have been thrilled to have him, had it been anyone else. Knowing what waited for him made it complicated and hard to know how to feel. As much as we wished we could help, or try something different, we knew we couldn't. So, I understood Amber's expression, mirroring my own inner conflict. I simply nodded.

For several weeks, the security cameras in and around Nuclear Engineering had been malfunctioning. They would randomly cut out for a few minutes, sometimes a couple of hours. When the camera by the bike rack shut down earlier that day, it wouldn't be seen as unusual if anyone investigated. By the time Kiernen—no, Kasey—stepped through the portal, Crystal had already unlocked his bike and ridden it away. It would be found at a hiking trail that, coincidentally, also had no security cameras. The night before, Mitchell locked Crystal's bike at the other end of the trail. A missing person investigation would happen eventually, and we needed to protect everyone involved one last time. Bikes and pedestrians were much harder to track with traffic cameras.

Amber spoke again and pulled me out of my thoughts. "Dinner reservations are at seven, right?"

"Yeah. I have a few things to finish here, then I'll pick up Mitchell and meet you at the restaurant."

"I hope it's not too odd a thing to celebrate, but it's like we can finally breathe a sigh of relief."

"No, I get it. I do. The loop is finally closed. Dinner and drinks sound great."

I heard her out in the front room on a call with Crystal. Who's driving and when to be there and all the ordinary domestic stuff one's life contains in middle age, comforting, if only from the normalcy of it and the constant presence of that other person in their life. Helmet on, she waved through the window on her way out.

When the door closed and relocked, I opened my desk and took out a single piece of paper from the very bottom of the drawer. On it was a set of temporal coordinates I'd scratched down, before deleting, long years in the past. Afterward, unknown to anyone else, I'd written an app that ran the formula backward to produce a destination from the coordinates. Across the bottom in a different pen, I'd written a date. I didn't need to read it. I'd memorized it long ago. Eventually, I figured out where I'd seen it before and what it meant. The coordinates had extra digits to include the time of day, 6:00 p.m.

In the lab, I verified that the portal was in standby, even though I could tell it was by the sound. Unable to concentrate on actual work, I did some unnecessary cleaning. I had one last card in my hand and was excited to play it. I'd kept it close to my chest for ages.

When the analog clock on the wall in the lab approached 6:00 p.m., and the second hand swept toward the top, the equipment ran through its automated start-up routine. A louder hum sounded, emitters glowed purple, and arcs jumped between them, followed, as always, by a shimmery silver field in the arch.

When Kurtis stepped through, he looked exactly like I remembered, not that I expected anything else. For me, more than twenty years had elapsed, but his trip through the portal took less than a twentieth of a second. How much did those years show on my face to him?

"Tia?" He looked surprised to see me.

I smiled. "The one and only. I couldn't let you return to the world alone." He bent and gave me a quick hug. "It's so good to see you again," I said.

"Amber and Crystal?"

"Married."

"Oh, that's great!" He pointed at my ring. "You too?"

"Yeah. Mitchell teaches physics at the same high school where Crystal's the orchestra director."

He nodded, then looked unsure how to ask his next question. "Vanhanen?"

I shrugged and shook my head. "Nothing. Not a sign. It's been peaceful at TE since you left."

He let out a breath and leaned on the edge of the counter. "Whew. That's a relief."

"I spent the first few years constantly looking over my shoulder, but I slowly came to believe he was truly gone."

The portal timed out, wound back down to standby mode, and I keyed in the shutdown sequence. As we turned and left the lab, the lights went out behind us.

In the front office, I tapped my watch and sent Crystal a text.

> **Tia**: *Can you change the reservation to a table for five? I'm bringing a guest.*

I opened the hallway door and gestured for Kurtis to lead the way.

His return brought our family back together, but was it the end?

The school where Mitchell and Crystal taught had plaques in the lobby with quotes chosen by previous graduating classes. One of them said, "You can't go back and change the beginning, but you can start where you are and change the end." Through all the folds and twists, I didn't know if we'd proved that, or if we'd disproved it.

Was this the end, or somehow only the end of the beginning?

I didn't even know if Amber still wanted to dismantle the equipment in the morning.

For the first time in a very long time, the future was uncertain.

A Note from Crystal

Across the timelines, we all mentioned songs that created a soundtrack to this narrative, flowing from one era to the next. Assembled here is "The Time Travelers' Playlist".

The Doors: "Five to One"
Jimi Hendrix: "Purple Haze"
Depeche Mode: "I Feel You"
Pink Floyd: "Time"
Pearl Jam: "Porch"
Alice in Chains: "No Excuses"
Nirvana: "Come as You Are"
David Bowie: "Within You"
U2: "Trying to Throw Your Arms Around the World"
Garbage: "Stupid Girl"
Green Day: "When I Come Around"
Soundgarden: "Room a Thousand Years Wide"

Toad the Wet Sprocket: "Fall Down"
Cranberries: "Dreams"
Chris Cornell: "Seasons"
The Clash: "Guns of Brixton"
The Breeders: "Cannonball"
The Warning: "Money"
Red Hot Chili Peppers: "Higher Ground"
AC/DC: "Moneytalks"
Led Zeppelin: "Going to California"
Jefferson Airplane: "Somebody to Love"
REM: "Losing My Religion"
The Animals: "House of the Rising Sun"
The Cure: "The Blood"
Blind Faith: "Can't Find My Way Home"
Bauhaus: "Hope"

Acknowledgements

I want to thank Carrie Vaughn and Lyndsie Clark. Without your friendship, encouragement, and advice, this book wouldn't exist.

A huge thank you goes out to NineStar Press for seeing the potential in my story and bringing it to the world. Your help has made this book so much better!

To anyone who recognizes certain locations in the book and knows the real-world places that inspired them, good for you!

Lara, I love you. You're the best!

About the Author

Jeff is an architect, archer, author, costumer, hiker, home-brewer, re-enactor, woodworker, etc. etc. etc. He lives in the suburbs of Denver, Colorado, with his family.

Email
jeffwomack.author@gmail.com

Instagram
www.instagram.com/jeffwomack.o

Bluesky
jeffwomack.bsky.social

Connect with NineStar Press

Website: NineStarPress.com

Facebook: NineStarPress

X: @ninestarpress

Instagram: NineStarPress

BlueSky: NineStarPress

Threads: @ninestarpress